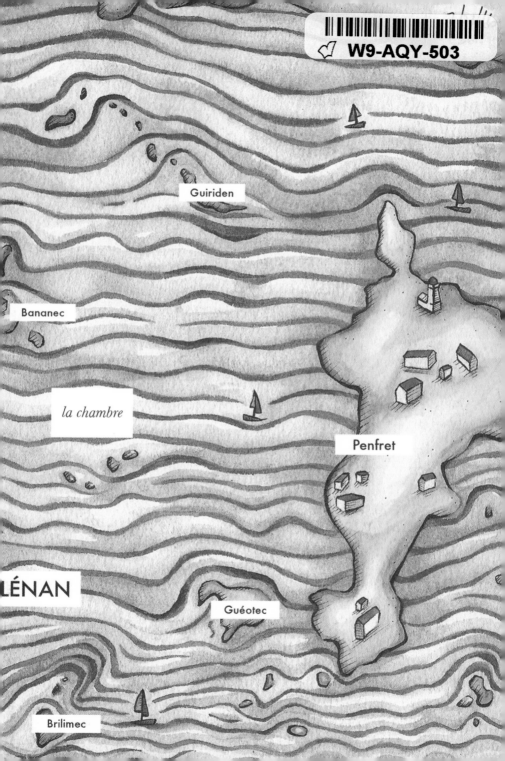

Guiriden

Bananec

la chambre

Penfret

LÉNAN

Guéotec

Brilimec

Murder on
Brittany Shores

Also by Jean-Luc Bannalec

Death in Brittany

Murder on Brittany Shores

Jean-Luc Bannalec

Translated by
Sorcha McDonagh

Minotaur Books

A Thomas Dunne Book
New York

A THOMAS DUNNE BOOK FOR MINOTAUR BOOKS.
An imprint of St. Martin's Publishing Group.

MURDER ON BRITTANY SHORES. Copyright © 2016 by Jean-Luc Bannalec. English translation copyright © 2016 by Sorcha McDonagh. All rights reserved. Printed in the United States of America. For information, address St. Martin's Press, 175 Fifth Avenue, New York, N.Y. 10010.

www.thomasdunnebooks.com
www.minotaurbooks.com

Library of Congress Cataloging-in-Publication Data

Names: Bannalec, Jean-Luc, 1966– author. | McDonagh, Sorcha, translator.
Title: Murder on Brittany shores : a mystery / Jean-Luc Bannalec ; translated by Sorcha McDonagh.
Other titles: Bretonische Brandung. English
Description: First U.S. edition. | New York : Minotaur Books, 2016.
Identifiers: LCCN 2016004320| ISBN 9781250071897 (hardcover) | ISBN 9781466883123 (e-book)
Subjects: LCSH: Police—Fiction. | Murder—Investigation—Fiction. | BISAC: FICTION / Mystery & Detective / Police Procedural. | FICTION / Mystery & Detective / Traditional British. | GSAFD: Mystery fiction
Classification: LCC PT2662.A565 B7313 2016 | DDC 833/.92—dc23
LC record available at http://lccn.loc.gov/2016004320

Our books may be purchased in bulk for promotional, educational, or business use. Please contact your local bookseller or the Macmillan Corporate and Premium Sales Department at 1-800-221-7945, extension 5442, or by e-mail at MacmillanSpecialMarkets@macmillan.com.

First published in Germany under the title Bretonische Brandung by Jean-Luc Bannalec

Previously published in Great Britain under the title Death on the Brittany Shores by Hesperus Press Limited

First U.S. Edition: July 2016

10 9 8 7 6 5 4 3 2 1

'An douar so kozh, med n'eo ket sod.'
'The earth is old, but not mad.'

Breton saying

à L.

The First Day

The long, flat islands floated on the deep opal sea as if by magic, a little blurred, shimmering. The famous archipelago lay before them like a Fata Morgana.

The contours of the larger islands were already visible to the naked eye, not much to distinguish between them: the fortress shrouded in mystery on Cigogne, Penfret's long-serving storm-lashed lighthouse, the abandoned farm on Drénec, the occasional weather-beaten house on Saint-Nicolas which was the main island in the almost circular archipelago. The Îles de Glénan. A legend.

They were ten nautical miles from the mainland, from Concarneau, the magnificent 'Blue City' of Cornouaille, whose residents had been calling the islands their 'guardians' for as long as anyone could remember. Day after day they were their unshakeable horizon. From morning onwards you could tell the weather from how they looked, clear, sharp, blurred, pale, whether they shook or lay still in the water, and on certain days, you could tell the weather for the rest of the year. For hundreds of years there had been fierce debate in Brittany about how many islands there were. Seven, nine, twelve or twenty were the most common counts. Seven 'large' ones, that was the only undisputed thing. And large meant a few hundred metres long – at most. It had all been *one* island once, a very long time ago, then little by little the tossing sea and the constant breakwater had torn them apart. Some years ago, a committee from the *département*, following the official criteria for determining an island – land in the sea that is permanently above water and features equally permanent vegetation – had identified 'twenty-one islands and islets' with absolute authority. Besides these, there seemed to be an almost endless number of jagged rocks and rock formations towering upwards. This number was also surprisingly variable, depending on the state of high and low tides, which in turn varied significantly themselves, depending on the positions of the sun, moon and earth. Some days a high tide was three or four metres higher than other days and at an extremely low tide an island could be many times larger and, perhaps, linked to a sandbank above water that usually lay hidden beneath the surface. There was never a 'normal' situation. That's how the archipelago's landscapes came to be in a constant state of flux and nobody could ever say: that's them, the Glénan, that's how they look. The Glénan were not clearly land, they were an ambiguous middle-ground, half land, half sea. During raging winter storms, huge waves occasionally rolled over the islands, the heavy sea spray turning everything into sea. 'Almost lost in the nothingness, in the great expanse,' that was the people's poetic, but precise description.

It was an extraordinary, early May day, indistinguishable from a true summer's day, the same absolutely unbelievable temperatures, the same strong light, the same magnificent colours. Even the air was already summery – it was lighter, it carried a little less salt, less iodine, seaweed and algae; yet it had that Atlantic freshness that is so difficult to describe. Even now, at ten o'clock in the morning, the sun created a gleaming, fitfully flaring horizon with a silver funnel below that narrowed down and down towards the observer.

Commissaire Georges Dupin from the Commissariat de Police Concarneau wasn't paying much attention to any of this. He was in an extremely bad mood this Monday morning. Only moments before he had been sitting in his café, the *Amiral*, having just ordered his third coffee and with his newspapers lying in front of him – *Le Monde, Ouest France, Télégramme* – when his phone had startled him with a shrill ring. Three corpses had been found on the Glénan. Nothing was known at this point – just that. Three corpses.

He had set off immediately. His regular cafe, where he began his day every day, was right at the harbour and just a few minutes later he had found himself on board a police speedboat. Commissaire Dupin had been on the Glénan just once – on Penfret last year, the island on the eastern edge of the archipelago.

The speedboat had been travelling for twenty minutes. They were halfway there. Commissaire Dupin would have been glad to be more than halfway. Travelling by boat on the open water was not his cup of tea, no matter how much he loved the sea like a genuine Parisian from the sixth Arrondissement loved the sea– because that is what he had been up until his 'relocation' almost four years ago now – the beach, watching, ideally bathing, the feel, the smell, the excitement. Even worse than boat travel itself, was travelling in one of the two new speedboats which the marine police had acquired after long, bitter struggles with bureaucracy and which were their pride and joy. The latest models were impressive high-tech miracles with probes and sensors for everything. They positively shot across the water. One boat had been christened *Bir* – 'arrow' in Breton – the second *Luc'hed* – 'lightning'. These were not good names for boats as far as Dupin was concerned, but in naming them, only the meaning had counted.

Commissaire Dupin was also lacking caffeine, which made him thoroughly grumpy. Two coffees weren't even close to enough. He was rather stocky in stature, not fat, but definitely not thin either and had suffered from very low blood pressure since his youth.

He had got on board reluctantly, mainly because he didn't want to show any weakness and because Inspector Riwal, who was one of his two young inspectors and looked up to him (which Dupin generally found unpleasant) had also got on board.

Dupin would have been prepared to drive the half hour to the little airport in Quimper and fly to the Glénan in headquarters' pitiful, rickety two-man police helicopter, even though it would have taken longer overall and flying was in no way enjoyable for him. But his boss, the Prefect, was out in the helicopter – a 'friendly meeting' with the Prefecture of the British Channel Islands (Guernsey, Jersey and Alderney), in Bordeaux, a sleepy backwater on

Guernsey. Police cooperation should – this was the firm English and French wish – be stepped up: 'Crime should have no chance, no matter what its nationality.' Commissaire Dupin couldn't stand the Prefect, Lug Locmariaquer, and even now, having known him for almost four years, still couldn't pronounce his name (Georges Dupin generally had a difficult relationship with authority, completely justifiably, in his view). For weeks he had been taking calls from the Prefect, who was 'collecting ideas' to be discussed at one such illustrious Prefecture meeting, annoying at first, then tortuous. At Locmariaquer's request, Nolwenn, Dupin's infinitely patient assistant, had had to research 'unsolved cases' from the last decade that 'perhaps, conceivably, in some way' presented a lead to the Channel Islands, cases which could 'perhaps, conceivably, in some way' have been 'capable of being solved' if there had already been closer cooperation. It was absolutely ridiculous. Nolwenn had baulked. She could not grasp why, here 'in the south', anyone had to concern themselves with the channel far to the north where icebergs drifted through the sea and it rained all year long. Files had been pored over by the metre and they hadn't found a significant case – which the Prefect had not be at all happy about.

What had not improved Dupin's mood on the boat had been the little 'accident' which had come about shortly after they had cast off to sea. He had done what only the worst landlubbers do – at that speed, stiff wind from the port side and a somewhat roughsea in that exact place, on the port side – he had cast a glance at the islands while Inspector Riwal, along with the two crew members of the *Bir*,

11

had taken care to stand close to the starboard side. It hadn't taken long for an enormous wave to get him. Commissaire Dupin had been soaked through. His permanently open jacket, his polo-shirt and jeans – his work uniform from March to October – clung to his body, only the socks in his shoes had stayed dry.

But what was making the Commissaire particularly foul-humoured was not having any information apart from that one fact: that three bodies had just been found. Dupin was not a man of patience. Not at all. On the phone, Kadeg, his second inspector, with whom he was generally at loggerheads, had only been able to pass on what he in turn knew, based on an agitated call that had come into the Commissariat shortly before, from 'a man with a strong English accent'. The bodies lay on the north-eastern beach of Le Loc'h, the biggest island in the archipelago – and 'the biggest island' meant four hundred metres long. Le Loc'h was uninhabited, with the ruins of a convent, an old graveyard, a dilapidated soda factory and – the greatest of the island's attractions – a laguna-like lake. Kadeg had needed to repeat that he had no other information a dozen times. Dupin had peppered him with all kinds of questions – his almost fanatical obsession with insignificant-seeming details and circumstances was notorious.

Three dead bodies and nobody knew anything – understandably, the Prefecture had been gripped by excitement: it was quite a big thing here in Finistère, the picturesque 'End of the World' as the Romans had called it. For the Gauls, the Celts – and the people here considered themselves as such to this day – it was the exact opposite – not the end of the world, but literally the 'beginning' – the 'Head of the World'. 'Penn ar Bed', not 'finis terrae'.

The boat had slowed down – they were only going at a moderate speed now. There was some difficult navigating to come. The sea was shallow here and dotted with towering rocks – above and below the surface of the water – and driving a boat in these waters was essentially only for extremely experienced captains. It was even trickier at low tide, as it was now. The least dangerous way to access the archipelago was the 'entrance' between Bananec and the large sandbank in front of Penfret. Through it, you could get to the section of sea in the middle of the archipelago, protected from storms and rough seas by the surrounding islands called 'la chambre' – 'the chamber'. With smooth movements, the Bir was expertly manouevred between the rocks and made for Le Loc'h.

'We won't get any closer.'

The captain of the police boat, a young, gangly chap in a high-tech fabric uniform that flapped fiercely about him, called down from his raised captain's booth without looking at anyone as he did so. He was fully absorbed by the navigating.

Dupin started to feel queasy. It was still a good hundred metres to go to the island.

'Spring tide. Coefficient 107.'

The lanky captain called this into the great unknown too. Commissaire Dupin looked at his inspector quizzically. After the incident with the large wave, he had made his way over to stand right next to the others and not moved from that spot. Riwal moved very close to Dupin. Even though the boat was barely moving, the motors were still deafeningly loud.

'We have extreme tidal amplitude at the moment, Monsieur le Commissaire,' he said. On spring tide days, the water level is significantly lower again than during a normal low tide. I don't know whether you...'

'I know what a spring tide is.'

Dupin wanted to add 'because I've been living in Brittany for nearly four years and have already experienced quite a few spring tides and neap tides,' but he knew it was pointless. He would also have had to admit that although he had had the thing about tidal coefficients explained to him many, many times, to this day he had never really been able to remember how they worked. To Riwal, and to all Bretons, he would still be a 'foreigner' for decades to come (although this was not necessarily meant in a nasty way). And on top of this, the worst kind of foreigner for Bretons – a Parisian (which could in fact be meant in a thoroughly nasty way). He had to have it spelt out to him again, every time: if the moon, sun and earth are in alignment and this results in the forces of gravity adding up...

The motor suddenly died away and the two employees from the marine police who looked, Dupin only noticed now, hilariously like the captain – the same wiry stature, the same narrow face, the same uniform – were immediately making their way forward to the prow.

'We won't get any closer to the island. The water is too shallow.'

'And what does that mean?'

'We have to get out here.'

It took a few seconds for Dupin to respond.

'We have to *get out* here?'

As far as Dupin could tell, they were still very clearly at sea.

'The water isn't deep any more, maybe half a metre.'

Inspector Riwal had knelt down and begun to take off his shoes.

'But we have a dinghy.'

Dupin had only just noticed it. To his relief.

'It's not worth it, Inspector. We wouldn't get much closer to the beach in that either.'

Eyebrows raised, Dupin looked over the ship's rail. It seemed a lot more than half a metre deep to him. The water was incredibly clear. Every shell, every pebble was visible. A school of tiny pale green fish darted by. The boat was off the northern coast of Le Loc'h. Nothing but dazzling white sand, shallow turquoise water and the sea lying completely still in the chamber. With the addition of a few coconut trees – probably the only kind of palm tree that didn't grow in Brittany, it seemed to Dupin – the scene would have been indistinguishable from the Caribbean. Nobody would ever have dreamt of associating this landscape with Brittany. But the sight could be marvelled at in hundreds of postcards – they were no exaggeration.

By now, Riwal had taken his socks off too. The boat's crew had dropped anchor, leapt neatly into the sea without the slightest hesitation and were now in the process of turning the boat so that the stern, with the wooden step that was only just above the water, was pointed in the direction of the beach. Riwal, in pale-coloured slacks, jumped into the water too, as though it was the most natural thing in the world. And, directly after him, the gangly captain.

Dupin hesitated. It looked absurd, he thought. The young police officers, Riwal and the captain had stopped and were waiting. It looked as though they were forming a guard of honour. All eyes were fixed on him.

Dupin jumped. He hadn't taken off his shoes. He was standing up to just over his knees in the Atlantic, which at the beginning of May was at most fourteen degrees now at the beginning of May. His eyes were fixed on the floor of the sea. The school of tiny pale green fish, now much bigger than before, approached inquisitively and swam fearlessly around his legs. Dupin made a half turn to follow the fish with his gaze – then he saw it: a magnificent crab, twenty or thirty centimetres long, in attack-ready position and staring right at him – a real 'tourteau', eaten with enthusiasm here on the coast, by Dupin as well. He stifled both a small cry of fear and his culinary enthusiasm. He looked up and realised that everyone was still standing motionless, watching him. Dupin straightened up his upper body with determination and began to wade in the direction of the beach, taking great care not to meet the gaze of Riwal or the other three police officers. His colleagues quickly overtook him on either side in the water.

Dupin was the last to reach the beach.

The lifeless body lay partly on its stomach and partly on its side, the shoulder wedged unnaturally underneath the body. It looked as though it had lost its right arm. Its left arm, which must have been broken, was severely bent. The head was resting almost exactly on the brow, as if someone had deliberately positioned it like that. The face could not be seen. Its blue jacket and the jumper were extremely ragged – on the back and throat, on the back of the head and on the left arm you could see the terrible wounds, superficial and deep. The lower body, by contrast, seemed practically unscathed. It was covered in algae in a few places. The sturdy sailing shoes, both still on the feet, looked new. The man's age was hard to judge in this pose, perhaps somewhat older than himself, Dupin guessed. Late forties, early fifties. The dead man was not very tall. Dupin knelt down to examine him more carefully. The sea had carried the body far up the beach, a few metres from the line where the white sand stopped sloping gently upwards and the bright green vegetation began.

'The two others are over there, quite close together. They're in a similar state.'

Riwal pointed along the beach. Dupin saw his young colleagues from the marine police standing next to something bulky, a good hundred metres away. Dupin had not realised that he was not alone. Riwal's voice was a little thin.

'The corpses look terrible.'

Riwal was right.

'Which pathologist is coming?'

'Docteur Savoir should be here any moment. He's on a different speedboat. With Inspector Kadeg.'

'Of course. That works out well.'

It was well known that there was little love lost between the Commissaire and Docteur Savoir.

'Docteur Lafond has a commitment in Rennes this morning.'

Nolwenn usually always arranged things behind the scenes so that old, grumpy – but superb – Docteur Lafond was called when Dupin was investigating.

The captain of the *Bir* strode towards them.

'There are three men, all probably early fifties,' the young man said gravely and calmly. 'Identities as yet unknown. The corpses very likely washed up with the last tide. They are lying quite far up the beach. We record powerful currents on the Glénan and on spring tide days they are even stronger than usual. We are photographing and documenting everything.'

'Is this the lowest low tide reading now?'

'Almost.'

The police officer glanced at his watch.

'Low tide was an hour and a half ago. The water has already risen again since then.'

Dupin did some calculations.

'It's now 10.45 am – so the low tide was at...'

'The last low water mark was this morning at 9.15, the one before that was yesterday evening at 8.50pm. Twelve hours and twenty-five minutes earlier. The high water mark was attained at 3.03am at night.'

It had taken less than three seconds. The police officer was looking at Dupin without the least sign of triumphalism.

'Have we got any reports of missing persons? At the station or with the sea rescue service?'

'No, Monsieur le Commissaire, none have come in yet, as far as we know. But they could still come in.'

'Le Loc'h is uninhabited, isn't it?'

'Yes. Saint-Nicolas is the last inhabited island in the archipelago. But there aren't even many people living there. Ten at most, fifteen in the summer.'

'So that means nobody is here on the island overnight?'

'Camping is strictly forbidden on the archipelago. A few thrill-seekers do it some nights in the summer anyway. We're going to inspect the whole island. And there might have been some boats lying in the chamber off Le Loc'h last night. It's a popular place to drop anchor. We'll find out.'

'What's your name?'

Dupin liked the unflappable, meticulous young police officer.

'My name is Kireg Goulch, Monsieur le Commissaire.'

'Kireg Goulch?'

Dupin's question had just slipped out.

'Exactly.'

'That... that is a very... a... I mean, a Breton name.'

Even this comment didn't seem to annoy the young man at all. Dupin cleared his throat quickly and made an effort to focus again.

'Inspector Riwal said that the Englishman who discovered the bodies was travelling by canoe.'

'Lots of visitors go on tours in sea kayaks around here, it's extremely popular. Even though there aren't as many at this time of year, there are already some.'

'Even in the morning? They go on tours at this hour?'

'It's the most popular time. By midday the sun is already beating down on the sea.'

'But the man didn't land and get out?'

'As far as we know, no. There are no footprints visible on the beach here.'

Dupin had not even thought of that. The sand that was virginal again after every high tide would show any mark perfectly and any attempt to blur anything out.

'Where is the man?'

'On Saint-Nicolas. He's waiting on the quay there. Our second boat is taking one of our colleagues to the island. He's going to speak to the man. Inspector Kadeg ordered it.'

'Inspector Kadeg *ordered* it?'

'Yes, he…'

'It's okay.'

Now was not the moment to let an emotion get the better of him. With some difficulty, Dupin fumbled one of his red Clairefontaine notebooks out of his still wet jacket. It was one of the ones he traditionally used for making notes. Well protected, it had stayed halfway dry in the sea incident. With the same stubborn awkwardness, he rummaged around for one of the cheap bic pens that, because they were always going missing on him so quickly, he bought in large stockpiles.

'Has there been a shipwreck somewhere then?'

He immediately knew it was a pointless question. They would have long since heard about it. The young police officer greeted the question with gracious patience.

'We don't know anything about that yet either, Monsieur le Commissaire. But if a boat did capsize yesterday, it could take a while for its absence to be noticed. Depending on how big the boat was, what technical equipment was available to it, where it happened, where it was going, who was expecting it...'

Dupin made a few half-hearted notes.

'So was there bad weather last night? Was there a storm out here?'

'You shouldn't be fooled by the weather today. Last night a storm tracked along the coast. Headquarters will be able to tell us exactly how severe it was, and where and how it moved. It was hardly noticeable in Concarneau, but that doesn't mean anything. We have access to all the records. The sea is actually still a bit choppy today, even though it's calm here in the chamber. Clearly, you noticed that yourself on the boat just now.'

It was a neutral observation with no undertones. He was getting to like Goulch more and more.

'It wasn't the storm of the century, but it was clearly powerful,' the captain concluded.

Commissaire Dupin was well aware of that – he himself had long since become too much of a Breton to be taken in by the blue, cloudless sky and the perfect atmosphere of good weather. The Breton peninsula and its furthermost, rugged outcrop – Finistère – lay far offshore in the *middle* of the North Atlantic, as Nolwenn was always explaining to him. 'Armorika sticks its jagged head out like a primeval monster. Like a dragon's tongue.' He liked the image – and you could actually make out the dragon on a map. Not only was Brittany exposed to the elemental force of the wildest of the world's known oceans, but also to the chaotic, constantly changing weather fronts that developed between the east coast of the USA,

Canada, Greenland and the Arctic; and the western Atlantic coasts of Ireland, England, Norway and France. The weather could switch from one extreme to another in an instant. 'Four seasons in one day' was the way they put it. The Bretons liked to quote this with pride.

'Maybe there wasn't even a shipwreck.'

Riwal's voice had regained some of its strength.

'The high tide may have taken them by surprise. Or the storm. While fishing or mussel-picking. Especially if they were tourists. Lots of mussel-pickers come when the tide is particularly low.'

That was true. Dupin noted this point in his notebook.

'Why do they not have any life jackets on? Does that not point to a hypothesis like that? That they weren't even on a boat?'

'Not necessarily,' Goulch replied firmly. 'Many of the locals go around without life jackets. And if alcohol comes into it too... I wouldn't attach any importance to it.'

Dupin made a gesture of resignation. So this was how it was. They knew nothing – especially not out here.

'Alcohol is generally a big issue at sea. Especially here on the islands,' Goulch added.

'People claim that the bottles on the Glénan are smaller than on the mainland – that's why they empty so quickly here,' said Riwal.

It took Dupin a moment to understand the joke – he assumed it was one – Riwal had rattled it off like a matter-of-fact explanation.

Goulch continued unperturbed. 'The bodies have definitely been drifting in the surf for a while, that's probably how the serious injuries came about. If it was a boating accident, they might have sustained at least some of the injuries during it.'

'Could they have lost their lives far from here? I mean, how far could the current have carried them?'

'That depends entirely on how long they were floating in the sea. Perhaps they were still alive at first and tried to save themselves. And only drowned later. They don't appear to have been drifting at sea for days on end. Bodies like that look different. Still, the currents vary in speed. Some are eight kilometres an hour, so the dead bodies could have covered a significant distance in just one night. But depending on where they went into the water, they may have drifted in circles. The course of the currents change depending on tide level, weather and season.'

'I understand: no assertions can be made yet.'

'It's a quirk of the archipelago that under certain configurations of the sun, moon and earth, many currents lead to Le Loc'h. Castaways have always been washed up here. In accidents involving large ships there were sometimes dozens of corpses found on the beach. Which is why a graveyard was built on the island in the nineteenth century, right next to the chapel. So the dead did not need to be brought especially to Saint-Nicolas, where the only graveyard in the archipelago used to be. They were all buried here. They have even found graves from early Celtic times on the island.'

'They were always washed up here?'

Dupin couldn't help looking around with a strange feeling.

'For centuries, the island was regarded as the mythical lair of Groac'h, the witch of shipwrecks.

She was rich beyond measure, richer than all kings put together, apparently. And her treasure chest was the lake, which had a subterranean link to the sea. That's how a magical current brought her the treasure from every ship that sank. Her palace stood on the lake bed.'

Riwal was smiling when Goulch finished, but his smile looked decidedly strained.

'She likes to feast on young men,' added Goulch. 'She seduces them, transforms them into fish, fries them and eats them. Many have set out to search for the legendary treasure. No one has ever returned. There are countless stories.'

That's how it was in Brittany. Beneath the surface of normality and naturalness, obscure powers were at work. And every village had its own supernatural stories. Even if the Bretons themselves made fun of them – and Dupin knew no other race of people who could make fun of themselves so confidently and brilliantly – during these stories the laughter suddenly died away and everything was very real. It was buried too deep – for thousands of years the supernatural had been the most natural way of making sense of the world – should it be different suddenly, just because they now found themselves in the twenty-first century?

'I want to see the other two bodies.'

Dupin walked along the beach, Goulch and Riwal following him. The first and most crucial question right now was: had the men been victims of an accident? Drowned? Were there any clues that it might have been anything other than an accident?

The lifeless bodies were lying on their sides, facing one another, their arms reaching out to each other. It

24

looked a little macabre, as though they had still been alive and, in their agony, tried, with the last of their strength, to creep towards each other. The creepy impression the scene made was intensified by a row of large mother-of-pearl shells that lay around the bodies as though arranged there, shimmering with all the colours of the rainbow. Goulch's colleagues were kneeling between the corpses, one of them taking photos with a digital camera. Without a word, the small group positioned themselves next to them and observed the two bodies.

Dupin broke away after a moments, walked slowly around the bodies several times, stooping down several times as he did so. The same severe flesh wounds, almost exclusively to the upper body on one, scattered all over the body on the other, badly tattered clothes (cotton trousers, polo-shirts, fleece jackets, sturdy shoes) and a little bit of algae and seaweed on and in the wounds.

The police officer with the camera straightened up slowly.

'Just like the dead body over there, on first impressions, they don't present any injuries apart from the kind that the sharp rocks could have caused to them in the surf.'

'At sea, you don't need to injure someone to kill them.' said Goulch. 'A little shove is enough, a fall into the water. In storms and heavy swells even an experienced swimmer doesn't have a ghost of a chance. Try and prove a small push some time.'

All that Goulch was saying was correct. You had to think differently out here.

'The second boat is coming.'

Dupin jumped. Goulch pointed to the sea. The *Luc'hed* was approaching the *Bir* at high speed, only slowing down just before it reached it. It stopped right next to the *Bir* and positioned itself parallel to it.

Dupin was watching the process, which he was familiar with from earlier. He could make out Kadeg and Docteur Savoir, the captain and also another police officer, who was already standing in the sea and straightening up the boat. Everyone got off the boat without any fuss and waded towards the beach, Kadeg a little way in front. Of course.

'We dropped a police officer off on Saint-Nicolas to question the Englishman who discovered the bodies. We will have a report soon. Three bodies, this is a substantial case.'

Before he was even out of the water, Kadeg had already launched into it, in the eager tone that he liked to adopt and that Dupin absolutely could not stand.

'We still have no idea whether this is even a case, Inspector.'

'What do you mean, Monsieur le Commissaire?'

'For one thing, it all looks like an accident.'

'And that means we shouldn't record everything there is to record, to find out what happened here?'

An impressively idiotic sentence, Dupin thought. He realised how irritable he was. It was because of the whole ruined morning – and the arrival of the second boat. Kadeg and then this cack-handed pathologist Savoir who would soon make a show of being like something out of a CSI series, even though he was unbelievably long-winded and never got to the point. Only now did Dupin see that the police officer from the second boat was carrying an enormous and evidently heavy suitcase, which would undoubtedly contain Savoir's high-tech equipment.

Dupin knew that he should just concentrate on the situation. Maybe this would all be over in a few hours and no longer his issue.

'Oh! Monsieur le Commissaire.'

Savoir's voice was laced with absurd pride, as though he had completed a demanding exercise just by recognising Dupin.

'Are there initial findings? What facts are there at this stage?'

He had walked past Dupin during these pithily expressed questions, without slowing his pace.

'I'll take a look at everything and then we will definitely know more. Although of course I can only make preliminary statements, I need my laboratory for anything over and above that. Equipment over here please, between the two bodies.'

Savoir cast a quick but theatrically professional gaze at the bodies and flipped the suitcase open.

'Has everything already been documented? Photographed?'

'Yes, those tasks have been taken care of. For all three bodies,' Goulch chimed in. 'Can whether the men drowned be determined, before an autopsy?'

Savoir stared indignantly at Goulch.

'Out of the question. Even in this case I will of course not be indulging in any speculation. It will all take time.'

Dupin smirked. Excellent! He was not needed here. He walked over to Riwal and Goulch.

'I'm going to have a look at the island.'

He himself didn't have a clue what he wanted to do.

'Should we take a systematic look around later anyway, Monsieur le Commissaire? See whether we find anything suspicious?' asked Goulch.

'Yes, yes. Definitely, Goulch. I'm just walking around a bit. And find out whether anyone noticed anything out of the ordinary here on Le Loc'h from a boat. Anything at all. Or elsewhere.'

'Are you getting at something in particular?'

Kadeg had positioned himself in front of him, uncomfortably close. He really liked doing this and knew that Dupin couldn't stand it.

'It's routine, Kadeg. Purely routine. I think we'll find out automatically about incoming messages about shipwrecks or missing people, won't we?'

Commissaire Dupin himself wasn't sure what he meant by 'automatically'. He had clearly turned to Goulch at this question.

'Of course, Monsieur le Commissaire. All police stations on the coast have been briefed and also those in the surrounding districts. We've requested the two helicopters from Brest, from the sea rescue headquarters. They were deployed an hour ago and are flying over the area.'

'Very good, Goulch, very good. – Riwal, you stay near Monsieur Goulch. I want to be informed about everything at all times. Kadeg, as soon as Savoir gives the green light, search the bodies for documents, for anything to help us identify them.'

'I – I.'

Kadeg fell silent. One of them had to do it. And the Commissaire could specify who. It was as if this simple thought process was displayed painfully on Kadeg's face. His features contorted.

'Be thorough, Kadeg. Do mobile phones actually work on the islands, Riwal?'

'A new mast was erected on Penfret last year. Although not a very big one. The coverage has mostly been stable since then.'

Riwal looked out over Le Loc'h, appearing to search for the mast on Penfret.

'What does that mean?'

'It depends on various factors.'

'And what does that mean?'

Dupin didn't think it insignificant.

'The weather more than anything. In bad weather you usually have no reception at all, but if the weather's good, you do. Although sometimes even then you don't for one reason or another. It's very much dependent on whether you're on the water or not – and of course especially which island you're on. On Bananec, you actually never get reception, even though it's not far away from Saint-Nicolas.'

Dupin wondered how that could be, purely from a technical point of view. And why Riwal knew it in such detail. He asked about both of these things.

'And here on Le Loc'h?'

'Probably stable today.'

'So I am – *probably* reachable?'

'And don't be surprised, Monsieur le Commissaire. You sometimes see things on the archipelago that disappear a moment later. Or hear strange sounds. It's always like that, it's totally normal.'

Dupin hadn't the faintest idea what on earth he was meant to say to that. He turned around, ran a hand through his hair and walked westwards along the beach towards the bulbous southern tip of the island.

It was truly breathtaking. Wherever you looked. The finest white sugar sand, beaches dropping gently away into the sea, seawater so translucent you couldn't even see where the waterline began. A pale, yet bright, turquoise that turned opal and then light blue in endless metamorphoses. It only started to get darker far out. Not that the sea wasn't bewitching in Concarneau – it was exactly that which distinguished the town after all – but this, the Glénan, significantly raised the stakes. You weren't by the sea, you were *in* the sea, that was how it felt, in the middle of the sea. It wasn't just the taste and smell, it was a deep, penetrating impression.

But the most enchanting thing was the light, a powerful, tremendous light, yet soft, not aggressive. It was a light from all quarters. It didn't seem to have a precise source, or at least not just one, not just the sun. It came from the whole sky – from all its breadths, heights, layers, spheres and dimensions. And, above all, it came from the sea. The light seemed infinitely multiplied in the various atmospheres, reflecting the water and thus becoming more and more concentrated. The small scraps of land were far too slight to absorb any of it. Dupin had never seen as much light as he did in Brittany – nor any sky that hung so high, was so free – but all that was surpassed here on the Glénan. It made you drunk, people on the coast said, it turned your head. Dupin understood what they meant.

He fished his mobile phone out of the left back pocket of his trousers. It seemed to have survived everything so far. And it actually had reception.

'Nolwenn?'

'Monsieur le Commissaire?'

Dupin had completely forgotten that his secretary had had a doctor's appointment this morning and hadn't even been in the office. Instead she had been at gnarled old Docteur Garreg's, who was also his own GP. He only recalled that now.

'Ah yes, you probably don't know what's happened yet?'

'No. I was just about to ring Inspector Kadeg. I saw that he'd tried me three times.'

'Three bodies. On the Glénan. On Le Loc'h. Washed up. Not yet identified. At the moment it looks like a tragic accident.'

'Yes, they're always on Le Loc'h. The Glénan have spelt shipwrecks in every era.'

Nolwenn remained absolutely composed, as always.

'"If you want to learn to pray, then go to sea!" is what we say round here.'

Nolwenn liked old sayings and passing them on formed part of her 'Breton lessons' that she had been giving the Commissaire since he'd arrived, in the interests of his 'Bretonisation' (that's really what she called her project). Dupin wasn't sure how to reply.

'Yes. One way or another, this is going to make big waves. Savoir has just arrived. I'm leaving the island now.'

'You're there already?'

'Yes.'

'By boat?'

'Yes.'

The second yes had sounded much more glum than Dupin had intended.

'Can I do anything right now?'

'No. First of all we have to investigate the identities of the deceased.'

Dupin hadn't actually had a specific aim in mind. He had just wanted Nolwenn to be up to speed. Nolwenn had been his anchor since his first day in his new 'homeland'. She was capable and pragmatic in all things, nothing in the world – or beyond it, Dupin imagined – could faze her. In three weeks she was going on holidays for the first time in two years, far away, to Portbou, on the Mediterranean border of the Pyrenees,. Since he had learnt about it, it had been making Dupin rather nervous. She was planning fourteen whole days at once.

'The Prefect will want to talk to you personally again today,' she said. 'Having had the initial discussions at his meeting on Guernsey. We had set up a telephone meeting for the afternoon. I'm afraid that will be completely impossible now. I will have a message sent to him via his office.'

'I – that is – wonderful! Yes. The coverage out here is really bad. He'll be able to understand that – I'm practically in the middle of the sea.'

'The Prefect will know about the new mast on Penfret. The dedication was an event. Although it could be more powerful... But – I take it that you will be in the midst of investigating. Three bodies, I mean, by Breton standards... No matter how they lost their lives. A swift resolution will also be in the Prefect's interests.'

Dupin's mood brightened for the first time that day.

'Great, yes. That's true.'

But only now did he take a moment to think about why the mast thing had been so much of an 'event' that everyone knew about it.

'So I'll pass on the message not to expect a call from you for the time being.'

'Excellent.'

Dupin hesitated.

'Was – how was it at the doctor's? I mean...'

'All okay.'

'I'm glad to hear it.'

He felt a bit silly.

'Thanks. What you really must bear in mind is to call your mother. She has left three answerphone messages already today.'

That was all he needed. He was always forgetting. His mother. For the very first time since his 'exile to the provinces' – this was what she consistently called it to this day – she was planning to visit him. This Thursday. And for weeks she had been calling – daily by now – to clarify yet another 'important issue', which always revolved around a single fear: whether, at so far away from the metropolis, there was still a sufficient degree of civilised standards. Dupin had of course booked her – Anna Dupin, the traditionally elitist Parisienne from an upper-class background, tyrannical when she needed to be, otherwise enchanting, and who only left Paris when it was unavoidable – into the best hotel in Concarneau. And naturally he had reserved the most expensive room, the 'Suite Navy', but she didn't seem to assumetake it for granted that there would be running water available.

'Will do.'

'Good.'

'Thanks, Nolwenn.'

Dupin hung up. He really needed to take care of a few more things for the visit, mainly his flat. Although it wasn't particularly untidy, he didn't want to show the slightest weakness. It would be best if they didn't even go into his flat. He would have the whole visit take place at other places.

Dupin had walked around a small outcrop of the land, this was where the white sandy beach came to an abrupt end. Unkempt, bushy, luxuriant greenery – stalks, grasses, ferns – grew down to the rocky waterline. Here, the island's rocks ran thirty or forty metres into the water and only here was there sand again. Dupin stepped onto the narrow, stony trail which had once led around the island, an old smugglers' and pirates' path, like the ones found all over the coast here. For hundreds of years, the Glénan had been the kingdom of renowned pirates, 'evil' English ones for instance, and 'good' Breton ones, the latter highly honoured to this day, regardless of any moral issues, because there was only one thing that mattered: they came from Brittany and were world famous. Nolwenn's heroine, after whom she'd called her first daughter, was the 'Breton Tigress' – the *'Tigresse de Bretagne'* – Jeanne de Belleville, the first authentic female pirate in world history. She was a breathtakingly beautiful woman from the nobility of the then still independent (!) Brittany, who had daringly destroyed countless well-equipped ships with a 'fleet' of just three boats in the thirteenth century – ships belonging to a mortal enemy: the French king.

The ruins of the soda factory could be made out at the western end of the island. Industrial soda had been extracted from algae here for manufacturing glass, and for washing and dying products. A valuable substance at the beginning of the twentieth century, unimaginable these days. Then suddenly, you saw the stunning sea too. A little surreal, it lay there like a smooth plane, you could see the incredible colour it was famous for: a vibrant, almost phosphorescent green-grey-blue. What was special about it was the shade's unique depth of intensity. Dupin couldn't help thinking, whether he wanted to or not – and he was struggling not to want to – of Goulch's stories about the sea. The witch. Groac'h. He understood immediately that this sea lent the imagination broad, strange wings. He shivered for a moment. Images of pitch-black labyrinths of underwater caves conjured themselves up unbidden in his mind's eye.

Dupin had thought it would be a good idea to walk around for a while. Have a look about. But there was no real reason for it. What should he be keeping an eye out for? Whatever had happened, it certainly hadn't happened on Le Loc'h, so there wouldn't be anything relevant here. He didn't have the faintest idea what else he ought to do on the island. They needed to investigate the identities of the dead and find out what had happened to the three men. Besides, he wouldn't be able to contribute at the scene.

So far, it had not been Dupin's day at all, this Monday. The Commissaire hadn't slept for long or well, although he had been sleeping quite well for some time, by his standards at least. He had been restless all night without knowing why. It was clear he needed a coffee now. Desperately. And immediately.

Dupin took his phone out of his pocket.

'Riwal?'

'Monsieur le Commissaire?'

'Could you ask Goulch to have the *Bir* take me to Saint-Nicolas?'

'To Saint-Nicolas? Now?'

'Precisely.'

There was quite a pause and in the silence, Riwal's unasked question about what the Commissaire was planning to do on Saint-Nicolas was practically audible. But Riwal didn't ask, knowing after years working with the maverick, occasionally pig-headed Commissaire what was sensible and what was not.

'I take it Saint-Nicolas will be the central point for all news here on the archipelago then? Goulch will have the chance to pick up his colleagues and I can have another word with the Englishman.'

'I'll speak to Goulch. You just need to come back to the beach, they won't be able to pick you up anywhere else on the island.'

'No problem. I'll be right there.'

'All right.'

'Riwal – the bar there will be open by now, won't it?'

'The bar?'

'The cafe.'

'I have no idea, sir.'

'Let's see.'

The wooden lobster cages with their pale blue braided ropes faded by the sea were strewn about by the dozen, piled artistically into towers here and there, and into downright mountains to the right of the main quay. Dupin was marvelling at the cages, as he sat in one of the wobbly, chipped wooden chairs scattered in front of the bar, along with some tables.

The *Les Quatre Vents* had obviously not been built as a restaurant, cafe or bar. It had been the boathouse for the first sea-rescue organisation on the coast, which had its headquarters in Concarneau but, due to the constant missions, had its most important branch here. The building was over a hundred years old and it had not been renovated at all on the outside and only slightly – and at no great cost – on the inside. To the left was a small, crooked, temporary-looking annexe made of wood, painted white like the stone main building, which was connected to the main room via a passageway. It had large windows and offered space for a few more tables.

There wasn't much available in the *Quatre Vents*, a small selection of drinks, mainly beer, wine and spirits; a changing *Plat du jour* – the fish of the day or an *entrecôte*; sandwiches with different fish rillettes; fish soup; and the seafood available from the Atlantic – crab, spider crab, various kinds of mussels and snails (bulots, bigourneaux, palourdes, praires, ormeaux). But especially, of course, Glénan lobsters. Above the main door there was a piece of wood with white handwritten letters that said 'Bar' and underneath that, 'Les Quatre Vents', with stylised seagulls flying to the right and left of the writing. The tracks which had been used to take the sea-rescue organisation's majestic boat out into the water until it could manoeuvre itself, also lay in front of the old boathouse, leading far out to the sea.

Dupin's mood had suddenly improved since he'd sat down in the *Quatre Vents*. It was wonderful here. It had been immediately obvious to him that he loved this place; straight away it was added to Dupin's list of 'special places', a list which he had been keeping for as long as he could remember. Places that made him happy. Everything was authentic in the *Quatre Vents*, nothing arranged or done up to be idyllic. And, in fact, it wasn't idyllic at all, it was – stunningly beautiful. And, just as importantly: the coffee was perfect. Dupin's second now. There was no table service, you had to fetch everything for yourself on wooden trays at a long counter in the bar, so you could sit wherever you wanted. Dupin had sat with his back to the wall of the annexe – from here he had a view of all the scenery.

To the left, perhaps thirty metres away, stood the island's largest building, the low lying former farmhouse that served as headquarters for the legendary sailing school: *Les Glénans* (with an 's', although the islands themselves are written without an 's' in the face of all grammar.) It had been founded at the end of the Second World War by a couple of idealistic young people from the Résistance and in the decades that followed it had developed into the most respected sailing school in the world. The school had spread quickly onto five of the other islands and now had branches in twelve countries. The building gleamed a dazzling white – it must have been repainted just recently. By the sea even the most resistant special paints lose their shine within months, the sun, salt, moisture and wind affect them so much. Opposite the sailing school, in front of which there was a small, oblong square, stood two oyster ponds. Their solid outer walls formed a kind of port wall facing the sea. The ponds had been half built over with a shed, which functioned as an oyster bar in the summer, not chic – nothing was chic here – no fuss and no hassle. Just marvellous.

A huge painting on the front wall of the shed added something whimsical to the otherwise completely harmonious scene. Painted in a deliberately naive way, it featured the typical landscapes of the Glénan – the best known landmarks of the individual islands and mythical subjects had been combined into a surreal panoramic picture. To the right you could see Groac'h's throne and the woman herself, represented as a pretty young queen with the tail of a fish. Right in the middle of the picture, on a beach, stood a large penguin, looking around cheekily. Penguins may have been Dupin's favourite animals, but he still brooded over what this one was doing here – a black-footed penguin, if he was not mistaken.

A massive, heavy, concrete quay ran along the side of the larger oyster pond, extending a good fifty metres into the sea. It was here that many boats docked in the summer months, shuttling back and forth between the islands and various places on the coast. The *Bir* had moored there half an hour ago too. The young police officer had long since completed the – utterly unsuccessful – questioning of the Englishman and was already waiting on the quay.

One of the Glénan's typical Caribbean-looking beaches began not far from the oyster ponds. At low tide – which was now – the most remarkable thing about this beach was that it extended out as far as an endlessly long sandbank, making Bananec – which was in fact the smaller neighbouring island to Saint-Nicolas – into an annexe of the main island. The most extraordinary beach in the archipelago lay between the two every twelve hours – and twenty-five minutes! – new and pure, washed clean by the sea.

Only two other tables had customers sitting at them. A group of English people,

sailors judging by their clothes, and a group of French people, Parisian by the looks of it. Dupin had a good eye for these things. There was a certain degree of excitement apparent in both groups, which wasn't surprising. Dupin assumed that they were talking about the washed up bodies. Of course.

They had not found any clues to the identity of the dead during their examination, no papers, no mobiles, nothing. There had been a little bit of change in two of their trouser pockets a slip of paper in one of them, already severely damaged by the saltwater and not yet possible to decipher. Kadeg had called him and delivered a rousing report just after Dupin had arrived on Saint-Nicolas.

Dupin was hungry. He hadn't eaten anything yet, other than the obligatory croissant with his first coffee. Why shouldn't he order something? He felt a little odd, three unknown dead people lay on the beach one island along, the investigations were underway, everyone was busy and he was just sitting here and – having a holiday, that's how it felt. He had just decided he would eat something – despite his scruples – when suddenly his thoughts were interrupted by an ear-splitting sound. A helicopter was flying eastwards in a long arc over Saint-Nicolas. It seemed like it had come out of nowhere, but Dupin recognised the sea-rescue service. It had to be one of the helicopters that Goulch had spoken about. As it was moving away and Dupin was just about to stand up, his phone rang.

'Yes?'

He hadn't taken any notice of the number. He hated when he forgot to do that.

'It's me.'

He sighed with relief. 'Nolwenn.'

'Good, I wanted...'

'Locmariaquer. He called from Guernsey. A friend of his is missing. Yannig Konan. An 'entrepreneur and investor', as they say. At first he got rich selling mattresses, then he ploughed his money into all kinds of businesses. He has a finger in everything imaginable. Seriously rich.' Nolwenn emphasised the 'seriously' with a wrinkled nose, which Dupin could practically hear. 'And an experienced sailor. Konan was on a boat trip with an acquaintance.'

'A friend of... a friend of the Prefect's?'

'Yes. Do you think that he...'

'Two of them? There were two of them out together?'

'Yes. Two of them. A criminal, this Konan, if you ask me.'

'A criminal? What do you mean by... Oh... He'll turn up again, this mattress entrepreneur.

We've got *three* bodies here.'

There was a suspenseful pause.

'How long has he been missing?' Dupin asked.

He was annoyed at himself for enquiring – he didn't actually feel like giving it any thought.

'He was meant to get in touch with his wife yesterday evening. And this morning he was supposed to be back in the port of Sainte-Marine. His boat is there, he has a house there too. Konan has a series of important meetings today. He has not turned up yet and hasn't sent word to anyone, which is why his office in Quimper contacted his wife, who...'

'And the acquaintance?'

'He's not answering the phone either, Konan's wife says.'

'Where were they on the boat?'

'His wife didn't know exactly. In good weather they spend the weekend on the boat quite often. Frequently on the Glénan. Fishing and diving. "Getting away from it all", as we like to say.'

Every second Breton, Dupin estimated, had a boat. And if you didn't have one yourself, then you knew someone who did. This only applied to the coastal Bretons of course. It would never even have occurred to an inland Breton to drive to the sea.

'They'll have absolutely no reception out there where they are. It seems to be tricky at sea, the reception.'

'Konan's boat is equipped with a satellite phone. But they cannot be contacted on that either.'

'They will...'

The helicopter had come back. Strangely, as before, it could only be heard when it was almost directly above Dupin. The noise was horrific.

'What's wrong over there?'

Dupin could only just make out Nolwenn's question.

'A helicopter!' he bellowed.

'A helicopter?'

Dupin was about to take the phone away from his ear and hold it right in front of his mouth and scream the explanation, when Nolwenn beat him to it.

'Of course. The coastguard.'

The helicopter was not showing any signs of flying on. On the contrary, it was clearly descending. Slowly at first and then faster and faster. It was going to land. The sound had become even more of a droning, it was absolutely impossible to make yourself heard.

'I'm hanging up now.'

Dupin had no idea whether Nolwenn had understood him.

The helicopter couldn't have been more than a few metres above the ground, it had disappeared from Dupin's line of sight. Dupin considered what to do. Should he check on it? He stayed seated. The sound continued for a minute or two, then the pilot killed the engine and suddenly the great, deep silence that reigned in the archipelago was back. Before Dupin could even sigh with relief, his phone rang again. It wasn't Nolwenn this time, it was Riwal.

'What is it?'

'One of the coastguard's helicopters should have just landed where you are.'

Dupin felt incapable of responding.

'We weren't able to get through to you – you were engaged the whole time. Objects have been sighted in the sea. Could be from a boat. At a small rock formation, Les Méaban, three nautical miles east of the archipelago. But somehow, it's still part of the Glénan. The other helicopter is still there and searching.'

In the centuries-old argument about how many islands, islets and rock formations the archipelago was actually made up of, and at which tides, there was always another question: which islands, islets and rock formations that did not directly belong to the archipelago, still counted as doing so? If needs be, even just geologically, geographically. that lay more or less off the coast between Trévignon, Concarneau and Guilvinec was often merrily assigned to them.

'Could the dead bodies have drifted here from there? What does Goulch think?' asked Dupin.

'Absolutely, he reckons. But he also says that's pure speculation right now.'

'What is the helicopter up to, here on Saint-Nicolas?'

'We couldn't – get through to you.'

'It's here for me?'

'The – the Prefect has – ordered it to fly you to the rock formation to have a good look at the objects in person.'

Riwal had clearly found it difficult to pass this on. He had beaten about the bush for what felt like a minute in the first half of the sentence and rushed through the second half in a split second.

'Fly? *Ordered*?'

Dupin could feel himself getting angry – entirely against his will, because it was his firm resolution to remain calm in everything relating to the Prefect and not let himself be provoked, in spite of the fact that he could recall few things, sentences or incidents relating to the Prefect that weren't a kind of provocation.

'And why should I fly there?'

'I was just meant to inform you of what he'd said. And he mentioned that it was an "order" repeatedly.'

It was clear that what Riwal wanted more than anything for the ground to open up and swallow him.

'Did he call you directly?' 'Yes, twice in the last ten minutes alone. He tried you, but, as I mentioned, it was engaged. He also said,' Riwal sounded utterly despondent now, 'I absolutely had to remind you, to activate the call-waiting function on your phone. He has already told you that several times, he can never reach you when it matters. He can only ever get through to Nolwenn.'

'Call-waiting service?'

This was a baffling conversation.

'It means that...'

'I'm not flying anywhere. What am I meant to be able to make out from the air? – – – What nonsense. Our colleagues will do a thorough inspection. What's more important is that we send one of the boats there.'

'The *Bir* is already on its way. They have diving equipment on board. Should we pick you up in the second boat?'

'I'm staying here.'

'And the Pref...'

'Let me worry about that, Riwal. Tell the pilot he can fly back. To wherever. Get in touch if there's news.'

'But...'

Dupin hung up. Riwal would understand him – he was used to him when he was in one of these moods. Dupin leaned back and took a deep breath. Tried to calm down again. Only now did he realise that the people at the other tables were staring at him, more or less openly. He didn't take offence. He was just attempting to make an effort to smile in the direction of both groups when his phone rang.

Nolwenn again.

'Yannig Konan's boat has been located. It is safe and sound in Bénodet harbour. He himself hasn't turned up yet – but even so, that is hugely reassuring. The Prefect has given the all-clear.'

Dupin wondered briefly how the Prefect managed to make so many phone calls within such a short time and to be up to speed to such an extent. It almost commanded his respect.

'Well that's good.'

'Only for the mattress manufacturer. The three deceased are still dead.'

Nolwenn had hit the nail on the head again.

'That's bad, yes.'

He had made an effort to find the correct tone of voice. It had only partially worked.

'Speak to you later then, Monsieur le Commissaire.'

'Yes. But also…'

The helicopter pilot started up the engine at that moment. The deafening sound was back. Dupin simply hung up. A moment later the helicopter appeared above the sailing school's headquarters, climbing at a remarkable speed and already moving in a southerly direction. Back to the Méaban, Dupin guessed.

These last few minutes had been ludicrous. But he wouldn't let himself be put off. In fact, he was going to eat a lobster now. In peace and quiet. It had gone noon. The clues were really piling up after all: they were probably dealing with a shipwreck. The *Bir* would examine everything thoroughly. The items seen from the helicopter. Kireg Goulch and his people would reconstruct the course of the accident reliably and quickly. The Prefect's tyrannical interest in the progress of the investigation had ended the moment it became clear that none of the dead was likely to be his friend. Excellent.

Dupin got up and went into the bar. The young woman he'd got the coffee from before was still standing behind the counter. She was still leaning – attractively bored – against the wall, near the passageway to the annexe. Short, not petite, but still slim, with dull shoulder-length black hair, remarkably deep brown eyes, snub-nosed, but, more than anything, majestically unconcerned and aloof. Dupin could have sworn she had been wearing a dark red t-shirt with jeans before, not a blue one. He had tried to strike up a conversation earlier while ordering the coffee, but had failed spectacularly. He got nothing more out of her than a '*oui*' and a '*s'il vous plaît*'. Like last time, she only looked up at Dupin once he was standing right in front of her at the counter.

'I'd like some lobster.'

It took her a few seconds to respond.

'There's a half lobster. Or a whole one.'

'Good. I think I'll take a whole one.'

Till now she had been standing completely still, but now she moved sleekly, like a cat, walking through the narrow open door to the kitchen without a word. The kitchen couldn't be very big, you could see that

47

it went back at most twelve metres to the outer wall. An old man was sitting at the end of bar, absorbed in reading his paper. He had caught Dupin's eye earlier. He looked like he hadn't moved since. He was sitting in the exact same pose. He had short white hair that lay flat against his head and a face weathered by the sun and deeply lined. You could have sworn straight away: a dignified old sailor. As before, he only raised his head a touch, his eyes glancing at Dupin and he made a subtle, but friendly gesture of greeting. It didn't take long for the young woman to return with a rustic white ceramic plate, with both lobster halves on it, a large piece of baguette, a lemon cut in half and two little white dishes, one with mayonnaise and one with *rouille*.

'And a jug of water, please.' Dupin hesitated. 'And a glass of Muscadet.'

The young woman put the plate on a tray, took a jug from a long row of them and taking her time, poured out the wine.

'Twenty-two euro.'

Dupin got out his wallet. He was intrigued by prices here, every time. In Paris, it would have been sixty. Minimum.

'Have you heard about the – news, the incidents on Le Loc'h?'

'The bodies?'

It sounded as though there was other news that might turn out to be even more spectacular.

'Exactly.'

'Yes.'

Her face was absolutely impassive.

'And what do you think?'

She looked at Dupin, a little shocked.

'Me?'

'Yes. You live here.'

'You're the police officer questioning people here, aren't you.'

It hadn't really been a question. He knew that he didn't look like a police officer, even less so than usual today.

'Yes – no, he's already gone. I'm – a different police officer.'

The young woman was utterly unimpressed by Dupin's awkward answer.

'They're always on Le Loc'h.'

'I know. And what do you think happened?'

This time she looked completely baffled. There was a considerable pause and Dupin assumed that she would not reply again.

'It happens. The sea.'

Dupin liked her manner, even though the conversation was a bit of an effort.

'Thank you.'

Without a word, she went and stood in the same position as before, in the same place she had initially been standing. Dupin took the tray, one of the already somewhat dog-eared newspapers that lay on the counter, left the bar and sat down in his seat again. One of the two groups was noisily leaving. These weren't sailors, Dupin realised now, but divers. He could see their equipment in the large bags. The Glénan, all of the lagoons – he'd been told countless times – were among the most spectacular diving paradises in Europe. Especially the chamber of course, with its unique underwater flora and fauna.

And the Glénan's diving school was an institution, even though it wasn't as big and well known as the sailing school. The group strolled towards the diving school building, which stood a little further on from the *Quatre Vents*. There wasn't even a path, you had to walk on mossy vegetation to get to it.

The lobster was incredible. If the Breton lobster, which was a little smaller than the American kind and also dark blue, was already a particular delicacy with its delicious, white flesh, the culinary reputation of the Glénan lobster was – along with that of the other sea creatures of the archipelago – even more impressive. It was self-evidently the 'best lobster in the world' but even Dupin, who still smirked to himself sometimes about the proto-Breton tendency to comparatives and superlatives when it came to anything Breton (even though he himself had more or less internalised the habit by now) found the pride completely justifiable in this instance. The lobster was delicate and at the same time very aromatic, with the exquisite, nutty, bitter note that Dupin liked so much. You had everything that made up the sea on your tongue, magically distilled with every bite. He pondered whether it might be possible to get this on the mainland. He would ask Paul Girard, the owner of the *Amiral*. Maybe he even served it in the *Amiral* itself. And it would definitely be in the magnificent old market halls on the main square in Concarneau that was like Cockaigne anyway, a fairytale land of milk and honey. They reminded him of the halls in the 6th Arrondissement on the rue Lobineau which he had loved even as a child and which were also wonderful because they opened at six in the morning, shutting only at midnight – a huge advantage given his working hours, which were extremely unpredictable, even in Paris. But more than anything, they had been *their* favourite place for a long time – his and Claire's. It was here that they had sometimes met at ten or eleven at night, after work, at a bistro-type stand with a few old wooden chairs. The stand specialised in wine, cheese and mustard. They sat there, watched people, that special, wonderful atmosphere at the time. Drank wine, not talked much.

It occurred to Dupin that he needed to call Claire. Wanted to. That's how it was, if he were honest: he *wanted* to call her. He had arranged to speak to Claire on the phone a few weeks ago. He had called her at the beginning of April, she had been on her way into the clinic and they had agreed to talk again soon, but for longer next time. They had also done this after Christmas last year when they had spoken at greater length – also considering whether they might not meet up, but they obviously hadn't trusted themselves then. He wanted this. He wanted to see Claire. It had become clear to him in the last few weeks. Not that it wasn't clear to him earlier, but not to such an extent. None of the relationships he had begun since the break-up with Claire – and there had been quite a few –had become serious. Not because they weren't amazing women, but because it always became clear to him suddenly that it wasn't working. Not even last year with the art historian, who had helped him with a spectacular case and whom he'd met several times since. It had been really lovely. And they had been in the *Océanopolis*. And had visited Dupin's beloved penguins. Then she had gone to Montreal at short notice, an offer from the university, but in all honesty that wasn't the reason why it didn't go any further.

During the last two phone calls with Claire, Dupin had felt for the first time that she was also genuinely thinking of them seeing each other again. Dupin picked up his mobile and dialled her number, which he still knew off by heart. There was a pause.

'Hello, you've reached the voicemail of Dr Claire Chauffin of the surgical department at Hôpital Georges Pompidou. Please leave a message.'

She had forwarded her phone's voicemail to her clinic. As she nearly always did. Dupin hesitated.

'I – I'll call again.'

He hung up abruptly.

He was well aware this was not the ideal message. Dupin hoped she would at least recognise his voice. The connection, he realised, had not been the best.

She *would* recognise it. Without doubt. And – he had called.

While enjoying the legendary lobster, a question constantly bothered the Commissaire in spite of himself. It had been going round and round in his head since Nolwenn's last call and he'd been trying to push it aside more and more forcefully since then. In vain. He would have to redirect his thoughts somewhere else more forcefully.

He fixed his gaze on a boat that had just approached the quay which didn't look like the others. It was larger, longer – perhaps fifteen metres he estimated.

It had superstructures that looked industrial. The sun beat down. He could have done with a cap.

'Oh, crap.'

It was no use. Distracting himself wasn't working. He had spoken in a low voice, but a few people turned around to look at him. He reached for the phone, his mood almost as bad as it had been that morning. Dupin knew that people said he was a little surly and bad-tempered from time to time – he'd heard 'contrary' once on his last case and he'd liked this expression best. Depending on his mood, he reacted to these kinds of comments in a conciliatory, self-deprecating or even a somewhat gruff way, but in general he considered this claim completely unreasonable.

'Nolwenn?'

'Monsieur le Commissaire?'

'The ship belonging to that mattress entrepreneur, which was found in Bénodet. Has he been heard from by now? I mean, has he got in touch?'

'I don't know. The Prefect was reassured when he heard that Konan's boat was safe in the harbour. I'll ask whether there's been any word from him in the meantime.'

'And Konan's acquaintance? Has anyone heard from him? And does anyone know why the ship is in Bénodet and not in Sainte-Marine? And who actually saw this boat in the harbour and why did they report it?'

'I don't have the faintest idea.'

'Do we know the name of this friend?'

'No.'

'Does he have a boat too?'

'As far as I know, they always went out in Yannig Konan's boat. Do you want me to clarify all of these points?'

Dupin didn't even know. Everything was so mysterious anyway. He was worrying about a friend of the Prefect's whom Nolwenn considered a criminal and this despite the fact that, as yet, no conclusive evidence of any kind existed that there was any reason to worry. Konan was probably just with a woman. Some sleazy affair.

'I'm going to finish my lobster now.'

'Your lobster?'

'Lobster.'

'You're in the *Quatre Vents*?'

'Correct.'

'Lobster from the Glénan is the best in the world. Good thing you're there. If you need anything, ask Solenn Nuz. She's the owner of the *Quatre Vents*. She knows everything. Knows everyone. The Glénan are her kingdom.'

'Her kingdom?'

'Oh yes.'

'What's that meant to mean?'

'You'll see. Solenn Nuz bought the *Quatre Vents* from the council ten years ago with her husband, Jacques. A passionate diver. The diving school already belonged to him, but they still lived on the mainland at that time. Nobody wanted to have the old boathouse, it was empty for almost seven years. Everyone thought it would be too tough to open a restaurant out there. – Have you met Solenn Nuz yet?'

'No.'

'Then I'm sure you'll have met one of her two daughters. Louann and Armelle, they work in the bar too. You can barely tell the three of them apart, they look so similar, it's amazing. One lives with her mother on the archipelago, the other with her boyfriend on the mainland, but she's often there. They have a cottage on the island, diagonally behind the sailing school.'

Dupin imagined it was not an easy life out here.

'And the husband, the diver?'

'Oh, it's a sad story. Drowned. Just after they'd bought the *Quatre Vents* and were about to move to the Glénan. It was their great shared dream. Solenn went to the islands anyway. She rented out the club. To a girlfriend of hers.'

During his years of close cooperation with Nolwenn, Dupin had become used to her knowing a huge amount about a huge number of people from Cornouaille – the coast between the most western point in France, the Pointe du Raz, and Quimperlé – without making the least bit of fuss about it. Sometimes he was gobsmacked though, and and a question slipped out.

'And how do you know all this?'

'The 'End of the World' isn't big, Monsieur le Commissaire. And also, my husband…'

'…once did a a few jobs for Solenn Nuz.'

'That's right.'

Dupin had no idea what Nolwenn's husband did for a living – he had also decided early on never to ask – but his job was clearly of a universal nature. There couldn't be many people in the region, Dupin reckoned, for whom Nolwenn's husband hadn't 'done a few jobs'.

'She is an attractive woman. Dour. A rugged beauty. Stayed young. Very young.'

Dupin wasn't sure what Nolwenn meant by that. Or why they had even been talking about the owner of the bar for minutes on end.

He allowed a pause to develop.

'Forget I called, Nolwenn.'

Nolwenn was familiar with every detail of Dupin's abrupt shifts.

'Then let's speak later.'

'I'll be in touch.'

Nolwenn had hung up.

Dupin still had the phone to his ear and had only just pushed the red button to hang up when it rang again. He answered automatically.

'Monsieur le Commissaire?'

'Riwal?!'

'You were engaged again. I wanted to say that the bodies are being brought to the pathologist's office by helicopter now, if you're okay with that. We can't get anything more done here. Savoir can't either. He needs them in his lab. He's pestering.'

'Of course. Is there any news? Missing persons reports? Something on the shipwreck?'

'Not yet.'

'But how can that be? Surely the three of them have been missed.'

'They could be from anywhere. Maybe they were foreign nationals. Dutch, German, English or Parisians taking a trip along the coast. Lots of people do that. If they were holidaying here on their own boat or on a rented one, it could take a while for them to be missed. And then for someone to call the police.'

That was true. Dupin's brow furrowed and he rubbed his temple with his right hand.

'The *Bir* is at the Méaban now. There's some stuff floating in the water between the cliffs, probably plastic mainly. Still nothing directly indicating a wrecked boat. They're taking a good look at everything now. Kadeg and I can come over to you on the *Luc'hed* now. And then go round the boats in the chamber and ask questions. About whether anyone noticed anything. Even if it's highly unlikely to come to anything.'

'Over to me?'

'Absolutely.'

'Feel free.'

Dupin said these words slowly – he had been thinking about something else as he spoke. Frankly, he didn't know what he was still doing on Saint-Nicolas, or indeed on the Glénan at all – except that it was very beautiful here, he was eating the best lobster of his life and the coffee was perfect. He could just as easily fly back with Dr Savoir and coordinate everything from Concarneau – which had the distinct advantage of meaning not having to get onto another boat today.

'Are you still there, Monsieur le Commissaire?'

'Riwal – the helicopter is to pick me up. In half an hour, from Saint-Nicolas. You need to take the bodies on board first of course, I'm sure that will take a while.'

Riwal's answer, when it came, was hesitant.

'All right, there's nothing more for you to do here. I'll arrange that.'

'And you can start the interviews on the boats straight away. You really don't need to come to Saint-Nicolas first.'

He would still have the entire half hour to himself. Be able to finish his meal in peace.

He hung up.

Dupin looked around. The terrace had filled up all of a sudden. Almost all of the tables were full now, including one of the two closest to him. The couple must have heard what he'd said. Dupin put on an ostentatiously friendly smile, which didn't do a thing to change the fact that his neighbours were giving him suspicious looks.

It really was all go. The sailing and diving season had already begun. Every year the Atlantic made the crucial leap from ten or twelve degrees to fourteen or fifteen (then in June or July the leap to eighteen degrees and, in Breton 'heat spells', sometimes even up to nineteen or twenty. Apparently in 2006, the sea in Port Manech was actually twenty-two degrees celsius on the 23rd and 24th of August!) The people he could see were clearly water-sports lovers, mostly between the ages of twenty and forty. For the anglers too, the best seasons were now, in May, and then in September, when the huge schools of mackerel appeared. Then you only needed to let your line down into the sea with nothing more than a hook and they would already be biting – with the number five hook lines that they used here, there were five fat fish per line. Dupin had heard many stories about it.

He ate the last piece of lobster, the flesh from the broken open pincer. He had saved the best till last, he'd done that even as a child. And he drank the last mouthful of the very good, very cold, white wine.

Dupin leaned back. He picked up the newspaper. Almost the entire front page of *Ouest France* – one of the two large regional papers that Dupin loved and meticulously studied every morning – was devoted to the thirty-six dead wild boar, as it had been for the last few days. Thirty-six wild boar had been found dead on a beach in the north, in the Côtes-d'Armor *département*. Killed by poisonous gases released during the decomposition of green algae. It was a sad report and one which provoked extreme rage. The death of a wild boar touched Bretons to their core, they loved their wild boar – *Asterix and Obelix* was pure truth. For years, the plague of algae had been one of the most discussed topics in Brittany. It was also one of Riwal's favourite topics – just last Friday afternoon he had got worked up for a full half hour ('an absolute disgrace!'). The over-fertilisation of the fields through the years and the run-off of the nitrates through the streams and rivers into the sea often resulted in large algae build-ups in the summer months. Some beaches were strewn with it for hundreds of metres. It was harmless really, edible in fact, it only became dangerous if it decomposed in the summer sun. This year the first of the algae had already been washed up by the end of April, earlier than ever before. Suddenly the whole of France and half of Europe were discussing it. Maybe the deaths of the wild boar would actually affect the supremacy of the farming lobby and the barefaced way many politicians played it down. Maybe the wild boars would change things – it would be a very Breton story.

Dupin's phone rang. Nolwenn again.

'Konan's friend is called Lucas Lefort. A big name in Brittany. Co-owner of the sailing school

Les Glénans. The most famous sailing school in the world! It belongs to him and his sister, the two of them inherited it. Also, Lefort used to be a professional sailor himself. He was a member of the crew of the *Explorer IV* that won the Admiral's Cup eight years ago, the toughest and most significant sailing competition for ocean-going yachts. The open class – the unofficial world championship. Only Bretons on the team!'

Nolwenn did actually draw breath here, going on a little more calmly.

'Konan goes with him on his trips. The headquarters on the islands are right next to the *Quatre Vents*. He also has a house on Saint-Nicolas, one of those houses that are very ugly on the outside, towards Bananec.'

Dupin delved into the topic reluctantly.

'Does he live on the islands?'

'He actually lives in Les Sables Blancs, he's got a villa there, renovated in an extremely modern way by a top architect, with a pool and all that. But he also seems to spend the night on Saint-Nicolas quite often. A confirmed bachelor. If you ask me: a show-off, snob and womaniser. He makes headlines quite a lot.'

Dupin was again tempted to ask how she knew all of this and how she'd come by this information within such a short time. Not least, how she had come to this drastic characterisation of hers. He had sounded like a hero at first.

'By the way, Lefort didn't keep his two boats in Bénodet, of course, he kept them in Concarneau. He owns a luxury sailing yacht and one of those speedboats. He's always running between the Glénan and the mainland in them.'

'Hmm. And why are they not out in the luxury yacht on their trips, he and Konan?'

'No idea, Monsieur le Commissaire.'

'I'll see if I happen to run into him here. Or whether anybody knows anything.'

Dupin had uttered this sentence instinctively. Nolwenn had, apparently, been reckoning on that exact thing. She knew him.

'I've just asked at the sailing school whether he is there. They said they don't know where he is right now, but he's expected there at any moment.'

'All right. Tell Riwal there's no need for the helicopter to pick me up. I'm sure it'll come back again later. I assume. After it's taken the bodies to Quimper?'

'I don't know. But there's also the second sea-rescue helicopter.'

'Great.'

There was just one thing Dupin did not want: to set foot on another boat.

A few minutes later, Commissaire Dupin was standing in front of Lucas Lefort's house, which was indeed very ugly. It was the first in the row. The other absolutely identical houses followed at intervals of about fifteen metres – six of them, each one set a little further back than the last. They were each surrounded by a large, albeit barren garden, overgrown with nothing but bushy, wild island grass. For all that, they had an enchanting view of the lagoon of Saint-Nicolas and of Penfret, Drénec, Le Loc'h and – in the middle of the chamber – Fort-Cigogne. The gardens were separated from the seaside path by a knee-high, strange-looking and very plain concrete wall. The houses must have dated from the seventies and the architecture had surely been ambitious for the time. The slate roofs reached the ground, with windows and balconies built into them like niches, which must have been considered chic at the time. Probably, only the extremely strict coastal protection laws of the last few years had prevented them being torn down and replaced with new houses. Lefort's balcony was wooden and was the only attractive thing about the whole house, which was surrounded by large stones and furnished with – in Dupin's opinion – an excessively large wooden table and an equally excessive number of chairs.

You couldn't make anybody out through the light-reflecting panoramic windows. On the right hand edge of the property, there was a small wooden gateway, from where a narrow gravel path led towards the entrance at the side of the house. There was no doorbell visible on the gate. Just a small enamel plaque: 'L. Lefort'.

Dupin again toyed with the idea of letting Riwal know he was to be taken straight to the mainland after all. The whole situation was too awful. Here he was making enquiries about the clearly unpleasant friend of an equally unpleasant friend of the Prefect whom he hated. Perhaps Lefort was lying contentedly in bed after a long night and if not here, then in his villa in Sables Blancs. And what did that mean – 'They're expecting him'? Anyway: there were no indications of any kind that Konan and Lefort were two of the three bodies in the air on their way to the pathologist's office in Quimper at that very moment. And what was he meant to say to Lefort if he did runinto him here? 'For some reason I had a hunch you were one of the three water corpses, even though we had nothing indicating that – I'm glad that you're not'? Everything was pointing towards his immediate return to Concarneau. But no matter how much this all annoyed him, Dupin couldn't do anything about it. He opened the gate and walked along the gravel path.

The main door was just as ugly as the house – made of aluminium, with a frosted glass window in the upper third. No bell here either. Dupin knocked. Discreetly at first, but after waiting a while, with more force.

'Monsieur Lefort? Hello?'

Dupin called out several times. Louder each time. 'Commissariat de Police Concarneau.'

'I don't know if he's even in.'

Dupin jumped. There was a woman standing right behind him. He hadn't noticed anyone approaching and she couldn't have come up the pebbled path.

'I – Bonjour, Madame – Commissaire Dupin, Commissariat de Police Concarneau.'

The woman looked to be in her late thirties, with long, thick hair, dark blonde, set in a tidy plait. She was exceptionally thin, of average height, with elegantly high, yet completely harmonious, cheekbones, in a narrow face. Very narrow, but not ugly. Not at all. Guarded, alert, self-assured eyes. A visibly tight, mud-brown tweed skirt and an equally tight, severe blouse in a dark orange. It looked quaint, the way she was dressed, old-fashioned somehow.

'Has something happened to Lucas? What's this about? I'm his sister. Muriel Lefort.'

'No, not at all. I just wanted…'

This was even more difficult than if it had been Lefort himself. Whatever he said, it would make her anxious.

'I'm sure there's no need to worry.'

Dupin felt uneasy at this sentence.

'My brother and I had arranged to meet, but he hasn't turned up yet. I wanted to check if he was here. He's not answering his phone. His boat is in the harbour. So he should be on the island. He actually lives in Sables Blancs, but he's here now and again, although he doesn't stay overnight very often. He was still here last night anyway.'

'He was here last night?'

'Yes. I saw him briefly in the *Quatre Vents*. But I didn't speak to him. I was only there for a few minutes.'

'Was your brother alone?'

'I couldn't say. He was standing at the bar talking to a blonde woman. Why are you looking for my brother?'

Dupin had hoped to avoid this question.

He was confused. Lefort had been here yesterday evening. Had Yannig Konan been too? Had they been travelling in the area, did they stop off here because of the storm? Did the two of them stay overnight on the island? If Lefort had been alone, was that not really an indication that Konan had not been travelling with Lefort at all, but had actually been with a woman or something along those lines? But where was Lefort?

'Do you have a key to your brother's house?'

'Not here. I can get it, I live just next door.'

Dupin's telephone rang loudly. He saw Kadeg's number. He stood aside and picked up.

'We have a missing person's report. It just came in to Quimper.'

Kadeg was getting a bit flustered, even though he was desperately trying to keep his words under control.

'Who is it?'

'A Monsieur Arthur Martin. From Île-Tudy, not far from Bénodet. He...'

'What age?'

'Fifty-five.'

'I – wait a minute, Kadeg.'

Dupin turned to Muriel immediately, who was looking nervously at him.

'This is about something totally separate, Madame Lefort. About someone else. Categorically.'

'That's good to hear. – – – I think...' she broke off awkwardly, 'I'll go get the key.'

'Please do.'

Dupin waited a moment, then turned back to Kadeg.

'Who reported him missing?'

'His girlfriend. He was on the Île aux Moutons yesterday. It's not a part of the archipelago at all, but everyone counts it anyway. It's five nautical miles away, in the direction of the mainland, slightly more to the west. He was meant to be back tomorrow morning at the latest, travelling by boat. Not a very big boat, five metres sixty, that he was always going out in. With a cabin though. The girlfriend tried to get him on his mobile. Then she got more and more worried.'

'Maybe the battery is dead.'

'She drove round to his house and called his office. He hasn't turned up there yet either.'

'What was going to do on the islands?'

'Fish. He was an experienced fisherman.'

'Was he alone?'

'His girlfriend says he was always alone on the boat. I'm having a photo of Arthur Martin sent to us on my smartphone.'

Kadeg didn't use a mobile, of course, he used a smartphone. Dupin couldn't even stand how Kadeg pronounced the word 'smartphone', let alone watch how he showed off when he used it – with all of its sensational functions.

'I don't see any signs that the missing man could be one of the three bodies. Monsieur Martin is certain to turn up again soon.'

Dupin knew that the strictness of this conclusion was mainly due to his displeasure at letting Kadeg score a point here – but still: even sticking to the issue, none of this made any sense. There was one man involved. There was no evidence that he had met anyone. And it was actually very unlikely that several boats capsized last night, perhaps capsizing in several separate locations, each with one person aboard and that three bodies had floated onto the very same beach – wasn't it?

'I'd put it down to a strange coincidence,' said Kadeg. 'At the exact same time, we have three as yet unidentified bodies and one missing person. And the missing person's report relates to the exact area that we're talking about. It would be grossly negligent not to look into it.'

It sounded convincing when put like that, Dupin had to admit. 'All right.'

'We ought to let one of the helicopters know to take a look at the area around the Moutons,' Kadeg continued. 'And also request another boat from Bénodet or Fouesnant. The Moutons may be uninhabited, but there might be boats there that were also there yesterday and someone might have seen Martin's boat.'

'Please do that, Kadeg.'

Dupin hung up. Maybe for some reason they weren't aware of yet, there had actually been two more people on board the little boat belonging to the man from Île-Tudy yesterday? After all, they knew nothing at this stage.

He looked around. Madame Lefort was back in sight again, climbing skilfully over the low wall from the first house to the second. Soon she was standing next to him.

'The key.' She seemed absolutely composed again.

A moment later, she was unlocking the door.

Directly beyond it was a spacious, open room, which was the sitting-room and dining-room all in one. The panoramic windows were to the front and back and a small, premium-looking kitchen range was opposite the main door.

'Lucas? Lucas? Are you there?'

It wasn't meticulously tidy, but not untidy either. Madame Lefort was standing there a little uncertainly.

'This is a bit awkward for me, just going into my brother's house. I wouldn't normally.'

'In this case it's – appropriate.'

Dupin had spoken in a soft but firm voice.

'If you think so.'

Muriel Lefort moved toward the narrow wooden staircase that led up to the attic. Commissaire Dupin had stopped and was standing in almost the exact centre of the room.

'Lucas? A Commissaire wants to speak to you.'

She climbed the stairs and disappeared to the first floor for a few moments, before reappearing on the stairs.

'Nobody there, Monsieur le Commissaire. The bed looks unused. The bath too. He doesn't seem to have slept here.'

'So he must have travelled back during the night.'

'As I said, his boat is in the harbour. He owns one of those ridiculous speedboats. He has a space right on the mole.'

'Maybe...'

Dupin broke off. This wasn't going anywhere. Everything was pure speculation. They needed clear facts.

'Do you have a photo of your brother?'

Madame Lefort's unease returned.

'Do you now think it possible that my brother is one of the dead after all?'

'I would like to be able to say with certainty that he is not.'

'He might have stayed overnight with someone else. He...'

Now Muriel Lefort trailed off.

'I'll get you a photo,' she said.

She disappeared into the attic again, coming back a moment later.

'There was one hanging over his bed, with his current girlfriend, I think.'

She had emphasised the word 'girlfriend' in a strangely stilted way.

'The photo is quite recent anyway. Take it.'

She handed it to Dupin. It showed an admittedly attractive, tall, thin man. He had chiselled features, angular cheekbones and short, thick hair, shining black. He was wearing Bermudas and a dark polo-shirt, standing on a biggish sailing boat. He was laughing, his arms around a bikini-wearing, picture-perfect brunette. He was looking straight into the camera, confidently, penetratingly, challengingly. Dupin couldn't make out whether the man in the photo was one of the three dead on the beach. But of the three men, there had been only one face that was relatively easy to make out. And it wasn't him.

'I can't make a statement based on this photo. But it would be good if we could check it quickly. Then we'll have some certainty. I'll...'

Dupin reflected.

'There's a series of photos of my brother available on the internet. He is a well known sailor. The Admiral's Cup...'

'Can I keep the photo anyway?'

'If he turns up again straight away, you'll have to explain to him why the Commissariat de Police Concarneau is in possession of a private photograph of him and his girlfriend.'

Her smile was a little strained.

'I'll think of something. What is still important for us is this: you said you brother hasn't been seen since yesterday evening?'

Muriel Lefort answered slightly timidly.

'As far as I know. My assistant said she hadn't seen him all morning. I don't know what he had planned. As I mentioned, I didn't speak to him at all in the *Quatre Vents* last night. We...'

She seemed to be thinking for a moment.

'It is well known, that we weren't – that we're not close. We have a meeting today, there are some important things to discuss. We run the sailing school together, in theory, I mean... It belongs to both of us.'

'I see.'

'You still haven't told me how you came across my brother in the first place?'

Dupin had to keep a clear head. The situation with Lefort now seemed clearer than it really was.

'It's a bit complicated, Madame Lefort. We know that your brother often goes on boat trips with a Monsieur Yannig Konan and that they were planning one this weekend too. I take it you know Monsieur Konan?'

'Only superficially.'

'But you're aware that the two of them are friends and sometimes go out together in the boat?'

'Yes, why?'

Dupin hesitated.

'Yannig Konan didn't turn up to his office today,' Dupin said, quickly adding, 'but he has not yet been reported missing. He could be anywhere, there are indications that he is in Bénodet or in the area of Bénodet. His boat, which he was out in, is in the harbour there.'

Muriel Lefort's eyes widened.

'Konan is missing too?'

'At the moment we don't know where he is. Nothing more.'

Dupin was well aware that his sentence had not been particularly polished.

'So it could still be Lucas then.'

'I myself have only known since a short time ago that it was your brother who was out with Konan. I... this is really a very complicated story. But you'll see, it will all turn out to have been nothing. That's how it will go.'

Dupin had made an effort to infuse this sentence with all of the confidence he could muster. He hadn't done a great job.

Muriel Lefort turned towards the exit.

'I have to go back to the office, Monsieur le Commissaire. Maybe somebody there will have heard from Lucas after all.'

'Thanks for your help so far already, Madame Lefort.'

They walked outside and said goodbye. Dupin made a note of her phone number in case there was news. Then he walked slowly back down the gravel path. But he didn't turn right towards the *Quatre Vents*, he went left, towards the sandbank.

He had to make a call. In peace.

'Riwal?'

'Monsieur le Commissaire?'

'I'd like our colleagues to check immediately whether one of the dead is a Monsieur Lucas Lefort. Straight away. A famous sailor. World champion or something. You should look for a usable photo on the internet. Lu – cas Le – fort. I want to know straight away. Have the bodies arrived in Quimper yet?'

'The Admiral's Cup winner?'

Riwal sounded agitated.

'Yes, he hasn't been seen since yesterday evening.'

'I'll call our colleagues. I think they should be arriving in Quimper soon. How did you…'

'Call them, Riwal. Everything else can wait.'

'Understood, chief.'

Dupin hung up.

He walked over the picturesque wooden bridge that ran alongside the sea all the way round the island. The 'inside' of the island (and there wasn't much of it) was barren, austere – he liked it. Thorny undergrowth, raspberries, blackberries, a scanty covering of grass, waist-high ferns, heather flaring here and there, pockets of garish yellow gorse. The rising water had already washed over the sandbank between Saint-Nicolas and Bananec. Long, gentle waves glided into the chamber from the open Atlantic. Right in the middle of the sandbank, two men were visible. They were standing no more than ankle-deep in the water. It looked insane – like they were walking on water. The high tide was coming. The landscape was changing, which meant above all that land was becoming even more scarce.

The archipelago was an extreme outpost of the old continent. You could feel it, Dupin thought. The final stop at the end of the world. In fact, there was nothing more between the Glénan and the coast of Canada, not a speck of earth, not even a bleak rock formation. You would have to put five thousand kilometres behind you before you'd set foot on solid ground again. Five thousand kilometres of water. In the wildest sea in the world. And it wasn't much land, this very last piece. Dupin was thinking about last night's storm. This very last piece of land wasn't a solid landmass, not even close. These were desolately placed, chaotically torn, misshapen swatches of land

– which the popular aerial shots showed impressively. The last bastion of land was a very fragile bastion.

Dupin had walked slowly round the northern tip of the island. He looked westwards. The ringing of his phone broke the silence. It was Kadeg. Dupin answered.

'Negative.'

Kadeg sounded more frantic than usual.

'What do you mean, Kadeg?'

'It's not him.'

'So you're saying none of the three dead who have been examined is the missing angler? The man from Île-Tudy?'

Dupin had phrased the sentence in such detail so that he could gloat. Because his instinct had been right and Kadeg's wrong.

'No.'

'Has he turned up again then?'

'No. But they've examined the bodies carefully, using the photographs and he has been conclusively excluded as being one them.'

There was open disappointment in Kadeg's voice. And a little embarrassment. 'So we have a missing person who is not any of the three dead – and three dead, of whom none of them have yet been missed.'

Kadeg clearly didn't know how to respond to Dupin's bit of wordplay and remained silent.

'Right, Kadeg, that's where we are.'

Dupin hung up.

As macabre as it was and for motives different from Kadeg's, he would not have been unhappy if the missing person had been one of the three bodies washed up on shore. To have some kind of lead at least. Then they could probably find out who the other two dead bodies were quickly.

Dupin had come to a stop. He was contemplating turning around, but it seemed he would be back at the *Quatre Vents* sooner if he just followed the path. The bar might not have been visible yet – a sand dune ran lengthways across the island – but it couldn't be far now.

Dupin's gaze slid uncertainly into the distance, over the sea, which was a deep ultramarine at the horizon. He had stopped saying that the sea was blue. Because that wasn't true: the sea was not just blue. Not here in this magical world of light. It was azure, turquoise, cyan, cobalt, silver-grey, ultramarine, pale watercolour blue, silver-grey, midnight blue, violet blue... Blue in a good ten or fifteen different base colours and infinite numbers of shades in between. Sometimes it was even green, a real green or brown – and deep black. All of this depended on various factors: the sun and its position, of course, the season, the time of day, also the weather, the air pressure, the exact water content in the air, all of which refracted the light differently and shifted the blue into this or that tone. It particularly depended on the depth of the sea and whatever sea floor the light was falling on. It also depended on the wind, on the quality of the surface of the sea and the swell. And on the land that lay in front of the sea, the landscape and its colours. The most important factor was a different blue though – the sky, which varied in the same way and even contrasted with the clouds. It was this blue that found itself in an infinite interplay with the various shades of the sea. The truth was this: you never saw the same sea, the same sky, not once in the exact same hour and in the exact same place. And it was always a spectacle.

Dupin walked on, at a somewhat faster pace. He would have another coffee. And wait for Riwal's call. And if that didn't produce anything either – Dupin was assuming it wouldn't – he would fly back to the mainland for good. Despite how beautiful it was here.

The terrace of the *Quatre Vents* had emptied noticeably. Dupin saw the three women from the Nuz family together for the first time, they were clearing the tables in a practised, skilled way and sprucing everything up again after the midday rush. Nolwenn was right, they looked almost eerily similar. They all had the same deep brown eyes, the same matt black hair and most of all they had the same obstinate snub nose, the same slim figure. Unlike her daughters, Solenn Nuz wore her hair short, à la Jean Seberg, and had two pronounced dimples. The daughter who was younger – as far as Dupin could make out, although only with an effort – had whispered something to her mother when he had walked into the bar, without making the slightest move to hide it. A brief glance from Solenn Nuz hadswept over Dupin – she was sizing him up – before she busied herself again behind the counter with glasses and bottles.

He hadsat down in his old place with a coffee. The *Luc'hed* was in view now. It had lain docked by one of the boats lying quite close to the pier. They were clearly still busy with the interviews.

Dupin realised that he was not satisfied. He was finding everything too slow. He would simply call

Savoir himself. They needed to make progress. And he wanted to be sure they did.

It took some time for Docteur Savoir to pick up.

'Is there any news, Savoir?'

'And to whom do I owe the pleasure?'

Dupin was absolutely certain Savoir had recognised him straight away.

'Did you compare a photo of Lucas Lefort with the three bodies?'

'Ah, it's you, Commissaire! We are looking for more photos and are in the process of examining the corpses. There is only one who it could possibly be. He has serious injuries, even to the face in part. What we really need is a portrait, most photos show him on a boat, at prize-givings, with other people. And you look different when you're dead anyway. You have to take into account that...'

'I want to know what you think, Savoir.'

Dupin had got louder. For a moment, there was silence at the other end of the line.

'I think it could be him. The probability is high.'

'What?'

Dupin was gobsmacked. This was almost impossible to believe. Now there silence on his end of the line.

'You think one of the dead is Lucas Lefort?'

'I said the probability is definitely there.'

'So you're sure.'

Dupin was in no mood for Savoir's roundabout manner.

'I think so, yes. We'll do an identification anyway, just as a matter of form. He has a sister.'

'And why the hell did you not call me when your suspicions were first raised?'

'*I* work meticulously.'

Had the message itself not been so dramatic and significant and had it not set off a chain of thoughts in Dupin's head – he would have hit the roof.

'The sister lives on the Glénan. We will have to fly her over here.'

Dupin didn't reply. He was thinking. It really was Lucas Lefort. One of the three dead was the brother of the woman to whom he had just been speaking. In whose house he had just been.

'Did you hear what I said, Monsieur le Commissaire?'

Dupin forced himself back to the conversation.

'Do you have initial indications as to the cause of death?'

'No. We've only just brought the corpses into the lab and then have only focused on the question of whether Lucas Lefort could be amongst them. We'll examine the bodies immediately for possible lesions that cannot be explained by drifting in the sea. Then we'll perform the post-mortem and the toxicology tests, we...'

'I see.'

Dupin had spoken in a very aggressive tone of voice, which at least had something of an effect.

'I couldn't do much on the islands. What I saw looked like external injuries that might have been sustained on rocks and cliffs. But they are absolutely not conclusive statements that would stand up to all scientific scrutiny.'

'How long will you need?'

'If the bodies weren't in the water for more than a day, we will know within three quarters of an hour of opening the chest cavity whether the cause of death was drowning. In each case. I...'

'Lefort wasn't in the sea for more than twelve hours, I can tell you that already. So the others probably weren't either.'

'Then let's start with him. I've requested two additional assistants from the clinic. I...'

'We have to know what we're dealing with.'

'I'm aware of that, Monsieur le Commissaire, we are waiting...'

'Savoir.'

'Yes?'

'Look for photos of a Yannig Konan on the internet. Yan – nig Ko – nan. A well known big businessman from Brittany.'

'You suspect he's one of the other two dead?'

'We'll see.'

'What makes you think so?'

'They had planned a boat trip together. It may not...'

Dupin stopped short. He actually was not keen to divulge anything to Savoir at all.

'It's not significant. Just search for Yannig Konan.'

Dupin had almost hung up before Savoir could say anything more, but he paused.

'Savoir, another thing.'

'Yes?'

The 'yes' spoke volumes.

'I'm going to inform Madame Lefort myself. I've just made her acquaintance. I'll tell her how things stand. And also that she is needed in Quimper for the identification.'

'The helicopter will collect her. We mustn't waste any time.'

'No, we shouldn't. Get in touch with me

immediately – even if it's just about a 'suspicion', I...'

Now Savoir had hung up.

Dupin got up. Even though they hadn't been close, Muriel Lefort and her brother, it would be a shock. And an identification was always horrible.

He walked past the mole. To the right of it, at the first buoy, there was a speedboat. Bright red, narrow, long. He hadn't noticed it this morning, despite how much it stood out. It belonged to a dead man.

He was just a few metres away from the sailing school now. The unusually broad door was standing wide open. To the right of the entrance was the 'Accueil'.

He went inside. At that moment – he wasn't even fully over the threshold – his mobile trilled. Savoir.

Dupin turned round on the spot and answered.

'You were right, Monsieur le Commissaire!'

Savoir's voice quivered slightly, even though he was clearly trying to come across as calm.

'It is Yannig Konan. It's him. In this case, it's definitive. The body has no significant wounds to the face. He's clearly identifiable based on the photos we found on the internet.'

Dupin had walked in the direction of the oyster bar.

'No doubt of any kind?'

'There's no doubt in my mind. None.'

Dupin ran his hand roughly through his hair a few times. Then he stood still.

'Bloody hell.'

'Excuse me?'

'Excellent. This is going to be a sensation. A good friend of the Prefect's. And we are still taking stabs in the dark.'

Dupin had been speaking more to himself than to Savoir.

'A friend of Locmariaquer?'

'Yes.'

'Oh. He's going to make a big issue of this then. I assume that you'll inform him straight away, Monsieur le Commissaire. I'm going back to work. We'll progress with our investigations as quickly as possible.'

That's what he got for his persistence and really for his being absolutely hell-bent on eating the lobster – he would certainly never have started his aimless snooping around on the mainland. Dupin had got things moving. Now it was up to him to deliver the message to the Prefect *personally* about the death of his friend and this after the Prefect himself had given a relieved 'all clear'. And also after he had *personally* notified Muriel Lefort of her brother's death. Of course, an identification of the body would have happened at some point anyway – but it would definitely have been much less unpleasant for him.

And quite apart from the Prefect: what did all of this mean? Who was the third dead man? Konan and Lefort had wanted to go out as a pair. As far as the police knew anyway. That seemed to be what they always did. And why was Konan's boat in Bénodet? They hadn't been out in Lefort's boat either – had they taken the third dead man's boat? And again: what about the missing angler, the man from Île-Tudy who was not the third dead man?

Dupin let out a bad-tempered curse.

As expected, the conversation with Muriel Lefort had been extremely difficult. They had gone into her small, simple office in the sailing school, right next to the 'Accueil'. Initially she seemed composed. Eventually she had broken down in tears and not been able to keep talking. In an odd way, Dupin had felt guilty. Then Madame Lefort sat there silently for a few minutes, paralysed, her head and eyes lowered, staring into the distance. You couldn't even tell if she was breathing. Dupin was sitting just as still. Then Muriel Lefort suddenly stood up and asked to be alone. She had tried to make her voice sound firm. Of course, Dupin agreed.

Without any fuss, she haddeclared herself prepared to fly to Quimper to identify the body as soon as she felt able. She had given Dupin her assistant's name and asked him to arrange everything through her. Dupin had obviously had some urgent questions, but it hadn't been the moment. He would speak to her again later.

The phone call with the Prefect had been even more hideous than he'd feared. A long, very ponderous, very stressful conversation. Dupin had walked exactly once round the island during it. Again and again, the Prefect hadcried out dramatically how terribly tragic and devastating this was, again and again he had wanted to know why Dupin had even kept on investigating what was going on with the various boats and how and why the accident had happened in the first place – all things which Dupin himself didn't have the faintest clue about yet. It had been an impossible conversation. If it hadn't been so clear how deeply the death of Konan was affecting the Prefect – it was now up to Locmariaquer to call Konan's wife, whom he had confidently reassured at length earlier – and if Dupin had not, surprisingly, felt a trace of sympathy, it would have ended in a sharp exchange of words. And this would not have done him any good at all. He'd been through this before. Each time, he had pulled himself together at the last minute with all the psychological strength he could muster. The Prefect had spoken constantly about Dupin's 'case' and Dupin had noted every time that it wasn't even a case in all likelihood – rather, it was an accident. That there was no evidence indicating otherwise yet. Only once Dupin had loudly interrupted to this effect had the Prefect reacted at all, bellowing that this 'accident' and its 'complete resolution' were now Dupin's case. Dupin and all other employees of the Commissariat in Concarneau should, the Prefect said, drop everything else in the meantime. And he, the Prefect, would personally and with immediate effect organise all of the reinforcements necessary. Then the phone call had ended.

Dupin was fed up, his mood at rock bottom. Shortly before the *Quatre Vents*, he turned off to the beach, going down the broad wooden steps and then to the left over the rocks. The sun had passed its highest point, you could feel it. It didn't have the full power of summer yet.

So that was that. This was now his *case*.

Dupin had declared the *Quatre Vents* their 'headquarters' on the spot, which had lifted his mood (if only briefly). They had taken one of the tables and six chairs from the terrace and put them next to the annexe, facing the diving school. It was quarter past four. After the conversation with the Prefect, Dupin had called them all together, his little troop, with the firmly worded order to come immediately. He hadn't felt like conducting the investigation as an endless series of telephone conversations, even if it would mostly be that way under these local conditions. He had also asked Kireg Goulch to come and so had sent the *Luc'hed* to the Méaban. All they had found on the Méaban so far were six large canisters used on boats for drinking water or other fluids. Nothing more.

The table was not big. They all – Riwal, Kadeg, Goulch, the two other young police officers from the *Bir* and Dupin – sat squashed uncomfortably close to one another, which looked decidedly odd. There were two large trays in front of them with coffee, water, coke and a few crab and mackerel rillette sandwiches.

'What have we got?' Dupin began. Somewhat awkwardly, he got his arms into position, opened his notebook, scribbled a few words – making the others wait – and then continued.

'We have identified two of the three bodies at this point. Lucas Lefort and Yannig Konan. There are no clues as to the identity of the third dead man so far. Lucas Lefort was still on the Glénan last night. In the bar here. We know this from his sister, Muriel Lefort. How long for, whether he was on his own or not, and if not, who he was with, we don't yet know. Or how long he was here for. Or when he left. Maybe he was actually with Konan and the third dead man. We…'

In the middle of his sentence, Dupin's mobile trilled. He saw Savoir's number. He had expected the call much earlier. He took the call.

'The body wasn't in the sea very long,' said Savoir. On the basis of a macroscopic examination we can conclude that no fine tissue examination is necessary. Although...'

'Savoir. Get to the point.'

Dupin didn't have the patience to listen to Savoir's endless preliminaries.

'Lucas Lefort died by drowning. Definitively. That much is clear. We're examining Yannig Konan's body right now, but I thought I'd let you know now.' Savoir sounded offended.

'I'm much obliged, Docteur.'

'Aside from that, we have not yet found any pre-mortem injuries. I'll be in touch again.'

Savoir hung up.

Dupin looked around, all eyes were fixed inquisitively on him. He briefly recounted what Savoir had said and tried to marshal his thoughts.

'That would fit with the idea of the accident. Or to be more specific: right now we've got no clues that could allow for a conclusion of anything other than an accident. Probably an accident in a boat. But not in Konan or Lefort's boat. Potentially, in the boat belonging to the third dead man.' Dupin was speaking mechanically, summing up. It sounded resolutely uninspired. 'We have initial indications of where the possible shipwreck took place. That seems to me to be the essence of it. What we still need to do is reconstruct exactly what happened. And find out who the third dead man is.'

Dupin had tried to compensate for the vagueness of his comments with the lively certainty of how we was phrasing them. He was holding his baguette in his left hand the whole time, but had not yet taken a taken a bite.

Goulch spoke. 'The storm will probably have had an effect. And the low tide. At high tide the Méaban are six or seven sheer towering rocks, nothing more. They're even visible in bad weather. At low tide, however, there are dozens of rocks just above and below the surface of the water, over an area of a good half kilometre,' he recited in his pleasantly matter-of-fact way.

'Right now we're dealing with pure speculation on all sides,' Kadeg interjected curtly.

While on Le Loc'h this morning, Dupin had already suspected that Kadeg would cope badly with not playing first violin. Goulch was clearly the one playing it out here, remaining absolutely unfazed.

One of the two other police officers piped up now, almost shyly.

'I've requested the information from the weather service,' he said, sounding increasingly certain as he spoke. 'The storm reached the Glénan at around 10pm and was over by midnight. The storm moved very quickly along the coast, in a slight zigzag. Almost only over the sea, it just grazed the coast at Penmarc'h. It reached wind speeds of nine or ten and up to eleven in the peaks.'

Dupin looked questioningly at the young police officer.

'Up to a hundred or a hundred and ten kilometres an hour.'

'Well that's – worth noting,' said Goulch. 'But these kinds of storms happen in the summer too.'

It was less Goulch's continued use of well chosen

words than his way of intoning 'worth noting' that made Dupin aware that it really had been a serious storm.

'Maybe they saw the storm coming and wanted to get back to the mainland in good time,' Dupin was making a few cryptic notes as he spoke. 'I'm sure we'll find out when they left the bar soon. Somebody will remember.'

'What is strange though, is this,' said Riwal. 'Monsieur Lefort was one of the best sailors in France, he was at home at sea and knew the Glénan like the back of his hand. And the Méaban too. He grew up here. Monsieur Konan was also extremely experienced at sea. And, of course, both of them were aware of the dangers of spring tides. And of what storms can mean here on the Atlantic.'

Riwal had put forward his reflections quite thoughtfully. An extended silence set in. He followed it up in an utterly Riwal-like way.

'The Atlantic is a *real* ocean.'

Riwal could be highly analytical, precise, very practical and pragmatic and then suddenly whisper dark, mysterious sentences. It had sounded full of emotion. Solemn.

The line about the 'real ocean' was not just a typical 'Riwal sentence', invoking the sea was an ancient Breton mantra. It was done in all kinds of situations and Dupin only occasionally understood what it actually meant. But it always came from 'very deep inside'. And, apparently, meant many things at once: respect, fear, anxiety, elemental force, fascination, love. A disaster. And pride. *Ar mor bras*, 'the great sea', as the ocean was actually called, in Celtic that is, before the Greeks had called it *Atlantis thalassa*, 'Sea of the Titan Atlas'. Even for them it was explicitly the 'End of the World'... And the Bretons would then immediately add superlative figures: a fifth of the world was covered by *their* ocean (106.2 million kilometres, squared!), it was almost ten thousand metres deep, with gigantic mountain ridges. This 'real ocean' was meant to highlight its difference from the 'harmless' Mediterranean Sea, which to Breton eyes was utterly overrated – nothing more than an inland sea belonging to the Atlantic. And, the Atlantic was growing. By two centimetres every year, by a metre in fifty years and, in a thousand years (by the standards of the Breton sense of time this was nothing) by twenty metres! What pained the Bretons a little though was this – the Pacific Ocean was – still – a little bigger. But other statistics made up for that immediately. So for instance the average salt content of the Atlantic Ocean was around 3.54%, while in the Pacific it was a mere 3.45%. And was salt not one of the central elements of life? And did they, the Bretons, not therefore have the most delicious and famous salt in the world: the *fleur de sel*, the flower of salt? There was no famous Pacific *fleur de sel*.

'It's not uncommon for us to fish experienced sailors out of the sea,' said Goulch. 'Thinking you know it all and are capable of anything, can sometimes be the greatest danger. The Atlantic is totally arbitrary. Nobody knows what currents result from the combination of storm and spring tides. At a moment's notice mountain waves tower up ten metres high, currents of eight or ten kilometres an hour appear out of nowhere – the Atlantic is a place of extremes.'

Goulch was explaining what the 'real ocean' statement meant this time.

'Isolated waves reach twenty or twenty-five metres,' added Riwal, 'and run against the direction of the normal swell, with narrow, deep troughs and a powerful crest. Then there is the "kaventman", the three "sisters", the "white wall".'

In his voice there was a mixture of awe, a profound thrill and fascination. It sounded very poetic, Dupin thought, even though it made him cast a quick look at the absolutely flat sea of the chamber.

'We should be concentrating on concrete things right now,' said Kadeg. Finding out as quickly as possible who the third man is. Whether anyone knows what the three of them had planned, where they were headed.'

Kadeg was playing the hardworking, business-like man, a role that he loved. Dupin slid backwards slightly from the table. His spoke tetchily, even though he didn't mean to sound that way.

'Then let's split up. The issues are clear. Kadeg, you concentrate on Konan. His circle. Wife, friends, colleagues. The harbour where his boat is. The harbourmaster and so on.'

The fact that Kadeg was taking on everything to do with Konan would mean that he'd need to get back to the mainland.

'Riwal, the two of us will speak to the people here on Saint-Nicolas. Find out who else was in the *Quatre Vents* last night. If Lefort was sitting in the bar with Konan and the third man, they'll have been seen. Maybe somebody knows him. I...' Dupin's brow creased, 'I will speak to Madame Lefort again in person.'

He hesitated for a moment.

'And Goulch, you lead all investigations on the water.'

Kadeg's mobile rang loudly. With a pompous expression, he eagerly checked the number.

'The Prefect!'

It sounded like 'His Majesty'. Kadeg answered before Dupin could say he shouldn't dare.

'Monsieur le Prefét? What can I do for you?'

Dupin's blood pressure shot up instantly. He banged his baguette down on the table. All heads were turned to Kadeg. The Prefect was audible, distant and muffled, but incomprehensible.

'Well naturally, Monsieur le Préfet. – – – I will tell the Commissaire again as a matter of urgency. – – – This is a case and it has the highest priority. – – – You want to be kept in the loop constantly about absolutely everything, by him personally. And also via me, yes. – – – That you are expecting results as soon as possible. – – – What? Monsieur le Commissaire just hung up when you were on the phone to him just now?'

This was simply too much.

'Kadeg, this is an important meeting. You're being disruptive! We need to get on. The Prefect is expecting progress immediately.'

Dupin spoke so loudly that Locmariaquer must have heard.

'I... yes, all right, Monsieur le Préfet. We'll be in touch. *Au revoir.*'

After Kadeg's slight gloating at the beginning of the phone call, he now looked just as glum as before and also somewhat confused – he had obviously been expecting a different reaction from the Prefect to Dupin's remarks. Dupin decided not to pay any attention to the phone call.

'And the missing man. We also have the missing angler from Île-Tudy. Kadeg, he is staying on your list.'

'You yourself implied earlier that you don't see a connection.'

'Now, I think you've heard the importance the Prefect is attaching to our investigation. We're going to get to the bottom of all, and I mean all, reports. The coincidental timing is strange, isn't it? It would be negligent to ignore it.'

From Kadeg's round face – so round that the eyes, mouth and nose looked distorted, not made any more attractive by his advanced baldness – it was plain to see that he was struggling hard to find a retort. Dupin beat him to it.

'No discussion now – there's too much to do, we don't have any time to lose. To work.'

Dupin was the last to stand up and was wrapping up the baguette to take it with him when his gaze fell on a diver leaving the quay and making a beeline for their little group. The others stood still too and were staring at the man, who looked a little like an alien in his full-body neoprene suit. Just a small area of his face – between the lower lip and eyebrows – was exposed. There was something very funny about the scene, Dupin thought.

A few moments later the man was standing in front of them, audibly out of breath.

'Somebody told me you're from the police?'

He kept breaking off to take deep breaths.

'Correct. Can we help you?'

Dupin still found the scene funny.

'I spotted a sunken boat on a dive. A Bénéteau. A large Gran Turismo.'

'What? You did what?'

'I was diving. Spider crabs. Between Penfret and Brilimec, not far from Guiautec. The boat must only have sunk recently. It wasn't there yesterday anyway. I'm sure of that. It's badly damaged on the bow. You can't make out the name of the boat.'

The expression on Dupin's face – like on everyone else's –changed abruptly.

'Could you show us the exact place, Monsieur?' Goulch was straight to the point immediately.

'I marked it with my buoy. The boat is right at a small rock formation. I was out in my dinghy.'

'How far down is it?'

'Four or five metres. You can see it from the boat.'

The diver started to peel the head part of the neoprene suit down, which looked far from easy. There was a small pause. Dupin looked at Kireg Goulch.

'What do you think?'

'If it's as he says, the probability is very high that we're dealing with the boat the three men were on. They wouldn't have got far, if they set out from here and sank at Guiautec.'

This whole investigation, the way it was going, the whole day in itself – it was ridiculous. Strangely topsy-turvy. Dupin was absolutely fed up.

'I want to know what's what. Goulch, take the boat and go with –'

Dupin turned to the diver who understood immediately.

'Monsieur Tanguy. Kilian Tanguy.'

'Go out with Monsieur Tanguy and take a careful look at the boat. I want to know straight away and with one hundred per cent certainty whether it's the boat that the three men were out in. Find out who it's registered to. Where it comes from. Then we'll also know who the third dead man is. It's probably his boat.'

'We'll set out immediately. Come with me, Monsieur Tanguy.'

Goulch was already walking towards the quay.

'One more thing: Monsieur Tanguy, you said you went diving in the same place yesterday? What time were you out till?'

'Five maybe, no later than that.'

'And what time were you there today?'

'I think around half three. My boat is on one of the beaches on Penfret. I came from there by dinghy.'

'Do you dive here often?'

'All season long. I'm a member of the diving club.'

Monsieur Tanguy openly scrutinised Dupin for a moment.

'You're the Commissaire from Paris.'

He said it in a very friendly and approving way. Dupin normally objected sharply in these kinds of situations, even though it was utterly pointless. And there were all too many of these situations. He was not the Commissaire from Paris – he was the Commissaire from Concarneau. But to Bretons, you were either a lifelong Breton or 'totally new here'.

'Yes, that's me.'

All the same, Dupin was impressed by the diver's astuteness. Commissaire Georges Dupin had become a real name in Finistère due to solving the sensational double murder in idyllic Pont-Aven last year. Yet he wouldnever havethought that people knew him out here.

'The people down at the quay told me that the Commissaire from Paris was on the islands. And since you have such a quizzical look on your face right now – the "season" runs from April until the beginning of November. The Atlantic has to be warm, over fourteen degrees, or else you need completely different equipment.'

'That – is very helpful to us, Monsieur Tanguy. Please accept our warmest thanks. We are in the process of clearing up an – accident.'

'The three bodies.'

'Exactly.'

When Dupin was wrapped up in something, he occasionally forgot the outside world and was surprised when it then reappeared. Of course the whole archipelago already knew, everyone who moved in its circles in some way. More than that, Dupin was certain that the press had long since got wind of it and that the report about the three dead washed up on the beach of Le Loc'h had already made a splash on the homepages of *Ouest France* and *Télégramme*. The report would already be on the radio too – radio that, with its many local broadcasters here at the end of the world, still played a considerable part in spreading news. He was actually surprised nobody from the press had turned up yet. It wouldn't be long now.

'It's almost impossible to comprehend that Lucas Lefort suffered a shipwreck in these waters. It's a horrible irony, he could navigate his way round here blindfolded.'

Dupin was shocked again. But of course – the fact that one of the dead was Lucas Lefort, even that had already got around, the news was too sensational. The only remarkable thing was how swiftly it happened here on the islands. Monsieur Tanguy must have noticed the stunned look on Dupin's face this time too.

'The people on the quay. They said that Lucas Lefort is one of the dead.'

This was true.

'Thanks again. As I said, you've been a great help to us.'

'The sea is unpredictable.'

The diver hadn't said this sentence to Dupin at all, but to himself. Dupin assumed he was thinking of the Atlantic mantra.

'Keep me up to speed at all times, Goulch.'

'Of course, Monsieur le Commissaire.'

Riwal and Kadeg positioned themselves to the right and left of the Commissaire.

'And now?' Kadeg actually managed to infuse two such banal words with a sweetly sarcastic tone of triumph.

'And now, what?'

'What will we do now?'

The stupid thing was – Kadeg's question was valid. The situation, it seemed, had thoroughly changed. The tasks he had given were largely no longer relevant. It now seemed possible to reconstruct much of what had happened. It *had* been a boating accident. And when they knew who the boat was registered to, they would in all likelihood know the identity of the third man. Potentially even before that. From a few conversations in the *Quatre Vents*. First and foremost with Solenn Nuz. Then all that would be left to clarify would be why they were all on *this* boat, the exact sequence of events, things like that. With Savoir's final autopsy findings they would be in possession of all the necessary facts to present a satisfactory report to the Prefect. That left the missing angler from Île-Tudy – probably just a second accident.

There really wasn't much left for them to do on the island now.

'Kadeg, you go on the *Bir* too, you can try to investigate the owner of the sunken ship straight away from the boat. As a top priority. And Riwal, you come with me. And...'

Dupin's mobile rang and he answered it.

'Muriel Lefort here. I'd like to apologise for my lack of composure just now. I know that it is important for you to find out certain things quickly. And I'd like to help.'

She had spoken at considerable speed. Without any apparent emotion. Dupin was familiar with these kinds of reactions, they were not uncommon in the initial shock. But emotions 'on display' or 'not on display' were, he knew, not an indicator of anything. Dupin had taken a few steps to one side and was now standing next to the first of the two oyster ponds.

'I feel ready to carry out the identification of my brother. As quickly as possible.'

'I will arrange for the helicopter to come and collect you immediately.'

There was a long pause from Muriel.

'My assistant will be coming with me.'

'Of course. I will also ask one of my inspectors to fly with you.'

'Thanks very much.'

'And as soon as you're back, I would like to speak to you again.'

'I'll call you.'

They hung up. Dupin had briefly contemplated telling her about the boat that had been found, but then he left it. He wanted to be absolutely certain.

He still had the phone to his ear when the horrific ringtone pierced deep into his eardrum again.

'Yes?'

He had practically roared.

'Yannig Konan drowned too. That's also clear. Death by drowning.'

'I...'

'We're opening the chest cavity of the third man now. I'll be in touch.'

Savoir had hung up before Dupin could react.

He saw that Riwal had walked to the mole with Kadeg. He followed them. Kadeg leapt on board the *Bir* and took up a position in the bow with Goulch's colleagues. The engines were already running.

'Riwal?'

'Yes, boss?'

'Go with Madame Lefort to the identification. Let Savoir know. He's already waiting. Meet Madame Lefort behind the sailing-school building.'

'All right, boss.'

'Call me afterwards.'

Dupin turned around and walked along the rusty old tracks that ran from the quay right to the bar.

Everyone at the *Quatre Vents* was sitting inside by now, the terrace was completely deserted. Even though the sun was still quite high, it had become 'a little nippy' – and for Bretons, Dupin had noted in the last few years, not without amusement, anything under fifteen degrees was 'a little nippy', which meant that at their latitude and in this Atlantic position, it was often 'a little nippy'. At this time of year, the switch from being summery outdoors to being cosy indoors happened quite quickly. Someone had closed the windows, the guests were sitting cosily close together at the small wooden tables. The old room had a high ceiling, a good four metres high and the rough stonewalls were whitewashed.

The Nuz women had their hands full. Solenn Nuz had greeted Dupin with a slight nod when he came in. Dupin had signalled that he wanted to speak to her. Putting down the bottle of wine that she had just skilfully opened, she hadpointed left, to the very end of the long wooden counter where nobody was standing. That was fine.

'Bonjour, Madame Nuz, Commissaire Georges Dupin from the Commissariat de Police, Concarneau.'

He hadn't meant to be so formal. Solenn Nuz smiled anyway, a big, open smile. She was a beautiful woman, he had to agree with Nolwenn there. And it would actually have been hard for him to guess her age.

'I know.'

Dupin had of course known that she knew.

'We are about to investigate what happened to the three men whose bodies were washed up on Le Loc'h this morning.'

'I know.'

'You also know who they are then?'

'Lucas Lefort. And probably Yannig Konan. They were here together yesterday evening. They're often out together. Mostly on Konan's boat. But in fact only ever the two of them. Do you know who the third person is yet?'

Solenn Nuz spoke in a very familiar way, as if they already knew each other.

'No, we don't know yet. I had hoped you might be able to help us. Was it just the two of them, Monsieur Lefort and Monsieur Konan, the whole evening? Was nobody with them?'

'I saw them talking to a few people. But in an evening here almost everyone speaks to everyone else once. At the bar. At the tables. Also, because you always fetch your own orders, there's always a lot of commotion.'

Solenn Nuz gave him a meaningful look.

'Lucas Lefort was interested in very young women and there are a huge number of them here during the season. The sailing courses. You understand.'

'I understand. But did Monsieur Lefort not a "steady" girlfriend recently?'

Solenn Nuz cast the Commissaire an amused look. It was clear that she would not answer this ludicrous question.

It took Dupin a moment.

'What's really important is this: was there someone who was recognisably a part of their group? Who came or left with them?'

'No. Definitely not.'

'Can you tell me the time span the two of them stayed at your bar?'

'I think from about seven to nine. Thereabouts. In the evenings things really kick off at around six. And we close at one. But a storm started up last night. Anyone who still wanted to get back made a move quite quickly. So a bit before nine. The two of them left then too. They were amongst the last to get going, if I'm not mistaken. But you should speak to my daughters again. And to other customers. There was a lot to do yesterday evening.'

'Was it as full as today?'

'It was pandemonium.'

Dupin estimated there were about thirty people there that day. There wasn't room for many more.

'The annexe isn't open in the evenings?'

'There's a terrible draught. And there's no heating. It's just something for during the day. For the height of summer. We have plans to change that by doing a bit of renovating,' she said, an open laugh crossing her face again, 'but it's going to be a while. The bureacracy...'

'Did you speak to Monsieur Lefort and Konan yourself, did they say anything to you?'

Dupin had to make an effort the whole time to speak quite loudly. Solwenn Nuz, it was clear, did this as a matter of habit.

'No. I didn't speak to either of them. I didn't speak to anyone for very long yesterday, a few words here and there.'

'Were Konan and Lefort here often?'

'Lefort was here regularly and Konan came maybe every third or fourth weekend. Konan was rarely here on his own, once or twice a year perhaps.'

'Who did the two of them speak to? Maybe they told someone what they had planned.'

Solenn Nuz reflected for a moment.

'I'm sure I wasn't aware of everything. I'm constantly in the kitchen. Sometimes for long stretches too.'

She made a curt gesture with her head towards the passageway behind her.

'Lefort with a young woman. A sailing school student probably. That was right at the beginning and, I think, again at the end. Also with Maela Menez briefly, as far as I could see. Muriel Lefort's assistant. His sister, the head of the sailing school.'

'I'm aware.'

Dupin had fished out his notepad, placed it on the counter along with the bic and begun to make notes in his notoriously idiosyncratic style, which made the pages into a kind of chaotic work of art.

'In theory, Maela Menez is Lucas' assistant too, but Muriel handles the sailing school's affairs, not her brother. Maela is accompanying Muriel to the pathologist on the mainland as we speak.'

When Solenn Nuz said 'mainland', it sounded like she was speaking about a continent far away. But it had seemed that way to Dupin all day too.

'Does anyone else come to mind?'

'They were sitting in the corner then. The new mayor of Fouesnant, Monsieur Du Marhallac'h, was sitting at the table directly beside theirs. I think they chatted too.'

'Du Marc...?'

'Du Marhallac'h. It's simple.'

She of course pronounced the tongue-twister without any trouble.

'During the season, he's also out here almost every weekend, a keen angler. That's how it is – during the day they're at sea and on their boats, in the evenings at my bar. He's here this evening too. He's sitting over there. At the same table as yesterday.'

She pointed openly at an unremarkable, middle-aged man at the other end of the room, who was clearly having a heated conversation with another man. The affable old sailor from midday was now sitting right next to him, this time without a newspaper, but alone as before.

'Yes, we have a series of regulars here in the *Quatre Vents*.'

She said this last sentence with undisguised pride. It was clear she knew her customers. Knew them well.

'Half of our world here is absolutely familiar, the other half is made up of participants on the sailing and diving courses and the tourists who come to go boating, fishing or snorkelling.'

'Do you remember Lefort and Konan speaking to anyone else?'

'Konan also spoke to Kilian Tanguy. A member of the diving club. An amateur archaeologist. And to his wife. He was standing at their table, I don't know how long for.'

'Monsieur Tanguy was here yesterday evening too?'

'Oh yes, with his wife. Lily. They're practically always out here in good weather. And we had a fantastic weekend. The loveliest of the season so far. Like today. And then the severe storm came. But even that's normal. – I think that's as much as I can remember off the top of my head. But I'll have another think. And I'll ask my daughters.'

'Thanks very much, Madame Nuz. This is really important. We will speak to all of these people soon. From that we really might learn something that will help us make progress. Did you know Monsieur Lefort well?'

'We didn't have much to do with each other. Even though I've known him a long time. I've been living on the islands for ten years now. And I used to come here a lot, even before that.'

'Incidentally, who is the old man sitting next to Marcha... sitting next to the mayor.'

Dupin had asked the question out of sheer curiosity.

'That's Pascal, my father-in-law,' she responded with great warmth in her voice. 'He was here yesterday evening too. He's always here. He lives with us. Has done for some years now. Since my mother-in-law died.'

There really were quite a few conversations to be had now. Dupin was annoyed not to have brought Riwal or Kadeg with him. Madame Nuz watched him.

With the noise level, Dupin could only hear it faintly, but his mobile was ringing.

Savoir again.

'Where are you, Monsieur le Commissaire?'

The noise of the bar was of course audible, even at the other end of the line.

'One moment. I'm going outside.'

Reluctantly, Dupin stepped outside.

'You want to tell me that the third man drowned, like the two others?'

It sounded more sarcastic that he'd intended. Investigating the death was the right thing to do.

'The serum is headed towards pink. The blood is already slightly haemolytic, the corpuscles have begun to dissolve. That means that the detectable substances have already diminished somewhat, it...'

'Savoir, what are you saying?'

'Benzodiazepines. Benzodiazepines can be detected in the blood serum in a reasonably significant concentration.'

'What does that mean?'

'I had the toxicology tests done using high-pressure as a quick method. Normally…'

Dupin raised his voice.

'I want to know what that means!'

'Benzodiazepines were detected in Lefort's blood. They're a group of strong sedatives. You'll know Valium. Or Lexotanil. Another twenty-four hours and and it would no longer have been possible to detect, the corpuscles would have been…'

'What? He had what?'

It had not been a proper question.

'He had a not insignificant amount of benzo-diazepines…'

'I understood.'

Dupin stood as though rooted to the spot. Savoir took up the thread again.

'I don't think he took that kind of dosage inten-tionally, he would have had to know how that ends, in combination with the alcohol that we could detect…'

'Was it a lethal dosage?'

'As I said: he died by drowning. But the dosage was undoubtedly high enough to produce severe disorientation and a serious loss of coordination. And that definitely has considerable consequences if you have to handle a delicate navigation by boat with an impending storm.

'How severe do you think the effect was?'

'It's hard to say. It depends on too many factors and the exact amount of benzodiazepines in the blood can no longer be determined. The only thing that can be said is that it was considerable and definitely manifested itself in the symptoms I just mentioned. And as I said: you must take into account the additional alcohol consumed in no small quantity, it was a good 1.5 millimetres...'

Dupin had not really been listening during Savoir's last few sentences.

It was murder. They were dealing with a murder!

'Bloody hell.'

'Excuse me?'

Dupin rushed to try and get his thoughts in order.

'Have you analysed all three of the men's blood?'

'We could detect benzodiazepines in Monsieur Lefort and Monsieur Konan, that alone makes an accidental misuse unlikely. We couldn't detect anything in the blood serum of the third dead man.'

Dupin's thoughts were racing. In all directions.

'How long do these drugs take to work? I mean, after taking them: how long before an effect occurs that you really feel?'

'Half an hour. Not longer. But then things go quite fast. At first you just feel a bit odd.'

'Can these substances be dissolved in liquids? In drinks, I mean?'

'Very easily. They dissolve quickly. You can dissolve them in a small amount of liquid and add them to something else without any difficulty – food or drink for instance, neither would be a problem. You can't taste it.'

It was a cunning murder, carefully thought through.

'Can you comment on the time of death yet?'

'No, and it won't happen quickly either. Can you narrow down the timings from your end yet?'

'At the moment I would say that the boat might have capsized after around quarter past nine yesterday evening. And probably not later than quarter to ten or ten o'clock. But please keep this new information to yourself for now, Docteur Savoir.'

'As you wish.'

'Thank you, Docteur.'

Dupin hadn't moved an inch. He was staring motionless at the staunchly majestic chamber lying there and at Fort Cigogne opposite. Everything was exactly as it had been a few minutes ago. But for him and for the case, everything had changed. Dramatically. Dupin broke away and walked towards the beach. He felt slightly dizzy. Mechanically, he felt about for his phone.

'Monsieur le Commissaire, good to...'

'It was murder.'

'Excuse me?'

Nolwenn's 'Excuse me?' came very softly.

'I need Riwal and Kadeg. I want to see the two of them here as quickly as possible. But don't say anything about the new situation yet. I want it to stay between us for the time being.'

There was no specific reason for this, it was essentially Dupin's way of keeping some things back for now. To have everything under control.

'I will have to inform the Prefect immediately – urgently and on your behalf.'

That was unfortunately true, there was nothing for it.

'All right, good.'

Dupin almost hung up. But Nolwenn needed some more information. For the Prefect, but especially because it was always good when Nolwenn was up to speed.

'Somebody administered a large dose of valium or something similar, benzodiazepines, to Konan and Lefort, presumably here in the *Quatre Vents*, probably some time between half eight and a little before nine, enough to result in severe coordination difficulties relatively quickly, which would explain a shipwreck. At Guiautec, on the edge of the chamber, a diver discovered a sunken boat. We must establish as quickly as possible who it's registered to. Then we'll have the third man.'

'And were there no benzodiazepines present in the third man's blood?'

'No.'

'Then Lefort or Konan must have been steering the boat. But why wasn't the third man, who owned it, doing that? If one of the two had noticed that they were coming over strange, wouldn't they have been able to hand the steering over?'

That was a good question.

'That... no idea. They were probably the insured sailors, especially Lefort of course – Lefort knew every rock here. They had already seen the storm looming. And then the drugs quickly started to take effect. And on top of that they had been drinking and we're not talking a small amount. People overestimate themselves even more when they've been drinking.'

He thought it sounded plausible to a certain extent, this on-the-spot improvisation of his. Even though it was pure speculation.

'And why didn't the third man have benzodiazepines administered to him?'

'That obviously wasn't necessary.'

Dupin had improvised again – and again, he found it plausible.

'But we're not at that stage yet.'

'The Prefect is going to be very involved, Monsieur le Commissaire. I mean: personally involved.'

Dupin was fully aware of the scale of this case, he was under no false pretences.

'He will definitely want to speak to you personally. I will tell him – truthfully – that you are already in the midst of important interrogations. You should speak to him later. When he has calmed down again somewhat.'

'Thanks, Nolwenn.'

Without realising it, Dupin had kept walking during the conversation. He now found himself on the northern tip of the island. He was still grappling with the new reality.

The chance of this murder ever being discovered at all had been slim. Everything had – the murderer could be sure of this – pointed towards the deaths of these three men being considered an accident forever. Just a few hours later and the strong sedatives would no longer have been detectable. And had the boat not wrecked here on the archipelago, but somewhere on the way to the coast instead, or had the bodies stumbled into a different current here in the vicinity of the Glénan during the severe storm, they would, like the majority of people lost at sea, never have been found. It was, you had to admit, without doubt a cold-blooded and cleverly conceived murder.

It had not been a spontaneous act, Dupin was sure of that. No sudden escalation of emotion. It appeared somebody had been waiting for the right moment. It was an act that betrayed great discipline. But had the murderer had all three men in mind? Or just one or two of them, tolerating the death of the other or others in the end? Only Lefort and Konan had been seen in the *Quatre Vents*. Also, perhaps there was not just *one* murderer.

New questions and possibilities kept occurring to Dupin. All kinds of things, all at the same time. He had to get his thoughts in order. Ask himself what was the most urgent thing now. Above all he had the vague feeling he needed to be quick, very quick. But he had nothing under control yet. Nothing at all. He was right at the beginning.

Dupin switched his phone to vibrate. And to 'call divert in case of unanswered call' – during hours of studying the crazy menu and sub-menu commands, he had taught himself this one skill in handling his phone. He wouldn't answer any more calls where he didn't recognise the number. It was always the old familiar drama: not just the Prefect, but also other 'important' people would absolutely 'desperately' want to speak to him now and, of course, want to know how the investigations were going. Especially to emphasise urgently how tragic this case was and what devastating consequences it had already had. And also what consequences there would be for every minute that it remained unsolved. Dupin hated this and from now on he could easilybe busy all evening having that kind of conversation.

The air had become heavier, closer and, of the little oxygen that had been present before, there was now even less left as Dupin walked back into the *Quatre Vents*.

It seemed absolutely surreal to him now – in the spot where he had eaten the best lobster of his life earlier in an almost holiday atmosphere, a capital murder had in all likelihood taken place. That was one of the thoughts that had just gone through his head. Of course, it was possible that Konan and Lefort, without suspecting it, had ingested the sedative after their visit to the *Quatre Vents*, perhaps the perpetrator had mixed it into water bottles on the boat, but Dupin considered that quite unlikely. It would have been difficult for the murderer to predict in advance whether they would ingest it – and whether it would be at the 'right' time. Incalculable. It seemed most likely that somebody had mixed the drug unnoticed into the food or drink in the *Quatre Vents*. But that meant: the murderer must have been here yesterday evening.

Riwal and Kadeg hadn't arrived yet. Solenn Nuz, who was dealing with the coffee machine with her left hand and, at the same time, topping up a wine glass with her right – an impressive formation of glasses was standing in front of her on the counter lifted her head briefly and threw Dupin a friendly, knowing look as if to mean: 'Work...' It only crossed Dupin's mind now that they had been in the middle of a conversation when Savoir's call came. No matter how inconvenient it might be for her right now, he needed to speak to her. Her above all. She and her daughters would most likely know who had been in the *Quatre Vents* yesterday evening. At this stage, they were interested in *all* customers. They needed a complete list as quickly as possible.

Dupin wound his way between the tables and approached the bar.

'Something urgent?'

'Yes, unfortunately.'

Solenn Nuz had good intuition, which did not surprise Dupin in the slightest.

'Come with me.'

With the same minimal head movement as before, she gestured towards the kitchen and turned around. Dupin followed her. The elder daughter was just unloading the dishwasher. In the opposite corner of the room there was even space for a little table and four chairs, the same as on the terrace, although they had been painted a deep Atlantic blue. It was cramped, but homely at the same time, cosy, there were two open bottles of wine on the table, a few half-full glasses and next to them lay half a baguette and two candles in empty wine bottles. Solenn Nuz stood by the table for a moment.

'You and your daughters might be very helpful to us. We need an exact, complete list of all customers who were in the *Quatre Vents* yesterday evening. Between seven and nine o'clock. Nobody can be missed off. And we need it as quickly as possible.'

As before, Dupin had tried to sound calm, to convey it as routine, but Solenn Nuz had already realised that something had changed. Really changed this time. What could Dupin say? He couldn't minimise the urgency of course, just so that his request didn't come across as suspicious.

'If you could discuss this your daughters?'

It was clearly on the tip of Solenn Nuz's tongue to ask what all of this meant. But she didn't. For which Dupin was very grateful. After a brief pause, she answered in a considered tone.

'As I said, a proportion of the customers who come here, we don't know. The participants on the sailing and diving courses, for instance. You see some of them several days in a row, some just once. And the visitors with their own boats, day trippers and so on.'

'We will also make enquiries at the sailing school and in the diving centre.'

'It's important, is it?'

'Yes.'

'My daughters and I will be able to get a significant list together. There were lots of regulars there too. I've already mentioned some of the people to you.'

'That would be very kind, Madame Nuz. And another pressing issue: do you or your daughters remember what Konan and Lefort ate and drank last night?'

'What they ate and drank?'

Her eyebrows shot up. Dupin was aware that this question – even more obviously than the request for the list – was likely to betray that something was absolutely and utterly wrong here.

'Exactly.'

'We'll try to remember. I think Konan had the lobster. But I'm not sure.'

'And who has access to the drinks and the food?'

'Apart from us, you mean?'

'Yes.'

'We prepare the drinks behind the counter and then put them on the trays on the counter. We fetch the food from the kitchen. Sometimes the trays sit there for a moment before the customers collect them or we bring them to the table. We do that if it's taking a relatively long time. It's always pandemonium at the bar. People cluster together there. You just saw it for yourself. We can't keep any track then.'

'I see. We...'

The younger Nuz daughter was suddenly standing in front of them.

'There's a police officer, an Inspector Kadeg. He's looking for you.'

'I'm coming.'

Dupin turned back to Solenn Nuz.

'I would be grateful if you could make a start immediately.'

She looked resigned. Dupin understood this well – thirty cheerful and happy paying customers were sitting out front and it was dinnertime.

'I'll start straight away,' and she added in her younger daughter's direction, 'you'll have to manage by yourself out front for a few minutes. And then I need you back here for a few moments. Both of you.'

'Thanks very much, Madame Nuz.'

Dupin turned around and went back into the bar. Kadeg was standing right at the counter with a typically desperate look on his face.

'There's quite a lot to discuss, Monsieur le Commissaire.'

Dupin could almost have laughed, Kadeg's sentence seemed so absurd in light of the new situation.

Kadeg followed Dupin, who had walked straight past him, heading towards the door. Outside, Dupin walked a few more metres at the same pace , only coming to a standstill once he was in front of the naïve surrealist mural, right in front of the penguin. He hadn't even turned around fully when Kadeg blurted it out.

'We know who the third man is, in all likelihood.' Kadeg left a small dramatic pause, then intoned almost solemnly: 'Grégoire Pajot! A developer, a Breton, from Quimper, now has the headquarters of his company in Paris, where he probably lives most of the time. He owns a house in Bénodet. The Breton branch of his company is in Quimper. The sunken boat, the *Conquerer*, is registered to him, if only for the last three months. It's a brand new boat.'

Everything was delivered in the eager staccato that Kadeg loved.

'How do we know this?'

'Goulch and his people went down to the boat and found the registration. Pajot had a mooring spot in the Port de Plaisance in Bénodet and one across the way in Sainte-Marine.'

'Has Savoir been informed? He will need photos for an initial identification.'

'Goulch informed him straight away.'

'Does he have a wife, family?'

'Unmarried. We don't know anything more yet.'

'And how do we even know that?'

'In the harbour office you have to deposit the permit for the boat and a copy of your boat-driving license. I spoke to the harbour master in Bénodet on the phone. He told me what he knew, which wasn't much. He barely knows Monsieur Pajot, he said, because he's only had his space for a short time after all. One of the best, most expensive spots, by the way. The harbour master at Sainte-Marine knew even less. Nothing at all, really. I also spoke to him directly on the phone.'

'Has his company not been in touch, was he not missed?'

'We don't know that yet. Who were they meant to get in touch with? The police? So most people wait, to begin with. I've asked Bellec to sound out initial findings about Pajot from his company – he'll definitely have a secretary.'

Much as it pained him, Dupin had to admit Kadeg was right. And Bellec was still inexperienced but he was an intelligent police officer who had impressed Dupin on a number of previous occasions. He was ridiculously quick, forthright, athletic, with impressive arm muscles and a long scar on his right cheek, the origins of which he kept shrouded in mystery.

'Why did Pajot have two mooring spots for one boat and so close together?'

Like Bénodet, Sainte-Marine was in the mouth of the Odet, where the river had long since become a three- or four-hundred-metre wide fjord and then gradually turned into the open sea. The two places were directly opposite each other. Sainte-Marine was – along with Port Manech, which was at the mouth of the Aven – the most beautiful place on the whole coast, Dupin thought. He loved it, including the two restaurants right on the quay, which he knew very well. Bénodet was also pretty, much larger and had more shops, hotels and restaurants, but Dupin preferred Sainte-Marine.

'Some of the "better sort" here have spots on both

sides so that they don't need to drive to the large bridge if they want to do something on the other side.'

'Did Pajot own a boat before this?'

'Apparently not. Not in these two harbours anyway.'

'First he's got no boat, then suddenly a really expensive one and two mooring spots at the same time?'

'He must be very well off. His construction company is one of the two largest in Brittany and is also known throughout the country. He has had the boat driving license for a long time, since 1978. The boat, the *Conquerer*, is a Gran Turismo 49 by the way. Bénéteau.'

The tone of this last remark made it clear that it was meant to be significant. Everyone here on the coast was knowledgeable boats – one of their favourite topics. Dupin didn't have a problem not being knowledgeable about them, but from time to time he was sorry when it was made into esoteric secret knowledge.

'And that means?'

'15.6 metres long, 4.3 metres wide, around 12,000 kilograms in weight. Two 435 PS. About half a million euro.'

Kadeg was putting this as cockily as if it were his own boat. It sounded like old times, playing Top Trumps.

'Half a million?'

None of the other figures meant anything to Dupin.

'Boats are expensive. And as I said: Pajot will have been seriously rich.'

'When were you on the phone to Savoir?'

'From the boat. A few minutes ago.'

'Did he say anything?'

'What do you mean?'

Savoir had apparently not hinted at anything to do with the murders yet.

'Nothing. Call him again. I want to know whether this man is the third man beyond all doubt.'

'The Gran Turismo is registered to him, it's definitively his boat.'

'I want the absolutely cast-iron facts.'

Far too much in this case was obvious and then turned out to be not so obvious after all.

Clearly in a bad temper, Kadeg got out his phone. Suddenly they could hear the infernal noise of the rotors – and the helicopter was right above the island again. Riwal was back. That was good.

Kadeg had to raise his voice considerably.

'Yes, Docteur, exactly, Inspector Kadeg. Exactly. I...'

You could tell how much of an effort Kadeg was making to understand. The noise was getting increasingly ear-splitting, the helicopter was about to land.

'You have to speak louder, Docteur. I...'

Kadeg broke off again. In despair, he pressed the phone to his ear, doing acrobatics to try and shield it with his other hand as he did so – which didn't even help. It looked rather bizarre. He was pacing back and forth the entire time as if he was looking – also, inevitably, to no avail – for a place where the noise would be less loud. He suddenly stood still, taking the phone angrily from his ear. Then he walked right up to Dupin, leant in and shouted:

'It's him! It's Pajot! They've...'

The helicopter had landed, but the engines were still running.

Dupin waited, he knew the procedure. It took less than half a minute for the great silence of the archipelago to return without warning. Dupin was ready more quickly than Kadeg.

'And there's no doubt about it?'

'No. Docteur Savoir is certain. They found a series of usable photos online.'

'Good. Then we have our third dead man. *Voilà*. The full set.'

Kadeg looked at the Commissaire in bewilderment.

Dupin was simply happy to be on more solid ground. To know the starting point of the case at least.

'There's news, Kadeg. We need to talk. With Riwal. Right away.'

'We should find ourselves some other place. The *Quatre Vents* is absolutely inappropriate for our discussions. It's a public place.'

'Out of the question. We're staying here.'

Dupin's spontaneous reply had arisen out of deep indignation.

Quite apart from Dupin's style of developing rituals straight away, everywhere and always, the real reason not to want to look for a different place was that there was also *de facto* no alternative. Where were they meant to go? Sit on the quay, on the beach, in a dune? On a boat? Commandeer a room at the sailing school or the diving centre? Dupin would have, in all honesty, done this without hesitation if it had been his preference – but, and this was definitely the second, important reason: there would be no coffee there.

'We'll sit down out here, right where we were sitting just now.'

Dupin headed straight for the table that was still as it had been before. Kadeg followed with visible reluctance, but stayed silent.

'We'll make it quick,' Dupin said firmly.

Inspector Riwal, Inspector Kadeg and Commissaire Dupin had not sat down for very long. Not because it really had become 'nippy' – by now 'seriously nippy'! –, but because Dupin was uneasy. He was well known for his urgent sense of restlessness when he was on a case.

In just a few words, he had conveyed to Kadeg and Riwal the news that changed everything. The colour visibly drained from their faces. They asked a few questions first and then in turn – and only just – extracted from Dupin exactly what Savoir's report had said and how the conversations with Solenn Nuz had gone. Dupin wanted to get to work.

Kadeg and Riwal also thought it most likely at the moment that Lefort and Konan had been given the benzodiazepines in the *Quatre Vents*. And that the culprit had therefore spent time there the previous evening, briefly or at length. They thought it necessary to find out very soon exactly who had been in the *Quatre Vents*, what Konan and Lefort haddrunk and eaten and whether anyone had seen anything suspicious. Dupin wanted a list of people categorised into 'regulars and/or known persons on the archipelago' and 'unknown persons'. The other category was obvious: which of the people had a connection to which of the three dead. And what kind of connection had it been? Another priority was to learn as much as possible, as quickly as possible, about the three victims, their lives, their work and the links between them and come across something of substance. Potential leads, potential conflicts, a potential motive, people who might have had some interest in the deaths of the three men.

Dupin had put Kadeg on Pajot, Riwal on Konan and he himself had taken on on Lefort, although he had asked Riwal to put him in touch with the man's girlfriend as soon as possible. The houses belonging to all three on the mainland were to be searched and Pajot's home in Paris. All of the 'routines' had to begin, the gathering of information about will and inheritance matters, looking into assets and property matters, bank transactions, phone line evidence... they would need more people in addition to the team from their own Commissariat.

Kadeg had wanted to have the *Quatre Vents* declared a crime scene. Dupin, who was otherwise known for sealing off crime scenes for long periods at will and for as long as he liked, had been dead set against it – even though Kadeg had raised arguments that were criminologically relevant, such as the issue of whether they should have the counters, glasses and kitchen examined for traces of the sedative. It wasn't just because Dupin was worried about the steady supply of coffee (which he was!) that he had been against it. No: if they closed the *Quatre Vents*, they themselves would be boycotting the scene of their enquiries: they would be forcing everyone to make themselves scarce. *Here* they actually came together: those who could say something about the world out here, who might know something – who maybe even knew the perpetrator. It had not beena long exchange, Dupin hadexpressed his position categorically, whereupon he hadmarched into the *Quatre Vents*.

For a few moments the customers' attention had been directed entirely at the small group of police officers coming in. The conversations at the tables had faltered briefly. People knew who they were of course. Dupin, Kadeg and Riwal had moved across the room at a decidedly calm pace and stood by the wall to the left of the bar. The conversations at the tables had quickly resumed their earlier liveliness.

They stood very close to each other, practically squashed together. Dupin hated it. Riwal and Kadeg were having an incomprehensible conversation about the bad air, the incredible bustle in the place, you could tell that they were feeling ill at ease.

Dupin, however, was content. From here, you could observe exactly what was happening at the bar. The trays sitting on the counter. The drinks being added, the food. The trays occasionally sat for several minutes absolutely 'unsupervised'. It was this exact place at the counter where the majority of customers lingered. It was all just as Solenn Nuz had said: a closely packed, chaotic swarm. Anyone, it was clear at a glance, could have come over here at any time without attracting any suspicion or attention at all. Anyone could have got close enough to the trays.

Or else it had happened at Konan and Lefort's table. Of course they would painstakingly try to reconstruct that decisive half an hour before they had left – they would question everyone about whether someone had noticed anything unusual during this time – but the likelihood of finding out more in this way, Dupin felt, was not very high,. It was clear they were dealing with a very intelligent perpetrator.

Dupin's forehead was deeply creased. He didn't like this one bit. And drawing up the list was also taking too long for his liking.

'Monsieur le Commisssaire, we should...'

Kadeg began loudly in his self-important tone, but Dupin interrupted fiercely.

'Riwal, Kadeg, watch the customers carefully over the next few minutes.'

Dupin was not quite sure whether what he was about to do was right. It had suddenly occurred to him, even though it might seem theatrical and he couldn't stand theatrics. In theory it might be – and he had already been thinking this at the table outside – a technical advantage, if the murderer didn't know for as long as possible that his deed had been discovered to be murder. But that was an absolute pipe-dream. It would do the rounds anyway. Probably quite soon, too.

Dupin wove his way to the centre of the counter and stood still. Without preamble, he began to speak to the whole room in a powerful voice and official tone:

'Commissaire Dupin from the Commissariat de Police Concarneau. Bonsoir Mesdames, Messieurs.'

The room was instantly as silent as the grave. Because of the clear words certainly, but certainly also because of his impressive physical presence, which could lend his words, when Dupin wanted, a considerable emphasis. Riwal and Kadeg's heads had whipped around in his direction and they stared at him in disbelief for a few moments.

'Last night three men were murdered on the Glénan. The three dead, who were found on Le Loc'h this morning are, categorically, not the victims of an accident. It was a cold-blooded triple murder. A capital offence. And we have reason to believe that two of them had strong sedatives mixed into their drinks or food right here in this bar, the effect of which led to the fatal shipwreck,' he broke off artfully. 'We are now investigating a murder case and would like to ask you to give all the support you can to our work.'

He paused again.

He went on, in the unmistakable tone of a police briefing:

'First of all we want to know which of you were here yesterday evening in the *Quatre Vents*, no matter how briefly, where you were sitting and whether you noticed anything suspicious. Especially here at the counter, by the trays. Regardless of how trivial or irrelevant it might seem to you. We're asking you to speak up. The smallest circumstance could be significant. The two men in question, Monsieur Lucas Lefort and Monsieur Yannig Konan, were sitting at this table.'

Dupin pointed to a table in the corner.

'I also want to know whether anyone was here yesterday evening who is not here today. Furthermore, whether you knew the victims and where every single one of you comes from, whether you are on a diving or sailing course or taking a sailing trip. Another pressing question is whether you saw one or both of the victims in the company of the third dead man, a certain Grégoire Pajot? – – – Thank you for your cooperation. We will take down your details. This is police procedure.' Dupin paused for a long time and let his gaze wander openly over the customers. Most of them looked stony-faced and didn't seem to have breathed during his speech. Even the two Nuz daughters stood as though rooted to the spot.

'My inspectors will now go from table to table and speak to you. If everyone could please not leave the room until the end of this questioning.'

Dupin had a feeling this had been the right decision. Now the case was real. It was out in the open. They needed to be fully alert now. To watch carefully. The game had commenced.

Dupin strode over to Riwal and Kadeg. There was still absolute silence in the *Quatre Vents*. Dupin murmured: 'Riwal, you take the left hand side, Kadeg, you take the right.' The two inspectors turned around and got down to work without any further ado. At first there was a gradual, tentative whispering from the customers, which slowly increased.

Solenn Nuz had been in the kitchen while Dupin was speaking. She only came out now, but stopped barely beyond the doorway, a sheet of paper in her hand. Dupin signalled something vaguely in her direction and then went over to her. Even though she had shown barely any agitation just before in light of the accidental deaths of three men – and she had known two of them after all – she looked distraught now.

'This is difficult to believe. Are you sure, Monsieur le Commissaire? That it was murder?'

'Absolutely certain. We have received credible blood analyses.'

She was silent for a moment.

'Who owned the boat that was found?'

'Grégoire Pajot. It's called *Conquerer*, a Bénéteau. Gran Turismo. No doubt – very large. They went out in his boat, or they did yesterday evening anyway.'

'The name Grégoire Pajot doesn't mean anything to me.'

'Even we can't say anything on that yet either. How the three met, where they were beforehand and so on,' something occurred to Dupin that he had just forgotten: 'We'll show you and the customers a photo of Monsieur Pajot. One moment please, Madame Nuz, I'll be right back.'

Dupin went to Kadeg, who was standing at one of the tables on the right hand side.

'We need a photo of Pajot straight away. You have that thing after all.'

Kadeg's eyes lit up with glee – now his smartphone was suddenly urgently needed. For once Dupin didn't care – he wanted the photo. Kadeg had already whipped out his handset and was typing away on the tiny screen with his far from delicate fingers. Dupin raised his powerful voice again:

'Mesdames, Messieurs, one more thing. We will be showing you a photo of Monsieur Pajot – we would very much like to know whether anybody knows him or has seen him recently.'

Kadeg was standing in front of him with a proud smile and holding the phone under his nose.

'A photo on one of his companies' websites.'

Before Kadeg could say anything else, Dupin had taken the phone out of his hand and turned away. He went back to Madame Nuz.

'Could we perhaps sit back there in the kitchen like before? That would be ideal.'

'Of course. Come with me.'

They sat down at the little table.

'This is Monsieur Pajot.'

Madame Nuz studied the photo closely before she said anything.

'No. I've actually never seen him here before. Maybe he came to sail or dive. But not to the *Quatre Vents*. You should ask at the sailing school. And Anjela Barrault too, the head of the diving school. She's a friend of mine.'

'We will.'

'My daughters and I sat down and drew up the list of people from yesterday evening.' Still holding it in her hand, she now placed it on the table in front of Dupin.

'So did someone occur to your daughters whom you hadn't thought of?'

'Just Muriel Lefort. She was apparently there briefly and also spoke to her brother. I was probably back here in the kitchen then. It must have been around half eight. Or thereabouts.'

Dupin knew that already. Just not the time. Dupin got out his Clairefontaine and made a note.

'My daughters also remembered what Konan and Lefort ate and drank. They are practically certain. First some draught beer and then red wine. They got themselves a bottle several times, spread out over the course of the evening. Anyone can help themselves to water at the front, the carafes are right there. Both of them ate fish soup, then Konan had the lobster and Lefort the *entrecôte*.'

Dupin made a note of everything.

'And nothing struck you or your daughters as unusual that evening? Something up at the bar, a person who behaved in a striking way?'

'No. But I'll speak to my daughters again.'

'Was anybody in the kitchen apart from you?'

Solenn Nuz hesitated.

'No.'

Dupin switched into a neutral tone.

'Now that we know that it was murder and that we are dealing with a whole new situation – does anything occur to you generally that you consider relevant, Madame Nuz? Do you have an idea of what may have happened here? I…'

'Um.'

There was a pointed throat-clearing. Kadeg planted himself right in front of them.

'My smartphone. We could do with the photo.'

Dupin held it out to him mechanically.

'Madame Nuz has drawn up an initial list of people. She is going to complete it. I also want a detailed sketch of the room with every table, every chair and the bar – mark everyone on it. Who stood or sat when, for how long, where, along with timings.'

Kadeg and Riwal were familiar with these impossible tasks. What was astonishing was – they had learnt this over the years with Dupin – how often it was in fact possible to achieve what seemed absolutely out of the question at first. And the purposes it could have. Kadeg made no comment on the task, not a word and even his expression was remarkably neutral. He turned around and left.

Dupin turned back to Madame Nuz.

'I had asked whether anything had occurred to you in general in relation to this murder.'

'You will find a whole series of people with motive. People tell nasty stories about Konan. I can't say what there is to them. And Lefort – people hate him. I know only a handful of exceptions.'

She had uttered these sentences in her distinctive, calm tone of voice. But it was clear that she felt the same way.

This was something new anyway. The deceased usually only had friends, never enemies, they had been admired by everyone, cherished and loved.

'And what was the reason? Why was he hated and by whom? By whom specifically?'

'There would be a lot to tell there.'

'Go ahead.'

Solenn Nuz looked serious.

'There really are a lot of unpleasant stories.'

'I want to hear them all.'

She took a deep breath.

'For over ten years, Lucas Lefort has been trying, using every means possible, to make the Glénan into a great "tourist scheme". With hotels, sports facilities, bridges between the islands. Four of the islands belong to him in any case. To him and his sister. He has always failed in his schemes, although only just. The former mayor of Fouesnant rebelled against it. He was one of his arch-enemies. Lefort then changed his plans two or three times. Purely

127

strategically. He attempted to do it with a gigantic extension planned for the sailing school. He also always wanted to buy the diving centre from me and extend it. His latest idea was: "sophisticated ecotourism". He is,' she paused for a moment, 'he was not above even the most brazen lie.'

Dupin was making notes. As well as he could. This was a big issue opening up here. These were the stories he had been waiting for.

'The former mayor often wished him dead. Lefort fought back hard, Lefort slandered him maliciously, accused him of corruption. He tried to make a fool of him. Yet the mayor was a man of integrity.'

'What is the situation now?'

That was vague, but Dupin had to get familiar with the subject first.

'Lefort's plans died down for a few years, but then he started on ecotourism recently. Apparently, he was on the point of submitting the revised concept. It's been talked about everywhere for months already. The new mayor hasn't spoken out yet. We all assume that he will advocate the same firm position as his predecessor. The local council is largely still the same as it was a few years ago. It also voted against, although only by a narrow majority. The district council was similar. The new coastal protection laws make it impossible really. Which didn't in the least deter Lefort from trying anyway.'

'But he was there yesterday evening too, wasn't he? The mayor, I mean. Monsieur...'

'Du Marhallac'h. Indeed.'

'You mentioned that he in fact spoke to Lefort too.'

'Yes.'

Solenn looked away from Dupin and contemplated her hands.

'It would destroy the Glénan. Everything here. Yes, there is tourism, but it only affects the archipelago on a superficial level.'

To an extent, Dupin understood what she was trying to say.

'And his sister? Muriel Lefort?'

'She has always been firmly against all of these plans.'

'So there was serious conflict between the two of them?'

Solenn Nuz hesitated for a brief moment.

'Incessantly. They fought bitterly, there was a real battle between them.'

'The Leforts must be very well off.'

'Indeed they are.'

Dupin made another note.

'Apart from these plans, were there any reasons for disagreements between them?'

'It's impossible to imagine siblings being more different. In every respect. Muriel embodies the "original spirit" of the sailing school. Her brother trampled all over that. He was only interested in how to make more money, he...'

'Could you explain that in more detail: the "original spirit"?'

'An attitude. Certain values. Volunteering, living collectively, solidarity, self-reliance. The sailing school is a global institution. It was founded at the end of the Second World War, out of the spirit of the Résistance. Lucas and Muriel's parents were leading members of the resistance in Finstère. The sailing school was initially a kind of commune of idealistic young men and women.'

'And then?'

'Over the course of years, it kept being expanded by Lucas and Muriel's parents. Cautiously. Very shrewdly. And always in keeping with the old ideals. It was about great ideas. Even today it's the opposite of a "posh yacht club", the normal sailing schools. The course participants still stay in the most basic conditions here. Everyone is equal. No matter how much money they have. They sleep on cots in dormitories, use communal showers like when camping, they eat together outdoors. They don't just learn to sail, it's about much more than that. – That's what Muriel Lefort stands for. And Maela Menez.'

'She's the assistant.'

'Yes.'

'What's her exact role?'

'She is Muriel's right hand woman. She does everything. She runs a few things on her own too. The boat park for instance. She embodies the spirit of the sailing school in a very, how should I put it, rigorous way. Ruthlessly. She is very – idealistic.'

'So she had a strained relationship with Lucas Lefort too.'

'Oh yes.'

'Did the two of them not chat yesterday evening too?'

'They were standing next to each other. At the bar. I don't know exactly how long for.'

'Still speaking to each other in any case.'

'Don't get the wrong idea. Even Muriel and her brother weren't shouting at each other the whole time,' she seemed to be reflecting, 'the conflicts went far deeper than that. And don't ever forget that it's a very unique world here. And very small.'

Solenn Nuz reminded Dupin of Nolwenn in some ways, which was something that had already occurred to him before. Yet it wasn't their names sounding similar, or the extensive knowledge that they both gathered about people, but, more than anything, it was their way of observing, how and what they observed.

'Are you aware of whether there was some escalation between the siblings recently?'

'Muriel always tried not to keep the conflict behind closed doors. Not doing that would have been distasteful to her temperament. She is a highly discreet person. I don't know exactly what happened. Only she knows.'

Dupin's forehead creased.

'Who else? Who were Lucas Lefort's other enemies?'

'As I mentioned, there were quite a few. And I'm sure there were more than I'm aware of. Marc. Marc Leussot. A marine biologist and journalist. He was here last night too. A radical opponent of all tourism plans. He has written critical articles about the potential consequences of a further increase in tourism on the Glénan.'

Dupin made a note of everything. He had such a dreadful scrawl that he had to be exceptionally disciplined with himself while writing and keep his speed under control, otherwise he himself couldn't read things properly later. He had had unfortunate experiences of that.

'He's sitting over there.' She moved her head brusquely in the direction of the bar. He's here very often. – – – And all of Lefort's women. You can't forget them. Many broken hearts. It wouldn't surprise anyone if one of them had taken their revenge. Especially his latest girlfriend. He cheated on her constantly, right underneath her nose.'

'Do you know the name of his current girlfriend?'

'No.'

'What else comes to mind?'

'You should also bear his sailing in mind. Apparently he wangled his place in the Admiral's Cup boat with ruthless methods. He was utterly cold. Unscrupulous.'

That had sounded like a résumé.

'You know this world here like nobody else.'

'Inevitably.'

For a moment, the warm, open smile that Dupin already knew returned to Solenn Nuz's face.

'But in fact there's very little I can really say. I have no idea what Lucas Lefort's life truly looked like. He was always away for days at a time on the mainland. But as for what deals he was involved with right now or whom he might have fallen out with, no idea.'

'You said that you personally didn't have much to do with Lefort?'

'If he was on the islands, then we said hello and goodbye. Perhaps had some small talk. Not even that yesterday.'

This case had been strange from the beginning and was continuing that way. By the end of his first proper investigative interview, Dupin would have a list of between five and seven serious suspects. And that was in relation to Lefort alone.

'And Konan? What do you know about him?'

132

'He started out with mattresses, but within a few years he had built up an empire. Then he expanded his businesses and became a big name in the export of Breton products. He founded a few societies. And he has a company for deep sea exploration, for scouting out oil deposits in the deep sea. He has close links with politics apparently. That probably "helped" him in all of his successes.'

'How do you know all of this?'

'He is extremely unpopular here. A power player. Snooty. He once wanted to buy an exclusive, private mooring spot at the quay. That kind of thing doesn't even exist here. He put two lawyers onto it.'

'But he did keep coming here?'

'Yes, with Lucas.'

This was really a very curious world, Dupin thought. They hated each other, but the place bound them all together somehow.

'And in private? Do you know anything about his private life?'

'We knew each other to say hello, that was all. He's married. But his wife never came with him on any trips. I barely know anything about her. She might be a primary school teacher. She's obese, apparently.'

'So what happened to the former mayor?'

Solenn Nuz hesitated for a second, which surprised Dupin.

'He died two years ago. His heart. Collapsed at a Fest-Noz.'

Amongst the varied tasks of a Breton mayor there was of course this one: taking part in the endless launches for regional, local and very local festivals in the summer. Drinking festivals.

Dupin was waiting to see whether she wanted to add anything else. There was a rather long pause.

'It's clear to me that I'm one of the suspects too. You know my opinion on Lucas Lefort. For me and my daughters it would have been simple to put something directly in their food or drink. Simpler than for the others.'

'I've just had an insight into how simple it would have been for anybody.'

'Maman?'

The younger daughter had come into the back.

'Yes?'

'Some customers want to leave. They want to get back to the mainland this evening. The two inspectors have said nobody is allowed to leave the bar until they're finished their interviews.'

It hadn't been a question and she had spoken to her mother, as if Dupin had not been present at all. Dupin answered directly.

'Yes, that's correct, it's what I ordered. Unfortunately, we have to do it this way. We are solving a murder.'

'Fine.'

The 'fine' had had no trace of resignation or sarcasm at all.

She was already gone when Riwal appeared in the doorway. He hurried over to Dupin, stood next to him and stooped down.

'Monsieur le Commissaire, Madame Lefort is going to land any moment.'

Riwal was whispering, but Solenn Nuz could still hear every word (which made the situation unnecessarily ridiculous in Dupin's eyes).

'Quimper called. Muriel Lefort has confirmed the identity of her brother. Our colleagues are taking care of the formal identifications of the other two. They haven't said anything to Madame Lefort about the murder yet – as you instructed. If you don't want her to find out about it from someone after she lands, you should be there to meet her.'

Dupin reflected. He had completely forgotten about that. It was very inconvenient just now. But he had to do it. And he wanted to do it. For several reasons. He looked at his watch, having lost all sense of how late it must have been. Half past eight.

'Fine, I'm already on my way.'

He stood up and said goodbye to Solenn Nuz.

She smiled in a very friendly way. Dupin took it to be a heartfelt gesture.

He left the room, Riwal at his side.

'You and Kadeg finish the interrogations here and call over to the sailing school and the diving centre. Speak to Madame Barrault, the head of the diving centre and Madame Menez, Muriel Lefort's assistant. The sketch with all customers from last night is still the priority. Don't forget any of the questions.'

'We won't, boss.'

'A Monsieur Leussot was also one of the regular customers there last night.'

'Got him already.'

'Great.'

'Will you be contactable, Monsieur le Commissaire?'

'Of course. Yes.'

Dupin fished his phone out of his pocket. It was still on vibrate.

'All right.'

If it rang, he would need to check the number. Which he had not done for a long time now: nine calls received. Riwal once, Nolwenn once, a number he didn't know, two withheld numbers – and the Prefect four times. Dupin growled quietly. Grimly.

The helicopter had just landed. The pilot had switched off the engine at the moment that Commissaire Dupin, a little out of breath, had reached the field behind the old farmhouse. Madame Lefort was about to climb out of the cabin, while Madame Menez had already disembarked and was helping her. Muriel Lefort looked absolutely worn out.

'It's kind of you to meet me, Monsieur le Commissaire. It was – very difficult.'

'In fact I should speak to you again, Madame Lefort.'

There was a vague yet intense fear in Muriel Lefort's gaze, her eyes narrowed. Dupin briefly considered whether he should tell her one on one.

He decided to do it in the presence of Madame Menez.

'Your brother was murdered. It was not an accident. We can say this without any doubt. I'm sorry.'

Dupin knew he had expressed this kind of message with more empathy on previous occasions.

Muriel Lefort looked at him as though turned to stone. She didn't say a word. The fear in her gaze had subsided, her eyes now looked absolutely blank. Madame Menez was silent too. After a few moments Muriel Lefort looked away. She took a few steps, walking around aimlessly. Madame Menez was obviously undecided as to whether she should follow her, but left it.

Dupin was watching Madame Menez, who looked him directly in the eye a few times and who, despite her silence, made no effort to give the impression she was shocked.

'I'm not really surprised,' Muriel Lefort said dully. She had slowly come back over to Dupin and Madame Menez.

'But it's still beyond me,' she added in a rather formal tone. As though she had felt duty-bound to add this.

'Your brother had quite a number of enemies.'

'Yes.'

'How was he murdered?' asked Madame Menez.

Dupin had expected the question earlier. And not from her.

'Somebody administered strong sedatives to him and to Yannig Konan. Combined with the alcohol, they had no chance...'

Muriel Lefort put her hands over her face. There was another long silence. Again, Madame Menez did not show the slightest emotion.

'We've also found the boat they were on when they capsized. It belongs to a Grégoire Pajot. A Gran Turismo. A very expensive boat. They sailed onto rocks at the exit of the chamber. – – – Does the name Grégoire Pajot mean anything to you, Madame Lefort?'

Muriel Lefort did not answer straight away.

'Yes. I've heard it before. One of my brother's "friends". An investor, I think.'

'The three of them were probably out in his boat over the weekend.'

Muriel Lefort closed her eyes, taking deep breaths in and out.

'Would it be possible to continue our talk at my home? I would like to have a drink. And sit down.'

'Of course. There are a few important questions.'

'Naturally.'

Madame Menez walked ahead at a brisk pace. Madame Lefort followed, almost catching her up but not quite. Dupin let himself fall back a few paces. They took a lightly trodden path over the sparse green towards the ugly triangular houses standing about a hundred and fifty metres ahead of them. All three were silent. Dupin was glad of it.

The sun had already sunk far down to the sea, the play of colours had long since begun. A gentle kind of magic, without any garish effects. Imperceptibly at first, a fine, delicate orange had blended into the light, clear blue, with a little red that had now become a watery orange glow and took up the whole western sphere: the sky, the sea – even the sun itself. Another few minutes and the clearly delineated ball would calmly disappear into the sea, quietly, tranquilly – for tonight at least. It was, Dupin thought, as though the sun was sometimes completely content to set, but other times not content at all. On those occasions, the sun seemed to have an internal struggle, ending in dramatic cosmic battles, apocalyptic colours, scenes and atmospheres and in the end it drowned in the sea like in one final global catastrophe. Within the next half hour the delicate orange would gradually fade and ultimately be swallowed up seamlessly by a deep black. Dupin knew it well. An almost physical black, which was much more than a lack of light.

As they approached the first house, Muriel Lefort took the lead. She started rummaging in her handbag as she walked, drawing out a small bunch of keys with a flourish.

They climbed over the low wall and stood in front of the door briefly until Madame Lefort had unlocked it. Still nobody spoke. They went inside.

'If you excuse me a moment, I'd like to freshen up. I'll be right back. Madame Menez will look after you.'

Muriel Lefort went upstairs. The house was absolutely identical in design and layout to her brother's – probably to all of these houses – but furnished more simply. Old wooden furniture, a beautiful, clearly well-worn oak parquet, an open-plan kitchen that you could tell was used. A small, neat table stood in it, a larger one by the east-facing panoramic window. Dupin walked over to the window. The sunset had already happened here. The difference between the hemispheres was profound at the End of the World when the sun was setting. Night was obviously here already, the last of the orange still glimmering in the west.

'It doesn't surprise me at all that it was murder.'

In Maela Menez's sentence, more thrust out than spoken, there lay deep emotion, which she seemed to have been holding back at first, only for it to come pouring out now.

'If I were capable of the murder and Madame Lefort wasn't his sister – I would have killed him too, under certain circumstances. He was a disgraceful character. It's disrespectful to say it, I know. But I don't care.'

Dupin turned around and scrutinised Madame Menez with interest. She was a peculiar mixture: the somewhat stilted, somehow old-fashioned way of speaking on the one hand and the rather lively, undeniably pretty looks on the other. Dupin would have put her in her early thirties. There was something extremely determined in her dark eyes – just a few forlorn bright spots blazed in the deep brown of the iris – and in her facial expression. In those eyes there was an impressive, alert intelligence.

'I've already heard that Monsieur Lefort was clearly very unpopular.'

'For which there was a multitude of reasons.'

'And for which of these reasons would you have wanted to murder him? For example?'

She didn't flinch for a second, even at this pointed phrasing from Dupin.

'I witnessed how he treated Madame Lefort. All these years. It was difficult to bear. I would gladly have intervened, but Madame Lefort didn't approve of that. The worst of it,' she paused for a moment and she seemed to be realising for the first time, what she was saying, 'I mean, it was loathsome, that he corrupted everything that comprised the Glénan at their heart, the original idea, the spirit. He would have destroyed everything without thinking, he wouldn't have cared a jot about it. He was selfish and his only interest was said to be megabucks.'

After the brief pause, her voice reached an impressive climax again.

'He wanted the jetset lifestyle. He had…'

'Maela, you shouldn't speak like that. You know that. Especially now – he's dead. Murdered.'

Even though it sounded like an admonishment, Muriel Lefort had not been brusque at all. She was standing on one of the top steps.

'I know. But it's the truth. And the police should know everything.'

'But we don't have a clue whether the murder attempt was meant for my brother. It could just as easily have been meant for one of the other men. Maybe even two of them or all three – in fact that's how it must have been. Otherwise the murderer would have had to tolerate the death of innocent people.'

Muriel Lefort seemed to have composed herself again to some extent. And her interjection was justified. And important. Here on the islands everyone and everything was automatically fixated on Lucas Lefort. Everyone assumed that the motive for murder was to be found in his life. Which of course was only because almost nobody knew Yannig Konan or Grégoire Pajot. Lefort on the other hand was an important figure here, a real celebrity.

'I'll leave you alone now, Muriel, Monsieur le Commissaire. You need to talk.'

Madame Lefort threw Dupin a questioning look and only replied when he nodded slightly in agreement.

'Thank you. Yes, Monsieur le Commissaire and I have things to discuss. And I'll go to bed afterwards. Or take a little walk. There's a full moon. See you tomorrow, Maela.'

Muriel Lefort had come all the way downstairs by this point. It was clear to see that she still looked haggard, no matter how composed she sounded.

'When the moon rises, it becomes almost as bright as day here on the archipelago, you've never seen the like, Monsieur le Commissaire. It's like a dream.'

Madame Menez glanced at her watch, gave Dupin a cursory nod and turned to leave.

'I hope you get some sleep tonight, Muriel. You've got to recover, you're going to need a lot of strength.'

'Thanks, Maela. Thank you for everything. You were a great support to me this evening.'

Maela Menez was almost at the door already.

'Madame Menez – wait. We need to ask you some urgent questions too,' Dupin was speaking very matter-of-factly, 'if you could please call in to one of the inspectors? They are in the *Quatre Vents*.'

She seemed confused for a moment. But she recovered immediately.

'Oh yes, of course. The investigations.'

'Thanks very much,' Dupin fixed his gaze on Madame Menez, 'and I had a question of my own.'

'Absolutely.'

Maela Menez was completely confident again now.

'Yesterday evening in the *Quatre Vents*, you spoke to Lucas Lefort briefly. What was it about?'

She answered without hesitation.

'I manage the boat park. He wanted to borrow the transport boat for a few days. This week.'

'The transport boat?'

'We have an old motor boat that we use for transporting other, smaller boats, bulky equipment or building materials.'

'And why did he need it?'

'I didn't ask him.'

'And what did you say?'

'That he didn't stand a chance this week because we needed the boat.'

'How did he react?'

'He said "We'll see about that". That was it.'

Madame Menez's words made it clear that she

considered her obligation to give information fulfilled and she turned to leave again. Dupin let her.

'Thanks very much, Madame Menez. See you tomorrow.'

Still standing, he got out his notebook and wrote a few things down.

'Oh, sorry, Monsieur le Commissaire. Let's sit down. Come, let's sit right here at the kitchen table.'

'Thanks.'

'I need something to drink. Will you join me? An old cognac?'

'I... yes.'

That was a good idea.

'And a coffee?'

That was even more vital. His caffeine levels were critically low.

'I'd love one.'

In front of Dupin on the old wooden table there was an – already empty – antique-looking espresso cup and a bulbous, generously filled cognac glass. In between lay his notebook, his bic and, dangerously close to the edge of the table, his mobile. Muriel Lefort was sitting opposite him, glass in hand, having already drunk a few mouthfuls from it.

She had wanted to know everything in detail, the course of events the accident might have taken – everything the police could say at this point. Dupin had reported what he knew. But that was not much.

'We actually don't know any more than what I've just told you. The boat belonged to a third man, Grégoire Pajot.'

'Why were they on his boat?'

'We're still taking stabs in the dark.'

Muriel Lefort's forehead creased.

'Perhaps because they thought they wouldn't get far in my brother's speedboat with the high waves. If the sea is rough, a boat like that is no use. Perhaps that's why they were on Monsieur Pajot's boat.'

'We found Monsieur Konan's boat in Bénodet. Your brother must have embarked here, on the Glénan. We have no knowledge of where the three kept the boat afterwards and for how long. I hoped you would perhaps know a little more.'

'No. Nothing at all. I've also spoken to Madame Menez already, she saw him just yesterday. You should speak to his girlfriend.'

'We will. Is there any other family? Do we need to inform anyone else?'

'Oh no. There's only a distant uncle, with whom we haven't been in touch for more than ten years. What else do you know, Monsieur le Commissaire? It's important for me to find out everything. It makes it more real.'

'We are assuming that someone mixed the sedatives into their food or drink in the *Quatre Vents*.'

'In the *Quatre Vents*? Unbelievable.'

Suddenly there came a strange buzzing sound, his mobile was moving across the table. The Prefect. Dupin kept speaking, undeterred.

'You yourself were in fact in the *Quatre Vents* at the time we suspect it happened, around half eight?'

Dupin's tone of voice didn't match the sharpness of his question. Muriel Lefort sat up straight and moved back a little in her chair. She didn't reply.

'Has something unusual crossed your mind?'

'Mine? No. I was only in the *Quatre Vents* briefly.
I got something to eat. An *entrecôte*. You can get it
to go too. I do that sometimes when I have a lot on. I
spent the whole evening doing paperwork. In the office.
I exchanged a few words with Leussot beforehand.
Small talk. Armelle Nuz served me. I didn't see Solenn
at all.

The word '*entrecôte*' had not had a good effect on
Dupin. He could feel how terribly hungry he was,
he was practically dizzy. And *entrecôte – entrecôte
frites* – was by far his favourite food. He tried to
concentrate on the conversation.

'Where was your brother standing or sitting when
you came into the *Quatre Vents*?'

'Near where you get the drinks, by the bar, but
later also on the other side of the passage. To the
right. With a blonde woman.'

'So you were only two or three metres apart. You
and your brother.'

'Yes.'

'But you're saying you didn't speak to him?'

'I don't think he even noticed me. He was absorbed
in his – conversation. There really was a lot going on
in the *Quatre Vents* yesterday evening.'

'We know that. Who else was standing nearby? At
the bar? Who was waiting for their food or came to
get drinks?'

Dupin knew that his question would not lead
anywhere.

'You're asking too much there.'

She paused for a moment, it was clear that she was
trying very hard to think.

'Leussot was coming towards me with a bottle of

wine when I went to the counter, we spoke there briefly. Maela was sitting right at one of the two tables to the left of the bar. Along with two of our colleagues,' she faltered and obviously felt obliged to add, 'two reliable young men, above all suspicion – then – there were definitely five or six people ahead of me, although the queue was moving quickly. People I didn't know, no doubt they were from the diving centre, or even some of ours, I don't know all the course participants after all. Oh yes, and Kilian – Kilian Tanguy was at the top of the queue when I came over, he had a big tray in his hands, Armelle had just put something else on it for him.'

Dupin had noted down a few things. Muriel Lefort had seemed nervous for the last few minutes, in some indefinable way. Her voice sounded distinctly more shaky than it had before. Perhaps it was just the exhaustion.

'I'm terribly sorry to wear you out with all these questions under these circumstances.'

'Personally, I want everything to be cleared up as quickly as possible of course. You know that we truly did not have a harmonious relationship, my brother and me. We had conflicting ideas. But – he was my brother.'

It sounded like more than an empty phrase.

'Do you have any idea who might have killed your brother then, a theory of what it might have been about?'

'It's been a long time since we've spoken to each other about personal things. Many years. As I said, there was a series of people he was at loggerheads with, but I don't know of anyone specific in recent weeks or months. I can't actually tell you anything about my brother's life.'

'What was the contact like between you in the last few months?'

'In February and March we met for about an hour at a time maybe and we also talked on the phone a few times, every three weeks or so. We never talked about anything private, only about things related to the sailing school. And it always led to arguments. He usually just hung up. And at the end of last year he started on about his plans again.'

'The new tourism plans?'

'Yes. He's always had megalomaniac ideas. He wanted to make the archipelago into a modern water sports and adventure tourism centre. He submitted his plans for the first time ten years ago. This time it was under the pretext of 'ecotourism'. After the old mayor of Fouesnant died, whom he'd battled against all these years, he thought he would have another chance with Du Marhallac'h, the new mayor. He was probably willing to have everything submitted to him again.'

'Was he?'

Madame Lefort looked at the Commissaire in shock. 'Yes.'

'I heard he hadn't commented on it yet.'

The shock on her face grew.

'Lucas told me, back in February, I think.'

Dupin made a note.

'What exactly did he say?'

'That the mayor had informed him, with regard to his renewed request which he had submitted at the beginning of the year, that what he'd presented sounded "interesting" and that they wanted to looked at the plans in detail.'

Muriel Lefort had spoken noticeably more quickly.

'I'm sorry to be so insistent – a bad habit of mine, please forgive me.'

Madame Lefort smiled with relief.

'Even the new or "ecological" plans would have required not just approval from the municipality and the region, but also, due to the strict coastal protection laws, approval from Paris. Strangely, Lucas was always certain he would get them. I think Konan played a part in that, he probably had good political connections in the capital. He lived there most of the time after all.'

'Was Konan caught up in all of these plans, I mean, were they pursuing this together?'

'I couldn't say. It seemed that way to me. At the beginning anyway. Ten or twelve years ago when my brother started it.'

'So Konan's money was at stake too?'

'I think so.'

Dupin made another note in his notebook – there had been a lot of notes since this morning, which was never a good sign.

'Besides, my brother wanted to expand the sailing school. "Internationally" – he wanted to open even more locations. Five more branches in the coming year. I was categorically against it. I think his idea was to become the manager of the international sailing business in the event of his plans here on the islands falling through again and, as they say, "to expand globally".'

'Will the entire sailing school belong to you now?'

Dupin had asked the question – one of his preferred methods – extremely abruptly.

'Purely a routine question,' he added and took a swig of cognac, which tasted extraordinary, as he'd already noted earlier on.

Again there was an unchecked, anxious cast to Muriel Lefort's features for a moment.

'I don't know whether he made a will. And if so, what it contains. For my part, I drew up a will a long time ago now, providing for the transfer of my share to a not-for-profit foundation in the event of my death. The foundation is then supposed to support the sailing school. A notary acquaintance of mine wrote it up – I've always wanted to convince my brother to join me. He had no interest in doing so.'

'So the whole sailing school will probably belong to you.'

'I really don't know,' she wrinkled her forehead, 'I – probably, yes.'

The simple question of who had a material benefit after a murder case – everyone always wanted to deflect it of course – might have seemed old-fashioned, but it was still elementary. Who got something out of the death? And what, exactly? 'Traditional' motives for murder still ruled the world: envy, humiliations and hurts, revenge, jealousy and greed dominated all statistics by a wide margin. Even though the murderers in films, television series and books these days were only ever psychopaths.

'How much would you say your company is worth?'

Muriel Lefort's gaze made it clear that she deemed the word 'company' inadequate.

'It's hard to say.'

'You must make a certain turnover every year, all things considered. And the company will be worth a multiple of that.'

'I'll give you the figures later. I'll speak to my head bookkeeper.'

'What do you know about Konan's relationship to your brother?'

'Almost nothing. They were here together maybe once a month, at the weekends. I always thought they went out in Konan's boat. He has quite a stylish boat. They liked to show up at the *Quatre Vents* or at the parties in the sailing school.'

'Didn't they sail together?'

'Not at the weekends. I think my brother has been taking longer trips in recent years. With his former teammates. I haven't seen his sailing yacht in ages. It's in Concarneau.'

'We've heard that already.'

It had become a long conversation after all. He would leave Madame Lefort in peace now.

'There might even have been a new treasure hunt. I just don't know.'

Muriel said this in a serious way, but also somewhat off-hand. Dupin didn't know quite how to reply.

'Treasure hunt?'

'Yes.'

'You mean the search for actual treasure? Gold, silver and all that?'

'It's a kind of sport here on the archipelago. Even if nobody talks about it. It's more serious than it might sound. There's a group of underwater archaeologists in the diving club. Scientists and amateur archaeologists. They cooperate with the official departments of the universities of Brest and Rennes. Everything seems very makeshift, but don't let that fool you. We don't set much store by appearances out here.'

'What's that meant to mean?'

Dupin ran a hand through his hair. Treasure-hunters. It sounded absurd.

'I mean, what kind of treasures are involved?'

'There are dozens of capsized boats lying around the Glénan. Some famous ships. Especially from previous centuries. The waters are dangerous here. Lots of wrecks have already been discovered, there are special sea maps they're marked on. With other wrecks, people know more or less where they're supposed to be, but haven't found them yet. And obviously there must be many more.'

'And what are people looking for in the wrecks?'

'Last year a diver found a chest from the seventeenth century with half a ton of well preserved silver coins. It's about anything valuable. Jewellery, gemstones, coins made from gold, silver, bronze. Old weapons, even cannons. Handcrafts. For the archaeology departments it's about science of course.'

Dupin didn't know what to make of this information; it sounded like a sailor's yarn.

'You said nobody speaks about it?'

'Nobody would give away a good lead.'

'But the treasures – I mean, discovered and salvaged objects from sunken ships actually belong to the state, not to the member of the public who finds them.'

'Ten per cent of the value goes to the finder, that alone can be attractive. Can you imagine how many valuable things have been hidden here in secret? Nobody understands this.'

'And your brother was a treasure-hunter too?'

'Oh yes.'

She said this as if it were the most natural thing in the world.

'Even as a child it fascinated him. He has discovered some ships. But nothing of value. As far as anyone knows. As I said, here on the archipelago and in the surrounding waters, treasure hunting is very popular. You should speak to Anjela Barrault some time – she's the head of the diving centre. And to Monsieur Tanguy, he's an amateur archaeologist himself.'

Dupin was still inclined to dismiss the issue as fantastical.

'What was the value of this chest? The one with the silver?'

'Over half a million.'

That was a significant amount. And very real.

'Konan picked a fight with the old mayor a few years ago – it was about some kind of salvaging rights.'

'Excuse me?'

Muriel Lefort had adopted an off-hand tone again.

'I only remember vaguely. Kilian Tanguy was talking about it.'

'You don't know any more than that?'

'No.'

'And that crossed your mind again just now?'

Madame Lefort, her exhaustion visible again, looked at him quizzically.

'I've asked too much of you in this situation. You should rest.'

'Yes, that would be good. I'm really exhausted.'

'I'll be in touch tomorrow during the course of the morning. I still have a few questions.'

'Of course. Get in touch, I'll be in the office.'

Muriel Lefort stood up before the Commissaire and Dupin followed her.

'*Bonne nuit*, Madame Lefort.'

'*Bonne nuit*.'

She soundlessly closed the door behind him.

It was like a wonderful dream. Madame Lefort had not exaggerated about a night with a full moon. It *was* a whole new world, produced by an extraordinary light with unfamiliar colours. A world in a faraway universe, with different laws and realities. The moon shone with a silvery-white power that Dupin – he was sure of this – had never seen before. Just like sunlight during the day, the moonlight reflected off the sea. It was bright, really bright. But it was not the brightness of daytime. The whole world looked changed: the rocks, the beach, the small stone wall in front of Muriel Lefort's garden. The light cast vague shadows that melded together around the edges. The moon world and the things in it gleamed dimly, a gleam somewhere between a secret, beauty and eeriness. The craziest thing was the sea: an absolutely motionless surface, like frozen mercury, the bizarre black shapes of the islands slipping into it. It was a perfect, mystical setting. If you were to see Groac'h, the witch of shipwrecks, right here and now, floating over the water to her legendary palace, it would have looked absolutely natural.

Dupin had walked a few metres and already had the mobile to his ear when he suddenly stopped. Everything seemed infinite – even the silence, which was now even more powerful than during the day. The sea itself was just a steady, uniform, harmonious roar.

Dupin shivered. It was excessively 'nippy' now. It was late and he was very aware that he had not eaten anything since the lobster and so had drunk a fair amount of cognac on an almost empty stomach and that it had generally been an extremely stressful day. But he needed to pull himself together again and concentrate.

He tried to get through to Riwal and Kadeg.

Riwal was engaged.

'Kadeg?'

'Monsieur le Commissaire.'

'Where are you?'

'We've just finished off the interviews and lists here in the *Quatre Vents*.'

'It took that long?'

'There were thirty people and plenty of questions and queries. We made thoroughness a priority. I believe that was what you wanted. Whatever you miss at the beginning, you never make up for. Now we have a serious list.'

Kadeg still seemed completely alert and ready for action.

'And the diving centre and the sailing school?'

'I've just spoken to the head of the diving centre, Madame Barrault. I firmly requested that she prepare a complete list of all current participants on courses and enquire which of them were in the *Quatre Vents* yesterday evening. We will have those tomorrow morning. Madame Barrault was in the *Quatre Vents* herself yesterday evening, by the way,' Kadeg deliberately paused in an artless-seeming way. 'She only went later, after work.'

'The diving teacher was there too?'

Neither Solenn Nuz nor Muriel Lefort had mentioned her. Muriel Lefort may have just missed her.

'We have somewhat vague, contradictory statements on the timing. She thinks she arrived around quarter to nine. Solenn Nuz's daughters testified to quarter past eight. In any case she stayed during the thunderstorm, until midnight. Until the worst of it was over. Riwal will get the list of sailing students from Madame Menez, the assistant to…'

'I'm up to speed. Where is Goulch anyway?'

'He tried to get you, but couldn't. You didn't answer…'

'Correct, Kadeg.'

'Goulch and his people examined the boot again. Then they came here to Saint-Nicolas, they ought to be in the harbour now. He wanted to organise everything for the immediate salvaging tomorrow morning. The *Luc'hed* went back to the mainland after unsuccessful dives at the Méaban. They didn't find anything, apart from more canisters. Goulch decided it unilaterally, after he couldn't get you…'

'I understand. Fine.'

Kadeg would touch on this many more times in one way or another.

'How many customers from this evening were there yesterday evening too?'

'We have identified twelve.'

That was quite a few.

'We let the people go a quarter of an hour ago, lots of them were getting seriously bad tempered.'

'You did what?'

That had not been agreed upon. There were strong words on the tip of Dupin's tongue.

'Objectively, we had no reason of any kind or any tangible evidence to continue to hold them. Of course we have taken note of all their personal details.'

Dupin had to relent, much as it wasn't convenient – and as much as he would have liked to speak to some customers himself, ignoring police regulations on such things. But Kadeg had acted correctly.

'Has anybody noticed anything suspicious then?'

'Not a thing so far. The mayor of Fouesnant, Monsieur Du Marhallac'h was desperate to speak to you, by the way. He was there yesterday and this evening.'

'What did he want?'

'He wanted to know the status of the investigation.'

Dupin was not far from the *Quatre Vents* now.

'We'll sit down again Riwal, you and I. I'll be right there.'

'I think we should.'

'Who is still in the *Quatre Vents*?'

'Madame Nuz, Riwal and me.'

'Good. Just one thing: Konan got into an argument with the former mayor a few years ago about salvage rights. To a ship, I gather. Speak –' Dupin leafed through his notebook and found what he was looking for, 'to that diver, Monsieur Tanguy. And to someone in the *mairie*. I want to know what it was about.'

'Incidentally, the Prefect was trying to get hold of you. He was highly indignant again.'

'Let me worry about that. It is absolutely inappropriate to insert yourself into the – fully functional communication between the Prefect and the lead Commissaire.'

'He...'

Dupin lost his nerve. He hung up. And sighed deeply.

He knew he wasn't going to get out of a quick conversation with the Prefect. No matter how hard he fought against it. He stood still for a moment and dialled Nolwenn's mobile number. It took a fraction of a second for her to answer.

'Monsieur le Commissaire?'

'Everything is okay, Nolwenn. The investigation is in hand.'

There was resignation in his voice.

'The investigation is in full swing.'

This time he deliberately infused the sentence with energy.

'*Abred ne goll gwech ebet* – quick never loses!'

This answer was one of Nolwenn's favourite sayings and probably intended as encouragement.

'Have you picked up the trail yet?'

Dupin hesitated for a moment and reflected. He set off again. Slowly.

'I don't know.'

He really couldn't say. Nolwenn knew that there was a point in every one of the Commissaire's cases when he picked up a scent – at different times and he was not always aware of it himself. But he only knew how to do one thing then: follow the trail, no matter how crazy it might seem. Everything else became – in his obstinate and occasionally pig-headed way – utterly irrelevant. Dupin defended himself vehemently every time somebody talked about his 'method'. He definitely operated highly systematically, this was true, but swiftly one had to add: unsystematically systematically. He practised careful observation and examination of the facts obsessively (a passion of his since childhood), combined with logical analysis, but then he'd act in a way that seemed completely intuitive again, suddenly and impatiently following an idea, a feeling, an impulse, occasionally combined with a coincidence. Absolutely self-willed. And always decisive.

'What does Solenn Nuz say about the case?' asked Nolwenn.

'She…' Dupin did not quite know how to answer. Nolwenn's question had sounded almost as though she thought all he needed to do was ask Solenn Nuz if he wanted to know who the murderer was.

'She is a huge help.'

'I'm sure she is. The Prefect has spoken to Monsieur Konan's wife, by the way. It was a difficult conversation, the marriage was probably not in – good shape.'

'Which means?'

'Apparently they have been considering a divorce for a long time.'

'Why?'

'I don't know.'

A rare sentence from Nolwenn.

'The Prefect is going to cut short his trip to Guernsey and be back in Quimper tomorrow lunchtime. I think,' Nolwenn's voice became suspiciously gentle, but without losing its firmness, 'I think that you should call the Prefect. It's definitely the biggest case of his time in office and he is, as discussed, personally very involved.'

'I know.'

He really did know.

'This is a vast case for Brittany.'

'I know.'

'The president of the Breton National Council has tried the official commissariat number twice. And journalists from *Ouest France* and *Télégramme* and one from *L'Equipe*, from the regional office in Rennes.'

This didn't surprise Dupin – of course the biggest sports newspaper in the country would be interested in the death of an Admiral's Cup winner. Along with practically every other paper in France. Undoubtedly, a few national newspapers would feature the case. An ingenious triple murder! Even on the basis of Konan and Pajot's contacts in the capital alone.

'Four callers hung up. Withheld numbers.'

'Nolwenn?'

'Yes, Monsieur le Commissaire?'

'Have you ever heard anything about treasure hunts – here on the coast I mean, on the Glénan?'

'The Breton waters are a unique, historical treasure trove, Monsieur le Commissaire.'

This was just the topic for Nolwenn, Dupin recognised the intonation from her 'Breton lessons'.

'Myriad ships from all eras lie on our seafloor – magnificent merchant ships, warships, expedition ships, cargo ships, passenger ships, private yachts, everything. Even Roman galleys!'

'I'm thinking of treasure on board old ships. Valuable things – like in books and films.'

'There are always significant salvages of valuable cargo. Even of precious metals. The largest find near the Glénan was made in the sixties. An old corsair, with half a ton of gold.'

Dupin was impressed. Now that *was* a treasure.

'Even the "Tigress of Brittany" crossed the waters of the Glénan.'

Dupin didn't fully understand what she meant by that – perhaps solely due to the Tigress, numerous sunken ships were to be reckoned with here. Nolwenn herself didn't elaborate.

'If you like, I'll research the most valuable finds for you.'

'You don't need to.'

'There are a significant number of treasure-seekers, even some veryprofessional ones. Even a few companies. But most of them are amateurs. There is an association of underwater archaeologists on the Glénan, which formed in the diving club. Is there something specific you want to know? Do you see a link to the murders?'

'I don't know.'

It still sounded absurd.

'How would you find out whether someone's got a good lead? Here on the Glénan?'

'You wouldn't, I suspect. Nobody would let a single word cross their lips. Unless the real archaeologists in the diving club were involved, the Université de Brest or something. But I would only vouch for them up to a certain point.'

So, it was highly likely. If real treasure was at stake, nobody would blab about it.

'You're right, Nolwenn.'

He hadn't actually intended to ask, but now it slipped out.

'There are Roman galleys here?'

'Tons of them! We fought the decisive sea battle against Julius Caesar in these waters. An unfair fight! We dealt him a devastating blow in 57BC, on land, man to man! Then the Romans holed up for a year and had hundreds of warships built in the Loire estuary. A huge, much stronger side. Yet it was a closely run battle.'

Dupin had shown a gap in his knowledge. He realised during the story that Nolwenn had already told him this episode in the course of the 'Breton Lessons'. He hoped she would let him away with this.

'I still need to see Riwal and Kadeg, then we'll call it a day. I'll be in touch tomorrow morning.'

'How are you getting back to the mainland? Shall I take care of that?'

Dupin was relieved that Nolwenn had given up on the Romans.

'There's still a helicopter on Saint-Nicolas. I think.'

Dupin realised that this was just an assumption on his part. But he would have heard if it had flown off. Or perhaps not, if he had been in Muriel Lefort's home at the time.

'I really hope so.'

'Good. And stick to your guns, Monsieur le Commissaire.'

'Thanks, Nolwenn. *Bonne nuit.*'

Dupin had long since arrived at the *Quatre Vents*.

Riwal and Kadeg were sitting at a table near the door and both of them swivelled their heads towards Dupin and nodded as he came in. They looked exhausted, Kadeg even more so than Riwal, despite sounding so eager just now. Solenn Nuz was nowhere to be seen.

Dupin joined them without a word. Riwal pushed four sheets of A4 paper stuck together towards him, a sketch of the room with the counter, clearly drawn tables and people represented by circles.

'We have investigated nineteen customers from yesterday evening. Of those, seven come regularly and are known here. The rest are sailors and divers.'

Dupin leant over the sketch and got out his notebook.

'The regulars?'

'Madame Menez, the sailing-school assistant; Marc Leussot, a freelance journalist from *Ouest France*, he was there just now too, we've spoken to him; Kilian Tanguy, the diver, and his wife – in each case we've noted the times when they arrived and when they left,' Riwal pointed to tiny, painstakingly recorded figures in the circles, 'then Du Marhallac'h, the mayor, whom we've also already spoken to; Madame Barrault, the diving instructor and head of the diving school.'

Dupin groaned softly. Sometimes it happened that he – for various reasons – actually thought himself unsuited to his job. That he had always had significant trouble remembering names was one reason, a serious one. People and faces however, he could remember without a problem.

'That's quite a few.'

'On top of that there were two people who were only here briefly, Madame Lefort and a doctor, Docteur Devan Le Menn, a GP.'

'Nobody has mentioned him yet.'

'Yes, that is a little odd. Only the two Nuz daughters remember him. Nobody else. They say that he also spoke to Lefort. Both of them think he was only there for a short time, ten minutes perhaps. Around quarter past eight.'

'Docteur Le Menn is the name?'

'Yes. He has a practice in Sainte-Marine.'

'And he wasn't there this evening?'

'No.'

'Any other leads?'

'Not yet.'

That wasn't much. The pickings were decidedly slim.

'We've got further with the list than I expected, chief.'

Riwal had probably delivered this sentence to combat his own fatigue and to prevent the atmosphere getting worse.

'Is Madame Nuz in the kitchen?'

'She left about ten minutes ago. She would rather clear up in the morning.'

'Did she give you the key?'

'She said we should just switch off the light and close the door behind us. And she sends you her best wishes.'

Dupin smiled in spite of himself.

'Let's make it quick, it's already late.'

He hadn't even finished the sentence when an idea came to him.

'Riwal, the helicopter is here on Saint-Nicolas, isn't it?'

'Yes, Monsieur le Commissaire. I gave it instructions to wait here. I assumed you'd be okay with that. Goulch has already gone off in the boat.'

'Excellent.'

Dupin thought it would be better to go outside quickly.

'I'll be right back.'

He left the bar and closed the door carefully behind him. He fished out his mobile.

'*Amiral, bonsoir.*'

'*Bonsoir,* is Paul there?'

'Just a moment.'

It really did take just one moment for Paul Girard, owner of the *Amiral*, to come on the line. Dupin liked him a lot – something like friendship had arisen between them over the years, because Dupin began each day with a coffee in the *Amiral* and usually also ended it there too. They didn't talk much, but an unspoken understanding had grown between the two of them.

'Georges here.'

'We heard about what happened. *Mon Dieu.*'

Dupin knew that he needn't say another word about the case. Which was wonderful.

'I'll call in tonight, but it's going to be late.'

The *Amiral* closed at half twelve at the latest. But Girard knew that during a case it sometimes got very late.

'I'll let the cook know. The usual.'

'The usual' meant: a large *entrecôte*, chips, a rich red Languedoc, *Château Les Fenals*.

'Wonderful.'

'See you soon.'

Dupin already felt a good bit better. Psychologically. He had solid ground beneath his feet again.

He went back into the *Quatre Vents*. Riwal and Kadeg stared at him quizzically.

'Excellent, gentlemen. We'll start early tomorrow morning. I say we have a meeting here at eight. We will need both boats in the coming days, Goulch and his crew – and the *Luc'hed*. Also, the helicopters should be available at all times. We have to be able to react quickly to everything, it cannot make a difference that we're out here in the middle of nowhere.'

There was something cheerful to Dupin's tone now, which he himself found amusing.

'Then let's meet tomorrow morning at the airport in Quimper at half seven?'

'Absolutely, Kadeg.'

The prospect of sitting with an *entrecôte* in the *Amiral* so soon was giving Dupin renewed energy.

'Have we learnt anything new about Konan or Pajot yet? Under no circumstances can we make the mistake of concentrating too much on Lefort, that would be negligent.'

He wasn't sure whether he himself believed what he was saying.

'We also need to focus on the issue of what connections there were between the three of them – what they got up to together, had planned, whatever. Whether someone had it in for all three of them. The same goes for each of the pair combinations: Lefort – Pajot, Pajot – Konan, Lefort – Konan. That the murder attempt might have been meant for just one person is,' Dupin broke off for a moment and wrinkled his forehead, 'the least likely. But cannot be disregarded of course.'

'Of the customers we've spoken to this evening, nobody knew Monsieur Pajot personally, not even any of the regulars. Monsieur Du Marhallac'h knew the names, the others didn't even know that much – even Solenn Nuz didn't,' Riwal reported. He also spoke about Solenn Nuz as though she were the ultimate authority on all things.

Now Kadeg butted in too, looking eager.

'We showed them the photo of Pajot, but nobody has seen him on the islands, anywhere. A little mysterious.'

'Perhaps he'll have been on his boat. That wouldn't be out of the ordinary after all. The boat was big enough to spend evenings on comfortably.'

Kadeg looked offended in his typically childish way. Dupin had really only said this to make a point to Kadeg, but suddenly thought it seemed very logical.

Riwal took over again:

'All of the regulars knew Konan, indeed he was frequently here with Lefort. But none of them know any details about him, just a few general things that we already know. Everyone knew that he was a keen angler. Madame Barrault, the diving instructor, knows his boat and says she met him and Lefort at sea a few times. Near the Moutons. At the spots where there are mackerel. Nobody knew him well enough to have heard about potential conflicts. Everyone just thought of him as "Lefort's friend".'

'Kadeg, I want you to pay a visit to Konan's wife first thing tomorrow morning. The Prefect has phoned her personally. Her marriage was possibly at an end.'

Kadeg obviously considered this a suitable task.

'Will do. I spoke on the phone to Pajot's secretary in Paris at around 10pm. She was dumbfounded. We're going to speak again tomorrow morning. He had no siblings and neither of his parents is still alive. But she wanted to ask around again, about whether someone else knows something. She said he was a rather "distant person". She didn't know much about his private life.'

'The sensational news is out in the world, soon we'll know whether there is any more family. If there are, they'll call you and complain that they weren't informed.'

It sounded more cynical than Dupin had intended. 'Let's call it a day.'

Riwal looked visibly relieved. Even Kadeg didn't seem unhappy.

'Did anyone mention something about a treasure hunt to you?'

They both looked at Dupin in bafflement.

'Something about a sunken ship, a discovery, salvage?'

'I – no.'

'Nor me.'

Both inspectors seemed too tired to ask. And Dupin wasn't in the mood for more explanations either.

'Let's head.'

That had been an order.

The helicopter had lifted off at exactly 11.15pm.

The three police officers from the Commissariat de Concarneau were sitting, strapped tightly into their seats – Dupin particularly tightly – each one lost in his own thoughts about the events of this strangely dramatic day. Something people on the coast said about the Glénan popped into Dupin's head: time expanded on the islands. As soon as you were there, under this world's spell. More could happen here than anywhere else; in a minute, an hour, a day. Incredible as it sounded, that's exactly how he felt too.

The helicopter threw a strange shadow on the silver sea, like something out of a surrealist film.

Several times, Dupin thought he saw the shadow of a bird of prey in a nosedive, so clear suddenly, that he was starting to get the creeps.

They would reach the mainland soon, the lights of Sainte-Marine and Bénodet were already glittering before them. It was strange, it seemed as though their shimmering marked an elemental border: the peculiar kingdom of the Glénan and the Atlantic here, and the normal world, reality, there. Dupin was glad, but also a little melancholy. And he didn't fully understand why he felt either emotion. With the monotonous noise of the rotors, which were muffled astonishingly well by the headphones, he almost nodded off a few times. Yet the attempt to make progress with some of his thoughts kept him awake. Besides, he would never have taken a nap in front of his inspectors! Except in front of Riwal.

They would have solid ground beneath their feet any moment now. He would climb into his Citroën, drive far too fast and be in Concarneau thirty minutes later. In his *Amiral*. He would park on the large square right at the quay – and everything would be okay for the time being. For a brief moment. After he'd walked into the bar, it would take less than five minutes for the *entrecôte* to be in front of him and he would already have drunk his first glass of Languedoc.

The Second Day

It was half past six. Still dark, the moon had long since gone down. In the westernmost part of the 'united' European standard time zone – even this was seen as a minor invasion by Bretons – it only got light at seven o'clock at the beginning of May. Commissaire Georges Dupin was sitting in the *Le Bulgare* and drinking his second coffee, having just ordered his third from the energetic waitress. His little notebook lay open in front of him. Things were loud and robust. The day had long been in full, unsentimental flow, there was nothing leisurely here early in the morning. The far from idyllic cafe was right on the *Route Nationale*, on the fourth of the closely laid out *rond-points* on the approach to Quimper. From here, it was just five minutes to the little airport. Dupin did not come here often, but he was fond of it and it had been his saviour today.

As early as it was, Dupin had already got quite a lot done. He had got up at twenty past five – after only getting to bed at a little after half one and then lying awake practically all night, tossing and turning every few minutes. At one point he'd felt like he had a fever. He had gone over the events of the day again and again, the facts, the little that they knew. Might there not be clues that they hadn't seen? A lead.

He had been very sure that it would have been better to get some rest, to sleep. That it was completely preposterous to rack his brains in that state.

He would have got up even earlier if he had known how to get his hands on caffeine. The *Amiral* only opened at quarter to seven, which he had discussed very seriously with Girard on a number of occasions. Dupin's disgracefully expensive espresso machine from Paris had suddenly given up the ghost, which he had only realised during the last emergency – because the *Amiral* was always closed on the second of January.

At a quarter to six, Dupin had called Riwal because he wanted the mayor of Fouesnant's number. Dupin could not remember his exact thought processes now, but at some point in the night he had been determined to talk to him.

And then, finally, Dupin had indeed called the Prefect, at five past six. He would need to get in touch quite regularly from now on. Besides, he had realised that the Prefect himself was relevant to this case, although only peripherally: he had been friends with Konan. For the first five minutes, Dupin had let the usual tirade wash over him – why had he not got in touch the day before and then now suddenly did so in the middle of the night, that this was not a proper way to work... Dupin had not actuallylistened for a second. He had agreed, absolutely passively, to leave all press statements to the Prefect and especially to report at least three times a day on this 'wholly exceptionally important case, which urgently required as quick a resolution as possible'. The Prefect had outlined all the potential 'disastrous scenarios' in store for Dupin, himself, the Finistère police, the whole *département* if they couldn't manage a quick and complete resolution to the case. Dupin had waited for the choleric fury to subside and then begun to ask questions of his own. Always 'in the interests of a quick resolution'. At first Locmariaquer had, with some astonishment – Dupin could not tell if it was genuine or not – asked to what it extent it was significant, what Konan's businesses were and whether he had enemies. But then the Prefect noticeably relented, so that for some stretches the phone call had turned into a genuine investigative talk with a 'witness'. In the end, Dupin left his superior thunderstruck with an overly friendly and formal 'Thanks for your help' and hung up. The Prefect had apparently felt more and more uneasy as the conversation went on. From a certain point onwards it had suited him to make it clear that Konan had not been a close personal friend in the strictest sense, but rather an 'acquaintance – a significant figure in Brittany and beyond', with whom he was on good terms for unavoidable professional as well as social reasons. Astonishingly, Dupin believed him. A few times the Prefect had even let a critical distance from Konan develop. He had mentioned that Konan had had 'problems' with the Inland Revenue from time to time and that his web of investments seemed a little unclear. He had known nothing about a specific, acute or simmering conflict with anyone in particular. He had seen Yannig Konan for the last time three weeks ago, at a party given by the 'Friends of Breton Beer-brewers Club', of which there were more and more in recent years – both

171

regional beer producers and their friends. (Dupin himself was one of them now, although he would not admit it and was always making the case for his beloved 1664.) The Prefect was certain that Konan's wife knew little about her husband's current life. Up until a few years ago, the Locmariaquers had invited the Konans to dinner once a year. Until the marital crisis had become official. What the Prefect had also confirmed was this: Pajot really was a close friend of Konan. Locmariaquer knew of regular evenings the two spent together in Paris. He had only seen Pajot a handful of times at some receptions.

In any case, Dupin had already learnt a thing or two this morning.

At either end of the *Bulgare*'s counter – it was five or six metres long – two televisions were on at the same time, each on different stations. 'TV Breizh' was on one of them – the Breton channel. Of course, it was about the murders. A photo of Dupin was shown for a few seconds, 'the young, yet experienced Parisian Commissaire from the Commissariat de Police Concarneau, who has solved a series of sensational cases in recent years, is leading the investigation.' Thank God the people in the cafe were too preoccupied with the beginning of their day to take any notice of the Commissaire. It must still have been possible to read about the 'tragic accident' in the papers today – the news about the murder had arrived after the editorial deadline. There were multiple copies of *Ouest France* and *Télégramme* lying on the counter, not very far away from him. Dupin did not feel like reading the articles.

Dupin finished his third coffee and contemplated ordering a fourth, he had a feeling his brain still wasn't functioning quite right. And he needed a croissant for his stomach. He had just made eye contact with the waitress when his mobile shrilled.

'Who's this?'

He had sounded unintentionally rude.

For a moment, nothing happened.

'Hello?' Dupin was annoyed.

'Check out the activities of Pajot and Konan's company, *Medimare*, and the *Institut Marine de Concarneau*.'

The voice sounded artificially disguised, muffled and low, far away. Deliberately montonous.

'Who's there? Hello? Hello, who's speaking?'

'This is about *Medimare*. Yannig Konan and Grégoire Pajot's company.'

This was no joke.

'What exactly is this about? Talk to me.'

No answer. Dupin waited. Nothing more, the caller had hung up. Suddenly, Dupin was wide awake. He froze, momentarily motionless.

Before he had even had time to think any more, his mobile rang again.

'Where are you, Monsieur le Commissaire?'

'I – – – Nolwenn?'

'Yes?'

It took Dupin a moment to pull himself together.

'What does *Medimare* mean to you?'

'Hmmm – nothing at all.'

So the company couldn't be well known.

'I've just received an anonymous call.'

'Oh?'

173

Dupin was glad to be able to tell Nolwenn about it, so it became more real.

'I got a call a minute ago, asking me to examine the activities of Pajot and Konan's company *Medimare* and the *Institut Marine de Concarneau* with a fine-tooth comb. He...' something occurred to Dupin, 'where did he get my number from?'

'Before I left yesterday, I myself transferred your personal extension to your mobile, that's what we always do at night during a case. He probably called your number in the Commissariat. It's easy to get.'

'Please check, Nolwenn.'

Dupin was still feeling the after-effects of this strange call.

'We'll know that very soon. But surely it was a withheld number.'

That was true, nobody would be so stupid.

'I don't know the name *Medimare* but that's definitely one of the companies I was talking about yesterday. I'll take a look at that straight away. What do you make of this call, Monsieur le Commissaire? It sounds extremely vague.'

'No idea. But we have to find out everything about this company at once.'

The caller had told him very little. Still, it was a clue. If there was something fishy going on with the companies the two of them owned and they had made enemies from it, there might have been a motive – and people who had one. And sometimes an anonymous person did give a tip. But sometimes these calls meant nothing at all, they were sick jokes by people not involved. Or they turned out to be well-aimed diversions.

'And the voice didn't seem familiar to you?'

'No. It was disguised. Although not very professionally.'

'Was it a man's voice?'

'Yes.'

'You know the *Institut Marine*, don't you?'

'Yes of course. I mean, I know as much as the next person.

Dupin's apartment – given to him by the city – was around hundred metres away from the institute. If he stood on his narrow balcony and looked out to sea, it was directly to his right. The institute had a branch on the other side of the harbour by now, the '*rive gauche*'. An institute for marine biology – in all honesty, that's as much as Dupin knew.

'It's the oldest research post for marine biology in the world. Which is no coincidence of course. Breton!'

Of course.

'Well regarded, a large number of renowned scientists work there. The head is Professor Yves Le Berre-Ryckeboerec.'

'Berk-Rib...?'

'Professor Yves Le Berre-Ryckeboerec.'

This was the ultimate escalation for Dupin: complicated Breton names clustering together in double-barrels. He noted 'Director, Institute' in his notebook.

'Is he based in the main building? Where the *Marinarium* is?'

There was a not very large but lovingly equipped *Marinarium*, no comparison with the *Océanopolis* in Brest, but Dupin liked it, even though it didn't have any penguins. He'd visited an exhibition there only three or four weeks ago. The purpose of the exhibition was immediately obvious: 'Fish on my plate, what's your name?' It was about the numerous types of fish in the area that you found at local fishmongers and on the restaurant menus. It demonstrated what they looked like before they ended up on the plate – alive, in their proper maritime habitat. There had been an incredible, colourful range, Dupin hadn't been able to get his head round it.

'I assume he's based in the main building. I'll check that.'

'Yes. Get in touch.'

'What are you going to do now?'

'I'll see.'

Dupin hung up.

Should he take the anonymous phone call seriously? His instinct told him: yes.

He felt a bit better anyway – the caffeine was doing the trick. Riwal and Kadeg would surely already be on their way to the airport. He had in fact intended to fly to the islands with them, to begin by speaking to Solenn Nuz. Then to the diving instructor. But he also wanted to talk to the mayor of Fouesnant. And the doctor from Sainte Marine, who was probably one of the last people to have spoken to Konan. Dupin had a series of urgent questions.

He reached for his phone.

'Riwal?'

'Yes, chief?'

'Fly without me. I'll come later. I'm paying a quick visit to the *Institut Marine*. You and Kadeg get to work on what we discussed yesterday evening. I want to know immediately if there's anything interesting. No matter what. You're aware it's about every detail, every irrelevant-seeming circumstance.'

'Understood.'

Riwal probably knew these sentences off by heart already. But he had not sounded resigned.

'The examination and salvaging of Pajot's boat, who is going to supervise that? Goulch?'

'Definitely. How are you going to get to the Glénan, chief?'

'We'll see. I'll be in touch.'

Dupin hadalmost hung up.

'Riwal, wait.'

'Yes, chief?'

'One more thing, I want to know the situation with Lucas Lefort's estate as soon as possible. Whether Madame Lefort will inherit everything. And talk to Madame Menez again, the assistant.'

'Anything specific?'

'Lucas Lefort wanted to have some cargo boat or other for the coming week. Take a look at that. And ask what the boat can be used for. And find out what led Madame Menez to end up on the Glénan. Her story.'

'Her story?'

'Exactly.'

Those were two things that had been going through his mind yesterday. Two among many other things.

After they ended the conversation, Dupin took his notebook and pen, stood up, placed ten euro on the little red plastic plate and left the *Bulgare*.

His car, an old, much-loved, boxy and unwieldy Citroën XM, which he had not replaced with a new official car yet, against all of the Prefecture's instructions, was right in front of the door. The sun had come up now and the traffic heavy *Route Nationale*, which was ten or fifteen metres in front of him, ran eastwards towards Concarneau, into a dazzling orange-pink sky.

It was eight o'clock on the dot. The director had arrived at almost the exact same time as Dupin. For science, the working day began early.

It was an impressive office that the director was sitting in, impressive for its size alone, a good forty metres square Dupin guessed, but especially impressive due to its view: through the panorama window you could see far out over the open Atlantic. The fifth floor of the dignified, dark-grey, stone building – which looked all of its hundred years and had resisted the tossing surf with its rear side built directly into the sea – boasted a view like that from a lighthouse.

Director Le Berre-Ryckeboerec was an angular, not exactly tall man in his late fifties with a gaunt, wan face and not much hair, whose pale appearance was only lent vitality by his extremely lively, light green eyes. He was sitting behind an intimidatingly sharp-edged wooden desk, wearing a dark grey suit that had obviously been elegant once, but was now worn-out.

It was clear the director's secretary was a little shocked by the Commissaire's unannounced visit. She was sure to have heard about the triple murder. Without announcing him, She had led Dupin into the Director's room after a brief, hasty knock. He had, it seemed, only just sat down and obviously thought her behaviour inappropriate.

'I would have liked to make a call first, Madame Sabathier. And since when do we accept visitors who do not give any notice?'

He was pointedly acting as though Dupin was not in the room at all. His voice was – in contrast to his outward appearance – powerful and authoritative.

'I'm terribly sorry, Monsieur le Directeur, it won't happen again. I just thought – Monsieur le Commissaire Dupin is in fact investigating this awful murder case on...'

'I know perfectly well about the murder case.'

The conversation was still taking place without any acknowledgement of Dupin's presence.

'But that is no reason to suspend etiquette and manners. Or to upset my working day.'

Dupin felt an angry buzzing in his solar plexus. His rage was growing from second to second. 'I think it is, Monsieur,' he said. 'A triple murder thoroughly upsets everything.' Director Le Berre-Ryckeboerec looked him coldly up and down.

'And the investigations in this murder case lead you to the illustrious *Institut Marine*? Well, the institute, along with its one hundred and fifty international scientists, welcomes you warmly. How can we be of help?'

On the journey here, the anonymous call had already started to seem like a bizarre dream to Dupin. He had to admit that the vague hint at some kind of 'activities' was shaky ground for questioning, especially under these hostile conditions. And apart from the minimal information available online about

Pajot and Konan's business, which Nolwenn had sent through to him shortly before his arrival, Dupin knew absolutely nothing. All in all, an extremely weak starting point. There was nothing for it but to take the bull by the horns, an option that was very much in keeping with Dupin's character anyway.

'It's about the illegal business transactions between the institute and *Medimare* – the company that belonged to the two of the three men who have just been victims of murder.'

Dupin's insinuation was not backed up by anything. But he needed to know whether he was on the right track and caution was hardly going to get him anywhere here. The director sat up straight, his face becoming even more pointed, his mouth more thin-lipped, his eyes, now fixed keenly on Dupin, had narrowed into slits.

'I don't think I quite understand what you just said.'

'I'm happy to repeat it.'

Dupin needed to persevere now. It wasn't difficult for him, the antipathy had been spontaneous and strong. Dupin knew these kinds of characters.

'I understand – there's a method to your humour.'

Now Le Berre-Ryckeboerec's irritation was clear too. Dupin was on the point of losing his temper. He tried to regulate his breathing (he was proud that he had learnt this, the basics at least: take a deep breath into the stomach, wait five seconds before breathing out slowly, then five more seconds before breathing in – this delay was important!). All of the life had drained out of the secretary's face in the last half a minute, standing motionless as though rooted to the spot.

'I don't think I will be having this conversation, Monsieur le Commissaire.'

Le Berre-Ryckeboerc knew that he needn't say a word now, here.

'I will be consulting our lawyers immediately about your outrageous insinuations. We have maintained excellent business links with Mr Konan and Mr Pajot's company for many years. Like other companies, they have acquired patents and licenses from us. If you are interested in these topics, go ahead, that will be a matter for communication to our lawyers. I suggest that we bid each other farewell now.'

'Yes, that would be best for all of us.'

Le Berre-Ryckeboerec turned to Madame Sabathier as if Dupin had already left the room:

'I will place my call now, as planned. And if you could inform Monsieur Daeron that I wish to speak to him here in the institute.'

Dupin's thoughts were racing, but he couldn't think of any more tricks that he might have had up his sleeve.

'We will,' Dupin said softly, almost whispering, yet harshly and acidly, 'we will look at every tiny detail of this cooperation with *Medimare*, everything that has existed and exists,' a subtle smile showed in one corner of his mouth, 'we'll take this opportunity to put the entirety of your business activities under the microscope. I'm looking forward to this, Monsieur le Directeur.'

Dupin didn't wait for a reaction, but turned on his heel and left the office. He took the lift, which was unbearably slow.

He already had his mobile to his ear as he left the building.

'Nolwenn?'

'I was just going to...'

'I need a search warrant. For the institute. Doesn't matter how. Does not matter at all. And immediately. We have to check the institute's business links to *Medimare*, especially the sale of licenses and patents, all of the research output.'

'Are you in the institute already?'

Nolwenn sounded slightly confused.

'I – am already outside again.'

'You're outside again already?'

'It was a very short conversation. As I said: we need a search warrant.'

'Did any new suspicious facts come out of the – very short conversation with the director?'

'I think so.'

'We ought to have something more than a vague tip from an anonymous caller.'

'The director of the institute acted completely uncooperatively. I've got *the well-founded suspicion, that he has made false statements and is covering up the truth – that delaying would be dangerous. That he will immediately get rid of incriminating documents.* – That's got to be enough.'

In these last phrases, Dupin had – albeit incoherently – put together the formal requirements for obtaining a search warrant.

'Call the Prefect, Nolwenn. Say it's about an acute suspicion and there is explicit, acute danger of the suppression of evidence,' Dupin was absolutely resolute, 'I want this search. Tell him it's indispensable in solving the murder of his friend. The first good lead. He's to call the investigative judge in charge personally or try the public prosecutor's office. We will also need to take a look at the business premises of *Medimare*, Paris.'

'Fine.'

That was the 'fine' that Dupin loved about Nolwenn. The more difficult it got and the more hectic it got and the more the pressure grew, the more Nolwenn liked it.

'Wonderful. Speak to you later, Nolwenn.'

Dupin hung up.

He had reached his car, in the lower part of the large carpark in front of the Port de Plaisance, very close to his flat.

He dialled Kadeg's number.

'Where are you, Kadeg?'

'I'm at the diving centre, Riwal is at the sailing school. I...'

'Call Nolwenn. We've got an anonymous tip about illegal business activity between the *Institut Marine* in Concarneau and a company held jointly by Pajot and Konan. It's called *Medimare*. We don't know much more than that yet. It buys and sells patents and licenses for pharmaceutical and cosmetic products based on findings from marine biology. The headquarters are in Paris. Nolwenn is still researching. We are trying to get a search warrant right now. For the institute and for *Medimare*.'

'What concrete suspicion do you have?'

'I don't have a concrete suspicion,' Dupin was aware that that didn't sound very strong, so his voice sounded all the more determined, 'but I would like everything to be probed, all business connections. I have no idea what dodginess could be going on there – but find it! I want you to deal with this. Rigorously. I mean *really* rigorously.'

'I understand.'

Kadeg's tone, even more so than his words, made it clear to Dupin that he really had understood. The disagreeable part of Kadeg's nature, which was the majority of it – there was also a small other part – was made for tasks like this. Kadeg was like a terrier at times like these.

'As I said, coordinate with Nolwenn. She's also trying to arrange for us to have a team from headquarters for the operation. You are going to lead this, Kadeg.'

'I look forward to it.'

'Speak later.'

Dupin sat still a moment longer before starting the engine. Wait five seconds before breathing in, five seconds before breathing out. Deep in the stomach.

Dupin did not know whether they would actually get the search warrant, it wouldn't be easy, not matter how forcefully he had just expressed it and no matter how much Nolwenn would devote herself to it. What they had was anything but compelling. He also knew that his behaviour just now in the institute might not been very clever. He had not achieved anything for the time being. But would he have got more out of that man if he had been more diplomatic? In any case, he didn't have the faintest idea if this tip would lead anywhere at all or whether they would even find anything relevant during a search. Perhaps the vague hint at the business links was just to create confusion, a diversion. Waste time. The caller had not supplied proof of any kind that he was well informed and really knew something. But – he had existed. And one thing was clear: the director was an extremely unpleasant individual. Dupin was looking forward to the look on the director's face when Kadeg was standing in front of him with the search warrant. And there was another thought that pleased him about this – and it would also mean his approach wouldn't have been completely wrong: a search would really make waves. In the media too. It would be a clear demonstration that the police were determined to do everything possible and were proceeding with massive resources and the clearer this was, the more nervous the culprit would become. Nervous culprits act more rashly. And, ultimately, make mistakes. Though Dupin had to admit that the murder plan itself, as far as he could guess from the current state of the investigation, did not point towards a nervous personality.

Dupin turned the ignition key. He drove off, fumbling about at the tiny buttons of the car phone. If he were honest, he still had no real idea what *Medimare* actually did. Everything Nolwenn had said was very abstract. Patents and licenses for research results.

'Nolwenn?'

'I've already spoken to the Prefect, Monsieur le Commissaire. He is very uncertain, but he's trying. Personally. I'm to tell you that you hopefully know what you're doing – and that you will be in regular contact with him, he…'

'Tell me, in as much detail as possible, what *Medimare* does.'

'They buy research results from institutes, which enable pharmaceutically and commercially viable products to be produced from biological and biochemical research into living materials in the ocean. The research institutes partly finance themselves through these kinds of means, they...'

'You were reading that out.'

'Sorry?'

Nolwenn had a near photographic memory.

'Nothing – what does that mean, what kind of products would they be?'

'Biodegradable, synthetic materials for instance, a really big thing, or completely new kinds of antibiotics, innovative cosmetics, alternative energy sources, potential cancer drugs. All those kinds of things,' she raised her voice dramatically, 'Brittany's marine environment is teeming with lifeforms that represent incredibly valuable resources. It's very much up and coming, Monsieur le Commissaire. They're called *blue biotechnologies*. In Brittany...'

'I see. That's all I wanted to know. I take it there's big business at stake there.'

'Very big business, yes. Think of the cosmetic industry alone,' she broke off briefly, 'I brought you in a sample of hand cream last November. *Fluidum.* Do you remember?'

Dupin remembered. He found it embarrassing, he had never used it, not only because he never used creams but also because he had never understood the purpose of a cream specifically for your hands. Yet the memory was even more embarrassing because it had been a discreet hint from Nolwenn at a Christmas present for herself. He had only understood that when it was far too late, after he had already bought another of the ceramic maritime bowls from a factory in Quimper that he had been enthusiastically giving her for the last three Christmases running (Nolwenn had once carelessly implied that she liked them).

Dupin didn't answer.

'That excellent cosmetics range, based entirely on all-natural brown algae. That little light blue tube, do you remember?'

At least Nolwenn didn't lapse into her harsh tone of voice. Dupin was relieved.

'I remember. It makes your hands very soft.'

Nolwenn sighed gently.

'Unique across the world! A natural phenomenon for your skin. With all the vital minerals. A concentration of the whole Atlantic!'

Dupin wanted to reply that he was unsure whether it was even possible for minerals to be absorbed via the skin, but he knew that this wasn't about that.

'Kadeg will get in touch in the next few minutes, because of the *Medimare*-thing. I want him to lead the search. If we get it through.'

'Good. I'll be expecting his call. What are you planning now, Monsieur le Commissaire? Should the helicopter pick you up?'

Nolwenn was back on top of things immediately.

'I think I'd really like to speak to the mayor of Fouesnant.'

'I'll let him know you're coming.'

'I'm just at the last *rond-point*, heading towards the *Route Naitonale*.'

Nolwenn hung up.

La Forêt-Fouesnant was an idyll. And yet not too picturesque, Dupin thought, it narrowly avoided that. A wide sea inlet extended into the village, giving it a small quay. The local fishermen's pretty, Atlantic-coloured wooden boats were resting contentedly on their sides now that it was low tide. Gently curving, low hills rose up from the harbour, where the little village, which was part of the larger Fouesnant, was widely scattered. Lovingly restored stone houses in the typical Breton style, cosy cafes, a wonderful newspaper shop, a baker famous for miles around. And also: a small piece of the once typical ancient Breton woodland with large oaks, ivy, mistletoe, a druidic, mythical wood that you drove through on a scenic road. It was ten minutes to Concarneau, the same distance to Quimper. It was here that the mayor of the little ten thousand-soul community lived – Fouesnant and La Forêt-Fouesnant taken together – of which the Glénan were officially speaking a part.

Even this morning the sun was surprisingly strong and apart from a scattering of the typical fair weather clouds of immaculate white, the sky was a magnificent blue. It would hold up. Dupin's sincere admiration for the Bretons' incredible skills in reading and predicting the weather had prompted him to dabble in this art himself. He had made a hobby of it – and: he thought of himself as not unskilled. His knowledge had increased year on year: the definitive knowledge of what the signs consisted of and how they were meant to be interpreted.

Monsieur Du Marhallac'h – Nolwenn had got through to him straight away – hadasked Dupin to visit him at his home, where he had a small office. It was an unremarkable house, one of the few new ones. Sensible, not too big, not too small, not flashy or showy, but still impressive. It suited Du Marhallac'h perfectly, Dupin thought, it matched him in a curious way. He was also neither tall nor short, fat nor thin, had no very striking features, but not a greying ghost either – distinctly average.

The office was located in an angular wooden extension, built out into the garden. The office furnishings tended far past the 'unremarkable' and into the 'clearly ugly'. The wallpapered walls were a dreary pastel colour and, for no reason, decorated with a kind of light blue pattern at the top. They were covered in amateur photographs stuck in colourful plastic frames, showing scenes of Fouesnant and the surrounding area.

'I take it it's still too soon to ask for your initial assumptions about what happened on the islands, Monsieur le Commissaire?'

'Indeed it is.'

Dupin needed to concentrate. He was, of course, still wrapped up in thoughts of *Medimare*. But even yesterday evening he'd had a strong instinct that he should be speaking in-depth with all regular guests and residents of this 'wonderful world out there'. And the mayor was a central figure in this world. Dupin had some pressing questions for him.

'It's our mission *to know* – not to make assumptions.'

It took the mayor a moment to reply to this.

'It's absolutely unbelievable. Everything, the whole case! Especially the idea that the murderer committed the deed in full view of us all in the *Quatre Vents*. Indeed I was there myself, the evening before last, I mean.'

The mayor broke off for a moment, trying to meet the Commissaire's eye. Dupin made it clear with a movement of his eyes that this was nothing new to him.

'I was sitting at the table right next to the two of them. My usual table. It was a lively evening, like it always is in the *Quatre Vents* – and in this cheerful crowd, there was a murderer amongst us!! A person with such evil energy. It's beyond the power of my imagination.'

Dupin hadn't been listening properly to this last sentence. Something had occurred to him. He was looking for his notebook in his jacket pocket. He thought he had made a note of it. He leafed through the pages of his Clairefontaine. Du Marhallac'h continued talking, but kept looking at the Commissaire with increasing irritation. 'Marc Leussot, marine biologist, also journalist,' that was it. *Marine biologist*. Maybe it didn't mean a thing. But the words 'marine biologist' had – this morning – now gained a new significance.

'If you could please excuse me for a moment, *Monsieur Du Mar... Monsieur le Maire.*'

Dupin stood up and went – without waiting for an answer or signal from the mayor – to the narrow door of the extension and stepped out into the garden.

He dialled directory inquiries.

'Could you please put me through to the *Institut Marine de Concarneau*? Thanks.'

It only took a second.

'*Bonjour*. I would like to speak to Monsieur Leussot please.'

The high-pitched female voice at the other end of the line was incredibly friendly.

'Docteur Leussot does field studies on the Atlantic most of the time, he's not in his office currently.'

'We're talking about Marc Leussot, the researcher, journalist and – permanent employee of the institute, though?'

The answer came hesitantly this time, the question was unusual.

'Oh yes. Docteur Marc Leussot.'

'Thank you very much then.'

Dupin hung up. He had remembered correctly. And he had found out something interesting. Leussot was a permanent employee of the institute.

The garden, to which Dupin had not paid much attention earlier, was not so small after all and it was clearly meticulously well cared for. But despite all the calculated grandeur, it seemed fussy and impersonal and the plants looked as though they had been counted: two camellia bushes, one in white, one in a delicate pink, a rhododendron, some mimosas, a sky-high dog rose, a smattering of cowslips, narcissi, azaleas, a stunted juniper. A prototypical Breton garden. Walking slowly, he returned to the mayor's office.

'Investigative duties. My apologies again.'

Dupin made a vague but conciliatory gesture and sat down again.

'So you were in the *Quatre Vents* yourself the evening before last. You were sitting at the table right next to Konan and Lefort, and nothing unusual struck you?'

There was a flicker n Du Marhallac'h's eyes, perhaps fear, Dupin couldn't say.

'No. I've already thought about it of course. It was like it always is. I remember Konan going to Monsieur Tanguy's table once. Monsieur Tanguy from the diving club. The amateur archaeologist. Lefort didn't sit at the table much, Konan did most of the time. Lefort spoke to a young woman who looked like a sailing student.'

'Did you see him speaking to Madame Menez, Madame Lefort's assistant?'

'No.'

The 'no' had come quickly and definitively.

'Monsieur Konan was sitting on his own for a while too,' said the mayor.

'And you didn't notice anything suspicious generally? At the table? Or at all?'

'No.'

'You were closer to the two of them than anybody else that evening.'

The mayor looked at Dupin a little uncertainly.

'We're especially interested in one half hour or three quarters of an hour. Between quarter past eight and nine o'clock.'

'If I recall correctly, they sat together at the table for a few minutes at the end, Konan and Lefort. And they were still eating something. But I have to admit that I'm not absolutely sure.'

'The two of them didn't seem different from usual to you?'

'Not in the slightest.'

Dupin flicked through his notebook.

'Did you see a Docteur Le Menn? Speaking to Lucas Lefort?'

'No.'

'Devan Le Menn, a GP, with a practice in Sainte-Marine.'

'Oh, I know him. Everyone here knows him. Most of them are his patients. A very good doctor. But I didn't see him. No. I don't think he was there.'

'The two Nuz daughters saw him. Just briefly. Speaking to Lefort. At the bar.'

'Funny, I didn't see him. But there's constant a coming and going in the evenings. Some people are just quickly picking up something to eat. You can get everything to go.'

'Le Menn is a regular?'

'Oh yes. A friend of Monsieur Lefort. And also his doctor.'

'A friend?'

That had slipped out of Dupin's mouth in surprise. Du Marhallac'h seemed confused for a moment, then he smiled:

'Of course, you've already heard a huge amount about Lucas Lefort already.'

'Do you think he was different from what people say about him?'

'I...' the mayor hesitated briefly. 'First of all I have to say: I've only known him reasonably well for the last two years. But really not very well. I try to see things in an impartial way, not to have prejudices, to be objective, to mediate, that's my disposition – and that's how I understand my role. It's an odd world out there – an odd community of odd people. So it's difficult to judge something from the outside. It's often a question of old stories. I try to stay out of that. Lucas Lefort was a prominent man. Well-off. A dyed-in-the-wool bachelor, I reckon. What's certain is that he was completely different to his sister. To everyone else out there. That is definitely true. But, as I said, I didn't even know him well.'

Dupin made a few scrawled notes.

'Apparently you announced you wanted to reconsider his new plans for a greater tourist development in the Glénan sympathetically – all earlier plans having been vehemently rejected by your predecessors.'

Dupin's voice changed at this sentence, not that he had meant it to. It became hard.

'*Reconsider sympathetically* is overstating it. I just made it clear that the council and I wanted to take a meticulous look at the new ideas and plans, and wouldn't toss them out wholesale ahead of time. What we received was a very ambitious project for sustainable, ecological tourism that, yes, does also concern the sailing school and the diving school, but goes a good bit further than that.'

'I didn't think the plans had even been received yet.'

'Not officially. They have not been submitted as of yet. But Lucas Lefort presented the project to us for the first time at a meeting a few weeks ago, informally. Which is absolutely routine,' Monsieur Du Marhallac'h had switched into a mayoral style of speech. 'As I say: we have not received any official proposal – and in any case, it's clear that an implementation is rather unlikely. The coastal protection laws are extremely strict on all French coastlines. And what's more, the Glénan are a designated conservation zone, which means, in fact, nothing is allowed.'

'If I understand correctly, hundreds of sailing and diving students stay the night where nothing at all is allowed, albeit in the most basic conditions. On several of the islands.'

'You know France. We have our strict laws – and we have what happens in practice.'

Dupin couldn't tell if there was a note of criticism or pride in this.

'Was Monsieur Lefort acting alone in this matter? I mean, was he running this project off his own bat?'

'I couldn't say.'

The mayor looked gravely at Dupin.

'You're wondering whether Monsieur Konan and Monsieur Pajot might have been involved? Financially?'

'For example. Monsieur Pajot was a building contractor, it would not be that far-fetched at all. And Monsieur Konan was an investor, amongst other things.'

'It is absolutely possible, Monsieur le Commissaire, but it's pure speculation. Lucas Lefort always spoke of "I" and an anonymous "we", but that didn't necessarily mean a plural.'

'Did you know Yannig Konan better?'

'No, just from the Glénan, from evenings in the *Quatre Vents* and the conversations there.'

'And Pajot? Did you know him?'

'No, not at all. I just know his name. And I know that he owns one of the two biggest construction companies in Brittany.'

The mayor's forehead furrowed in deep lines, a little theatrical, Dupin thought.

'You are wondering whether there could be a story at the bottom of this that could have been a motive for murder?'

'A big issue and lots of money is at stake with this project, if I understand correctly?'

Du Marhallac'h was silent.

'So what did Lefort's specific plans for the islands look like then?'

'He had a lot in mind. You must know that the sailing school is already one of the largest in Europe. This was about a tourism and sporting master plan. He was planning new developments on Penfret, Cigogne and Le Loc'h. Hotel complexes, sports complexes. Ecological, sustainable and exclusive. With a small harbour for yachts. He had a well-known architect from Paris on hand, he had plenty of connections at his disposal. Everything would have been run on wind and solar power, that's already the case on Saint-Nicolas, albeit on a smaller scale. A proportion of the revenue would have been put into the even more effective ecological protection of the archipelago.'

Du Marhallac'h was a perfect politician – and Dupin could hardly imagine anything worse. Slippery as an eel, ruthlessly elastic, a rhetorical show to hide other things, mostly personal interests and to pursue them uncompromisingly at the same time.

'The local council is against this project.'

'The *old* local council. There were utterly irrational entrenchments.'

'I see. "Irrational entrenchments".'

'A project like this needed to go through every authority first.'

'When did Lefort submit plans for developing the Glénan for the first time?'

'Ten years ago. Approximately.'

Dupin made a note and underlined it vigorously. Twice. Du Marhallac'h peered curiously at the notebook.

'Did he present them a second time in recent years?'

'No, he must have let them lie for a few years.'

'Who was amongst the opponents to this plans?'

'Almost everyone. Even though most of them probably weren't very familiar with the plans at all.'

'The most vehement opponents?'

'His sister. I'm sure you already know that. Madame Menez too, certainly, the assistant. The whole sailing school. The head of the diving school, Madame Barrault. She is very prejudiced,' the mayor suddenly looked quite uncertainly at Dupin, 'I mean: she has a very set opinion. Solenn Nuz too, of course. She is – she is the other owner of Saint-Nicolas. Bananec and Quignénec belong to her too. She – she naturally has her own interests...'

'What do you mean by that?'

'Nothing in particular.'

Dupin was aware that Du Marhallac'h was acting in a disloyal way. And Du Marhallac'h must have been aware that Dupin noticed it.

'I think the majority of the residents on the coast were against the plans. In the past the politicians were too, for the most part. Definitely the press, the *Ouest France* as well as the *Télégramme*. Monsieur Leussot for example,' the mayor hesitated, 'a marine biologist who also likes to work as a journalist, was passionately committed to opposing Lefort's plans. In my view it was a purely ideological fight, it doesn't interest me. My concern is to make everything more objective.'

There it was again. That unspeakable ways of a politician. Dupin glowered.

'Did Monsieur Leussot write articles opposing Lefort's plans?'

'Biased, drastic articles.'

'And against the new plans too?'

'As I said, Lefort had not yet presented them to the public, just to us, orally. An absolutely routine procedure. The media obviously got wind of it, it was not a clandestine meeting after all. But since not much is known yet, there have just been short reports in the papers so far. You mustn't forget that Lefort is still a famous person in Brittany – the great sailor. No matter how unpopular he may have been with some people.'

'The marine biologist wasn't involved in these short reports?'

'No. Not as far as I know.'

The shrill ring of Dupin's phone made both men jump.

It was Nolwenn.

'If you could please excuse me again, Monsieur le Maire.'

It wasn't a question, Dupin had already stood up and was hurrying towards the door and into the garden. He picked up there.

'That was complicated, Monsieur le Commissaire,' Nolwenn's voice was, by her standards, a little flustered, 'the Prefect called them both: the public prosecutor and the investigative judge in charge. I'm to tell you he felt very uncomfortable doing it. He had to claim that there was an acute danger of suppression of evidence. He assumes the Director will lodge an appeal immediately. He knows Le Berre-Ryckeboerec. In fact he has a lot of respect for him, he...'

'We've got the search warrant?'

Dupin felt an almost childlike joy.

'We are already organising the operation.'

Dupin was relieved, although it was all still making him quite nervous, because there was no truly incriminating evidence to justify the search yet. He would need something watertight soon.

'That's great, Nolwenn. Perfect. I'm still in the interview with DuMall... With the mayor.'

Dupin hung up. He thought for a moment and dialled Kadeg's number.

'It's starting. We can get going on the search.'

'I know.'

'As I said: I want to know everything about the deals with *Medimare*. There must be papers, documents, data, find out everything. Don't hold back.'

'I never do, Commissaire.'

'Wait, one more thing, Kadeg: I want us to probe all of the business activities of the three men meticulously. Beyond *Medimare*. Every company and also every share, every investment. As far back as we can trace. Get someone on it.'

'Will do.'

This time Dupin walked back through the garden very slowly, opened the door to the office and sat back down on one of the four simple chairs standing around the angular formica table. All with a marked lack of haste. Du Marhallac'h looked as if he was expecting a short explanation at the least. Which Dupin did not feel obliged to provide.

'What does *Medimare* mean to you?'

The mayor looked quizzically at Dupin.

'That means absolutely nothing to me.'

'A company belonging to Pajot and Konan that buys and sells research results from marine biology. Patents and licenses.'

'Oh, I've heard of that. Not of that company, just that the institute sells research results to companies.'

'You don't know anything about the two of them owning a company like this?'

'No.'

Dupin had the impression that he would not find out anything more of interest at this point. Not that he entirely trusted and believed Du Marhallac'h – he absolutely didn't – but there was nothing more to be done at the moment.

'Thank you very much.'

The mayor was clearly at a bit of a loss at this abrupt end to the conversation.

Dupin stood up. Du Marhallac'h followed suit.

'I'll see you to the door, Monsieur le Commissaire.'

'These plans, the papers from Lucas Lefort's presentation – do you have a copy of them?'

'No. Monsieur Lefort had everything on his laptop.'

'You don't think that anybody is in possession of these plans as of yet and only you and the local council know them?'

'Yes.'

'When exactly was the meeting?'

'The end of March. The twenty-sixth I think.'

They had already reached the garden.

'I'm sure you'll be hearing from us again.'

They shook hands.

'I'm at your service. I have a personal interest in a speedy resolution to the case. As the mayor of the community affected, I mean.'

'I totally understand.'

'*Au revoir.*'

Du Marhallac'h had already turned his back on Dupin.

'I have one last question actually.'

The mayor turned back round, a carefully friendly expression still on his face.

'What were your conversations with Lucas Lefort and Yannig Konan about on the evening in question?'

There was a vague, somewhat strange undertone to Dupin's question.

'My conversations? Oh – we exchanged a few words every now and again. Seeing as we were at neighbouring tables. The usual. Very banal.'

'And that was?'

'We talked about the mackerel. About the scalloping now at spring tide. The weather, the coming storm. Things like that. Oh, and about the elections. Of course. The elections! And the price of langoustines. And finally about the *pousse-pieds.*'

'The what?'

'They are the rarest of all seafood, people say: the king of seafood. They grow in extremely difficult places to get to for three months of the year. The

Japanese buy them from us for three hundred euro a kilo, a sushi delicacy. You won't have heard of them, in Paris...'

'Three hundred euro a kilo?'

'Three hundred and more. Really delicious, really iodine-rich. The ones from the Glénan are considered to be the greatest delicacy.'

'*Pousse-pieds.*' Dupin repeated the word with something approaching awe.

'Did either of them talk about what they had done that weekend? Or did of either of them mention Pajot?'

'No and no. But there wasn't any reason to anyway.'

'What does that mean?'

'It was an absolutely normal evening, like always.'

'Fine. Then thanks again. *Au revoir.*'

It seemed as though Du Marhallac'h still had something he wanted to say, but Dupin had already turned away.

He urgently needed a coffee. He had needed one even before the conversation. It had smelt a bit odd in the mayor's office, a little like in the Commissariat, maybe it was the same cleaning product. Dupin was grateful for the fresh air, perfumed here in Fôret-Fouesnant at the beginning of May by the hortensia bushes in bloom.

He went straight back to his car, got in, fiddled with the ludicrously small buttons on the carphone and drove off.

'Nolwenn? I want to talk to Docteur Le Menn. Devan Le Menn. He has his practice in Sainte-Marine. He lives there too.'

'It'll be best if I send you the numbers as a text message, Monsieur le Commissaire, then you can dial the number directly. The practice one and the private.'

'Great. And I want to see a Monsieur Marc Leussot, a researcher from the *Institut Marine*, it doesn't matter where he is. The secretary of the institute told me he was doing "field studies" at sea.'

'I'll be in touch straight away. We've also sorted everything with our colleagues in Paris, they are taking a look at *Medimare*'s office space there. The company has its headquarters right in the 6th, not far from Luxembourg.'

Dupin had to admit that he always got a bit sentimental and filled with yearning when he heard about the Jardin du Luxembourg. In the end he had lived three minutes away from the park, on Place Saint-Sulpice – and had grown up two minutes from the park, on Place de l'Odéon. The park was full of wonderful memories.

'Great.'

'Your mother tried again just now.'

'Damn.'

He had forgotten his mother yet again.

'I told her that you were on a complicated case. She's very much – I'm just quoting here – assuming that you will at least make one quick call anyway.'

It was unbelievable. But not surprising.

'She asked whether there are bath towels in the *Hotel des Sables Blancs*. And a "lounge". And "a good restaurant"?'

Her tone of voice made it clear that Nolwenn did not find this funny.

'She wanted to arrange to meet "an old girlfriend" there. She says she's coming in two days anyway – and there are still some important issues to clarify.'

'I'll call her. Definitely.'

'Good.'

He really did need to call her. Otherwise, everything would just go from bad to worse unnecessarily. In fact he needed to tell her honestly that right now he didn't even know whether he would have any time the day after tomorrow. He had no idea how long he'd be on this case and he could not imagine a bigger nightmare than having his mother to visit during it.

Dupin had arrived at his destination: a large Total petrol station at the last *rond-point* in La Forêt-Fouesnant. It was big enough to offer coffee to take away, which was not particularly well thought of in Brittany and nobody did it apart from at petrol stations.

Dupin stopped right in front of the entrance. By the time he was back in the car again a short while later with two small paper cups, a croissant and the *Petit Indicateur des Marées Bretagne-Sud*, Nolwenn had already called back. The *Petit Indicateur* was a legendary institution: a fire-engine red booklet in a pocket-sized format, which reported details of all low tides and high tides with their coefficients for the whole year. It was sure to be useful.

'Monsieur Leussot is in fact on his boat. Between the Moutons and the Glénan. He has no reception there though. But he can be reached via radio. If you want, I'll radio him.'

'Please do,' Dupin hesitated. 'No, leave it.'

He would prefer to visit unannounced.

'Okay. Shall I arrange for a boat to pick you up?'

'A boat?'

Dupin had of course been thinking of the helicopter. Which was absurd, if Leussot was on his boat in the middle of the ocean.

'Good – it's to be waiting in Concarneau. Where we cast off yesterday.'

'I'm to tell you from Riwal, that he's finished with the list. He still wants to talk to you about a few things.'

'I'll try to get hold of the doctor. Speak to you later.'

Dupin hung up. He took a foolhardy gulp of espresso – it tasted absolutely revolting.

Lovely. Everything was just lovely. What a great morning. He needed a proper coffee, this just wouldn't do. Considering what it was made from,, he turned the ignition key with a vigorous movement and stepped on the accelerator. The tyres screeched. It was just a small detour. It wasn't far. And he could could talk to Riwal on the phone...

Four minutes later, Dupin was turning the engine off again. Just a stone's throw from the *Café du Port*, which was right on Sainte-Marine's stone quay. The pretty village's old town was in a gently kept bay on the bank of the Odet, which was almost sea here already, half a kilometre wide, very close to the open Atlantic and with subdued tides. It was lined with willows and chestnut trees, camellias, wild jasmine, a few bushy palm trees – a typical Breton scene – an old chapel, picturesque fishermen's cottages. The fine shingle beach in the little bay stretched almost as far as the *Café du Port* at low tide.

Dupin had always liked the bar and restaurant; everything was simple, plain, made of wood, all in the Atlantic's primary colours: blue, white, red. This was where – apart from the *Amiral* – the best coffee in the area was. He'd liked it even more since he'd become friends with Henri, the *Café du Port*'s proud owner. They had met at the large Citroën dealer in Quimper when they were both making enquiries about the new C6, which they had not bought in the end, because they were both attached to their old XMs – even though both cars were extremely old and probably wouldn't last much longer. The intervals between his visits to the mechanic had been getting shorter and shorter over the course of the past year, they were now four weeks apart, Dupin estimated. Nolwenn would say two. She had been on at him for quite a long time about getting round to buying a new car. Sometimes brochures lay as if by chance on his desk, for Breton cars only of course: Citroën, built in Rennes. Dupin had come in to the *Café du Port* more often in the months that followed, usually in the evening or if he had something to do in the area. He also like Héloise, Henri's wife, the chef, who with her bushy black curls looked funny next to Henri's almost bald head. Apart from the old Citroëns, they were united – more so than by any other affinities they had with one another – by the fact that Henri was also 'new' here. Not a Breton, but a Parisian like Dupin, although he had been living in Brittany for thirty years (which still qualified as 'new').

Henri was standing behind the counter, thoroughly absorbed in a list and hadn't even made a move to raise his head.

'I need a coffee. Double espresso.'

'Bugger. Just a moment, Georges.'

Henri had answered warmly, but still hadn't looked up.

'Jeannine, a double espresso for the Commissaire!'

He had called this in the direction of the stout young girl who often helped out in the afternoons and sometimes in the evenings too.

'The drinks delivery just came. I hate it, these lists are always utterly baffling.'

There was a moment of intense silence.

'Damn it! Something's not right.'

Henri's sentence had ended in a laugh – he was glad to have a distraction.

'I'll be on my way again soon, Henri.'

'Sure,' Henri knew the score of course. Dupin would not need to say much.

'Hell of a case.'

'I think so too. Nasty guys. Konan, Lefort,' Henri made a serious face.

'Really?'

'Oh yes.'

'Good. If so, the baddies are already dead. Maybe I'm looking for the goodies. In any case. I'm groping around in the dark.'

'Don't let the Bretons confuse you,' Henri laughed.

Dupin was glad he'd come here. The young woman had brought the coffee. They never talked about work, he and Henri. Which Dupin liked very much. He drank the coffee down in one gulp. It was wonderfully strong and not in the least bit sharp. Delicious smells streamed into the restaurant from the kitchen. Dupin liked Héloise's cooking, which, of course, was thoroughly Breton. Holy confession went like this: 'If you are a true Breton – then you take butter. Morning, afternoon, evening: butter.' Héloise was a passionate adherent of the 'olive oil/butter border', which Bretons really did take very seriously: the question of how successful the Roman invasion of olive oil as a universal tool in the kitchen had been and to what extent it had been possible to defend the Celtic–Gallic butter line, were regularly discussed in the two large regional papers. They doggedly published new reports about scientific studies on the clear medical superiority of butter, which had, apparently, been wrongfully brought into disrepute. Initially Dupin had been, as he was with everything, very sceptical, but through the 'empirical evidence' he had almost become a rebel himself.

'I need to get going.'

'Héloise has a marvellously crisp joint of Breton salt-lamb in the oven with thyme, *fleur de sel* and *piment d'espelette*. With fresh butter beans. A tiny plate perhaps?'

'I really need to get going.' Dupin sighed heavily.

'Come again another evening!'

He hoped to. He always enjoyed sitting down with Henri. They talked about everything under the sun; about the world, which had been going off the rails for some time now. Even in France. Some time ago Chinese people had, after sending the prices of French wines soaring dramatically (a Chinese man had recently paid 167,000 euro for a bottle of Lafitte), finally bought the best vinery in the Bordelais. After thirty months of negotiations,

the Château in the middle of Lalande-de-Pomerol
had gone to a Chinese firm, *Mingu*, which had
corneredChina's mass market with a 'wine' called
The Great Wall. And it was clear that that had
only been the beginning, further deals were already
underway, including with corporations in other
countries. This was in a country where wines, along
with certain culinary delicacies and creations by
great chefs de cuisine, naturally occupied the same
class of cultural assets as great paintings or pieces
of music. And of which, Dupin thought, France
should be truly very proud. This was the ultimate
surrender to commerce, the selling off of France, it
was blood-curdling. Both Henri and Dupin, could
get impressively riled up about it and it was their
ritual to do so together.

'I'll come by some time next week. Depending
on when I'm finished with the case. And in fact my
mother is coming the day after tomorrow for a few
days.'

'Ah yes. I'd forgotten. Works out well. Come
together then.'

'I'll probably need to cancel on her.'

Henri laughed, his deep, rather soft laugh, that
spread over his entire face.

'You'll solve the case quickly. For your mother's
sake if nothing else.'

Dupin took his car key from the counter.

'*Salut!*'

'And call Claire.'

Now Dupin had to laugh. They had spoken about
it. Never for long. But a handful of times.

'I left her a message.'

'Romantic!'

'See you next week.'

'Yes, see you next week!'

They were in the middle of the deep Atlantic blue, the Glénan were shimmering in front of them, the Île aux Moutons behind then. Although not far away, the Moutons could only be made out vaguely. They blurred hazily into the sea. It was misty, in a way. Dupin was familiar with this by now: the effect of the water in the air was enormous. The blue became gentle, soft, smooth, it was still a rich blue, but it didn't have the lucid luminosity of yesterday. The haze changed the light, sun, colours, taste and smell of the air, it became very soft itself – and at the same time more powerful, more intense. It muffled the sounds, even the silence. It also became velvety. At the horizon to the west – far away – there was a thin, sharply outlined layer of dark cloud masses, a fine, firm line, so long that there was no end in sight.

The captain of the *Luc'hed* had turned off the motor. The crew was busy with the dinghy. The sea seemed almost perfectly flat – 'like oil', the Bretons said – not even the slightest movement was visible and yet the boat was being rocked, as if by a ghostly hand, in a vigorous, albeit strangely slow motion way.

They were about thirty metres away from Marc Leussot's boat, the *Kavadenn*, which had a normal hull, but whose partially misshapen structures and installations made it clear that the boat had a specific function. It took a moment before Dupin recognised it as the boat that he had noticed at the quay

210

yesterday while sitting in the *Quatre Vents* eating the delicious lobster.

Docteur Le Menn hadn't been contactable at the practice or at home or on his mobile. He didn't have consultation hours until the afternoon, he spent Tuesday mornings making house calls, if there were any – which today, according to the practice receptionist, hadn't been the case. Dupin had driven back to Concarneau where the *Luc'hed* had been waiting for him. Nolwenn had arranged everything. He had spoken to Kadeg – who had already got his first meeting with the Director of the institute over with – on the phone again, but who seemed unimpressed and reported that two experts from Quimper had already disabled the institute's server. The Director was currently consulting with his lawyers.

Nolwenn had then had Leussot radioed, to find out his exact position. So it had, like yesterday, been a speedboat that had lived up to its definition by tearing through the groundswell with Dupin onboard.

'Over here, Monsieur le Commissaire.'

One of the police officers was already in the very small dinghy, which was rocking violently. This really was not Dupin's habitat, no and he was extremely sorry to have thrown his justified decision of yesterday morning – to drop the whole boat thing – out the window so soon. He should simply have ordered Leussot to come to Saint-Nicolas. Dupin gave himself a shake. He mustered all his psychological strength and, thanks to his agility, which he generally wasn't thought capable of due to his rather large build, he was soon on the tiny rowing boat. The outboard motor showed off its impressive horsepower, and soon they were approaching the *Kavadenn* with stunning speed. Leussot was standing on the stern where wide wooden steps led down into the sea.

'*Bonjour*, Monsieur le Commissaire. Come on.'

Leussot held out his hand, but Dupin heaved himself on board without any help, in a not every elegant, yet precise way.

'*Bonjour*, Monsieur Leussot.'

Leussot was a tall, very athletic man with fine facial features, lively eyes, rather long hair. He was, perhaps, mid to late forties. He was wearing short, washed-out shorts and an open black jacket with a white t-shirt underneath. The built-on bits of the boat looked even more misshapen up close.

'I've just been taking care of lunch.'

Leussot spoke with a deep sense of calm, which perfectly suited the supreme, gentle strength which he radiated in general. Two fishing rods lay on the long bench that ran underneath the railing.

'A *vieille*, wonderful, a magnificent specimen, look.'

Leussot lifted up a battered plastic bucket which had a large fin peeping out of it.

'You won't get this fish in any restaurant, in any fishmongers, or even back home on the coast. You have to eat it within a few hours of catching it, otherwise it spoils straight away. It's one of the best edible fish in the world and found in healthy numbers here – still.'

Flecks of gold shimmered and diffracted the sunlight into soft rainbow colours on the forty-centimetre long, fat, green-orange-red speckled fish.

'Impressive.'

Unfortunately, Dupin couldn't think of anything else to say. The *Kavadenn* was rocking just like the speedboat. He had hoped that it would be slightly less bad, since it was several metres longer.

'I have some questions, Monsieur Leussot. You're aware that we are investigating the murder case of Lefort, Konan and Pajot.'

'I'm up to speed. If you like, we can go below deck, it's not very spacious down there, but we'll have some quiet.'

Dupin took this as a joke. Yet Leussot was looking at a narrow door behind the helm and was getting ready to make a move. He meant it seriously.

'If you agree, I would prefer – to remain on deck. Out here in the open air.'

Having to sit cramped in a tiny room now was a traumatic thought.

'Okay. Then I'll see to the fish while we talk.'

The dinghy was almost back at the *Luc'hed* already.

'What do you know about the business activities of the institute and *Medimare*? Are you involved in these activities in any way?'

'Well, you get right to the point.'

Leussot didn't let himself be thrown.

'We have evidence of something amiss about these dealings.'

Dupin's was very keen to keep this conversation, out on the open sea, as short as possible.

Leussot raised his eyebrows, his deeply tanned forehead furrowing.

'Okay. I'll tell you what I think: Konan and Pajot defrauded the institute, systematically, over and over, in conjunction with the Director, they were in things together – but I doubt that they were really actionable things. It's all taking place in a grey area, nobody will be able to touch them, legally. No matter how much some researchers in the institute hated them, they acted skilfully. – That, for me, would be the quintessence.'

'How did you come to this *quintessence*?'

Leussot had flipped open a long Laguiole knife and at that very moment the boat made a particularly severe movement, making the situation – Leussot half toppled onto Dupin – seem threatening for a moment. Dupin was too busy keeping his balance to worry about it. Leussot realised the strangeness of the little incident and smiled. With his left hand, he picked up the large, shiny fish which was still thrashing fiercely and set to work with practised movements. Quickly and precisely, he placed the knife to the underside of its head.

'My research was also involved sometimes. Yes, you're surely wondering that. They buy the results at a very early stage, at the risk of them not in fact being as viable as they initially appear, sometimes at prices that are far too low. The individual researcher doesn't have any control over the business side of course, they are employed by the institute. Le Berre-Ryckeboerec profits from the deals from, amongst other things, the fact *Medimare* sponsors the institute – which provides the legendary third-party funding.'

The fish's innards fell into the bucket. Leussot had taken them out with a few artful flicks of the wrist.

'Pajot and Konan got patents at extremely reasonable prices. That was the deal. When in doubt, it was to the disadvantage of the researcher. Only, of course, if large discoveries were involved. But as I say: there won't be proof of anything illegal there, is my guess,' he fell silent for a moment, but then picked up the thread again immediately. 'I also don't think that they greased the director's palm, that he personally received money in return. Even if he is a slippery asshole.'

Leussot stood up and went to the bow, leaning down dangerously far and holding the fish in the water – in a way that made it clear that the conversation with Dupin could continue in the meantime. The fish carcass was still twitching violently every few seconds.

'How come you're so sure of that?'

'Intuition.'

For a moment, Dupin wanted to enquire as to what exactly Leussot meant by 'asshole' in reference to the director, but in fact it was already obvious. Leussot came back, placed the fish in a second bucket and sat down again.

'What is this research specifically about?

Dupin had got out his notepad. Even on his first attempt to note something down, he realised that this was not a good idea on the boat. He went ahead anyway, although he already knew now that he would be puzzling over what he had noted down here in the coming days.

'The seas are brimming with treasures of immense value for humans. We should use them before we've laid it all to waste. Take, for example, the wonderful *Chondrus Crispus*, a red algae that we are researching currently. A crazy life form. If it's attacked by microbes, this algae literally transforms into a high performance factory for fatty acid oxides, which can be used in medications. So far, fifty thousand substances and organisms from the sea have been identified that are suspected to have therapeutic potential. And that's just the beginning. Many of them are already undergoing clinical testing, a series of them have already passed.'

'Marvellous.'

Dupin was indeed impressed. He liked topics like this, sometimes he bought himself natural science magazines, which he eagerly read, even if he strictly speaking didn't actually understand a word of it.

'Life comes from the sea – evolution had over three billion years here. It produced a great deal more shapes and functions in the oceans than on land. The biological variety is immense,' Leussot was absolutely in his element, yet it didn't seem like a show at all. 'It's estimated at three million different species.'

Leussot paused for quite a long time.

'And right at the moment when people are beginning to grasp the sheer, infinite potential the oceans harbour, they themselves are destroying it. All of it.'

'You mean the Glénan?'

'I mean the bigger picture. The oceans are ill.'

'And are you doing something about it?'

Leussot was clearly thrown for a moment, he wasn't sure how Dupin meant that.

'I am. I'm taking action.'

He fell silent again, but then a broad smile appeared on his face again.

'Yes, I'm doubly, triple suspect. I was an enemy of Lefort, I opposed his destructive plans, wrote critical articles and am amongst those defrauded by Pajot and Konan's company – and I was in the *Quatre Vents* yesterday evening. You've got to admit, that's not too shabby.'

Suddenly his face grew serious.

'Finding someone else who had the motive to kill all three of them will not be easy.'

'If you're also one of the people who go on treasure hunts, looking for sunken boats, coins, gold and silver...'

Dupin had remained pointedly matter-of-fact. He had suddenly remembered a dream just now that he'd had in his few hours of sleep last night. It had been utterly bizarre. So embarrassing that Dupin would have preferredit never to cross his mind again. He, Riwal and Kadeg had been worn-out old buccaneers. On a ridiculously small frigate, which was letting off valiant sustained fire nonetheless, they were chasing three majestic sailing ships overflowing with stolen treasures, helmed by Lefort, Konan and Pajot. But the best thing about the little frigate had been this: it could dive. Descend and then emerge again here or there at breakneck speed. That's how they hunted down one after the other.

'That's child's play,' Leussot responded earnestly.

'If I understand correctly, discoveries do sometimes happen.'

'It's not my thing.'

There had been something brusque about this sentence, Dupin thought.

'So you don't know of any "treasure hunt" going on at the moment – in this area?'

'No.'

'Did you personally come into contact with Pajot and Konan?'

'I knew Konan by sight, from the *Quatre Vents*. He always came with Lefort. I've never said a word to him. Why would I? I've never seen Pajot all. I only know the name through *Medimare*. I don't want to have anything to do with any of that.'

'And Lefort, how was your relationship to him?'

'There was none. The idea wouldn't have occurred to me either. He was an awful guy. End of story. That would be my summary.'

Dupin was having some difficulty staying upright, the boat had rocked dangerously a few times.

'And do you have a theory on the murders? Some idea of what might have happened here?'

'One of the dirty tricks they pulled will have made someone angry. Truly angry.'

'Do you know Docteur Le Menn? Did you see him in the *Quatre Vents* the evening before last?'

'Le Menn? No. As far as I know, he wasn't there.'

Leussot's expression had darkened, he didn't even try and hide it.

'A friend of Lefort's?'

'Yes.'

'Did you know him personally?'

'No.'

'You know that he's a doctor.'

Yes.'

Even this was a waste of effort. Leussot didn't want to do this.

'The new mayor appears to be another friend of Lefort's, he...'

'In his case, it wouldn't surprise me if his favourable

attitude towards Lefort's plans had been motivated by money,' this seemed to be weighing heavily on Leussot's mind, 'or else it was enough for him that, as the mayor, he would profit from the huge investment. Prosperity, growth, image, a tax income increased many times over. Those are the currencies of reality. Nature – the animals, the people, nobody gives a shit about any of that. Terrible that it sounds so cheap, like painting by numbers. But that's exactly how it is. There's no difference.'

'The old development plans – were you very familiar with them?' Dupin asked.

'Yes. They were made public. I wrote extensively about them, several times in *Ouest France*, once even for the *Libération*. Interestingly, the plans were then never officially submitted. So never officially rejected either. It was probably clear after an intense discussion that they didn't have a shadow of a chance and I believe Lefort didn't want to show any weakness.

'How long have you been working for the institute?'

Dupin was aware that his way of steering this conversation sometimes swayed back and forth as much as the boat – it must have been because of the sea, he had been feeling dizzy and little unwell the whole time. And something else had been distracting him since he'd got on the boat: an erratic, loud splashing that kept coming back every few minutes, accompanied each time by noises that were difficult to identify. At first, Dupin had looked around, not found anything and assumed that it must have been seagulls. They performed daring flight manoeuvres over the boats in the hope that there would something for them to take. Now the sounds were louder than before. Dupin looked around yet again. A group of dolphins was swimming past them, less than ten metres away, at breathtaking speed, diving down for a moment before coming back up, as quick as a flash. It was absolutely surreal. Dupin was dumbfounded. It was only with an effort that he managed to suppress the cry, 'Real dolphins!' He had never seen any in the wild before. They actually looked like they did in films.

Leussot had noticed Dupin's surprise – although the word did not even come close to describing it.

'They've been keeping me company since last week. These ones are very playful.'

This sentence could hardly have been uttered in a more off-hand way. Leussot had smiled smoothly as he said it.

'I...' Dupin really didn't know what to say.

'The tourists always lose their minds. They are great animals after all.'

The second sentence sounded conciliatory.

'But the sea is full of wonderful creatures that are just as fascinating. Even more fascinating than dolphins. Take the tychoplankton, for instance.'

The group of dolphins had swum in a semi-circle around the stern of the boat and then, after what looked like a final jump, they went under and disappeared. The whole thing had lasted perhaps fifteen seconds. Dupin tried to compose himself again with all the strength he could muster.

'Yes, I think we should get back to where we were. Back to our conversation, Monsieur Leussot. I had asked you how long you'd been working at the institute?'

Leussot looked quite mischievous, but then answered very matter-of-factly.

'I came here as a young man, fifteen years ago. After studying in Paris, I started my research here, got a PhD, then went to Brest for a few years for larger projects and have been back for four years now. When Lefort tried to push through his plans the first time, I was still in Brest, but came here regularly. Lefort's plans were my impetus for working as a science journalist. People have got to know what's going on.'

It was evident that Leussot hadn't given the dolphins another thought. Dupin had been forcing himself – reasonably successfully – not to scan the sea with his eyes again. He already felt ridiculous.

'Fifteen years. And a journalist too. In Brest.'

Leussot looked seriously irritated. Dupin had to control himself.

'Muriel Lefort, Madame Menez, Madame Barrault, Monsieur – the mayor, Solenn Nuz and her daughters, Monsieur Tanguy. Do you know them all personally?'

Now Leussot looked at the Commissaire for a moment, like a gormless young schoolboy.

'You know – the Glénan. It's a world of its own. It's hard to explain, you have to experience it yourself. And in the *Quatre Vents* they come together: the inhabitants of this world and their constant stream of guests. We all know each other. Not as the people we are outside of this world, only as the people we are here.'

Dupin didn't understand the literal meaning of this exactly, but he guessed what Leussot meant.

More importantly: he had found a way back into the conversation.

'And do you think anyone had a motive for an act like this?'

'The village forces you close together, the sea, the Atlantic – into each other's pockets, much closer than you'd like.' It was as though Leussot had not even heard Dupin's enquiry. 'Even against the individual's will. Sympathies and antipathies don't come into it sometimes, not enmities, not even hatred. And more importantly: the archipelago may in fact bring people together – but in the end everyone is on their own.'

Even these sentences were cryptic, but Dupin had the feeling that they contained something important.

'Hatred?'

Leussot draw a sharp breath in through his nose.

'Yes.'

'Who do you mean?'

'Don't get me wrong, I don't mean anyone specific.'

'Muriel and Lucas Lefort? You mean the siblings? Or Madame Menez and Lucas Lefort? – You yourself and Lucas Lefort?'

'I don't mean anything in particular.'

'It would be very helpful to us.'

Leussot was silent. Not an unpleasant silence. But one that made it clear that he would not answer.

'And you didn't speak to Pajot or Konan two evenings ago, I assume.'

Leussot looked almost amused.

'I wouldn't have made such an effort with the murder, believe me. Definitely not.'

He laughed. Leussot was very good. If it had been him – it would be impossible to behave more skilfully.

'It's quite a feat! A brilliant plan really,' Leussot now contemplated Dupin's question, 'No. I sat as far away from them as possible, I always do that. I didn't notice anything suspicious all evening. Nothing at all.'

Of course not, Dupin almost blurted out.

'Depending on whom I had noticed something suspicious about, I might even forget it again, I have to admit.'

He smiled again. Dupin guessed that Leussot meant this sentence seriously.

'Fine, then I'll leave you to prepare your fish. It's lunchtime after all. And I know what I wanted to know.'

That was true. He had learnt a lot.

Dupin raised his hand and looked over to the *Luc'hed*. The observant young police officers understood the gesture immediately and climbed into the dinghy without wasting another moment.

'Yes, I'm going to eat now. And get back to work. Red algae are impatient creatures.'

'Will be you be out at sea all day, Monsieur Leussot?'

'We'll see.'

He pointed towards the west with a minimal movement of the head, where the wisps of cloud had become undeniably denser, although they were still far away.

'Actually, yes. At the moment, I'm more or less at sea all week,' he smiled, 'so you'll know where to find me.'

The dinghy had come to a stop alongside the stern.

'*Bon appétit*, Monsieur Leussot.'

'*Au revoir*, Monsieur le Commissaire.'

Dupin climbed nimbly back into the little boat, which turned around just a moment later and travelled back to the *Luc'hed*. As it did so, he contemplated the sky with raised eyebrows. It was – apart from that growing dark streak in the west – the same unchanged blue. Dupin was slightly uncertain about his own weather forecast. But not overly so. The signs were too clear: Grand Marée, spring tide, full moon, then for thirty days the weather stayed the way it was on the evening of the full moon, that's how he'd remembered...

'Monsieur le Commissaire, Inspector Riwal has just radioed us. He needs to speak to you. You were already in the dinghy.'

The captain bent down to Dupin and offered him his hand, which Dupin accepted this time. He had forgotten that he had no reception here.

'You'll be with him in less than ten minutes, at top speed.'

'Good. Full speed ahead then.'

Dupin couldn't believed what he'd just said.

The air was absolutely still, even the ubiquitous Atlantic breeze could no longer be felt. Yet it was even hotter than yesterday. At the last moment, the islands had materialised in front of them, as if out of nowhere. And strangely, all of them did so at once. You were left with the impression: this is the last second before you're dashed on them.

Dupin was briefly overcome by a vague suspicion which he quickly pushed aside. He was busy going over the conversations he'd had today in his head. And the dolphins came into his mind again too.

They were going past Guiriden's long sandbar. To Dupin it was perhaps the most astonishing thing about the entirety of the Glénan. A few rocks at high tide, a little bit of land and green all around them, perhaps twenty metres by twenty and then – at low tide – suddenly two or three hundred metres of dazzlingly bright sandbar. Unbelievably white sand, falling gently away, even forming Caribbean-like lagoons. It was fantastic. Just like Henri had described it to him last year, on what have been his only trip to the Glénan before yesterday. Dupin had let himself be talked into a day on Henri's brand new boat – an Antares 7.80 – which he had regretted enormously, as beautiful as it had been on Penfret. This was no normal sand here! It was coral sand! It was not a Breton exaggeration, as Dupin had initially suspected. This really was genuine coral sand. And there was only one instance of it in Europe and that was on the Glénan. Nolwenn had explained it vividly to him a few times before too. The sand on the archipelago consisted of chalky coral skeletons ground down over the course of millions of years. Snow white, fine, yet solid, not fly-away like powder. 'This bears no relation to sand – little, crystalline pieces of coral,' he recalled Nolwenn's words. Of course, Breton sand in general was no ordinary sand, not some run-of-the-mill sand from some normal sandstone; it was mainly *flawless* granite sand. Sand that had broken away from the elemental granite ridges that made up Brittany, geologically-speaking. But if the coral thing sounded spectacular enough already, the real highlight of it was the explanation. The sand, or rather the corals, hadn't been washed up somehow, no – they had once grown extensively right here: large, splendid corals. Right here – when Brittany was still in the tropics. This was not a joke or a metaphor or an analogy. It was reality. Dupin remembered the first time that Nolwenn had proudly said this: 'For a long time we were an exotic, tropical landscape – in the heart of the tropics.' He had found it almost too strange to laugh, which Nolwenn had noticed with an indignant look and countered with a geography lecture that was all the more serious for it. The position of the earth's axis, Dupin had learnt, had shifted dramatically and with it, the climactic zones. So these really were tropical beaches here! Or at least they had once been. Bretons had, Dupin found, a special relationship with time, with the past, even the far-distant past. Which above all meant: it didn't exist for Bretons, the past. It had not passed. Nothing was past. Everything that there had been was also present and would stay that way forever. This didn't reduce the significance of the present at all, on the contrary: it made it even greater. It had taken Dupin some time to understand that. But at some point he had discovered that there was a truth in this that was very moving. And if you wanted to get by at the 'End of the World', you couldn't forget it.

In the chamber the *Luc'hed* was going at a slower speed. Soon the quay at Saint-Nicolas came into view, the ugly triangular houses, the sailing school's farmhouse, the diving school, the *Quatre Vents*. The captain moored expertly at the quay and soon Dupin was already on his way to 'operation headquarters'.

'What have we got, Riwal?'

The inspector was sitting at the same table they had sat at yesterday. He was so absorbed in his notebook that he hadn't seen Dupin coming. Lots of A4 pages were stuck into it. He straightened up with a jerk and looked a little sheepishly at the large plate on the table in front of him, with the meagre remains of a lobster piled on it. Next to it stood two bottles of water and several glasses. And an empty wine glass.

'You've got to drink a lot of water in this weather. I've conducted interviews with Madame Nuz and Madame Barrault. And with Madame Menez.' He added, slightly more quietly, 'I've just had something to eat.'

'Excellent, Riwal. I'm going to do that soon too.'

The solid ground beneath his feet was making Dupin feel, by his standards, practically euphoric.

Riwal burst out with the news.

'The doctor from Sainte-Marine, who apparently was also in the *Quatre Vents* briefly the evening before last, has been reported missing: Devan Le Menn...'

'Le Menn is missing? Le Menn?'

Dupin's mild fit of good cheer was evaporating.

'His wife informed the police half an hour ago.'

'Bloody hell.'

'He left his house around half seven this morning, he had a few errands to do. Amongst other things, he wanted to go to the bank in Quimper, he often does that on Tuesday morning if there are no urgent house calls. He was meant to meet his wife at twelve o'clock. He's always on time. His wife seemed anxious.'

'He's not even two hours late yet. There's no reason,' Dupin hesitated, 'to assume that something bad has happened yet.'

'I have a bad feeling about this.'

'Maybe there was a medical emergency, one of his patients. Something acute – and he hasn't found the time to get in touch yet. He's a doctor.'

Dupin himself didn't believe this. He felt, if he were honest, the same way Riwal did. Although there really were, of course, quite a few possible explanations and Le Menn could turn up again any moment. However: disappearing at this point in time was too much of a coincidence.

'Actually, what about the missing man from the Moutons, the angler?'

Dupin had completely forgotten him the evening before and this morning too, it was only as they were going past the desolate Moutons on the boat that he had crossed his mind again.

'No news. We've checked whether there were any links to the Glénan, whether he came here sometimes or whether there are links to the three dead men – no, no and no. Apparently, he always moored between the mainland and the Moutons. Usually near the coast. His wife doesn't remember him coming out as far as this in recent years. And she also didn't know anything about a relationship with Lefort or either of the other two.'

'That is strange.'

Riwal looked quizzically at the Commissaire.

'This coincidence is quite strange, I mean. The timing. The proximity to the crime scene.'

'But we're not aware of any connections yet. And we've had a severe storm. It's not uncommon for people to go missing during storms.'

Riwal was right. Dupin had been here for nearly

four years, but it still gave him the creeps: the 'lost or drowned at sea' statistic for Finistère far outstripped the murder statistic. Every coast-dwelling Breton had heard such 'fateful stories' first-hand from people they knew.

'How big are these Moutons exactly?'

'Very small, a main island about two hundred metres long, a little island about thirty metres long. Lots of rocks.'

Dupin didn't pick up where Riwal had left off. He was thinking. Riwal interpreted the short pause incorrectly.

'If you're wondering whether there are sheep there – no. The sailors call the white ridges of the surf "sheep", *moutons* – and they, on the other hand, are always there.'

That hadn't been what Dupin was pondering.

'Going back to Le Menn. I want a large-scale manhunt. Maybe we'll find his car. He must have parked it somewhere.'

Something was going on.

Riwal took a deep breath. 'That leads us right to the heart of the case.'

He had spoken very off-handedly, as though absent-mindedly. Nolwenn called him *the druid* at moments like this. If Riwal's 'mystical' side was essentially an amusing contrast to his appearance, his cheeky facial expression and his virtual youth (early thirties), it fitted with his new, decidedly stylish short hair even less. They had been speculating in the commissariat about whether this was the wedding haircut already. In two weeks' time, Riwal was going to marry the strikingly pretty daughter of one of the wonderful fishmongers in Concarneau's market halls. She worked for her father at the stall. Riwal was obsessed with langoustines, the medium-sized ones from Guilvinec, the 'best in the world'. For a while he had bought them nearly every lunch break. At some point people in the office had figured it out and had certainly done so by the time Riwal was buying so many langoustines that he had to hand them out liberally in the Commissariat.

'We have to talk to Le Menn's wife. I want to know everything about his links to Lefort, Konan and Pajot, down to the very last detail. Who can drive out to her immediately?'

'Our two colleagues from Concarneau, Le Coz and Bellec, are on the islands too and right now they are speaking to the last of the sailing and diving course participants who were in the *Quatre Vents* two evenings ago.'

'Take Bellec off that. This is more important now.'

Bellec did not waste any time. He came at things head-on.

Dupin was extremely uneasy. If Le Menn's disappearance was related to this case – what did that mean? What was going on here? Had there been another victim – or was the culprit on the run? Whatever had happened on this tiny speck of land – it had to do, Dupin felt, with its residents and regular guests. He would find the solution there. They had to look very carefully.

'What about Kadeg and the institute?'

'Nothing of interest so far. Kadeg last called half an hour ago. They have found the first documents and data relating to *Medimare*. But getting usable information out of them is no doubt not that simple. The press has got wind of the operation by the way, *Télégramme* and *Ouest France* are featuring it on their websites already. The radio station too. The director is acting like Rumpelstiltskin the whole time.'

'I especially want you to take a look at the business documents involving Leussot's research. You should also speak to the researchers Leussot dealt with.'

'I'll let Kadeg know.'

'What about the headquarters of *Medimare* in Paris? Is there anything on that yet?'

'Nothing relevant there yet either. Apart from the chief executive, the company officially only has scientific staff and a secretary, our colleagues are speaking to them right now.'

'We need to examine everything, the account balances and transactions. The director's too, and his private accounts. As soon as possible.'

'Nolwenn will sort it. *La tigresse.*'

Dupin smiled. Yes, Nolwenn would sort it. Even though there would be yet more trouble.

'I also want information about the mayor of Forêt-Fouesnant's accounts.'

'Do we have suspicious circumstances there? Without grounds, even Nolwenn won't manage that.'

'But hopefully we will have the bank statements for all of the three dead men's bank details soon?'

'Nolwenn is on it.'

'I want to know whether there were transfers from business or private accounts belonging to the three to anyone here on the islands. No matter who. No matter how much.'

Dupin got out the Clairefontaine and saw that three-quarters of the notebook was already full.

'Okay, let's look more closely at: Leussot, the mayor, Le Menn, the director of the institute,' Dupin leafed furiously, 'also Tanguy. And Madame Menez, Muriel Lefort and Solenn Nuz.'

'Madame Lefort and Madame Nuz?'

'Yes, everyone.'

'Then don't forget the two Nuz daughters. And the father-in-law.'

'True. And I want to know what plans Lefort ever actually officially submitted for developing the Glénan – if he did ever even submitted any? What is there at the council in terms of papers? Statements, appeals, we should check the files carefully. Also whether there were proposals for projects on the Glénan submitted by other people in the last ten years.'

'I could take that on, chief.'

'I want to keep you here.'

Dupin knew that sounded a bit odd.

'I want the two of us to have in-depth conversations with everyone out here again. What were the three men's relationships like exactly? I still need to know a lot more detail about who stuck by whom here, and and how. I'd like to have a precise picture of this world out here.'

'I'll do that.'

Dupin stood up.

'Just a few more things, Monsieur le Commissaire. We haven't been able to find out where Pajot was two evenings ago, nobody saw him. I suspect he was on his boat. By the way we now know when the three of them probably arrived on the Glénan. On Sunday around five o'clock in the evening, the Bénéteau attracted jealous glances, two boat-owners remember it. AndI finally spoke to Lucas Lefort's current girlfriend this morning. It was a bit complicated to get hold of her. She works in Brest in a luxury 'spa'. Salt therapy and things. Funny Daerlen, a Dutchwoman. She had already heard about everything obviously, she was astonishingly composed. They had only known each other two months. In fact, she had wanted to spend the weekend with Lucas Lefort, but he cancelled when the weather was so good. Just the day before, Thursday. So the three seem to have set out quite spontaneously.'

'Funny Daerlen?'

'Yes.'

'No joke?'

'No.'

So Muriel Lefort's assessment of this 'liaison' seemed absolutely correct. Mademoiselle Daerlen hadn't been a big part of her brother's life. Still. Coincidences were possible.

'She didn't know of any conflicts Lucas had had recently. But it was probably just not the sort of relationship where that kind of thing is discussed. They last saw each other on Tuesday evening, in his house at the Sables Blancs. He seemed on top form then, she says. He told her about buying a loft in London.'

'London?'

'In South Kensington, Chelsea. It's where the wealthy are buying property out of fear of the crisis. The French now too. – – – Disgusting.'

That was a harsh word, in Riwal's view. Somehow well-planned 'emigration' didn't fit with the picture that Dupin had gathered of Lucas Lefort. He didn't seem to have been particularly systematic. Not very rational in his actions.

'The mayor's wife comes from London. She has a house in South Kensington.'

'Excuse me?'

'We happened to find that out at Du Marhallac'h's questioning yesterday evening.' Although he still said this in an off-hand way, Riwal's voice then hardened: 'If you have a residence in England, you don't have to pay tax on a cent of your income here in France. Four hundred thousand French people "live" in London at this stage. France's sixth largest city! Many of them make their money here and then squirrel it away there. Seriously disgusting.'

Even though Dupin could understand Riwal's fury, he forced himself to return to the subject.

'What connection could there be?'

'None yet.'

'Not so far anyway. Anything else of interest from – Funny, Riwal?'

'No.'

'I think I should speak to Madame Barrault.'

'You wanted to eat something though, Monsieur le Commissaire.'

True. He desperately needed to eat something. And he needed a coffee.

'I'll just get myself a sandwich. – Riwal?'

'Yes, Monsieur le Commissaire?'

'Did you know that this place is just swarming with dolphins? We saw some just now.'

Dupin hadn't planned to talk about them. Especially not so excitedly.

'Yes, they like the Glénan. Shall I get you that sandwich, chief?'

'No need. I'll go myself. Maybe I'll see Solenn Nuz.'

Dupin took a few steps towards the bar, turned around and came back again. Riwal was already standing.

'Riwal, we'll keep Le Menn's disappearance to ourselves for the time being, for as long as possible.'

'Good. If I have news, I'll get in touch straight away.'

The bar was empty. All the customers were sitting outside in the splendid sunshine. The older daughter, Louann, was behind the counter, busy with some glasses, and smiled as Dupin came in.

'My mother isn't here.'

Dupin was amazed afresh every time – and almost shocked – at how similar the three women were.

'Coffee and a sandwich, please.'

'Cheese, ham? Or rillettes? We have mackerel, crab, spider crab and scallop rillettes.'

'Scallop.'

'Great.'

'The coffee first.'

She smiled again and set to work. In the wonderful hissing of the coffee machine, Dupin's mobile rang. It was Goulch.

'We've retrieved the boat, Monsieur le Commissiare. It was easier than we thought. It is now in one of the dry docks in Concarneau,' Goulch's voice spiralled upwards a little: 'The Bénéteau had a series of expensive special technological features built into it, a little high-tech arsenal – a sonar that goes far beyond normal sonars, a detector for metal on the seafloor and a laser underwater camera.'

Dupin started.

'What?'

He was certain he knew what this meant, but somehow it had wrong-footed him.

'One moment,' he said.

Dupin left the bar and went back to the table where they had just been sitting. Riwal had already disappeared.

'Do you think it was fitted out for treasure hunting?'

'There is definitely special equipment for examining the seafloor – not just the immediate surface of the ground, the sonic waves from this sonar penetrate even two- or three-metre thick layers of sand. They're expensive gadgets. Professional quality.'

'Anything else?'

'What do you mean?'

'On the boat. Other evidence or things to note?'

'Not so far. Everything is wet of course, in the stowage space too.'

'Maps, map materials?'

'It all works on digital maps. The navigation,' Goulch stopped himself. 'You mean maps that could have specific places in the sea marked on them?'

'Yes.'

'We haven't found any as of yet. Lots of things definitely went missing too, got washed out of the boat in the accident. During the storm and the hours on the seafloor.'

'Are boats like this equipped with a blackbox? Do we have a chance of seeing where they were at the weekend? Before they got to the Glénan?'

'Only larger ships. – What we can do, although there there isn't much chance it will work, is use the emergency frequency to radio everyone who is at sea in the area and ask whether someone saw the Bénéteau at the weekend. We'll send the request to all newspapers and radio stations too.'

'Do that, Goulch.'

Louann Nuz appeared in the doorway of the *Quatre Vents* and came over to him with the sandwich and the coffee, swiftly placing everything in front of him and disappearing again.

'We'll be in touch if there's any news.'

'Good.'

Dupin hung up.

He still wasn't sure what to make of this new information. He felt like he was in an adventure novel. Like in a Tim and Struppi comic, which he always read if he couldn't sleep. He loved Tim and Struppi. Might this cold-blooded triple murder be about treasure? An old shipwreck with gold, silver and jewels on board? Had the three of them been on the trail of a treasure and someone had found out about it? Or vice versa: had the three wanted to steal the treasure from somebody? As outlandish as it sounded – which didn't mean much in Brittany anyway – it sounded realistic to Dupin right now.

He stood up abruptly, ran his right hand through his hair and placed it on the back of his neck, his forehead deeply creased, his head lowered. Whenever he took up this position, his inspectors were in the habit of keeping a safe distance as inconspicuously as possible.

He needed to get moving. To think. Dupin picked up the cup with his left hand, finished the coffee in one gulp, grabbed the sandwich and headed for the beach on the other side of the island.

He didn't like this one bit. Three victims, who each seemed to have a minimum of half a dozen enemies and no fewer than four impressively big motives. They may have appeared somewhat outlandish in parts, but all contained enough dramatic potential for murder. The development of the sailing school and the fight about its 'spirit', an issue with a lot of money and conceptual values at stake. The tourist development of the Glénan, with as much money as high ideals at stake. *Medimare*'s license deals, which very likely involved huge sums too. And treasures on the seafloor, possibly worth millions.

Ridiculous. Yet they hadn't found out anything that was actually viable down any of these avenues. And the case was getting bigger all the time: two missing persons now too. And an anonymous caller who might get in touch again – Dupin was secretly already waiting for it. He had never had a murder case to solve where there were so many motives.

Without thinking, Dupin had walked down the wooden planks to the beach and to the western tip of the island, which was less than a hundred metres away now, at high tide. He stood still. Right in front of a temporary-looking sign that someone had rammed firmly into the sand on a simple wooden stake. In the middle of nowhere. A hand was sketched on it, throwing a wine bottle into a stylised landscape. There was an oversized red cross through it. It took Dupin a moment to understand. It was a 'don't throw your waste away in the countryside' warning, using the most common rubbish on the islands: an empty wine bottle.

On the left hand side lay one of the famous fields of narcissi that everyone talked about. Nolwenn talked about them too, very happily and at great length. They were at the heart of the regional pride of the Cournouaille (along with several hundred other things). At the beginning of the nineteenth century the pale yellow and creamy white, not even twenty-centimetre tall – Dupin had thought on Penfret last year: very unremarkable – narcissi had been classified for the first time an. In the hundred and fifty years that followed the botanical facts and genealogies had been hotly debated until it was confirmed: yes, of course, it was unique! They only existed here on the Glénan, it was a distinct narcissus species: the Glénan narcissus! After being under threat of extinction for a few centuries, on several islands protected meadows had been designated as strict nature reserves where the flowers flourished splendidly. Two hundred thousand individual flowers, protected by their own society: the *Association for the Prosperity of the Glénan Narcissus*. The locals were especially proud of the flowers' 'mysterious origins'. Apparently, nobody knew exactly where they came from, although it was agreed that the Phoenicians had brought them here as medicinal plants. Admittedly, 'mysterious origins' were more interesting. And more Breton. At the end of April or beginning of May, they bloomed for three or four weeks, forming yellow-white fields –

impressive in their abundance, Dupin had to admit. Unlike the nondescript individual little plants.

Dupin bit into his sandwich. He might almost have forgotten it again. And carried the baguette around the whole time like yesterday, until he'd felt stupid and dropped it discreetly into the waves. Which had proved to be incredibly careless: because the one seagull (a great black-backed seagull to boot) that had been on the spot and pounced on the sandwich a moment later, had turned into a swarm of gulls within seconds, flapping excitedly, screeching, aggressive. Dupin swiftly took to his heels.

Anjela Barrault's suit was opal blue, skin-tight with a metallic sheen. Dupin had never seen a wet suit like it, the long neoprene arms blended seamlessly into the gloves. Only her head was uncovered, the head-piece pulled down and snug around her neck like a poloneck. Around her hips she wore a wide, black belt with several large and small karabiners. Anjela Barrault was not tall and was clearly delicate despite the suit. Her mid-length, wildly tousled hair was different tones and shades of blonde, every strand different, from dark honey blonde to a cool, ashy, Scandinavian blonde.

Dupin was slightly embarrassed, he thought he had looked her in the eye too long and too hard when they had met. Her eyes had looked exactly the same colour and the same dazzling lustre as the wet suit. She was tanned. A mischievous, yet absolutely sincere smile was on her face. She was approximately early forties and insanely attractive. Dupin had resorted to fixing his gaze on the hair at the side of her face. This way, he wasn't rude, he wasn't looking past her and he didn't run the risk of falling under the spell of her eyes again.

'As I said, come with me.'

Dupin couldn't think of a suitable reply. He had been resolute in deciding that he'd had enough boats for one day – for the whole case in fact. For the whole year.

'I...'

'Just hand me the bottle.'

The *Bakounine*, an old fishing boat, was at the end of the long quay, moored in a makeshift way, the bottom half painted a vibrant orangey red, the top half in an equally vibrant light blue. Those were the Breton primary colours that Dupin loved so much: yellow, green, red, blue, everything in rich, warm tones.

Anjela Barrault stood on the boat, which only rocked slightly here in the chamber. Now, at high tide, the deck was at almost the same height as the quay where Dupin stood. Next to him lay a pile of equipment. Wetsuits, weight belts, flippers, masks. And a blue bottle which may not have matched the shade of the wetsuit exactly but came incredibly close. Dupin stooped down and, impressed by its weight, cautiously handed it down to her. There was just a small gap between the quay and the *Bakounine*, between him and the head of the diving centre. But it was two metres deep, the Atlantic lapping below.

'And the other things?'

'Those are for the second boat,' she pointed to a boat at one of the buoys near the quay. 'We have several.'

Dupin still had no idea what to say or do.

'I have to do my rounds. Collect people and bring them to Penfret. So come on.'

Without thinking, Dupin jumped. Anjela Barrault hadn't even waited, she simply untied the two ropes with a few quick movements and proceeded to the wheelhouse with its colossal helm.

'You're going to have to come closer, otherwise we won't understand a word each other is saying.'

Before Dupin could reply, there was a violent vibrating and the menacing sound of a heavy diesel motor starting up. Fountains of water spurted out of the two emission pipes and onto the stern. Dupin was already regretting his reckless leap onto the boat. The *Bakounine* puttered away from the quay in reverse. Dupin approached the wheelhouse uncertainly, the ship's vibrations spreading through his body. He felt a bit embarrassed as he eased himself into the narrow wheelhouse with Madame Barrault. The way she wore it, a suit had very little in common with clothes, in his opinion.

'So you've got to deal with the whole lot of us here now. With us strange beings on this magical archipelago.'

She had pronounced the 'magical' with pointed irony. Dupin had only just managed to make it out, although he was standing very close to her, right in the narrow doorframe in which he'd wedged himself with his elbows.

'I wouldn't like to be in your shoes, Monsieur le Commissaire.'

He couldn't help but smile. Which did him good.

Anjela Barrault was concentrating on putting the boat into drive, which seemed to be giving her some trouble. She gave the helm a hefty smack.

'I love this boat really, but it's really getting on in years.'

Dupin urged himself to concentrate.

'And what do you mean by "strange", Madame Barrault?'

'Oh I mean a lot by that. It's a crazy scrap of earth. The most beautiful I know. But tough. Extremely tough. You're far away from the world here. Far from civilisation. The eighteen kilometres between it and the mainland, the smooth sea today, the mobile reception in this weather, that you can get a coffee here, wine, something to eat – all of that is misleading. It's not a real place – when you're here, you're at sea.'

Anjela Barrault sounded like Leussot had earlier, thought Dupin. He had used very similar expressions. But everyone here did that when it came to the islands and themselves.

'And that makes people strange?'

'Without doubt. But, you already have to be slightly strange to come here in the first place. You don't come here without a reason.'

'What do you mean by that?'

Anjela Barrault shrugged. 'Everyone has their stories here. Their experiences. Their missions. A reason why they're here and not in a more comfortable place.'

'And – could all of this lead to a murder?'

'No, in fact. Things must have gone really wrong. In fact, people's life-paths rarely cross here, even though superficially it looks like they do. In principle, everyone lives their own life, side by side. We don't know much about each other. Often nothing at all about the crucial things. Do you understand?'

This was something Dupin understood surprisingly well, although it was expressed rather unconventionally. It corresponded exactly with his observations.

'Are you hinting at something specific that happened here? At something that you know, or witnessed? Or suspect?'

'No.'

The 'no' had been clear and firm.

'Did you know all three dead men personally?'

'I've never met Pajot. Konan, I know only to see. He came with Lefort.'

'And Lefort?'

'An idiot. Never interested me.'

For some reason the boat had listed hard to port side for a moment. Dupin lost his footing briefly, Anjela Barrault held him firmly by the shoulder. He recovered.

'You never came in contact with him?'

'Never. We didn't even speak to each other. Just said hello.'

Dupin wedged himself more firmly than before in the doorway. It must have looked bizarre.

'Do you know what discovery the three were on the trail of?'

That had been more abrupt than Dupin had intended. Anjela Barault's brow furrowed. She understood immediately.

'There's a lot of money at stake with some of these finds. You should take it seriously. Lots of people here take it seriously.'

'Do you know of anything specific?'

She burst out laughing.

'Then I'd have been involved myself.'

Dupin was intrigued to know what the furrowed brow just now had meant.

'You – are a treasure-hunter?'

'I'm a free diver. And diving instructor. Head of the diving centre. We have fifteen employees, twelve more in the summer, it's a very large operation.'

'Not on the hunt for treasure?'

'Maybe I will happen to find something some time.' She burst out laughing again.

Dupin had been concentrating so hard on the conversation and on staying upright that he had only just noticed they were barely fifty metres away from the island now. He looked around.

'Drénec. We're going to take a group of diving students on board here, then on to Cigogne. Do you see the old restored farmhouse made of stone?' She pointed in the direction of the island with her head.

'It belongs to the sailing school too. Even Drénec was inhabited once and the island is not really that big. People kept on trying, but they never stayed long.'

Anjela Barrault cut back the speed. Dupin now saw a small group of perhaps six or eight people, who were expecting them.

'During the really severe spring tides you can walk here from Saint-Nicolas.'

Dupin looked at the water in amazement. And at Saint-Nicolas. He still had not got used to the fact that the whole water and land issue out here was very unstable and unclear. At the moment, everything between here and Saint-Nicolas looked like nothing but Atlantic.

'With enormously high coefficients of over 115, you can nearly always hike across the whole chamber.'

That was an incredible thought. Dupin fished the *Petit Indicateur des Marées* out of his pocket to check when that would next be the case. He just saw a mass of numbers and understood nothing.

'In the last four decades that has only occurred twelve times. The spring tide yesterday only reached 107.'

'I see.'

'By the way there is a shipwreck up ahead, not deep, you can see it from the boat. A majestic ship. A large Greek brig, the *Pangolas Siosif*. Everyone drowned. 1883.'

Dupin almost have cried out 'where?'

'They wanted to take refuge here in a storm. It was that which proved to be their undoing. That's the Glénan for you. It has happened to so many people. Did you know that the souls and ghosts of the drowned have been gathering in the *Baie de Trépassés* since time immemorial, the "Bay of the Deceased"? And once a year, on all souls' day, they dart over the crests of the waves as fleeting sea spray. White flecks. Even far away from the bay you can hear the ghastly cries.'

Dupin hadn't known this. But it was a good story.

As she spoke, Anjela Barrault had kept her eyes fixed on a particular point ahead of her. Now she began to turn the boat. They were only fifteen metres away from the beach that looked Caribbean here too.

'We can continue our conversation very soon. This won't take long.'

Dupin cautiously loosened his grip on the doorframe and groped his way to the railing.

'I have to make a few calls.'

'Go up to the front, it's not quite as loud there.'

The engine was idling, the water splashing out through the expel pipe.

Anjela Barrault went to the stern and opened up a sort of hatch in the railing with skilful movements. The group of divers had already come over.

Dupin positioned himself in the tapering point of the bow. Behind him lay the bleak, not very large (at high tide) Quignénec and the two little neighbouring islands that closed off the chamber in a south-easterly direction; in front of him, a breathtaking panorama of the whole archipelago. He took out his phone.

'Riwal?'

'I just tried you, chief, you had no reception again. Where are you?'

'Has Le Menn turned up?'

'No.'

'What about the manhunt?'

'The personal description has already gone out on all radio stations. We're pulling out all the stops. We've already spoken to his wife and had her tell us everything. Every ritual. Where he usually gets petrol, drinks coffee, buys his newspapers, everything... Bellec and a colleague are out checking those places right now.'

'And his contact with the three dead men?'

'His wife confirmed that he was Lefort's doctor. And that she remembers him being out with Lefort three or four times in the last year. The last time was at the *Transat Concarneau*. On the day of the regatta opening. In April.'

Dupin remembered it – especially because he couldn't find a parking place for days yet again – it was one of the big festivals in the town. Not as large or significant as the *Festival des Filets Bleus*, but still very big. In the days before the regatta opening, the town was one big fairground with colourful stands and stalls. All of the boats taking part were at the quays, the teams were introduced on signs – great heroes. Hundreds of little pennants adorned the streets of the town centre. You could feel the good mood. It was one of the toughest regattas in the world – from Concarneau, straight across the entire Atlantic to Saint-Barth; the special thing was that all participants were in the exact same boats, there was no advantage in resources, Riwal explained it in detail again every time, extensively: a *Figaro Bénéteau*.

'But his wife doesn't think they were really friends. In fact, sometimes he even distanced himself from Lefort.'

'In what way?'

'He didn't approve of Lefort's behaviour towards women. And recently they were in disagreement when it came to Lefort's new Glénan plans, his wife recalls.'

Interesting. Apparently nobody knew the plans apart from the town council, yet everyone was talking about them.

'Did he have knowledge of these plans?'

'His wife thinks he did, Lefort told him about them a few months ago, apparently.'

'And what exactly did he tell him?'

'She didn't know that.'

'And why was her husband against them?'

'She just knows that he considers them dubious from an ecological point of view.'

'And his relationships with Konan and Pajot?'

'She couldn't say whether he knew Konan and Pajot. If he did, then not well in any case. She said her husband has been very agitated since yesterday. She assumed it was due to the news of Lefort's death.'

'Agitated in what way?'

'He wasn't speaking much, she says, he kept standing up and walking around. Yesterday evening he tried to call someone many times, but he didn't get through. His wife didn't know who it was. Apparently, he was up extremely early today. At six o'clock. An hour earlier than usual.'

'Hmmm.'

'Anything else?'

'No.'

'I want to know who Le Menn has been on the phone to recently, we need the phone records for all of his lines.'

'We'll need to claim that there is danger in delay on this one too. Otherwise we won't get it at this stage,' said Riwal.

'Danger in delay, Riwal. Absolutely.'

'Good. I've just received the report on the search of the three men's houses too. And the boats by the way. Nothing of note has been discovered yet. But we've removed all of their computer hard drives, we're analysing them now.'

'And nothing on the boats? Maps, nautical maps? Nothing remarkable?'

'No. Are we looking for anything in particular?'

'Tell them I want to see all nautical maps if they find any. I want to know whether one, two or all three went repeatedly to particular coordinates at sea recently. No idea how we are meant to find that out. We'll need some luck.'

'Everyone navigates electronically these days…'

'I'm up to speed.'

'You're genuinely thinking about a treasure hunt?'

'I'm thinking about everything that seems possible and impossible.'

'If there's a sunken ship involved, which the three men discovered, and if nobody was meant to know anything about it, then they will have been extremely careful.'

A loud bang made Dupin jump. Anjela Barrault had slammed the hatch in the railing shut and was already on her way back to the wheelhouse. There was a considerable hustle and bustle at the stern, the divers were in the process of stowing their things underneath the narrow wooden seats.

'I'll be in touch again very soon, Riwal. I'm on Drénec.'

'What are you doing on Drénec? Did you not want to speak to Anjela Barrault?'

'I'm on her boat.'

'You're on a boat again?'

'I'll be in touch, Riwal.'

Dupin had almost hung up.

'Wait.'

'Chief?'

'Has Kadeg found outanything about this dispute between the former mayor and Konan, regarding salvaging rights?'

'Bellec made enquiries at the mairie. No documents about any kind of incident were found. And even Monsieur Tanguy didn't know what Muriel Lefort might have meant by that story.'

Dupin sighed deeply.

'Speak to you later, Riwal.'

The diesel engine ramped back up, the low vibrations began again, Anjela Barrault put it into gear and the boat slowly, then more and more clearly, picked up speed.

Dupin groped his way back to the wheelhouse.

'Did you get reception?'

'Yes.'

'It's always the luck of the draw out here.'

'What do you know about the business links between *Medimare* and the *Institut Marine*, Madame Barrault? About conflicts that Leussot and other researchers have with the institute?'

'Nothing really. Just that Leussot and Lefort got into a fight once and it was about that amongst other things. And that the Director of the institute is a nasty character.'

'A fight? Leussot was in a fight with Lefort? An actual, violent altercation?'

'In front of the *Quatre Vents*. About a year ago. Alcohol was probably involved. But that's as much as I know.'

Her gaze seemed more mischievous to Dupin than before.

'Ask Solenn Nuz.'

'Why her?'

'She knows – the most.'

'And this is generally known? This issue of the fight?'

Nobody had mentioned it yet. Everyone out here only seemed to say what suited them in their respective situations.

'I'd say so.'

Dupin again pondered how he could manage to make notes in this position, he needed both arms for stability. He gave up.

'What's your relationship to Monsieur Leussot?'

The question did not seem unwelcome in the slightest.

'Let's put it this way: it was once – clearer, but it hasn't been like that for a long time. We're friends. Most of the time, anyway.'

'I see. Is Leussot also a treasure hunter?'

'Even he definitely takes a look, if something is lying on the seafloor. He's always out on the Atlantic. He has the best of everything when it comes to equipment. The latest technology. Even if it has other functions. Nobody can record the seafloor as precisely as he can.'

Dupin hadn't thought of that but it made sense.

'Is that his boat he goes out in?'

'No, it belongs to the institute. But he's been using it all the time recently.'

'Do you know it?'

'I've never been on it. But Tanguy has, the two of them know each other well.'

Dupin's mobile rang and he took it out with his left hand. He looked at the number, taking great care not to relax his wedged-in elbows. He knew the number from yesterday or today, but couldn't place it.

'Excuse me.'

Now he did ease out of his safety position, walking cautiously to the bow.

'Hello?'

'Muriel Lefort here. Can you hear me, Monsieur le Commissaire?'

'I can hear you, Madame Lefort.'

'Where are you? It's terribly loud where you are, I can hardly make out what you're saying.'

'I'm investigating right now.'

The boat bobbed strangely to and fro, in quick, short movements. For no apparent reason – nothing could be detected at sea which could explain this. It was extremely surprising how diverse and perfectly distinct the unpleasant movements of a boat could be; by this point, Dupin felt he was in a position to formulate a small typology of these movements: there was a rocking, a teetering, a bobbing, swerving, swaying, lurching, wavering...

'There are some – things I'd like to discuss with you in person.'

'Same here. It would be best if I came by later. I'll call you again.'

He desperately needed a coffee. Especially after this second adventure at sea.

'Great. Then I'll expect your call.'

Dupin hesitated for a moment.

'Madame Lefort. I have one quick question. Do you happen to know whether your brother was out at sea particularly often recently?'

'He was always out at sea a lot.'

'I mean...'

'You mean was he hunting for treasure?'

'Yes, that's exactly it.'

'People are saying you think that's a possibility.'

Dupin wanted to ask who was saying what, but left it.

'We are looking into all possibilities.'

'As I said: Lucas has been dreaming about treasure since we were children. Oh God. But I'm not able to give you an answer. I would definitely be the last person he'd have told.'

'I understand. See you later then.'

She had hung up.

At the same moment, Dupin's phone rang again. He took it away from his ear and glanced quickly at the number. Nolwenn.

'Yes?'

'The Prefect wanted to have it confirmed personally by you that the large manhunt operation for Le Menn is of "extraordinary relevance". I've explicitly confirmed everything. You should just know that that's why I called you. An hour ago.'

'I... good.'

'Are you making progress?'

'I don't know. There are lots of figures involved.'

'You don't have to drink the whole sea, even in this case.'

Nolwenn's untiring use of Breton sayings always reassured him – and he was very happy to hear Nolwenn's voice anyway (and, of course, to know that he didn't need to drink the whole sea).

'Do we have access to the three men's accounts? It's important.'

'I think we will very soon. You're quite difficult to understand, Monsieur le Commissaire, where are you right now?'

'On a boat, with Anjela Barrault.'

'You poor thing, on a boat, yet again?'

'Exactly.'

Dupin was now deeply regretting that everyone knew about his little boat phobia.

'Last week there was a big article about Anjela Barrault in the *Télégramme*. She is planning to win back the world championship title this summer.'

'The world championship title?'

The mobile was clamped to his ear again.

'She is a freediver. She has already dived the deepest twice. No other woman has reached a greater depth,' Nolwenn broke off briefly. 'You know what a freediver is?'

'Possibly. A kind of – diver.'

Anjela Barrault had mentioned it herself, but Dupin could not in all honesty have said any more than that.

'Diving without oxygen tanks, as deep as possible. A tough sport.'

Dupin had vaguely heard of it.

'And she is the world champion? Anjela Barrault?'

'A Breton woman. She was a yoga teacher actually. A very attractive woman. Absolutely stunning. She wants to make it to the hundred-metre mark in the summer.'

'A hundred metres?'

'A Breton woman. She will manage it.'

'I see. Nolwenn?'

'Yes, Monsieur le Commissaire?'

'On the boat this lunchtime… we saw dolphins.'

Dupin didn't know how he was getting onto this subject now, which had no place here. It was probably because of the diving.

'Interesting animals. But be careful.'

'Excuse me?'

'Do you not remember Jean Floch? The dolphin who deliberately tore fishing nets and attacked and sank rowing boats, so that the anglers were tossed into the sea? Four years ago, you were still in the capital then, but it went national across all the media. An aggressive maverick, spreading anxiety and fear along the Breton coast. Like a rabid dog. Three hundred kilograms!'

That sounded brutal. Dupin had always had a different impression of dolphins.

'A miracle that he didn't leave any widows or orphans behind. Swimming bans were imposed everywhere in southern Finistère. Then they drove him away with noise. Yes, sexually mature males can sometimes display extreme dominant behaviour and are excluded from the group.'

'They were all very clearly in the group. I mean: it was most definitely a group, not a single animal.'

Dupin had also wanted to say that the aggressive male was certainly the absolute exception and that overall they were peaceable creatures. After all, that was the very thing that they were famous for of all things – but then he left it. This was an absurd conversation in any case.

'Okay. Then let's speak later, Monsieur le Commissaire.'

Nolwenn sounded fully composed.

'Let's.'

She hung up.

Dupin stayed stock still. This was a crazy case. Not just the case itself. Everything.

The *Bakounine* had now come within fifty metres of Cigogne – the island in the middle of the chamber. The fortress, more or less round for the most part, could already clearly be made out. The legendary Fort Cigogne had a pointed, sharp bend in seven places, which is where it got its name ('*seiz kogn*', seven corners in Breton). Now it was used by the sailing school. Corsairs that had found perfect cover on the Glénan were chased out of here in earlier times. The worst of them came from the English island of Guernsey, of course. It was regarded as fact that there were hidden chambers and vaults both in and underneath the fort. Corridors suddenly ending in nothing. People spoke about widely branching secret tunnels underneath the seafloor that you could get to all of the islands through. Seeing the dark, atmospheric fortress, you believed it straight away.

It occurred to Dupin that he hadn't even enquired what 'doing the rounds' meant earlier. There were quite a lot of islands.

The dark band of cloud had pushed closer, it was deep black by now and much wider. That didn't mean anything in Brittany. Even so, Dupin had to admit that he wouldn't have suspected a few hours ago that it would move in their direction at all. You still couldn't class it as proper wind, but the weak draught that was palpable again this afternoon was clearly coming from the opposite direction, from the east. Dupin relaxed. A moment later he was standing in the wheelhouse again. Anjela Barrault greeted him with her bewitching laugh.

'This is an amusing investigation. The way you work, I mean.'

'I... you and Solenn Nuz are friends, I've been told.'

'Very old friends. We went to primary school together. Loctudy.'

'And how did you come to the islands and to this job?'

'You want to hear *my* story?'

She seemed genuinely astonished for the first time.

'I do.'

'After the death of her husband, Solenn Nuz considered buying the diving school. Lefort wanted to take it over. He made a very impressive offer. Likewise Muriel Lefort. She even outbid her brother. I was an amateur diver at the time, a yoga teacher really and before that I had been in Kathmandu for two years. When I came back, I happened to run into Solenn. We arranged to meet. Then she told me about her situation, made me an offer and, in a pub, at two in the morning, I said I'd do it. My then boyfriend had found someone else while I was away and my parents had died shortly before. The way it always is: everything happens at once. Life is chaos, more muddled than a ball of wool.'

Dupin liked the image of the ball of wool. It was very true, he thought.

'That is *my* story in one minute.'

This was expressed without sorrow, without flirtation.

'And then you become a world-class free diver?'

'Believe me. Strictly speaking, it's just a different form of yoga.'

She throttled the engine. They had arrived at her next stop. A small group was waiting on the beach again, this time there were just three divers.

'Just these ones and then off to Penfret. Have you done yoga before?'

Dupin had nothing against yoga, nothing at all, but he was certain that he was the most unsuited person in the whole world when it came to that kind of thing. Yoga, meditation, self-hypnosis, all relaxation techniques. He got nervous just hearing the words. Nobody could be less talented in matters of conscious relaxation. He deliberately ignored the question.

'So Madame Lefort had made Solenn Nuz a very high offer for the diving school?'

Muriel Lefort was more business-minded than he'd thought.

'Yes. She was really serious about it. By the way, since you're so interested in sunken ships: on this side of Cigogne alone there are four, all pirate ships. Immense treasures were found in the wreck of the *Double Revanche* in the thirties. It was buried deep in the sand, amid dozens of lobsters. The lobsters love the wrecks of the old wooden ships. Did you know that the Glénan have a mascot? A lobster, Charlie, over eighty years old. He lives in a wreck not far from the quay on Saint-Nicolas. Everyone knows him. The club set up signs under water at his favourite spots to sit. Every diving newbie has to pay him their respects once.'

She laughed.

'Charlie. There are some videos online,' in more of a scholarly tone she added: 'Lobsters are completely sedentary. A one-hundred-and-forty-year-old lobster was saved from the pot at the last minute recently – it was almost a metre long.'

With a powerful swing, Anjela Barrault turned the steering wheel right around and set the boat to idle. She looked expectantly to Dupin, who took a moment to realise – he was in the way. She wanted to get to the stern of the boat.

'The same procedure as just now.'

Dupin stepped aside and headed for the prow again. He was still occupied by the idea of the one-metre long and one-hundred-and-forty-year-old lobster: so it had been born around 1870, Charlie in at least the 1930s – he was older than Dupin's mother. He was anxious to keep it all abstract. He liked the taste of lobster too much.

His mobile had slid deep into his trouser pocket again. He dialled Goulch's number. The young police officer was on the line immediately.

'Monsieur le Commissaire?'

'Where are you?'

'Still in the docks, at the examination of the Bénéteau. But we'll be done very soon. We've also been able to save map stuff. Ordinary nautical maps, laminated paper. We'll take a good look at them. We haven't been able to find any markings yet.'

'I need you. Go to Monsieur Leussot's boat. He's probably still somewhere near the Moutons, or already on Saint-Nicolas. Take a look at his ship, check what technical equipment and technology he owns which would be suitable for hunting for treasure. And see if you see something that definitely indicates that he's actively – how to phrase this – on a hunt.'

'A proper search, am I understanding you correctly?'

'If need be.'

Even though this way of going about things had – like all the other actions today, in Dupin's opinion – something of a stabbing in the dark quality to it, he wanted to know now. And: even stabbing in the dark could be very effective. So long as he was not stabbing in the wrong direction entirely.

'And then look at Kilian Tanguy, Muriel Lefort and Du Marhallac'h's boats. And the one belonging to the doctor who disappeared, Devan Le Menn. Have I forgotten someone?'

'The Director of the institute? Anjela Barrault?'

'Anjela Barrault?'

'The head of the...'

'I know who she is.'

'She has her own boat too. She often uses it for the diving school.'

'How do you know that?'

'Everyone who is constantly out on the water here knows each other, at least to some extent. They know of each other.'

'I'll take care of that, about Anjela Barrault's boat. I'm having a conversation with her right now.'

'Are you on her boat at the moment?'

If he were honest, he had no idea if it was her boat.

'What kind of boat does she have? What does it look like?'

'A Jeanneau, Cap Camarat, open-topped, maybe seven metres long, an old model, but in good condition, white, recently repainted.'

'Then I'm not on her boat. – So inspect her boat too.'

'Good. I'll head out immediately.'

'And yes – the Director's boat should definitely be searched. And ask around about whether anyone knows of – treasure-hunting activity on the coast here.'

'Madame Barrault would definitely be best placed to know that. Or one of the archaeologists. Or Solenn Nuz.'

'Get in touch if you've got something.'

'Will do, Monsieur le Commissaire.'

Dupin hung up. And took a few deep breaths. It was astonishing, the air smelled and tasted even 'oceanier' today: salt, iodine, magnesium, iron, calcium – and algae. Dupin grinned to himself, he was reminded inevitably of Nolwenn: the health, oh no, the medicinal quality of the Atlantic air was among her favourite topics. 'Like a permanent saltwater bath. The nervous and muscular systems relax, blockages and internal clamps are loosened,' she liked to say. Dupin particularly liked that internal clamps stuff, even though he had no clear idea of what it meant. Of course people ascribed more 'banal' effects to the Atlantic air in general, like the detoxification of the organism, the harmonisation of the metabolism and various healing effects. In the initial period of his 'transfer' it had all seemed like esotericism or druidic healing rituals. But then he had done some research and been very impressed. The proportions of the individual components of the sea in fact corresponded almost exactly with how they were present in the blood and in the tissue fluid in the human body.

When Dupin turned round, he saw that Anjela Barrault was already closing the hatch. The loud bang followed and again she left the divers to their own devices, already making her way back to the wheelhouse.

'Now we'll drop them all off on Penfret. Our spartan accommodation is there.'

A moment later she was standing at the the helm again. And Dupin was in the opening of the wheelhouse once more.

'Are we going back to Saint-Nicolas afterwards?'

Anjela glanced at her impressive diving watch, which she wore over the sleeve of her suit.

'We should be at the quay around five p.m. And then maybe you'd like to go out with me again?'

'You're going out again?'

'The sun only goes down at nine. These are *my* hours.'

She smiled warmly.

'Are you going to be out in *your* boat?'

She wasn't in the least bit put out by Dupin's question.

'No, I'm staying on the *Bakounine*. I would only be wasting time. I just let them out at the quay and keep going.' Without changing her tone she added:

'You're well informed.'

'That's my job.'

'I'm sure you'll want to know whether my boat is suitable for hunting for treasure?'

'Indeed.'

'I have a perfectly normal sonar, but a hideously expensive underwater camera, the latest model. It's crazy. It's five times better than normal cameras. My assistants film me with it when I'm training. But you can only see what the camera lets you see. Things on the sand. On the seafloor. Do you want to look at it?'

'I think that's enough for the time being. It's possible a police officer will still want to take a look at the boat.'

'You really think that these murders are about treasure?'

'We'll see.'

'Did you always want to be a police officer?'

Anjela Barrault had asked this question in the same mild tone of voice that she had been using the whole time.

'I think so, although I never used to think about it. My father was a police officer. He died when I was six.'

Dupin had answered without thinking and was surprised he'd done so. It wasn't his way, talking about himself. Especially not on a case.

'What do you think happened here on the islands, Madame Barrault?'

Dupin was trying hard for a serious tone.

'Maybe it didn't happen on the islands at all.'

'What do you mean?'

'Maybe it involved things from the outside that have nothing to do with the people here. Perhaps it was a coincidence that this was where it happened.'

Dupin found this answer only marginally more comprehensible than the first one.

'Specifically?'

'I don't know. They must be terrible things. So much destruction.'

Dupin needed to bring the conversation back down to earth a little.

'And Lefort's tourist plans?'

Anjela Barrault laughed scornfully. More mischievously scornful than he would have thought her capable.

'Oh yes. His great plans. His great playground.'

'Do you know the new plans?'

'Nobody knows them yet. Except the amorphous bureaucrats from Fouesnant. I don't even believe in any *new* plans. They're always the same ones.'

'The mayor?'

'The mayor.'

'And what do you think?'

'About what exactly?'

'How do you view the idea of expanding the sailing school, the diving school – and tourism on the Glénan?'

'It's a big joke. A terrifying joke at the same time. I would rather the islands got swallowed up by the Atlantic. Which will happen very soon anyway, if the sea level keeps going up. This little bit of stone and sand.'

'You don't think that it can be carried out in an ecological way?'

'Bullshit.'

Anjela Barrault made no move to answer in more detail. She turned her head and looked Dupin firmly, almost sternly, in the eye. A moment later she looked ahead intently again. They had arrived at their destination. Penfret. They were right at the 'whale skeleton', the massive, still fully intact wooden frame of a mighty old ship that had run aground here, whose planks had decayed little by little, but whose solid wooden scaffolding still towered up out of the sand. Dupin knew it from last year.

As the divers got out, he let his gaze sweep over the island. The basic accommodation was visible, scattered far apart, low wooden cabins. They stood in close squares of four, there were perhaps twenty in total. They extended from the beach to the middle of the island where the ruins of the old farmhouses from the nineteenth century stood, which Henri had showed him last year. They were in fact absolutely normal houses, Dupin thought. To the right of the farmhouses stood two taller, two-storey wooden cabins. This was where the temporary canteens and bars, as well as the entertainment rooms were. Youth hostels were luxurious in comparison, Dupin had been impressed. The island was towered over by the famous white-painted lighthouse with the glowing red glass whose 175th birthday had been celebrated last year, by decorating it with festive bunting. It rose up out of the roof of a large stone house where the lighthouse keepers had lived with their families in days gone by. Nolwenn had told him some of the tragic stories that had grown up around the lighthouse. Only one had stayed with Dupin. And still gave Dupin a slight shiver. One day the glasshouse's red light shattered in a blustery storm and a new one had been installed in a huge rush to avoid accidents, but only white glass had been available. In the weeks that followed, four ships full of people had capsized on the archipelago. People had thought the lighthouse's white light was the lighthouse on Penmarc'h and during the night or in bad weather, navigation had gone terribly wrong. Hundreds of people had died. A terrible story.

Voices could be heard from the stern. He heard Anjela Barrault saying 'see you tomorrow' many times. It sounded warm each time.

Dupin felt dizzy. He probably had for a while now, but he had been distracted during the journey. For a moment he was so dizzy he was afraid he would lose his balance. Or stumble, fall. The boat was bobbing, but Dupin's feeling went far beyond than that. The sea itself seemed to be swaying. A great, sweeping swaying. He had instinctively taken hold of the railing with both hands and was holding on with all his strength. He tried to keep his gaze riveted on a fixed point on the island.

But what gave him a shock yet again was: the bang when Anjela Barrault slammed the hatch in the railing shut, clearly with even more force than before. It sounded like a gunshot. Dupin jumped. Yet the small fright helped him more than deep breathing.

He needed to distract himself.

Dupin went back to the wheelhouse. The boat was picking up speed, the vibrations going right through him, making his bones resonate right down to smallest one.

'What else do you want to know? We'll be at Saint-Nicolas any moment.'

As though to prove it she ramped up the engine to the maximum, along with the noise and vibration.

'That Sunday evening in the *Quatre Vents* – do you remember what time you arrived?'

'Your inspector has already asked me that too. Quarter to nine.'

'And did anything unusual strike you then? At about this time, someone was presumably slipping the sedative to Lefort and Konan.'

'I was sitting at the bar. I didn't even notice them properly. Most of the time I was talking to Solenn's older daughter. We get on very well. And to Solenn's father-in-law, Pascal.'

Dupin had clean forgotten him.

'He doesn't talk much.'

'No.'

'What did you talk about?'

'About a few strange currents there have been recently.'

'Strange currents?'

'Yes, oddly strong currents right at the western and southern exits from the chamber that immediately try and drag you southwards to the open sea. Now that it's spring tide. We're familiar with currents like these at coefficients of 120, but always towards the land. Now suddenly they're tugging you towards the open sea.'

'So you didn't particularly notice anything that evening?'

'No.'

'Who else was at the bar?'

'Oh God, it's always chaos there. Maela Menez. She's tough. But wonderful. I like her. I think a few diving students too. Louann Nuz. Armelle Nuz. I stayed a long time. Most people left before the storm got going. I don't like to be alone in thunderstorms like that,' this was very confidently expressed. 'Later, I sat by myself, most of the time.'

'The two Nuz daughters state you were already there around quarter past eight.'

Something flickered in her eyes for a brief moment.

'This is like an old crime novel. Poisoned drinks, a group of strange folks stranded on an island.'

Dupin looked intently at her.

'Then the two of them were simply mistaken. I can't tell you any more than that.'

'What do you mean by "Madame Menez is tough"?'

'Relentless. Unyielding. She has completely internalised the old values of the sailing school. She marches fearlessly into every battle for them. But with an open visor. She works day and night.'

'Which battles?'

'The one with Lefort for instance.'

It all sounded a bit vague to Dupin's ears, he wasn't sure if that was intentional.

'She shows the feelings that Muriel Lefort holds back. Muriel is always composed.'

'What feelings are these?'

'Hate. They are familiar with that.'

'You mean she truly hated Lucas Lefort?'

'It was no secret.'

'How close are you to Muriel Lefort?'

'We get on well. Even if you couldn't say that we are friends. We women have to stick together out here. Solenn, Muriel and I. Muriel represents something big. She takes it seriously.'

'And Muriel *hated* her brother too?'

'Deeply. She always wanted to buy him out – and he wanted to buy her out. Both of them thought: at some point the other one will give in. Only Muriel suffered. He had his fun. And trampled on all that was sacred to her.'

'Do you know of a man in her life?'

Dupin himself didn't know how he'd got onto this topic.

'No. The women here live without men. Without fixed men. We're almost there by the way.'

He looked ahead. The quay was in fact not much further.

'I wanted...'

Dupin heard his mobile amongst the loud engine noise as though it was coming from far away. He dared to relax his wedged position in the door. It was Riwal.

'They've found Le Menn's car, chief.'

'Where?'

'In the big car park in Sainte-Marine, at the harbour, not very far from his house. His boat is missing. He owns a Merry Fisher by Jeanneau, nine metres twenty-five, a popular boat here on the coast.'

Inspector Riwal was – of course – a boat expert too. Along with his 'druidic' streak, he also had a practical and very well-developed interest in technology.

'So he's out in his boat?'

'Looks like it. So shall we call off the manhunt?'

'No. We don't have Le Menn yet.'

'But he's at sea.'

'Let's wait it out, Riwal. It could be a different story. Perhaps he's trying to trick us. Maybe he has gone ashore somewhere else. In Fouesnant or Concarneau. Or he went up the Odet and left his boat behind there. If he were on the run, that wouldn't be implausible.'

'You're right,' Riwal's pondering was almost audible. 'So you definitely suspect Le Menn then?'

'I suspect everyone right now. Especially if someone was at the scene of the crime at the time it was being committed and disappears the next morning.'

'Or, he is another victim.'

Dupin answered with some hesitation.

'Or, he is another victim.'

'I'll inform the coastguard.'

'Please do. And – Riwal?'

'Yes.'

'There was something else I'd forgotten just now: find out when our biologist, Leussot, is going to get back on land. Whether he's coming to Saint-Nicolas. I would like to hear from him firsthand what happened with the fight between him and Lefort and why he didn't say anything about it.'

'Will do.'

Dupin hung up and only now did he notice that the *Bakounine* had already moored at the quay. Thirty metres away from Riwal. Anjela Barrault was standing at the railing and looking in his direction. Having been able simply to jump onto the boat earlier, he would just have to climb up some rungs of the rusty iron ladder now.

'Thank you for your help, Madame Barrault. That information was important.'

'Only you can judge that.'

The smile that crossed her face at this sentence was even more entrancing than before. She was fully aware of its effect.

'Enjoy the diving, deep below the water.'

'I'm not going to go that deep today.'

'Speak to you very soon.'

That sounded more definite than Dupin had intended.

'It would be a pleasure.'

Dupin considered offering Madame Barrault his hand to shake, but then simply climbed up the ladder.

Even from a distance, Dupin could see that Kadeg was sitting next to Riwal at the 'operations table'. Dupin headed straight for the bar and left the two inspectors to their own devices. Which prompted baffled looks.

He was in desperate need of a coffee. And a large glass of water. After leaving the *Bakounine*, he had suddenly been overcome by the strong feeling that the world, although he now had solid ground underfoot, was swaying even more violently than on the boat. The dizziness had been more severe than the attack before. The older of the two Nuz daughters served him in a friendly way and started a conversation, but Dupin was not in any condition to show any interest. He was concentrating intently on regaining his balance. He ordered two coffees, drank one immediately standing up and moved very, very slowly and carefully through the bar with the second one and the glass of water, making for the two inspectors outside.

Kadeg seemed to have been staring at the entrance to the bar. As soon as Dupin emerged from the door, he leapt up and came hurrying over.

'The helicopter just dropped me off. We have come across a range of controversial information during the searches – the hard drives were conclusive,' Kadeg was too quick and too eager for Dupin to have been able to interrupt him. 'I had been trying to reach you, but it was always engaged. I wanted to speak to you directly. There are more companies owned by Pajot, some of which Konan was involved in. As an investor. One is a consortium belonging to the two them – and guess who else was involved and what the purpose of it was!'

This was how Kadeg was when he had *tracked something down*. Dupin was not in the mood for this over-enthusiasm. He sat down. Of course it had only been a rhetorical guessing game – after a short, dramatic pause, Kadeg came straight to the point.

'They set up a consortium for the development of tourism in the Glénan, which in turn has shares in Lefort's business.'

That really was an interesting piece of news. Dupin drank the second coffee. In small, but quick sips, so as not to burn his mouth again. He didn't know whether it would be good for him in this very unpleasant state, seasickness did have something to do with the stomach – but Georges Dupin essentially believed caffeine capable of anything. A medical miracle of course.

'What is the company called?'

'*Les Glénan vertes*. 'The Green Glénan. That was Lefort's new project. And there's even better to come.'

Another dramatic pause.

'It was extremely complicated to find out. They made every effort imaginable to cover it up. With numerous accounts and sub-accounts. An expert from Rennes had to take a look. Then I went through it with him, painstakingly. He obviously couldn't make out the hidden meaning.'

'What, Kadeg?'

'Transfers were made from one of Pajot's accounts to Du Marhallac'h twice, each for over thirty thousand euro, nine months ago and six months ago.'

Dupin was immediately alert, the dizziness completely vanished. He didn't say a word. Because his thoughts were racing – and because he did not want to show he was impressed by Kadeg. 'The transfers were marked "architect's services". We haven't found anything yet about any services rendered in any records or on the computers.'

'Architect's services?'

Riwal chimed in:

'Du Marhallac'h is an architect actually. He has had his own office for twenty-two years. But since he has been mayor, he has only worked as an architect occasionally. Before that he must have been extremely successful, he got commissions all along coast.'

Riwal's brother was an architect, just like Dupin's sister. He was well informed.

'Good.'

Dupin leant back. He himself didn't know what he meant by 'good'. It was clear from Kadeg and Riwal's faces: they didn't know either. It was getting more and more odd. He was familiar with this of course. Sometimes there were several substantial leads in a case, but normally a proportion of them cooled down over the course of the investigation, suddenly or gradually. The opposite was the case here – more and more kept cropping up.

'What about the director, Kadeg – and the institute? The deals between the institute and *Medimare*?'

That's what the searches had really been about for Dupin.

'The experts are still working on that. So far, all of the files look normal. On paper at least. We also have not found any suspicious transactions or anything like that yet.'

'And the deals involving Leussot's research?'

'Nothing unusual there either. At this point we have identified four such cases. Depending on what dodgy stuff went on, it will be difficult to impossible to prove anything actionable.'

Kadeg was all too openly enjoying explaining how Dupin's lead had so far come to nothing.

'Kadeg. You head off straight away. I want you to drive to Du Marhallac'h and grill him. Properly.'

'But I've only just arrived and along with Riwal, I wanted...'

'Tear him apart, Kadeg.'

From the gleeful flicker in Kadeg's eyes, it was clear that Dupin had now hit upon the right choice of words.

'All right.'

'This is corruption. And I want watertight evidence of it. The whole story. They bought him. No way did he just want to *simply examine them with an open mind*.'

Again, Dupin was proved right in his prejudices towards politicians – pathetically, it was sad.

'I'd also be interested to know how far along the plans for the development of the islands really were. What stage were they at? They must be on Lefort's laptop, Kadeg.'

'We've already found them there, but we haven't been able to take a look yet.'

'"Architect's services". – We're going to nail him!'

No matter how much he tried, Dupin couldn't manage to savour the moment properly. So far, the search had been anything but a triumph. He had wanted to get his hands on something against the Director of the institute. Above all: he wanted to solve the murder case. Besides, he was responsible for making use of the last resort in investigative tools, based on the vague hint of a mystery caller.

Kadeg leapt up, full of energy.

'The helicopter is still here. I'll hurry.'

'Be rough, Kadeg.'

At these words, Kadeg turned to Dupin with a look confident of triumph and an irrefutable sense of having the case in hand.

Dupin and Riwal sat together for a few minutes longer and had a discussion. Dupin made it brief, he wanted to speak to Muriel Lefort as soon as possible.

By now the press had arrived too of course, they were long since overdue. 'The press' meant the two chief reporters from the *Finistère-Sud*-editorial department at *Télégramme* and *Ouest France*. The old, well-loved and although not exactly tall, still practically round Drollec, a real gourmand, and the delicate, intellectual, mid-thirties Donal with her stylishly angular black glasses (Dupin liked the unusual duo somehow). They often turned up together out of necessity, whenever there was 'something big' going on. Both of them were very much people of few words, but when they met like this they were obviously not unpleasant to each other either. As if they had agreed to abandon the attempts to be 'the first' in order to get all the more information together. Their arrangement which, in the end, always led to a tie between the two papers, didn't work badly, Dupin had to admit. Right now, they were at the spot where the bodies had been found on Le Loc'h.

Dupin approached the ugly triangular houses via the same path as the day before, looking as he did so at the same breathtaking panorama beneath the still predominantly deep Atlantic-blue sky. Yet everything was different from yesterday.

Dupin noticed that Muriel Lefort's house was not in as good condition as her brother's, the roof was covered in moss, it must have been a while since its last coat of paint. As at Lucas Lefort's, you had to walk once around the house to get to the entrance. Even Muriel Lefort's garden consisted mainly of bushy lawn. Two camellia bushes, which had definitely never got very big or beautiful, stood a little sadly at the edge.

After a quick ring on the doorbell, Muriel Lefort opened the door. Her hair was dishevelled, her face severe, even narrower than before. Instead of the unconventional tweed skirt with the tight blouse, today she was wearing jeans and a wide, light blue tunic, which, oddly, did not make her appearance seem more casual. Dupin had an impression of old-fashionedness, a slight stiffness, and it didn't stem from the clothing.

'I'm glad you're here, Monsieur le Commissaire.'

She really did seem relieved.

'Of course. As I said, I have a series of questions for you too.'

Deep creases appeared on her forehead, which she didn't try to hide.

'Where should I begin?' It was clear that she was finding talking difficult. It took a moment before she was able to go on.

'I have to tell you something,' she broke off again. 'Maela Menez had an affair with my brother,' she sounded dramatic and downcast in equal measures now, 'seven years ago. She tried to keep it quiet, but of course I noticed.'

Muriel Lefort looked at the floor in embarrassment. They were still standing in the doorway, which she only seemed to realise now.

'Sorry – I didn't mean to be rude. Please do come in.'

Dupin didn't react at first. Then he stepped inside.

'Your assistant had an affair with your brother?'

That would never have crossed his mind. Madame Lefort led Dupin to the small suite of four armchairs right in front of the large panorama window that looked out on the terrace.

'I'm terribly sorry that I didn't tell you earlier, I'm finding this extremely unpleasant. The affair went on for months in fact.'

'And then it just finished?'

'Yes. She swore it to me. And I would have noticed, believe you me. She ended it. She almost collapsed when I confronted her, she was absolutely hysterical. She had embarked on this relationship even though she knew that it was not the same thing for her as it was for him.'

'What do you mean by that?'

'She was truly in love. And he wasn't interested in her in the slightest.'

'Your brother was the embodiment, if I understand correctly, of the opposite of Madame Menez's convictions in every respect, which are apparently very clear and strict.'

Dupin himself had enough experience to know that this didn't make any difference.

'It was a betrayal. Yes.'

The harsh word contrasted oddly with the way in which Madame Lefort had uttered it, almost off-handedly.

'Has there been any kind of contact between the two of them since then that went beyond business? Did something happen recently?'

'No. Nothing at all. She assured me that there had been no incidents of any kind since. No scandal, nothing. I believe her.'

'She didn't write to him, didn't try to talk to him?'

'No. We didn't even talk about it any more after a certain point. It was as if it had never happened. I think there was a tacit agreement between us on that.'

There was nothing unforgiving in her tone, in fact it was almost sympathetic.

'And what do you personally think about this affair?'

'Me?'

She seemed surprised. 'I was really hurt by it, as I'm sure you can imagine.'

Dupin wasn't sure whether this whole thing was so unpleasant for Muriel Lefort because she might be making Madame Menez suspicious in the eyes of the police by sharing it, or because she assumed that she herself was becoming more suspicious because she had held back this information until now. A long pause developed. Dupin wanted to let her talk. Muriel Lefort looked like there was something else she wanted to say. But nothing more followed.

'Thank you for sharing this. I don't know myself whether this story is relevant, but I am keen to gather as much information as possible about each person in a case as tangled as this one.'

She was still silent.

'You spoke of several points on the phone.'

'Yes.'

She sounded more composed now, Dupin's support seemed to be working.

'I wanted to tell you in person that I will profit hugely from the death of my brother. I was informed this afternoon that Lucas didn't make a will and that I will therefore inherit everything. We still have the same notary, he and I. So the sailing school and the properties will belong solely to me.'

These sentences practically came gushing out of her. She had looked Dupin right in the eye as she spoke. He tried to remain outwardly indifferent.

'Your inspector had already asked me about it twice.'

'We work together very closely.'

'I don't know whether you've also already found out that I offered to buy my brother out of his stake in the Glénan several times. Absolutely nonsense offers.'

'I already know that too.'

She looked anxiously and expectantly at him.

'I think that would indeed be a perfect motive: my brother sets sail drunk, in boundless hubris, during a gathering storm at sea and suffers a shipwreck – nobody would have been surprised. Everyone knew how arrogant he was. And the sailing school belongs to me the next day.'

Dupin was silent. A silence that Muriel Lefort couldn't stand for long.

'What do you think, Monsieur le Commissaire?'

'That would have been nearly a perfect murder, yes. Coincidence had other ideas.'

'Am I a suspect?'

'Yes, you are.'

Madame Lefort was silent now. It was a weighty silence, her facial features had become shapeless. Her voice cracked.

'I didn't hate my brother, believe me,' she was speaking very softly now, 'but I disdained him. Yes. And fought with him. Because he would have destroyed my parents' work if he had been able to, their great ideas. My parents were both in the Résistance as young people. They chose the Glénan for themselves and their lives in the spirit of their group and wanted to pass on this spirit through the sailing and the school. They believed in something, risked their lives for it. This is their legacy. That's what they and everything that they were, stood for. They never wanted to make a business out of it. Even when more and more people came from all over and they realised that you could earn a lot of money from it.'

'You don't just inherit the part of the sailing school that belonged to your brother, you also inherit the land – more than half of Saint-Nicolas, if I'm not mistaken and the islands of Cigogne and Penfret?'

Dupin deliberately posed his question nonchalantly.

'Yes.'

He looked at her. As neutrally as possible.

'And not only would you have disposed of your brother. In one fell swoop you would have got rid of everyone who threatened all of this here.'

'Yes. My motives must seem stronger and stronger to you.'

'That's true.'

'We're definitely talking a good – about sixty or eighty million euro all told.'

'And, did you do it, Madame Lefort?' Dupin asked calmly.

Muriel Lefort's eyes twitched for a moment, a twitch that spread over her entire face.

'No.'

'Did you know that your brother founded a company especially for the new plans? *Les Glénans vertes*? And that Pajot and Konan had a consortium that wanted to have a stake in this firm?'

Muriel was visibly confused. By the change of subject too.

'No. I didn't know anything about that.'

'How much was known about these new plans here on the archipelago then?'

'Nothing at all, I don't think. Lucas was aware that everyone here would have been against them – irrespective of exactly how the plans looked now. Even back when he submitted them the first time, everyone was against them in the end. Even though he did manage to make a few people fall for it at the beginning.'

'Who fell for it back then?'

'Several people, but at some point they saw through him. At first he pretended he wanted to save the sailing school and our whole world out here. He said that there was interest 'from outside' in investing in the Glénan and developing tourism. Solenn Nuz and her husband were fully on board at first and Kilian Tanguy, but then they swiftly and categorically distanced themselves. They originally thought everything would happen in a kind of collective. Like in the sailing school. Lucas had conveyed it like that. But then it became clear that they were simply to invest in his business and that he was planning to exploit the archipelago, which would have destroyed everything. Konan was already on board back then too. Plus Lucas was able to produce two further investors from the mainland, whom he lost again equally quickly. – The more famous he became as a sailor, the more he was in contact with all of these people.'

'And Devan Le Menn, the doctor – was he on board too?'

'Yes, he was one of the two.'

'Did he stay on board when the others turned away?'

'I couldn't tell you.'

'Was he already a friend of your brother's back then?'

'He had been his doctor for a long time. Lucas had a few serious accidents, mostly through recklessness and sometimes he only just escaped with his life. He liked to sail in severe storms. Le Menn patched him up over and over again. He also mentored him as a competitive sportsman. At some point they became friends. I don't know how close the friendship was.'

Dupin wondered whether he should tell her about Le Menn's disappearance.

'Did anything in particular strike you in relation to Le Menn recently?'

Madame Lefort looked at him, at a loss.

'No. But I don't see him often either.'

'He was also in the *Quatre Vents* on Sunday evening, if only briefly. Like you.'

Dupin had also said this in a deliberately neutral tone.

'I didn't see him. I was probably already gone by then. Or else he was.'

'We don't know...'

Dupin's mobile, which had been quiet for an unusually long time, shrilled loudly. It was Riwal.

'Excuse me a moment, Madame Lefort.'

Dupin answered the call.

'One of the helicopters has found Le Menn's boat. It's on the south coast of Brilimec. On the side facing the open sea. It's one of the smaller islands. Diagonally on the beach, so he must have got there hours ago, when it was still high tide.'

Riwal's voice was almost cracking.

'Hello? Hello, chief?'

Dupin was silent. This was serious news. It took him a few seconds to compose himself.

'Call Goulch. He can't be far away on the *Bir*. He's to pick us up straight away. We are going to Brilimec. Let's meet at the quay.'

'When?'

'Now.'

A quarter of an hour later Dupin found himself on a boat for the third time already that day, hurtling across the waves at top speed once more. This time he was so wrapped up in his thoughts that he barely took any notice. Things were escalating – whatever it was that was going on here.

Dupin was standing in the bow. He could feel the tension throughout his body and he was in a grim, determined mood. Riwal was positioned diagonally behind him. They stared, spellbound, at Brilimec, nowdirectly ahead of them. Neither really noticed that they kept getting hit by sea spray.

They began toscan the teardrop-shaped island carefully. Brilimec was barely a hundred and fifty metres long and absolutely overgrown with thick, scraggy grasses. In a few places the grasses soared to about ten metres – which was quite a lot for the archipelago – and some powerful and bizarre granite rock formations towered steeply upwards. At the wider end of the island stood an abandoned house, of which only the roof could be made out from the ship.

'I'll drive around the island, to Le Menn's boat,' called Goulch.

Suddenly something occurred to Dupin. He turned to Riwal.

'I need to know something.'

He had to shout.

'Yes?'

'Who do we have on Saint-Nicolas?'

'Only one person at the moment. Philippe Le Coz.'

'I need to speak to him straight away.'

Dupin moved into the stern and waited for Goulch to throttle the engine a little, because they had almost rounded the island. They could see Le Menn's boat clearly from here.

'Le Coz?'

'Monsieur le Commissaire, is that you?'

'Yes.'

'I can't hear you very well at all.'

Dupin shouted even more loudly into the phone.

'I want to know where everyone is right now. Do you hear me? Muriel Lefort, Madame Menez, the mayor, Leussot, Tanguy. Also Madame Barrault and Solenn Nuz. Call all of them immediately. Verify what they say. However you can. Have Bellec come and help you straight away.'

'I…'

'Straight away. And the Nuz daughters too. I need to know this about all of them.'

'Absolutely, Monsieur le Commissaire.'

'Keep in touch.'

Dupin hung up. He was already putting his phone away in his jacket when he hesitated and pressed redial.

'Something else, Monsieur le Commissaire?'

'I also want to know where they spent the day today. In great detail. Everyone. The last few hours. What they did. On the islands, or wherever they were.'

Goulch had throttled back the engines but Dupin accidentally screamed the last sentence, staring intently at Le Menn's boat, which looked absurd, lying so far up a small patch of beach.

'Do you have anything specific in mind?'

'No. I just need to know this about everyone.'

'Understood.'

Dupin hung up again and this time he stuffed his mobile deep into his pocket.

The engines died. It was perhaps fifty metres to the shore, the anchor was dropped, the two young police officers, were already in the process of lowering the dinghy with perfectly synchronised movements and a moment later they were coming aground on the beach at considerable speed. There was a severe jolt. The two police officers leapt out of the dinghy immediately and Dupin climbed after them, warning them: 'We have no idea what's going on here. Be careful.'

He pulled his gun out of his belt, a 9mm Sig Sauer, the national police-issue weapon. The others copied him.

The small group approached the boat quickly.

'Police de Concarneau – hello? Is anybody there? Please give a sign.'

No reaction of any kind.

The two young police officers climbed onto the Merry Fisher immediately. Riwal, Goulch and Dupin positioned themselves, without saying a word, next to it. The dazzlingly white boat, with dark blue just on the lower part of the hull, seemed surprisingly large to Dupin up close. There was nothing remarkable visible on deck.

'We're going in.'

The young officers' excitement was clear. They opened the door to the cabin and a moment later disappeared.

Still no one said a word. Dupin thought it was taking quite a long time for the pair to report back.

'There's nothing out of the ordinary here.'

Their voices were muffled.

'Come back out. We'll search the island.'

Dupin practically growled. He turned to Riwal and Goulch much more quietly.

'Riwal, you go clockwise. Goulch, you anti-clockwise. I'll take the abandoned house, we'll meet there. Goulch, tell your two colleagues to guard the boat.'

Dupin and Riwal set off straight away. Goulch waited.

First, Dupin had to scale a few tall granite rocks leading to a kind of plateau which fell gently away to the middle of the island after a few steps, where the terrain was relatively flat. That's where the house stood. It was possible to make it out clearly even from the plateau. Dupin stood still and looked around with a keen eye. To the left of the plateau Goulch was moving fast and nimbly over the stones close to the water, while a little further ahead, Riwal was walking on the right hand side of the island.

The house stood there inconspicuously, in complete silence. There was no one in sight. Dupin went ahead carefully, his gun grasped tightly in his right hand. He had to watch his step, the ground was uneven. He approached the house from behind. A small window was roughly boarded up with wooden slats. The slate roof on the other hand still seemed to be in astonishingly good condition, although covered in moss. The house was made of stone, built in the typical style for the region. It looked considerably more battered than the roof. Small pieces had broken off the walls in several places.

Dupin moved carefully around the house so that he was diagonally across from the front door. He waited there until Riwal and Goulch joined him.

'Nothing of note, no footprints, nothing.'

'Same here.'

Instinctively, Riwal and Goulch were speaking quietly.

'Let's take a look at the house.'

Dupin walked towards the door.

'Monsieur Le Menn?'

Dupin had called out loudly, insistently.

'Are you there, Docteur Le Menn?'

And again: 'Docteur Le Menn – this is Commissaire Dupin from the Commissariat de Police Concarneau.'

Riwal and Goulch were following half a step behind Dupin and almost collided with him when he suddenly stopped dead. They both followed his gaze. A broken padlock lay on the ground. The door, repaired in a makeshift way with two large wooden slats, was ajar.

All three remained motionless.

'We're going in.'

Dupin got his gun into position and gave the door a powerful kick, so that it burst open with a tremendous bang. A moment later he was inside and immediately leapt to the wall on his right.

'Commissariat de Police – is there anyone here?'

It was almost dark. It took a while for Dupin's eyes to adjust to the dusky light and for him to be able to make out details.

The room was empty, dust lay centimetres deep on the broken wooden floorboards. On the left hand side there was a passageway where a door once used to be. There were clear footprints in the dust. Several. They led into the other room. Riwal and Goulch had come in too and were standing shoulder to shoulder next to him, guns at the ready. Dead silence, nothing to be heard apart from their breathing.

'The other room,' Dupin whispered.

Again he went ahead, slowly, the gun pointed at the passageway, pausing for a brief moment as though to summon his strength and then making an impressive lunge into the adjoining room. Riwal and Goulch followed suit.

Here too: nothing. No one. No Devan Le Menn. In contrast to the front room, furniture was piled up here, including the remains of two tables and a wardrobe. Riwal and Goulch suddenly had torches in their hands. Goulch stooped down to the blurry prints that could also be seen here in the layer of dust. They hadn't uttered a word so far.

'There were at least two people, I think. Maybe three, it's hard to say. More than one anyway. We need forensics, we should move very carefully now. And somebody presumably stood here,' Goulch pointed to a spot next to the tower of furniture.

'Yes, call forensics. Tell them to come immediately.'

René Reglas, the greatest forensic expert in the world. Dupin shuddered at the thought of his pompous 'crime scene work'. But there was no way round it.

'I've already given them advance warning.'

Goulch left the room. Riwal looked around systematically with his torch, without moving from the same spot.

'This is bizarre. Where is Le Menn? He came to the island on his boat, but he's not here. How did he get away? Who else was here? And why did he come here anyway?'

Dupin didn't know whether Riwal was talking to himself or to him.

'Let's search the beaches again. Perhaps we'll find traces after all. A second boat must have landed somewhere. If Le Menn hasn't disappeared into thin air, then he must have left the island on that second boat! I want to know what happened here!'

Dupin was furious. Although he didn't know who or what with. With himself most likely.

'Such bullshit. This just doesn't make sense.'

All of this had happened right under his nose. Perhaps even this afternoon when he had been waltzing around the islands on board the *Bakounine*. Less than a kilometre away as the crow flies.

'Let's go.'

Dupin wanted to get out this stuffy dungeon. He left the stone house quickly and only stopped once he was a few metres away. Riwal and Goulch followed him. Silently, to be on the safe side.

In front of the house, about fifty metres away, was the island's largest beach. Just before the sand, there was a kind of wall made from rounded granite blocks. Dupin headed for the beach. He came to a stop above the granite blocks, then squeezed between two of them and walked in tiny steps along the high tide mark. Nothing. Nothing to be seen. Not even the beginnings of a lead.

Goulch and Riwal hadcaught up with him.

'If there was a second boat here, it definitely landed on the other side of the island, not here in the chamber. Whoever was here, he certainly didn't want to be seen. Let's go back. Maybe the others have actually found something,' Dupin said in a strained voice.

Goulch and Riwal nodded.

They walked back, past the house, up the gentle slope until they arrived back at the plateau. Apart from the beach directly in front of them, where Le Menn's boat and their dinghy lay, they could see three more small beaches from up here.

'Come on, Goulch, we'll take the beaches to the left, Riwal, you take the one on the right.'

They climbed carefully down the steep rocks.

Goulch and Dupin hadn't reached the first of the two adjacent beaches when they heard Riwal calling.

'Over here! – Over here!'

They turned on their heels.

Half a minute later, both of them were standing, panting, next to Riwal, who was on a narrow beach surrounded by flat rocks. The two young police officers had joined them.

Riwal had crouched down and was inspecting the sand in front of him.

'There are footprints here. Up ahead here, prints of a person running in this direction,' he pointed a little to the left, 'and there, of two people moving in our direction.'

It was clear. Dupin stood up and followed the tracks. They led towards the water and vanished where the sand was still damp from the high tide. On the other side they ended at a field of small stones. The big rocks began beyond it, which didn't rise quite so steeply upwards here.

Dupin ran a hand roughly through his hair.

'Le Menn really did come alone. As did a second person. For whatever reason, they spent some time together in the abandoned house and then left the island on the second person's boat.'

'Maybe they were at a different part of the island too.'

Dupin and Goulch stared at Riwal.

'What do you mean by that?'

'Well, maybe they weren't just in the house. Maybe the house wasn't the main reason for coming to the island at all. Maybe they – or one of the two – were looking for something? Burying something or digging it up?'

'What makes you think that?'

Dupin was irritated.

'I don't know,' Riwal's gaze swept over the water, he was murmuring now. 'What happens on the islands does not always conform to reality as we know it. We've known that for a long time.'

Dupin sighed.

'Forensics should take a look at the house – and search the whole island. Thoroughly. I have to make a call.'

He walked a few metres away. He needed to speak to Le Coz. To know what he thought he already knew anyway. He dialled the number. Nothing happened. He tried again. Again the connection went dead. He gaped at the screen. And went back to the group.

'Riwal, we've got no reception.'

There was real accusation in his voice and he couldn't suppress it.

'That happens on the islands.'

'This cannot be happening!'

This was no way to work.

'Unfortunately I wouldn't even know who to radio.'

It was impossible to have comprehensive conversations over radio anyway, in Dupin's opinion. But Goulch meant well.

'We'll go back to Saint-Nicolas straight away. And Goulch, radio the coastguard. A helicopter is to have the area around the island searched.'

Dupin marched resolutely to the beach where Le Menn's boat and the dinghy lay. Goulch and Riwal followed him. He checked for the reception symbol every few metres with increasing rage. In vain. It didn't even change on the water, not even at the spot where he had still been on the phone on the way there. It was enough to make you tear your hair out.

Shortly before they moored at the quay, the first bar had appeared on the screen and a moment later all of them at once. Dupin had stormed over to the operations table in the *Quatre Vents* as if he wanted to make an arrest.

'What have we got?'

A list lay in front of Le Coz. Dupin sat down next to him. No matter how hectic things were, Le Coz was calmness itself, without being slow. He was by far the oldest and the most experienced person in the commissariat. He still had two years to go till his retirement. His knowledge, his accuracy and above all his level-headedness had made made Dupin take to him from the beginning.

'I've just consulted Bellec again. Leussot, the biologist, was at sea from nine o'clock, on board his boat. He arrived here half an hour ago.'

'I'm concerned with...' Dupin reflected, trying to calculate the last high tide, 'with the time from half past twelve till four o'clock. What did Leussot do after I was with him? He would have easily had enough time to go to Brilimec.'

'He says he stayed at the place where you visited him all day. We won't be able to verify that.'

'Oh, wonderful!'

Dupin clasped the back of his head. Le Coz was right.

Riwal had now arrived at the operations table too and sat down.

'Keep going, Le Coz.'

'This diver, Monsieur Tanguy, has guests visiting from Brest, a delegation of marine archaeologists. They are sitting here in the *Quatre Vents* right now. Out the front on the terrace. He picked them up in Concarneau at three o'clock.'

'And before that?'

'Before that he was here, he says. Because of the preparations. He was also here overnight. On his boat.'

'When did he set out?'

'Around half past one, he said.'

'Alone?'

'Alone.'

Fantastic. How were they meant to find out whether he had taken a detour to Brilimec? He would have had enough time to do it. And even to take Le Menn somewhere too. As victim, perpetrator or accomplice. While Le Coz was speaking, Dupin had begun to make notes.

'The mayor?'

'He was working at home in his office almost all day, in...'

'I know.'

'Exactly, you visited him this morning, he told us. Then just between four o'clock and five o'clock he had an official engagement. In the local kindergarden. Monsieur Du Marhallac'h was very cooperative.'

'Witnesses? The kindergarden children of course. It will be difficult for the time in the office. He claims to have talked to his wife on the phone several times, she is probably in London. On the landline. That can be verified.'

'Brilliant.'

Dupin could not have enunciated this word with greater cynicism.

'The younger Nuz daughter was at her boyfriend's place, they were in Quimper, the older one was working here in the *Quatre Vents* all day. Solenn Nuz was on the mainland. Apparently she runs errands every Tuesday and Friday. She left at half past ten and only got back an hour ago. She was in Fouesnant, in the mairie and ended in Concarneau. She came back with lots of big shopping bags. She ate in the *Amiral* at lunchtime, we were able to check that.'

Dupin felt a brief feeling of joy at the mention of the *Amiral*.

'And Madame Lefort?'

'Bellec is speaking to her right now.'

'Madame Barrault – the diving instructor?'

Le Coz looked at his notes.

'She ran a course this morning, until one o'clock, then she ate at home. In the afternoon you were out with her of course and afterwards she went diving herself. She has also only just returned. Around the same time as Leussot.'

'Where does Madame Barrault live?'

'In the second house over there, with the triangular roof...'

'I know it,' he said. 'And she was alone at home over lunchtime?'

'So she says. She thinks there definitely aren't any witnesses.'

Dupin couldn't help smirking. That sounded very much like Madame Barrault.

'And what about old Monsieur Nuz, Solenn Nuz's father-in-law?'

'You didn't mention Pasacal Nuz. But I did just speak to him. He is – a little withdrawn. He was in the *Quatre Vents* in the morning, reading the paper at the bar, then he was at home. At four o'clock he headed for the Moutons in his boat, apparently he does that every day, his granddaughter vouched for that. Headed off towards the shoals of mackerel, he came back at six with a pile of fish.'

'Okay.'

A kind of high-pitched fanfare suddenly rang out. Le Coz answered the call straight away.

'Yes?'

He turned to Dupin.

'Bellec. He's got the additional information. Shall I put it on loudspeaker?'

Le Coz took Dupin's hesitation as agreement, pressed a button and placed the phone on the table in front of him.

'Bellec. We're all listening now.'

'*Bonjour*, Monsieur le Commissaire. I...'

This was always a horrific situation, Dupin thought, he hated talking hands-free like this.

'Fire away, Bellec.'

They needed to make progress.

'Madame Lefort was on Saint-Nicolas all day long, she was on the phone several times, including with her notary. She was in her office in the sailing school mostly, but walked back to her house several times. She went for a few walks. Madame Menez came over to her house for about half an hour at lunchtime. After their conversation she left to go to the sailing school on Penfret, to meet Madame Menez again, at around quarter past six.'

Even this was vague in parts and, where witnesses could confirm it in detail, they could only do so with a great deal of effort. This much was clear: for someone who was on the islands anyway, three-quarters of an hour would have sufficed for the Brilimec episode, depending of course on what had happened to Le Menn...

'Madame Lefort seemed very concerned that she is now the prime suspect, also because she was questioned again so soon after the long conversation she had with you. I assured her that these were all routine enquiries.'

In truth this was the least of Dupin's worries right now. She should be anxious.

'And the assistant, Madame Menez?'

'Madame Menez appeared to be remorseful, although she seemed stubborn. She had several meetings with various sailing teachers today, in the office. At lunchtime she was at Madame Lefort's house, as I mentioned. Then she ate in the *Quatre Vents* and then finally had long team conferences with the heads of accommodation on Cigogne and Penfret.'

'When did these team conferences begin?'

'One ran from half two till four and one from five till half six. Madame Menez is still on Penfret.'

Dupin was making detailed notes.

'When did she set out for Cigogne, I mean, when exactly after lunch?'

'According to her statement she was in her house for a little while after lunch. And so left around quarter past two.'

'Can someone confirm that?'

'Not yet. We should check.'

It was driving Dupin crazy that none of this information was helping him to make any progress.

'Please do, Bellec.'

Le Coz hung up.

'Should we be verifying other statements too, Commissaire?'

Dupin reflected. Le Coz and Bellec had done some good work in such a short time, as meagre as the fruits of their labour seemed at the moment.

'No need. Thank you.'

They were none the wiser. Everyone would have had the opportunity to make the trip to Brilimec. It would have to be a big, big coincidence for there to be witnesses. And it would probably be impossible to narrow down the relevant time further.

'I spoke to Le Menn's wife again just now. After we found out that he went to the Glénan. I wondered whether she associated anything with Brilimec.'

Le Coz had torn Dupin away from his thoughts. That had been a good idea.

'But there was nothing. Nothing at all.'

Dupin stood up abruptly.

'None of this feels right to me.'

Riwal chipped in for the first time.

'Goulch has taken charge of the forensics on Brilimec. He went back to the islands again too. Maybe they will find trace evidence in the house after all.'

'Maybe.'

Dupin realised that his thoughts were taking on a life of their own. He walked a few metres to one side. He definitely had a few theories by now, some more specific than others, but overall the picture that emerged was still much too blurry. He couldn't find the truly central element.

Dupin looked at his watch. It was coming up to eight o'clock now. He had been up since five. And the day would not be over for a long time yet.

From this side of the *Quatre Vents* there was a clear view to the west, which actually meant you could watch the sun go down. But not this evening. The band of cloud had come menacingly close, piling up into a gigantic cloud front, a monster, probably no more than ten kilometres away. Pitch-black. Only now did Dupin notice that the wind hadn't just picked up, at this point it was continuously sweeping powerful squalls over the islands. But he knew: even that didn't mean anything yet in Brittany, he'd been through it all before, he was no rookie any more. Dupin looked at the sea. There were already white horses. And proper waves. That had been quick. On the way back to Saint-Nicolas from Brilimec he still hadn't noticed anything. But apart from the first small stretch, they had been going through the chamber and he had been staring at his mobile the entire time.

He took a few deep breaths.

'You said that Kilian Tanguy is still here in the *Quatre Vents*?'

'Yes. Out the front on the terrace.'

'I'll have a word with him.'

'As I said, he's got guests. Underwater archaeologists.'

'So much the better.'

Dupin almost didn't recognise Kilian Tanguy in jeans and a colourful sweatshirt, instead of the neoprene suit, with a dry face and dry head. It was only the shape of his head that gave him away: it was like an egg. He had a bald head apart from a narrow, closely cropped hairline above the ears, which was still an untouched black; plus a fleshy nose and eyes full of fun. He was sitting with six men, all about the same age.

'*Bonjour Messieurs*, Commissaire Georges Dupin from the Commissariat de Police Concarneau. I would like to speak to Monsieur Tanguy, but since

I've heard that you're all underwater archaeologists, I'd like to put some questions to all of you.'

Dupin spoke firmly and low, which rarely failed to have the desired effect.

'You're the police officer from Paris, aren't you?'

A well-built man with a baby face looked inquisitively at him. As did the rest of the table.

Dupin was sick of answering this question.

'Did you know that Paris was called after the legendary sunken city Ys?' the man went on eagerly. 'Par-Ys! After the Breton Atlantis which was infinitely magnificent and rich and worshipped the ocean as their only God in extravagant ceremonies. The kingdom of Gradlon, his daughter Dahut, who was fiancée of the sea and his magical horse Morvark, which is the symbol of a free Brittany to this day. Ys was off Douarnenez! There are many very serious archaeological indications.'

Dupin had never heard of this, just as he had never heard that Paris was ultimately Breton, apparently. Luckily, Kilian Tanguy chipped in at this moment.

'I think that would be fine by all of us, Monsieur le Commissaire. You actually have a group of illustrious underwater archaeologists from the University of Brest in front of you, friendly associates of our small group in the club. How can we help the police?'

There was something mischievous in his voice. Something pleasantly mischievous.

'Do you know anything about treasure hunts going on at the moment here on the coast? Have you heard rumours?'

The divers looked at each other, unruffled. Kilian Tanguy answered again.

'You think a story about treasure hunting is behind the three murders?'

He clearly sounded proud at this.

'We are investigating various avenues. And that is one of them. Nothing more.'

'I haven't heard anything about a sensational find. Not even rumours.'

Tanguy added in a much more serious way:

'But you must know, Monsieur le Commissaire, that we, as we say, *dive for wood*, not for precious metals! Underwater archaeology has absolutely different aims. Scientific aims. For example, we look for settlement sites from the Mesolithic era. As early as four thousand years before Christ, a Dolmen was erected here on Brunec and graves were dug on Saint-Nicolas and Bananec too. We know next to nothing about this culture. So much has now lain beneath the surface of the water for such a long time.'

His facial expression almost betrayed a kind of outrage now.

'The sea has risen a hundred metres in the last ten thousand years! A hundred metres! A few thousand years ago, the British were still, God save us, coming to France with dry feet! – And if we take an interest in sunken ships, which we definitely do, then only in order to be able to study the historical boat architecture and techniques of their respective nautical epochs.'

A mild, tongue-in-cheek smile stole across his face.

'Last year two sunken ships were found, one from the seventeenth century, one from the twentieth. In the one from the seventeenth century there were silver coins. The other one was unremarkable. Maybe thirty kilometres to the south of here.'

Tanguy had uttered these last sentences with marked cheeriness.

'And there's no ship,' asked Dupin, 'that, due to some documents or other, people know in theory must be in the vicinity but hasn't yet been found?'

Every gaze fixed on Dupin in astonishment. Tanguy took charge of answering again.

'There are about two dozen of them – and that's within a radius of fifty nautical miles alone. And in at least a dozen cases the documents suggest cargoes of substantial value. Two of the ships are highly likely to have had large amounts of gold on board.'

'You're pretty sure you know of two ships with gold cargo near here?' Dupin was astonished.

'Don't go getting the wrong idea, it's more complicated than you think. Like a needle in a haystack. – In a wild, dangerous haystack.'

'So none of you heard that one of the three dead mean was on a specific treasure hunt? That's what I want to know.'

'No. Nothing.'

Dupin would have been interested to know whether one of the other divers would have had anything else to say. Apparently not.

'Thank you, Monsieur Tanguy.'

Dupin had had enough of the stories now (as fascinating as they were). And if he were honest, all conversations on this topic ended inconclusively, as they had all day long. But it was clear: if the three had been on the trail of something big, they would have given their all to make sure nobody found out anything about it. And, if someone had learnt something and this was the motive behind the whole case, then that would be the perpetrator. And he definitely wouldn't say a thing.

Besides, Dupin was also unfocussed, he couldn't stop thinking about the issue of what had happened to Le Menn on the island. He didn't have a good feeling about it.

'I'd really like...'

Dupin was suddenly interrupted by a noise. A sudden, strong squall had caught some of the *Quatre Vents* tables and chairs, knocking them over. The gust of wind had brought a smattering of fat raindrops with it. Considerable activity broke out. The previously quiet underwater archaeologists leapt up. One was in the process of rushing to the aid of a young couple whose table had fallen over, along with everything that had been on it. Tanguy and another man were protecting the things that were on their own table and hurrying to the bar with them. Everyone was moving swiftly, with precision and yet without any rush.

'It's all kicking off.'

Dupin turned around. Solenn Nuz was standing in the doorway to the bar.

She was looking around with utter indifference. Louann Nuz appeared behind her, then darted past her like a cat to take care of the tables.

'I've been waiting for this all day. The storm really did take its time.'

Solenn Nuz delivered these sentences with perfect calmness.

Dupin was still standing as though rooted to the spot, as if the group of archaeologists was still sitting in front of him. Solenn Nuz looked at the sky:

'This is going to be a big one.'

She went back into the bar.

The apocalyptic-looking bank of cloud was speeding over the islands. In the south and west it was already pitch-black – only far away in the east could you see a strip of light. Everything had happened so suddenly. Like an ambush. It was truly pouring with rain now and the temperature had dropped noticeably in the last few minutes.

Dupin shook himself out of his stupor. Louann Nuz was the last person still outside, everyone else had already fled inside the *Quatre Vents*. Dupin didn't hesitate and followed her into the bar. He closed the door firmly behind him.

'There's a big *cotriade*.'

Dupin was standing at the bar. Solenn Nuz was on the other side of the counter, pouring various wines into a whole row of glasses in front of her with impressive speed. One of the underwater archaeologists was standing very close to him on his right hand side, the oldest one in Tanguy's group. He was waiting for their order. To his left were Riwal and Le Coz. Solenn's father-in-law was sitting at the end of the bar.

Dupin was still dazed, moments ago the atmosphere had been that of summer evening terraces, now he felt like he was in an isolated research station, cut off from the outside world. There was a fire burning in the large stone fireplace – on his previous visits Dupin hadn't even noticed it existed, although it took up a whole corner of the room. The raging storm and the pelting rain outside could clearly be heard, but amazingly only as a muffled background noise, that was almost pleasant. It felt very cosy – even though Dupin was in anything but a cosy mood – but at the same time he found it menacingly cramped here, an odd mixture.

'There's traditionally a *cotriade* when storms come, Monsieur le Commissaire. It lifts the spirits. Would you like some?'

Dupin was focused on something else entirely – he urgently needed to make some calls. There were a number of things he definitely wanted to follow up. Besides, he couldn't conceal the fact that, in the back of his mind, he was bothered by the question of how Solenn Nuz could have been so sure that a storm was coming that she had got to work on the undoubtedly elaborate preparations for the *cotriade* hours ago – meanwhile he himself would have sworn he could make out the unmistakeable signs of a solid high pressure zone. But what was much worse was this: in a storm they'd need to call off the sea-search for Le Menn. And even worse: what about the forensics? And Reglas and his team? Even they wouldn't be able to work now. Dupin wondered where they'd got to – and also Goulch and his crew. Had they found a makeshift shelter on Brilimec? What about the helicopter? If Le Menn were on the run, he would be miles away by tomorrow – if he was in danger, everything would probably be too late now.

Solenn Nuz interpreted Dupin's silence incorrectly.

'Ah yes. Of course.'

She smiled gently.

'You're new of course – *cotriade* is our classic Breton fish stew.'

Dupin was familiar with *cotriade*, he had eaten it, at a rough estimate, once a month for the last four years. That made about thirty-five, forty *cotriades*, he guessed. It was among his favourite dishes. But he was too distracted to protest.

'In the south they copied it as bouillabaisse! Some rouille in there and in an instant, they elevate it to the national dish!' said one of the underwater archaeologists. The thin little man, who Dupin estimated to be in his late fifties, had an almost comically screechy voice, which didn't match the outrage that his face was expressing as he chipped in.

'The *cotriade* is the original! At least eight types of fish, plus shellfish *and* mussels! Leeks, Breton potatoes, Breton butter. Fresh herbs! Bay leaf! *Fleur de sel*! – In Marseille they only use six types of fish.'

It sounded like genuine contempt.

'It was invented by the fishermen's wives – in the evenings they used the fish and the fish pieces that their husbands hadn't been able to sell in the market that morning for it. You put some pieces of baguette fried in butter in a flat bowl, pour the broth over, add the pieces of fish, shellfish and mussels – and then, the crucial part, you top the whole thing off with a strong sauce. A secret recipe in every house! You...'

Dupin interrupted him.

'I urgently need to speak to my colleagues – excuse me.'

Solenn Nuz winked at Dupin and smiled knowingly.

Dupin made a signal to Riwal and Le Coz and they followed him. Dupin had taken a few steps towards the door when it occurred to him that it was not a good idea to go outside. They would have to stay indoors. But, although barely half of the tables were occupied, it was far too loud to talk on the phone, let alone be discreet. Even in the kitchen they wouldn't be alone.

'Let's go into the annexe, I'm sure Madame Nuz won't have a problem with that,' said Riwal. 'I'll ask her quickly.'

It was a good idea. Dupin headed for the passageway immediately, Riwal back to the counter, to Solenn Nuz.

Before he opened the door, Dupin looked around quickly to Riwal, who nodded. Dupin had to push down hard on the iron door handle before walking inside.

He almost shrank away in terror. The storm was making an ear-splitting din in the wooden annexe. Soon, Riwal and Le Coz were standing behind him. The room's lighting was much dimmer than next door.

'Madame Nuz says we would be very welcome to use the room, but she can't recommend it. We wouldn't be able to hear ourselves.'

'This is absolutely absurd. We will *need* to make a number of calls.'

Dupin's mood was darkening with every passing second. After all, they had no time to waste.

He headed for the furthest corner of the annexe, in the hope that it would be better there. He pressed himself against the massive stone wall of the old building. His hope was in vain. The raging storm and whipping rain could not only be heard throughout the annexe as though you were standing in the open air, but it seemed as though the wooden structure acted as a resonance box, increasing the sound even more. Stubbornly, Dupin got out his mobile. He dialled Nolwenn's number. No luck. And again. Again, no luck. He held the mobile up to his face. Nothing. No bars. Nothing at all. Not even the smallest one. There was no reception. Because of the storm.

Dupin hadn't thought of that. This was utterly unbearable.

'We'll need to use Solenn Nuz's landline then,' he said.

Nobody said a word for a few seconds. Riwal stepped in.

'There's no landline out here, Commissaire.'

'What?'

This came out so meekly and softly that nobody heard Dupin's reaction. He was thunderstruck.

'This cannot be happening. They've got to have a landline.'

'There's never been one here, chief. It would be an enormous expense – for a handful of people.'

Dupin gave up. This was a catastrophe. For many reasons. What would happen if they found Le Menn, somewhere on land and he had something something crucial to say. Or if Kadeg found out something relevant during the interrogation of the mayor. Even more importantly: if there were new results from the examination of the confiscated hard drives. He was at a critical point in the investigation, he needed to be contactable and in turn be able to get through to anyone he wanted to get through to any time.

'Then we'll need to go back to the mainland. There's no way round it.'

Riwal tried to calm the Commissaire down.

'There's no way we can do that. In a storm like this, we cannot leave the island.'

'What? This is not on.'

'There's only one thing we can do, as difficult as it may be: wait. We need to wait. Everyone on their respective islands. Us here, Bellec on Cigogne, the others on Brilimec.'

'How long for?'

Again, it was clear that Riwal was considering how to break the news to him as gently as possible.

'It doesn't look like it will be over quickly.' He tried hard to infuse the next sentence with confidence, 'but you never know. Breton weather is hard to predict.'

'How long?'

'Until we can set out from here without any danger – probably late at night. Or early in the morning.'

'Tomorrow morning?'

Dupin had difficulty speaking.

He was only gradually grasping the situation. It was far worse than he had supposed in his initial shock.

They were stranded. Here on the archipelago. Trapped. Cut off from the world. No matter what happened, come what may. Even in a medical emergency, even if there were another murder. They would not make it to the mainland. And nobody from the mainland would make it here. Only now did Dupin realise what the words that he'd heard so often in the last two days really meant: 'The Glénan are not a real place at all, they are a nothingness in the middle of the sea.' As though to underscore these thoughts, the annexe's wooden structure had begun to creak and groan alarmingly at the last strong gust of wind.

Dupin started to say something but then left it. They were losing crucial hours.

Riwal and Le Coz were clearly worried about the Commissaire's state. Dupin lowered his head and strode towards the door. He opened it very slowly and stood still in the doorway. In the last minutes, the number of customers had clearly grown, everyone was absolutely soaked through. He saw faces he didn't recognise, but also Madame Menez, Muriel Lefort and Marc Leussot. Everyone was looking for shelter. And was hungry. Leussot had probably come from his boat and Madame Menez would have just made it back from Penfret. None of the three had noticed him yet.

Solenn Nuz cast him a look from the bar that was not easy to interpret, but probably meant something like 'don't worry about it'. Then she smiled. That calm smile, friendly at the same time. Dupin went over to her.

'We're stranded,' he said.

'I know. And there's nothing you can do. It may last a while.'

'What do you think? How long will it last?'

'Definitely a night. I don't think it will be longer than that.'

Dupin was too depressed to respond.

'Madame Lefort will find a place for you and your colleagues to stay the night. She has a second house, right next to her own. There are two smaller apartments inside it. Madame Menez lives in one of them and she sometimes puts up guests in the other.'

Dupin wanted to decline. This was just too awful. He hadn't even thought of it. But, they would need to sleep somewhere, for a couple of hours at least.

Riwal and Le Coz had sat down at one of the last free tables.

'Lo and behold, Monsieur le Commissaire is one of the stranded too.'

Marc Leussot had positioned himself next to him, without Dupin seeing him approach. He was still wearing the faded shorts from lunchtime today, the same T-shirt. The conversation on the boat seemed to Dupin as though it had been days ago.

Dupin was not in the mood to talk. But he had a few urgent questions just for the marine biologist. Leussot kept talking before Dupin could get himself ready.

'Has Le Menn turned up again?'

Dupin started.

'You know about his disappearance?'

'You've had a large-scale manhunt for him running for a few hours, across all media. I listen to a lot of radio on the boat.'

Of course. Most of them would know. Even if Madame Lefort seemed not to have known anything about it just now. The same went for Tanguy.

'Yes. We're searching for Docteur Le Menn.'

'A bloody difficult case.'

'You have no idea what might have happened to Le Menn?'

'I would already have told you, believe me. This is serious.'

'Speaking of seriousness. You never mentioned that you beat up Lefort not so long ago.'

'That's not a secret. And I think I made it very clear what I think of him.'

'What else did you not share because you didn't deem it necessary?'

Leussot laughed, a deep, confident laugh.

'True. And that's me – as a suspect many times over.'

Suddenly there was the sound of a muffled bang. Someone had opened the door from outside and as they did so a sharp wind had caught the door and swung it open violently. Anjela Barrault burst into the room. It looked funny and dramatic at the same time. With some force, she shut the door behind her, stood still for a moment and smiled at everyone. Instead of the diving suit, she was now wearing jeans and a windcheater. And she was dripping wet.

'That was close.'

It didn't sound at all tongue-in-cheek and so, based on what Dupin had just got to know about her, it meant without exaggeration: I only escaped certain death at sea by the skin of my teeth.

All of this was getting to be like a genuine scene from a novel. Dupin would have found it funny if it hadn't been so serious. An alarmingly small island, cut off from the outside world, in the midst of a raging storm, in a creaky old house that had become a prison, where they were keeping vigil by the light of the fire. During the course of which, more mysterious things might happen. Crime, even a murder, might happen. In fact, the majority of the suspects were now gathered here.

Leussot seemed less taken by Barrault's entrance, he seemed to be waiting for the continuation of his little rhetorical battle with Dupin instead. However, Dupin had lost his appetite for that conversation.

'I need to consult my colleagues, excuse me, Monsieur Leussot.'

He left the counter without waiting for a response and wove his way between the tables. His gaze swept over Madame Lefort and Madame Menez who were sitting in the furthest corner and who nodded at him slightly bashfully. Solenn Nuz was standing at their table. Dupin supposed they were talking about how they could put him and his colleagues up. It made him uncomfortable. And Anjela Barrault, who had plumped for the next table, had now seen the Commissaire too and threw him a bold look.

He sat down with his colleagues.

'We've been – considering – eating something,' Riwal said cautiously. As if he wanted to sound it out first.

It still seemed inappropriate to Dupin somehow – although even he was ravenous, if truth be told, and besides, what were they meant to do? It was clear they would be spending the evening and night here in any case. And this was the only place there would be something to eat. No *Amiral*, nothing.

'Fine.'

It was a grumpy but acceptable 'fine'. Riwal looked visibly relieved. Le Coz positively jumped to his feet. Riwal likewise, a moment later.

They spoke almost in unison. 'We're getting ourselves a *cotriade*. Shall we get you one, Monsieur le Commissaire?'

Dupin gave in (only grumbling a little bit now). To his own stomach, more than anything.

'Riwal? And a bottle of red wine. The cooled pinot noir.'

That was the best with fish.

Riwal's eyes gleamed, even though he made an effort to hide it.

The two of them took up a position in the little queue that had now formed in front of the counter.

Something wonderful had just occurred to Dupin – if he wouldn't be contactable all evening and night, then he wouldn't be able to contact anyone either, not even the Prefect! Suddenly he couldn't suppress a grin.

Le Coz and Riwal had apparently agreed that only one of them would queue up. Riwal came back and sat up straight.

'What are we going to do now, chief?'

'We have a large proportion of the suspects here. This is going to be an interesting night, Riwal,' Dupin paused, 'we're best off watching and listening. Perhaps the murderer is sitting just a few metres away from us. Just like he or she was sitting here the night before last...'

Riwal looked around furtively.

'Do you have a hunch now?'

Dupin laughed.

'I suggest that after we eat, we sit down at a table with everyone who is stranded here.'

'Do you think that's a good idea?'

'We'll see.'

Dupin was in a strange mood, which was also due, at least in part, to his worryingly low blood sugar levels.

Le Coz came back holding a large tray with a bottle of water and the wine on it. Three glasses.

'The drinks. Madame Nuz is bringing the *cotriade*.'

'Great.'

Dupin finally gave in to being extremely hungry. He took the bottle of wine, poured some for Riwal and Le Coz, then for himself, and toasted with '*Yec'hed mat*' (he was always very proud of that) – then drank the whole glassful in one go. The others concentrated on the wine too. It had been a long day for everyone. Nobody said a word.

It didn't take long for Solenn and Louann Nuz to bring two trays with three ceramic bowls of *cotriade* on them, several little bowls of baguette toasted – in salted butter! – and the 'secret sauce'. In fact this was essentially a vinaigrette which varied depending on the family, village and region. Dupin had drunk his second glass of wine just as quickly as the first before he'd even taken his first bite. It was this very moment that Goulch's joke crossed his mind: that bottles were unfortunately smaller than usual on the Glénan.

Dupin felt decidedly better. The fish stew – you could never say fish soup – smelt indescribable. Dupin recognised all of his favourite fish: angler fish, sea bass, red mullet, gilt head, pollack, cod, hake and sole, his favourite mussels: praires, scallops, blue mussels, *palourdes grises* and even better – *palourdes roses* – along with langoustines of various sizes and crab. It was in fact a huge, deep soup bowl with an impressive mountain towering upwards. More hurriedly than he'd intended, he poured the sauce over the fish and the potatoes. And ate. He tasted the whole sea. Incredible – the fish, but especially the broth, a concentrate that had been reduced for hours and hours.

Rudely, he hadn't even noticed that Madame Nuz was still standing next to them. Silently. She could see that they liked it.

'Sorry, Madame. This is incredibly delicious. The best *cotriade* I've ever eaten. And I've eaten many.'

At times like these, when he had drunk some wine, it sometimes happened that Commissaire Dupin got a bit dramatic in his phrasing, without noticing it. He realised he should be careful about more wine.

'I spoke to Madame Lefort. You can have the apartment tonight. You're to arrange everything directly with her.'

'Thanks very much, that is terribly kind.'

Madame Nuz turned around.

'Excuse me, Madame Nuz – I have a question.'

She turned back around to him immediately.

'Of course.'

'This may sound unusual – but do you think we could all sit together soon? All of the residents of the island and the regulars. Once everyone has eaten.'

Madame Nuz smiled her typical smile. In agreement.

'We'd best come to your table then, Monsieur le Commissaire.'

'Let's do it that way.'

Madame Nuz went back to the counter. Dupin turned his attention back to the fish stew once more. And to the third glass of wine, which he swore would be his last of the evening.

They ate the *cotriade* right down to the last morsel – they really were large portions – without exchanging a single word with each other. Rapt. And despite the tense situation, a little bit blissful.

Every two or three minutes there came a hefty bang. Unpredictably, but never at long intervals. It sounded as if something big and powerful was smacking into the rear side of the building. The bangs were muffled, but were accompanied by high-pitched, metallic sounds that were impossible to identify.

The storm had picked up even more in the last half hour. It must have reached crazy speeds by now. The noise in the stone building had increased too, it was now almost as loud here as it had been in the wooden annexe. Dupin had stood up once and gone to the door, wanting, without thinking too much about it, to see how it looked outside. 'Don't do that!' Solenn Nuz had called across the room at the last moment. She had called out in a friendly way, but it was still an embarrassing scene. Dupin then remembered how Anjela Barrault had come into the bar – and realised what would happen if an even stronger squall blew through the open door. He walked to a little window on the right and looked out. He couldn't see a thing. No world. Nothing. Just a jet-black hole. Visibility disappeared after the first centimetres. If you focussed your gaze directly on the windowpane, the rain running down the glass made it look as if someone were spraying the window with a garden hose on full power. Dupin had never experienced a storm like it. They were completely at its mercy, there was nothing but these few old walls around them. The atmosphere had changed, the storm was playing on their nerves. Just a few voices and conversations were still to be heard at the tables. Even the underwater archaeologists had become noticeably quieter, having been by far the most boisterous at first. Only the people who lived in this world were not showing any sign of emotion in particular, least of all Solenn Nuz.

It was very cramped at the square tables they had put together to make space for everyone to sit. Solenn Nuz was on Dupin's right, Leussot next to her; to his left Anjela Barrault, Riwal next to her, Madame Menez and Louann Nuz diagonally opposite and directly opposite Muriel Lefort, with Tanguy and Le Coz next to her.

'What is that? Those bangs?'

Riwal's edginess was visible.

'Odd things sometimes happen during big storms,' Leussot grinned.

'Groac'h's greedy hand, it's knocking.'

Kilian Tanguy, suddenly taking on an unprecedented cheeky tone, had his fun too. 'Or it's the knocking that comes before the ancient disembodied voice. If she calls your name, you have no choice. She leads you to the *Baie des Trépassés*, the Bay of the Deceased. A boat is waiting for you. It's low in the water and seems to be heavily laden and yet it's totally empty. The Skiff of the Dead is waiting for your crossing. A sail hoists, as though by a ghostly hand, and you are tasked with steering it safely to the Île de Sein. As soon as the skiff reaches the island, the souls leave it. Then you may come back, to your family. Everything is just a shadow, but you are never the same.'

Tanguy opened his eyes wide, his face contorting into a grimace.

'And that's a lucky fate. If you're unlucky, it's shadowy Ankou himself who knocks, messenger of death and graveyard watchman, a skeleton veiled in a black cloak holding a scythe. On nights like this you can hear his ancient cart creaking.'

Leussot and Tanguy were acting out a grim duet.

'Or there's the dead themselves, the lost souls who trick you malevolently. On stormy nights they pretend to be sailors who have run into difficulties to lure the living out to sea.'

Dupin knew these stories by now, not all of them – that was impossible – but a great number. For hundreds, for thousands of years, people had been telling them to each other here at the storm-tossed End of the World and to this day they were 'real'. No Roman civilisation, no Christianisation, no Modern Age, no Enlightenment or any other fleeting innovation had been able to change anything about that. The large 'Festivals Paroles' where story-tellers gave dramatic recitations of the old epics, sagas, myths and legends had been in fashion again in the last few years. If these legends were typically Breton like little else, Dupin thought, what was even more typical was the wonderful way Bretons then suppressed the terror of these stories in their lives. The way they found very practical, very distinctive (and not infrequently: delicious) rites to minimise the terror and to incorporate it into life – for instance on All Hallows', crêpes were baked for the lost souls, huge numbers of crêpes.

It was clear Riwal did not find any of this funny. Le Coz's face betrayed noticeable anxiety too – and Dupin had to admit, that in places like this, in atmospheres like this, these stories had much more of an effect than usual.

But Leussot was already relenting.

'In daylight we'll see what was causing that noise. Believe us, we're not in danger. It's is completely normal.'

He had said this seriously and soothingly, and Riwal's facial expression really did relax a little, even though it wasn't clear what 'completely normal' meant.

Dupin had been expecting a lot from the idea of bringing everyone together at one table. However, the conversation was faltering – more specifically, apart from the gothic duet, no conversation of any kind had got anywheresince they had been sitting here. Now and again, somebody uttered a sentence that nobody really responded to. Most of them said nothing at all, not even those who usually talked a lot. And Dupin no longer felt – physically or mentally – capable of conducting a 'group interview' or continuing to stimulate the conversation. It had probably been a ridiculous idea anyway. The silence was surely only because none of those present knew where the Commissaire was going with this. It was an artificial situation.

'And Lucas wanted to establish a tourist's paradise here!'

Leussot burst out laughing. None of the others laughed with him. It seemed macabre.

'My brother went out into a storm like this,' Muriel Lefort stated suddenly, emotionlessly.

At first, this sentence also died away without any response.

'Quite a few people have gone out into a storm from here, wanting to make it to the mainland. Thought they could handle anything.'

This was the very first time Anjela Barrault had spoken up.

'But they hadn't had sedatives administered to them.'

Leussot sounded aggressive. His gaze had darkened for a moment. Dupin's hopes were raised, he had been counting on something like this. He waited. But nothing happened. Leussot regained his composure and it didn't seem as though anyone wanted to respond.

'How often has it happened that someone set out too late from here?'

Dupin knew that it was an awkward sentence. He didn't care. Maybe something was going to be revealed after all.

'It was mainly sailors stopping off here and underestimating the situation. Five years ago a baker from Trégunc, who was very experienced at sea,' Tanguy seemed embarrassed, 'that was particularly bad, he made the best baguette for miles around.'

'The most tragic was that time with the niece of the institute Director, Le Berre-Ryckeboerec. Alice. Three years ago, with her husband. Just married. And,' Muriel Lefort glanced at Solenn Nuz, 'Jacques of course, ten years ago.'

'Le Berre-Ryckeboerec's niece?' Dupin butted in.

'Yes. That was dramatic. She was in the process of becoming a professional sailor. I trained her. A terrible loss. She was never found.'

'Never?'

'Never.'

'How did the Director cope with that?'

'She was his elder brother's daughter, I don't think

that they were very close. He and his brother. But only he himself knows that.'

Muriel Lefort was clearly at pains to be accurate.

Dupin waited to see if the conversation would continue to develop.

In vain.

'Thank you all. That was an – interesting conversation.'

There was no point. Dupin could not go on. He didn't want to do go on. It was half past eleven now. And it had become four glasses of wine in the end. And, of the wine Riwal had poured out for him – despite a clear look declining it – he'd already drunk half.

Besides, it was still going to be a long time before they were in bed – somewhere. The accommodation surely still needed to be prepared. And, above all, they would need to go through the storm now. A good hundred metres.

To the others, even Riwal and Le Coz, the breaking up of the group had obviously appeared abrupt, they seemed unsure what to do. Only Anjela Barrault and Solenn Nuz stood up without hesitation.

'Good night all,' Dupin said and turned to Madame Lefort.

'Thank you for making your apartment available to us.'

'No problem. I'm glad to do it. It might be a bit cramped.'

'We'll manage.'

Dupin was by no means as easy-going as his answer sounded. The idea of potentially having to sleep in the same room as Riwal and Le Coz was horrifying to him.

Muriel Lefort tried to smile. Dupin couldn't even manage the attempt any more.

Commissaire Dupin lay in bed. More specifically: he was lying on a barely fifty-centimetre wide, aluminium fold-out bed that he had pushed right next to the front door. He had covered himself with two large beach towels. Le Coz was sleeping in the only proper bed in the tiny bedroom under the roof, 'ready for duty and dressed' as he emphasised, somewhat coyly and also sopping wet. Riwal had retired to the sofa that stood directly in front of the panorama window.

Dupin, with his fold-out bed, had sought to put some distance between himself and the sofa, insofar as that was possible. The gap wasn't big. He wouldn't hear any of the noises that Riwal might make in his sleep anyway, because the rain and storm were still pelting against the shutters outside the window, causing an infernal racket here too. Even as a child, on school trips to countryside camps near Chartres, Dupin had hated having to sleep in a room with other people. Whenever they went to the Jura to visit his father's family, who lived in a tiny backwater, he had had to sleep in his cousins' room. Three cousins (essentially very nice), all older, and him, split over two beds. That's also why he had a hang up about this, that much was clear.

He still had wet hair. Even his polo-shirt was wet, but he was in no mood to take it off, it had been unpleasant enough taking off his trousers and hanging them over a chair to dry. But what was really worrying was the state of his red notebook. He had been too tired to look carefully at the extent of the water damage. But it didn't look good. It was even worse for the *Petit Indicateur des Marées* – it was absolutely sodden.

They had been soaked to the bone, all of three of them, as well as Madame Lefort and Madame Menez, when they had ventured out of the *Quatre Vents* to battle the hundred metres to the houses. It had been crazy. They had walked in single file, one close behind the other, so that they were touching at every step. Muriel Lefort had walked in front because she knew the way best. The short path had taken them a full five minutes. After just a few seconds, the rain had been forced through even the thickest material by the gusts of wind. And it had not just been rain – after only a metre or two Dupin noticed that the water running down his face and into his mouth tasted salty. Sea spray was scattering like mist and mixing with the rain. The surf around them must have been metres high. Dupin had been glad not to be able to see that.

It was half past midnight now and even though Dupin was absolutely exhausted, he was under no illusion that he'd be able to fall asleep quickly.

The day was going through his head and it seemed like the longest day of his life. Mostly, he was, of course, thinking about what had happened to Le Menn. And the complete failure of the round-table in the *Quatre Vents* just now. A few times he saw the leaping dolphins, which now seemed like a surreal vignette. But something had crossed his mind. Something had occurred to him, a detail from the conversation just now, that had only come to seem significant little by little and that had resulted in an – as yet formless, unclear – thought. It was just an idea. One that was pure speculation. But he couldn't stop thinking about it.

Georges Dupin's thoughts became more and more tangled and incoherent.

The Third Day

Commissaire Dupin reached instinctively for his gun, which he had placed underneath his pillow. He tried to get his bearings. There was semi-darkness. He didn't even know which way to point his gun. Riwal, who was standing next to him in a T-shirt and underwear looking miserably tired, leapt to one side.

'It's only me, chief, it's me. Hello, chief, it's me!' he shouted. First and foremost, Riwal wanted – in his own best interests – to make sure that Dupin had realised beyond doubt where he was and what was going on here.

'It's okay, Riwal.'

Dupin had come to his senses. To some extent anyway.

'Your phone is ringing.'

At the word 'phone' he jumped up. A moment later, he was wide awake. He had been having another deep, juicy Caribbean dream until just moments before and was glad not to be able to remember it exactly.

He had only fallen asleep in the early hours, having spent hours tossing and turning with increasing despair. He looked at his watch with something approaching panic: seven minutes past seven.

'This cannot be happening.'

He should have been up and about much earlier. There was no sign of Le Coz. The mattress on the absolutely worn out steel springs, which had seemed millimetres thick to Dupin, was dank. Just like the horribly thick pillows and the two garish green beach towels that had not kept him warm in the slightest. The whole room was dank. The worst thing was, it smelt that way too. They had not been able to open a window. It had, without doubt, been one of the most wretched nights of his life.

His mobile was still ringing.

'Yes?'

'Monsieur le Commissaire.'

Dupin recognised Goulch's voice.

'Lefort, Konan and Pajot have in fact been seen at the same place in the same area a few times in the last week. Around twenty-seven nautical miles south-west of the Glénan.'

Goulch sounded, by his standards, worked up.

'I was just in the fish halls in Concarneau, where the local fishermen bring their catch from five in the morning. I was asking around. About the Bénéteau. Two of the fishermen are sure they saw it. It's an area where the seafloor suddenly and clearly drops away. The Gran Turismo 49 is pretty noticeable after all.'

Dupin stood up, which caused considerable pain throughout his body.

'Good work, Goulch.'

'That would make the hypothesis about the treasure-hunting much more likely.'

'Or else they were fishing. Because there were some schools of fish there.'

Dupin said it without thinking.

'The large schools are closer to the coast at this time of the year, where the water has already warmed up and where there is, therefore, more food.'

'Good. How do we find out whether there really is something lying on the seabed?'

'I've already ordered a special boat with the relevant equipment; it's leaving right now.'

'Good. Very good, Goulch.'

'Another thing: the forensics team had to call off their operation yesterday, they changed course in the helicopter when it was clear that the storm was hitting the islands. But they're already on their way today. They should be there by now.'

'I – we had no reception. We were totally cut off from the world.'

'That's not an uncommon occurrence on the Glénan. The storm wasn't that bad here on the mainland, but when I couldn't get through to you any more, I thought that it might be a bit more severe out there. I'll be in touch.'

'Thank you.'

Dupin had not really been concentrating. For various reasons. Because he felt extraordinarily uneasy this morning. Because he hadn't had a coffee yet – devastating. Because since he'd woken up he'd been thinking about all that might have happened while they had been cut off from the world. But especially because what had preoccupied him so much before he had fallen into his utterly unrefreshing sleep had just recurred to him.

During the short phone call he had used one hand to put on his – still very wet – trousers. Then his socks and shoes – equally wet.

Out of the corner of his eye he could see Riwal starting to squeeze into his clothes.

'I need a coffee, Riwal.'

He was already at the door. He needed to get out.

'See you in the *Quatre Vents* in a few minutes. Check on Le Coz. It seems he's still sleeping.'

With these words Dupin opened the door and walked out.

He had to screw up his eyes outside. He hadn't reckoned with how much light would greet him. It was phenomenal. The sky had been swept completely clean, not a cloud to be seen for miles and miles. Wafer-thin clouds of dust hung in the air, almost more palpable than visible. It was one of those 'silver mornings' as they were called in Brittany, when sun, sky, sea and the whole world possessed a shimmering silver aura.

He had stopped right outside the front door. He breathed deeply. Very deeply. The air was fresh, magnificent. He was shivering a little. Nothing, not a trace of the storm remained. As if everything had been a bad dream.

Solenn Nuz greeted him with a doubly warm, doubly cheering smile, as if she wanted to give him a sign that she knew what torture the night had been. She looked dazzling, well rested, in top form, she really was a beautiful woman. She was standing by the large coffee machine, the exact spot where Dupin was headed with a look of longing on his face.

'*Petit café?*'

'Double.'

She set to work at the machine straight away. The heavenly sound was interrupted by Dupin's phone.

Reluctantly, he took a look at the number. Kadeg. Of course.

'One moment.'

Dupin made for the door and stepped outside.

'Yes?!'

'You couldn't be reached all evening, Monsieur le Commissaire. Not even late at night.'

This sounded accusatory to Dupin's ears.

'What is it, Kadeg?'

'Du Marhallac'h claims he actually drew up plans for the extension to Pajot's private house, so did in fact provide architectural services. This was above board apparently. Absolutely normal and legal. Pajot had some luxurious renovations made to his house six months ago, with a new pool, a terraced landscape and an extension. Du Marhallac'h really did make out two invoices for exactly the amounts that were transferred from Pajot's accounts. I asked him to show me the plans that he drew up. He said he didn't have them in his office. And he also didn't see any reason to show them to me.'

Even this early in the morning Kadeg had already moved into his diligent reporting style.

'How was he acting?'

'At first he was behaving very reasonably, by the end he was bad-tempered.'

Sometimes Dupin was impressed by Kadeg after all – he had put it in a nutshell. It was just as Dupin had imagined it: that answers like this would come from Du Marhallac'h. That such behaviour was to be expected.

'I'm about to speak to the building contractor who carried out the work. He knows who prepared which plans. Let's see if this building work really existed.'

'Please do, Kadeg.'

This was important.

'I was also in the mairie yesterday and checked what applications Lefort submitted. There isn't a single one. Nothing. Officially, nothing was ever actually submitted.'

'You're absolutely sure, Kadeg?'

'Absolutely sure.'

Dupin was finding this more and more interesting.

'Have you read the papers yet this morning? There are extensive reports about Le Menn's disappearance now.'

'That doesn't bother me. I'm going to…'

'Just quickly on *Medimare* too. All the content from the hard drives has now been seized. But there are an immense number of documents, even if you narrow them down. They are being examined one by one. Four experts are working on it. So far nothing stands out from the documents relating to the deals that *Medimare* did with Leussot's research work or anyone else's.'

Dupin really did have to admit that Kadeg was doing good work on this case.

'And – – – the Prefect tried to reach you yesterday evening, but then only spoke to Nolwenn and me. He was really worked up, he…'

Dupin hung up. He'd really needed that. The same thing all over again – Kadeg was still Kadeg.

Dupin reflected. There were important things to do. He went back into the bar. The double espresso was on the counter. Next to it was a plate with a small *brioche nature* that he hadn't even ordered.

'Wonderful.'

His mood was improving.

Solenn Nuz was nowhere to be seen. On the counter, near the passageway, there was already a pile of newspapers. Dupin recognised the lettering of the *Ouest France* right at the top. He decided to keep his distance.

The brioche was fantastic. Melt-in-the-mouth, soft as butter, the way it was supposed to be and with the delicate hint of yeast in the milky flavour typical of a good brioche. But the most important thing was: the coffee was simply perfect.

But Dupin didn't linger. Two minutes later, he left the bar again.

On the terrace he saw Riwal and Le Coz coming towards the *Quatre Vents* from the left. He turned right. As on previous days, he made for the tip of the island without thinking. This time at the lowest tide. He got out his phone.

'Nolwenn?'

'Monsieur le Commissaire! I hope you haven't had too awful a night.'

Nolwenn's sympathetic words almost made everything all right again. 'Nolwenn, you've got to research something for me. I want to know everything about the death of Solenn Nuz's husband, Jacques. Everything. Check in the police files. He went missing at sea ten years ago. He set out from the Glénan shortly before a storm reached the island,' Dupin hesitated, his voice changed. He seemed to be speaking less to Nolwenn than to himself. 'A storm like last night perhaps,' he paused again, 'a storm like three days ago, like Sunday night.'

'I'll see what I can find. I'll take care of it straight away. You – you should…'

'I know. I really can't manage it.'

It didn't take long, but there was a moment before Nolwenn answered.

'I'll explain to the Prefect that you regrettably still cannot get in touch. That you yourself regret it the most. I think the Prefect… he himself has an interest of course, in light being shed on this darkness soon.'

Dupin loved Nolwenn. He loved her.

'Speak to you later.'

'Just one more thing, Monsieur le Commissaire. Your mother. This morning there were another four calls on the voicemail, all of which were rather indignant. She's arriving tomorrow evening, I'm to tell you that again. And that she absolutely must speak to you immediately.'

'I'll call her.'

Dupin hung up. This could not be happening. Tomorrow. He really did need to call her. He would have to cancel. But not now.

Jacques Nuz's accident. Four times, he had noted 'Jacques Nuz, in an accident' in his notebook. It had occurred to him last night on the fold-out bed. It wasn't, as he had first thought, the reference to the death of Le Berre-Ryckeboerec's niece that had put him on the alert in his utter fatigue. But in fact the death of Jacques Nuz, who had set out from the Glénan before a storm to get over to the mainland.

As he walked he pulled the Clairefontaine out of his jacket pocket – it was still damp, but its varnished cover had kept the rain off surprisingly well – better than he had feared last night. He leafed through and found his last notes. Yes. It was written here. 'Was in the mairie.' So in Fouesnant then. He put it back into his damp jacket pocket. And dialled Riwal's number.

'Riwal, what did Le Coz say yesterday about where Solenn Nuz had been? In the mairie, I wrote down.'

'That's what he said. He's sitting next to me. We're drinking coffee, do you want to speak to him?'

'Yes, pass me over to him.'

There was a rustling, then Le Coz was on the line. 'Monsieur le Commissaire?'

'You asked Solenn Nuz yesterday where she'd been all day, didn't you?'

'Precisely.'

Le Coz was a very conscientious police officer.

'She told you she was in the mairie in Fouesnant. Did she tell you what she was doing there?'

'No. Only what I've told you. I didn't probe any deeper because I thought it was only about the issue of where she had been between half twelve and four that day.'

'That was correct, Le Coz. So she she didn't say anything more about it.'

'No. Nothing.'

'Can you try and find out from the mairie?'

'Right away, Commissaire.'

Dupin hung up.

He had arrived at the tip of the island. Or more specifically: he had walked past the tip of Saint-Nicolas, over the seabed, which suddenly became stony and covered in blue mussels at this point and he had reached an absolutely tiny little island. Only forty metres away from Saint-Nicolas in fact and it was barely more than ten metres by ten. At low tide it was a small appendage to Saint-Nicolas. Dupin had been so wrapped up in his thoughts that he only realised where he was now. He turned on his heel immediately.

He got out his notebook again, flicked through, found what he was looking for and dialled Riwal's number again.

'Chief?'

'Give me Le Coz again.'

'Will do.'

The same rustling sound again.

'Did Madame Barrault tell you what she did between lunch and the time I met her on the quay?'

'No. Just that she was at home. Alone. So that couldn't be verified anyway.'

'Thanks.'

Dupin hung up. That had not been a productive telephone call. He was right between the two islands. He was moving very carefully. This was crazy when you thought about it, it could make a person from the 6th Arrondissement dizzy: he was walking over the seabed. Fish usually swam here. Like the ones from his *cotriade* yesterday.

Dupin's mobile rang. It was a Paris number. He briefly feared it was his mother, but he recognised Claire's number. He agonised for a moment. Then he answered it. And knew immediately that it had been a mistake. He would have to tell her that he didn't have time to speak now – and that was exactly what he needed to avoid. The biggest problem between them had been that he had so little time for Claire and for the two of them.

'*Bonjour*, Georges. Is this not a good time?'

'I. No. *Bonjour*, Claire.'

'Thanks for your message. I've had some insanely hectic days there, I was in the operating theatre all the time. Two of my colleagues were ill.'

'No problem.'

There was an embarrassing pause. Claire assumed that Dupin would say something. Finally she spoke again.

'And what are you up to? Where are you?'

She obviously hadn't heard about the case. Claire didn't often watch the news.

'I'm on an archipelago, eighteen kilometres off the coast. I'm standing on the seabed between two islands, it's low tide right now. There are blue mussels everywhere here, the ones you love so much. I'm walking over them.'

He had said all of these things because he had no idea how to resolve this situation. He even briefly considered whether he should tell her about the dolphins.

'That sounds wonderful. Are you on a trip?'

'I,' there was nothing for it, he couldn't avoid saying it, 'I'm on a case.'

'On a case on an archipelago?'

'Exactly right.'

It took Claire a moment to understand what he was trying to say.

'So you don't have any time to talk now.'

'No! I... No. You're right. But I'll call you as soon as the case is solved. Then we'll have plenty of time.'

'Oh right, yes,' another pause. 'I understand.'

That had always been the worst sentence.

'I want to see you.'

He had let that slip out. And it must have really surprised Claire. They had agreed to think it over together. Whether they wanted to see each other.

'What?'

'I'm absolutely certain. I want to see you.'

Dupin had taken the bull by the horns. This was his only chance. But above all: this was right. It was the absolute truth.

'Good.'

That had been a real 'good'. He was familiar with it. From their happy times. The best times he'd ever had.

'Then let's see each other.'

'Good.'

'I'm glad. That we've talked. That was a – good phone call.'

Dupin was truly exhilarated.

'So – call me when the case is closed.'

'I will, Claire. Straight away.'

She had hung up.

That had been rather incredible, Dupin thought. He needed to be careful, he had nearly slipped on some algae.

But he didn't have time to keep feeling pleased, his phone was ringing yet again.

It was Goulch.

'Yes.'

Dupin sounded more bad-tempered than he actually was. He would simply have liked to let the effects of the conversation with Claire linger.

'The forensic scientist has found two bullet holes. Shots were fired in the abandoned house on Brilimec. At least two shots.'

'Shots?'

'Yes, they found the bullets in the brickwork. They match the calibre exactly. About one metre to the left of the footprints that we saw. The two bullet holes are close together and were probably fired from the point where we suspected somebody had been standing.'

'So somebody deliberately missed.'

'Excuse me?'

The shooter could have been standing at most two or three metres away in the small room, Dupin thought, even if he had been standing in the passageway from the first to the second room. From that distance, nobody missed a shot by a metre twice. Le Menn? Or was Le Menn the one who had been shot at?

'They were intimidating shots.'

Goulch did not answer straight away. So when the penny dropped it was truly audible.

'Exactly!'

'Any other trace evidence?'

'The padlock and the door are being examined more closely.'

'Is that it?'

'Yes, for the moment.'

'Thanks, Goulch.'

A minute later Dupin was standing in front of the *Quatre Vents* again.

Riwal and Le Coz were sitting at the table they had all sat at yesterday evening. Solenn Nuz was still nowhere to be seen, but her elder daughter was there. Way over on the right, Pascal Nuz was sitting in his regular spot, absorbed in a newspaper. Leussot

339

was right next to him and he made a cheerful signal of greeting to the Commissaire. Small groups were already sitting at two of the tables, divers or sailors. And the 'press' was here again too. The remarkable partnership from the *Télégramme* and *Ouest France* were sitting in the corner right next to the entrance, two steaming *grands crèmes* sitting in front of them. They both looked glum. Although they really ought to have known. They had plenty of experience with his – in Dupin's view – very clear information policy: not a word before the case was solved. There was nothing to be got out of him before then. Unless he could see a specific advantage for his investigation – which he didn't see here.

Dupin didn't feel like having a conversation now either, ignoring them completely and walking straight toward the coffee machine, next to which Louann Nuz had just placed a fresh coffee. Clearly an order for one of the tables.

'Another coffee, please.'

'No problem. Good morning, Monsieur le Commissaire.'

'Good morning.'

With a few practised movements of her hands, Louann brewed the fragrant coffee and placed it in front of him.

'Thanks! Is your mother here?'

'She's just getting something from the house. She should be back any moment.'

Dupin wondered whether he should say that he wanted to speak to her. He decided against it.

Dupin took the coffee and went over to Riwal and Le Coz.

'Let's keep working outside.'

'We were planning that too, chief. But everything is still soaking there.'

'Doesn't matter.'

Sitting inside was a stupid idea. For all sorts of reasons, not just because of the press.

Outside, they shook the rainwater off the chairs as best they could and sat down.

'I spoke to the mairie in Fouesnant on the phone a minute ago,' Le Coz said quietly.

'Is it already open?'

Dupin was genuinely surprised.

'It's nearly half eight now and it's open from half seven. It's an office. I spoke to the employee responsible. Madame Nuz put in an application some months ago to be allowed to redesign the annexe on the *Quatre Vents*. She was there twice in recent weeks to clarify details. She just wanted to take another look at her file yesterday. Every organisation, every person, every company who submits applications gets their own file. A kind of folder. Everything goes in there, even intermediate notifications. The whole process.'

'Why did she want it? What does it have to do with the intended new construction?'

'I don't know. Madame Nuz didn't tell the employee why she needed it.'

'And everyone has access to their file at all times?'

'Yes. That's very much normal procedure.'

Dupin lapsed into silence. The suspicion that was taking up more and more space in his head was still very incomplete.

'I need a helicopter.'

Riwal and Le Coz looked at him in surprise.

'I need to go to the mainland. To Fouesnant. I want to visit the mairie.'

It was a while before there was any reaction.

'I'll request it.'

Le Coz stood up and walked a few metres to one side.

Riwal looked expectantly at Dupin.

'I want to inspect the file.'

'Are you looking for something specific? I mean, do you know what you are looking for?'

'No.'

It was true. He didn't know what he was looking for, but his instinct told him that this was exactly where he needed to look.

'The helicopter is on its way,' Le Coz reported. 'It was on Brilimec with the forensic team just now. So they'll just have to wait.'

Dupin was reminded of René Reglas and couldn't help grinning. As he did so, something occurred to him that he wanted to do. He took his mobile out of his jacket pocket and dialled Reglas' number. It took a while for the call to be answered.

'Ah, Monsieur le Commissaire. I would have thought it appropriate if we had been in touch directly and in person about the…'

'Can you say anything more specific about the footprints in the house yet?'

'I…'

'Large feet, small feet? Women, men?'

'It's extremely difficult to say, you've seen it yourself, none of the prints are clear. And the ground is firm and stony in front of the house. But even if there had been some, the storm destroyed all of the prints outside. Even on the beaches, Goulch showed us the places. We couldn't find anything there any more. Nothing at all. I can't commit to anything for the time being.'

Dupin hated the 'can't commit to anything'.

'I just want to know what you think. An initial guess.'

'They are neither significantly small nor significantly large imprints.'

Excellent. It wasn't a giant or a dwarf.

'A woman?'

'I can't say. I think there were shoe sizes between 38 and 44.'

That didn't really help either.

'We're finishing off the work right now. And are flying back immediately. Then we'll take the two bullets and...'

An ear-splitting sound started. Dupin knew it well by now. Rotor blades.

'It's starting... can you still hear me, Commissaire?'

Dupin hung up.

He turned to Riwal and Le Coz.

The helicopter will be here any minute. I need to get going.'

'You're welcome to sit down. Please.'

The employee of the mairie in Fouesnant, not just thin but almost scrawny, was extremely solicitous, in an exaggeratedly submissive, yet also authoritative way – a dangerous mix, Dupin knew. She had moulded the severity of her features into a smile with some force. Early sixties, he guessed.

With a brief nod of agreement, Dupin took the folder that she was holding out to him in her firm grip. He sat at one of the decades-old, dark yellow veneered tables scattered around in a ridiculously haphazard way. Dupin had chosen a solitary table in the corner – as a sign he didn't want to be disturbed.

It had taken them less than a quarter of an hour to drive here from the small airport in Quimper. Riwal had announced the Commissaire was coming and the deputy mayor – Du Marhallac'h was 'indisposed' – had practically welcomed him in state and accompanied him to the first floor. Followed by curious looks from the staff.

The folder practically looked like it was about to burst open. 'Jacques Nuz and Solenn Pleuvant, later Nuz,' it said on the typewritten index card. 'Jacques Nuz' had been crossed out by hand with a short, sharp, horizontal line. The 'and' had been left as it was, which looked strange.

The documents were in chronological order. The file seemed to have been administrated painstakingly well. The most recent documents nearest the top.

Dupin found the current application, the one Le Coz had spoken about. Twenty-four pages long. A form filled out by hand. Two construction sketches attached. Elevation, floor plan. By an architect called Pierre Larmont. From Quimper. A 'reconstruction of the existing annexe in wood in masonry construction'. The application was full of technical terms that Dupin didn't understand, but it was all thoroughly plausible and corresponded with the information that he had. He placed it to one side. Shorter applications followed – six- or eight-page long forms and the relevant decisions – from the last few years. 'New connection to the professional technical medium-format static-solar board of the Glénan', 'new construction of a demand-appropriate, independent soakaway system for gastronomic purposes'. Everything logical and self-evident.

Dupin came to the first applications that Solenn had submitted in conjunction with her husband. Opening the *Quatre Vents* had clearly entailed an impressive number of individual- and sub-applications for the then young couple and their great dreams. The 'internal structural redesign of the restaurant *Les Quatre Vents* (bar/cafe), formerly *Le Sac de Noeuds*', 'the renaming of the restaurant (bar/cafe) *Sac de Noeuds* as *Quatre Vents...*' Unbelievable. Besides applications for the diving school 'international association for the friends and patrons of the underwater sports of the island group Les Glénan'. And of these too: a considerable number. Dupin went through them quickly. They corresponded with his basic understanding too. Everything seemed to be in good order.

Dupin stood up, somewhat frustrated. Only now did he become aware that the office worker was still standing in the doorway. She was looking at him expressionlessly.

'Madame, was it you who handed the folder over to Madame Nuz?'

'Oh yes, I manage and administer the files for the entire archive.'

'Do you know why Madame Nuz needed these documents by any chance?'

'That's obviously a question I don't ask. Because I

don't need to ask it. Every citizen can have a look in their file at any time. And people make use of that.'

She expressed this as if she considered it the central achievement of a free citizen. Dupin would have gladly said something like 'So tens of thousands gave their lives in the Revolution for the right to free access to their file?' He was reminded of the Revolution whenever he was dealing with administration and management.

'Did you happen to see which document Madame Nuz needed? I'm asking you to recall carefully. And to give me an answer.'

Dupin had adopted his clear, commanding tone.

'I have no occasion of any kind to spy on people,' the woman retorted, before added in a more subdued yet still acid tone:

'She will have needed statements from earlier applications for filling out a series of forms that are still outstanding with regard to the new construction she applied for – there are still two due. Although they are just copies, we never give them out. You have to come here – these are important things.'

It made sense and would explain why Madame Nuz had come here. And the hot lead would instantly have cooled, the idea that he had had: illogical.

Dupin stood up and was on the point of turning away without a word when something crossed his mind that he hadn't paid any attention to before.

'Copies? You're saying these are copies?'

'Oh yes, what do you think? We can't in all conscience just hand over the originals. The originals are in our archive. All litigable documents!'

The horror was not feigned.

'I would like to see the originals.'

'That's not possible without authorisation. I'll need to ask the mayor. That's what the regulations say. We have to be very strict on that. No exceptions.'

Dupin felt the colour of his face changing and he involuntarily planted his enormous body in front of her, standing up to his full height. The way he looked left no room for doubt that he was going to explode within moments. Before Dupin could even lose his temper, she gasped out in a thin, aggressive voice:

'I'll get the file.'

She vanished with astonishing speed.

Dupin sat down again.

Had he made a mistake? He had hoped to find something surprising that would shed light on the case.

'Here you go.'

She had slapped the folder down in front of him, rather than placing it.

'I hope you are aware of the fact that you are now dealing with originals, the damage or loss of which would have serious consequences.'

She was tough. As much as Dupin would have liked to get into a war of words, he left it. He needed to concentrate.

He went through the documents in the same order as before. Backwards chronologically. Looked at them again meticulously one by one. After a few documents, he switched to making two systematic piles, one with the originals and one with the copies. This way he could compare and see if there was anything striking or anomalous. He didn't find any discrepancies. Why would someone have wanted to change something in the copies anyway?

He didn't find anything, not a thing. By now he had got to the applications for the diving centre, so he was back to the beginning. Left pile, right pile. One more document. He put it to the left. Dupin stopped short. Where was the copy? There was a document missing from the pile on the right. It only existed with the originals. He searched frantically for the heading. 'Construction of duly compatible hotel company on Saint-Nicolas in accordance with Regulation '16.BB.12/Finist.7', a particularly thick application on thin, faded paper. Date: '28.5.2002'. He leafed through it. 'Capacity/number of intended rooms in hotel company: 88'. That must have been part of the initial great plans that Lefort had had back then. Clearly. 'A hotel company'. And not a small one. Dupin leafed further through, 'Integral functionality of a water sports centre and marina for the purposes of tourist use/integration of existing institutions'. That was the big thing at stake. Dupin's gaze fell on the last page. 'Primary applicant: Jacques Nuz', then a difficult to read signature. And: 'Additional applicants for the purposes of § GHF 17.3: Lucas Lefort, Yannig Konan, Charles Malraux – that must have been the other participant from the 'mainland' – Kilian Tanguy, Devan Le Menn'.

Dupin knew that at the outset of Lefort's tourist plans, other people had been involved in the project. Initially, if he understood correctly, several young, enthusiastic people had thought they were pursuing a dream together. Then it had turned out that they were dreaming very different dreams – and a fight had erupted which had turned them into enemies for life.

Thus far everything corresponded with what was known. But the application raised questions. Dupin was not sure whether this was what he had been looking for and, if so, what it meant. One thing was remarkable in any case: the document was missing from the accessible folder. If it had not gone missing by chance, then it had been removed, which indicated real effort. And why had Jacques Nuz been the chief applicant? Nobody had ever said anything about that. Everyone had always spoken of Lefort's plans. And, finally, the application had indeed been submitted. The statements on it had been contradictory the whole time. Even Kadeg hadn't found anything about it. But Kadeg had only been looking for applications in Lefort's name. As had everyone else presumably. Dupin leafed backwards. On the first page he found a handwritten comment. Furnished with an official stamp of the 29th of June 2002: 'Applicant missing according to police'. What did that mean – had its processing been suspended? That would explain why the application had never become 'official' anyway. Why everyone thought it had never existed.

Dupin stood up. He saw that the office dragon had guarded the door this time too and was enjoying watching him suspiciously.

'If an application has several applicants, are the documents then only filed in the chief applicant's file?'

'Previously, yes. But we amended it two years ago, now there are copies under each applicant.'

'I need the files. I'm taking them with me.'

Dupin knew that for the office dragon, this was the worst sentence that a human being on this earth could utter.

'*Monsieur*!'

She was obviously having great difficulty keeping up with her own outrage linguistically.

'Those – those are our originals! Even taking the *copies* away is forbidden.'

She puffed herself up even more.

'This is completely out of the question. You – you need to make an application for this.'

Dupin made no move to answer. He walked straight past her. She moved abruptly and for a moment, Dupin was braced for her to try and snatch the folder from him. Instead, she turned around snappily on the spot like this was a military exercise and marched after him. Through the door. Along the corridor. Down the stairs. Wordlessly. She only piped again once they had reached the ground floor.

'I'm warning you, Monsieur, that you are committing a criminal offence. I'll demand this of you one last time: put down the documents. They are the property of the French state.'

Then she began to call for help.

'Hello? Monsieur Lemant? I need you! Hello?'

A friendly woman at reception was staring anxiously at the strange drama.

Dupin was walking with determination, taking his time. A moment later he was outside and signalling to the driver to start up the engine immediately. Within two minutes they were already driving down the motorway towards Quimper, back to the airport. Dupin had put his phone on vibrate in the office. It had vibrated several times in the last hour. He checked the numbers. The Prefect... five times in total. Along with Kadeg, Riwal, Goulch, Nolwenn.

The forensic star, Reglas.

Nolwenn was engaged. He tried her three times.

Then he dialled Reglas' number.

'You've got our helicopter. We're still marooned on Brilimec,' Dupin heard instead of a greeting.

'I really hope you didn't try to call me because of that.'

'I wanted to inform you of something – incredibly surprising.'

Reglas paused. Dupin knew his tendency towards the theatrical.

'Reglas, I'll...'

'The gun in question is probably an FP-45 Liberator. From the Second World War. A primitive but effective gun, which the Americans...'

'Reglas!'

'... it was then used by the French resistance.'

Dupin started. That was interesting.

'And that is indisputable?'

'As good as. The ammunition is very distinctive. Even though I could only examine it with the provisional means that we have on site, the...'

'So this weapon would be quite rare to come across?'

'On the contrary. There are still many specimens. Although the majority of them do not work any more.'

'What do you mean by "many specimens"?'

'At the time, the Résistance were gradually building up sizeable arsenals right here in Brittany. In quite a few houses one of these weapons remains in the attic or in the cellar to this day... Many kept them for sentimental reasons too and took care of them.'

All of this was very plausible.

'Get in touch when you know more, Reglas.'

Dupin hung up. He tried Nolwenn again. It was still engaged. Then Kadeg.

'Hello?'

'Kadeg, did you have them show you the original of Lefort's file in the mairie or just the folder of copies?'

'The original of course. I summoned the acting mayor especially.'

'Good. What other news do you have?'

Dupin was speaking quickly, but clearly and with focus. Kadeg adjusted to his speed.

'The building contractor states that he planned the terrace himself. Du Marhallac'h did butt in occasionally with ideas and concepts, but never drew up a concrete plan.'

'Brilliant.'

That would be enough. Even if Du Marhallac'h claimed Pajot had paid him the fee for oral consultations – he had nothing to show for it. That was sufficient for reasonable suspicion – of corruption.

'Hand it over to the Prefecture, they should get the state prosecutor involved. Immediately. – Oh yes, inform the Prefect personally.'

Although it had nothing to do with the case and Dupin was sure of that by now, the Prefect would nevertheless be a bit busy.

'And the Director of the institute?'

The driver had taken a particularly tight *rond-point* at high speed and Dupin was pressed against the door.

'Directeur Le Berre-Ryckeboerec?'

'Exactly.'

'That won't be easy. Our people still haven't found anything clear. Nothing that breaks the law. But since the institute, although largely funded by third parties, is essentially a state institution and partially even a European institution, there are regulations to be strictly adhered to regarding the sale of research. Studies, results, licenses and patents must come onto the market in a verifiable way. But it's probably complicated because it's not clear which regulations apply to which of the institute's platforms for which activities in each case. We need to look carefully at that. It will take a while.'

'And his accounts? The private ones?'

'I've spoken to Nolwenn a few times on the phone. It would be easier if we found something here. It was a miracle that we got the search warrant at all.'

'Get in touch as soon as there's news. One more thing: call Riwal and tell him someone is to go to Muriel Lefort and ask whether she is in possession of a gun from the Résistance, belonging to her parents – she, or perhaps her brother...'

'Will do...'

It was clear that there was something Kadeg still wanted to say. Dupin knew what it was too: he would want Dupin to bring him up to speed on things.

'I'll be in touch, Kadeg. And I'll tell you then.'

Dupin had hung up. He wanted to speak to Nolwenn. He tried again. And at last he got through.

'I have some information, Monsieur le Commissaire.'

They had arrived at the airport. Dupin got out, his mobile to his ear.

'I looked at the file on Jacques Nuz's accident in great detail. The story begins just like the story on Sunday. It's astonishing. The Glénan, a stunning day in early summer. Then a storm picks up. Jacques Nuz has urgent things to do on the mainland and wants to get across before the storm. According Solenn Nuz's statement, he leaves the island at half two. So says the report. The next morning she registers him missing with the police in Fouesnant. A search operation is launched immediately by boat and helicopter. He is never seen again, his body never discovered, just pieces of the boat two days later. Quite far in the east. Nobody knows anything about the accident itself.'

'The next morning?'

'Think about it, mobile phones weren't widespread here at the time.'

Dupin was still standing next to the car. Just a few metres away from the helicopter. The pilot was already sitting in the cockpit. Dupin made a vague gesture that was intended to mean: just a moment.

'And?'

'Here it comes: two other boats also leave Saint-Nicolas with Jacques Nuz, one immediately after him and one some minutes later again. And do you want to guess who owned those boats?'

That was a rhetorical question.

'Lucas Lefort and Devan Le Menn! And it gets even better, do you know who was on board with Lefort?'

'Yannig Konan.'

It had been more of a murmur than an answer from Dupin. He shuddered.

'That's right. Of course Lefort and Konan were questioned about Jacques Nuz's whereabouts. The statements are documented in the files. Nuz wanted to go to Fouesnant where he and Solenn still had a small apartment. Lefort and Konan wanted to go to Sainte-Marine. It's the same course at first.'

'And Le Menn?'

'He also testified he didn't see anything. Neither Nuz's boat nor Lefort's.'

'And other boats? Were there any others out, are there any more witnesses?'

'Nobody else is listed. Any sensible person would either have set out in good time – or else stayed put.'

'And there are no indications of any kind as to what happened? Did Nuz come aground on a rock? Capsize? What kind of boat did he have?'

'The pieces that were found didn't allow for any conclusions, although they were examined thoroughly. The reports are all enclosed. It was a Jeanneau, almost forty years old, but in good condition according to statements from Solenn Nuz and some others. Nothing pointed towards the possibility of the boat having a defect.'

'Hmmm.'

Dupin's mind was racing.

'You always need to remember: these accidents aren't uncommon here, Monsieur le Commissaire – and only in the very rarest cases are there clues as to the course of events.'

The helicopter pilot made a gesture of his own now, which Dupin understood as a request to get in. Reglas and his team were waiting. Dupin didn't care much about that, but he was in a hurry himself

355

now, to get back to the islands. To a – very important conversation. What he had just heard was in fact highly interesting. But he still didn't understand the story, even though he was sure that it was the key. The key to everything.

Solenn Nuz's small stone house was – when viewed from the quay – at the back of the island, where the piece of land, scattered wildly over the sea, was at its widest. It was at the island's western beach, the most beautiful beach, the one that had the most Caribbean-like atmosphere. The building had been built so low that it looked as if it wanted to offer the storms the least resistance possible and was surrounded by an impressive number of flowerbeds, big and small. Salad, potatoes, all kinds of vegetables, even artichokes were growing there, *the* great Breton speciality in vegetables apart from leeks. Dupin ate them in all forms and by now his favourite way was the utterly Breton way: with a chive-and-egg vinaigrette. Two large herb gardens adjoined the flowerbeds. Somehow it didn't suit the islands, that there was soil here at all, proper ground, not just sand, dunes, grasses, stones and rocks.

Dupin had walked into the *Quatre Vents* first, without thinking. Louann Nuz had informed him that her mother was at home.

He was now standing directly in front of her house. Everything looked very simple. He liked it. He looked for a doorbell but couldn't find one. The massive wooden door with the iron edges and hinges stood half open. He stretched a little, so that he didn't to have to go inside just to knock.

'Hello? Madame Nuz?

No answer. Dupin knocked and called a little louder.

'It's Commissaire Dupin.'

Again, no reaction.

Dupin was just considering what to do when Pascal Nuz appeared beside him as if out of nowhere.

'She's in the sea. Fishing for mussels.'

Dupin almost jumped. Her father-in-law must have been outside in the garden.

'I would like to speak to her.'

The sentence sounded very obvious, Dupin realised.

'You'll find her on the big beach.' With his right hand, Pascal Nuz made a vague gesture towards the west.

'I'll look for her. Thanks very much, *Monsieur*.'

Dupin found an elaborate zigzag path through the flowerbeds, walked around the house and quickly found himself on the flat dunes right before the big beach.

It was the lowest tide, the beach extended far down into the sea, a flat, even surface, perfect again after every high tide. The uppermost, finest layer of sand had already been dried by the sun and recovered its flawless, dazzling whiteness. It was still thin – here and there the wet sand underneath shimmered like parchment. His eyes peeled, Dupin spotted Solenn Nuz in the north-west. You could just see her silhouette. She was the only person for miles around, in a landscape that belonged to the sea for a large part of the day (Dupin understood why her father-in-law had said 'in the sea'). She was walking slowly towards the end of the low tide at the northern tip of the island. Dupin set off. It was further than he'd thought.

Solenn Nuz only noticed him once he had already come quite close. He hadn't called out. Suddenly she turned towards him. There was a dark green, woven-looking, plastic basket hanging over each of her shoulders. In her right hand she was holding a small shovel with a long handle.

She smiled when she saw the Commissaire, the calm, beautiful smile that he knew. She only spoke once he was standing directly in front of her.

'It's the season. *Palourdes*, praires, *coques*. And *ormeaux*. – The *palourdes* are in the sand, the *ormeaux* on the rocks, in the cracks where the algae are,' she pointed in the direction of Bananec where the impressive rocky landscapes began at low tide.

'The *palourdes* hide ten centimetres deep in the sand. You need to know that and recognise where to find them,' she spoke calmly to herself, as on previous days, 'I learnt it from my mother. There are very few clues. Do you want to see how to find them?'

'Show me.'

Dupin spoke just as calmly.

'You have to look for small holes in the sand, in a figure of eight, those are the female *palourdes*. And then for two even smaller holes of equal size two to three centimetres away, those are the larger, male ones.'

Solenn Nuz's gaze hadmet Dupin's for a moment. Now her head was lowered again, her gaze fixed expertly on the seabed.

'And then you put your hand carefully in the sand and feel for the mussels. And take them out.'

Dupin was walking next to her.

'Do you like *palourdes*? Or *ormeaux* – the mother of pearl mussels?'

'Very much.'

Dupin in fact loved both kinds of mussels, there were delicious *palourdes* in the *Amiral* – grilled with herb butter and white breadcrumbs. And he had to admit that, to this day, it still made him as happy as a child when he found an *ormeau*, an intact mother of pearl mussel that shimmered with every colour of the rainbow. He always stowed them away and he had already accumulated an impressive collection in his desk drawer.

'There are crêpes with *palourdes* tonight, maybe with *ormeaux* too. Pan-fried. We'll see.'

'What happened to the application that your husband had submitted at the mairie?'

The question had come without warning. But Solenn Nuz didn't look in the least bit surprised. Not at all. She answered without hesitation, in the same tone in which she'd just spoken of mussel-fishing.

'For a while we thought we had a shared idea. Lucas, Yannig, Kilian Tanguy and us. And also Devan Le Menn. Muriel Lefort knew her brother better, from the beginning she was not on board. We didn't listen to her, we thought she was old-fashioned. After a period of hammering out a plan together, it became clear to us that Lucas had something else in mind entirely. We wanted to leave the Glénan the way they were, modernise and expand the diving school and the sailing club a bit, build a hotel and restaurant, but no crowds, no luxury. For Lucas that was just the beginning, a tactic. We started arguing more and more. Then one day there was a big fight. Yannig never said much about any of it – but he was on Lucas' side. And he had the money. Charles

Malraux was on our side. Devan tried to keep out of it somehow.'

Suddenly she bent down.

'Can you see, here – the two tiny holes?'

Dupin stooped down low. He might have missed them. But there they were.

Solenn Nuz let her hand glide into the sand in a fluid, gentle movement and drew it back out moments later with a magnificent *palourde grise* on it. She placed it in the basket to her right and only now did Dupin notice that there were already a large number of mussels inside.

'Why was your husband the chief applicant?'

'Because the land on which the hotel was supposed to be located was his land and it was initially intended to be the centre of all of the plans.'

'I heard the application was never submitted. Why did your husband submit it following the final falling-out?'

It seemed now as if Solenn Nuz was holding back for a moment, but Dupin wasn't sure. She kept her head lowered, her gaze fixed firmly on the sand.

She was silent, then she seemed to pull herself together.

'He didn't submit it.'

Dupin didn't understand. It seemed Solenn Nuz was not going to elaborate.

'What do you mean, didn't he submit the application?'

'We hadn't completed the application. But we were already uncertain by that point, Jacques, Kilian and I. And were already fighting fiercely with Lucas.'

She was silent again. Dupin waited.

'We lived between two places at the time, the little apartment in Fouesnant and the islands. For a few months we lived on the boat most of the time, even though it was cramped. We didn't have the house here yet, we barely used the apartment any more. The boat was our real home. Everything we needed was there – we felt free, we were very happy. We kept our personal documents there too,' she paused again and finished the sentence in the same tone of voice, 'including the application.'

Dupin stood still. At first, he didn't realise what she had just said. Then he felt dizzy. It dawned on him. He felt slight goosebumps on his forearms.

'The application – the filled-out application was on the boat? It was on the boat that Saturday ten years ago when your husband set out from the Glénan one afternoon because the storm was approaching?'

Now it was Dupin who paused, his thoughts racing through his head at tremendous speed. Solenn Nuz kept on scanning the sand undeterred.

'The application was on Jacques Nuz's boat when it left Saint-Nicolas,' Dupin was speaking mainly to himself, 'and it was submitted directly after the accident. It didn't go down with the boat. The application – after setting sail from Saint-Nicolas,' Dupin was speaking more and more slowly, 'it made its way onto another boat, it didn't go down with Jacques Nuz.'

They walked next to each other in silence, Solenn Nuz half a step in front. It was appalling. Dupin tried to collect his thoughts.

'It was murder, wasn't it? It was murder. It was Lefort and Konan.'

Solenn Nuz still remained calm.

'They let him drown,' she said. 'The motor was defective apparently. Nobody knows exactly. Between the Glénan and the Moutons. The sea was already really churned up. He probably went overboard when he tried to fix something. They saw what happened, Lefort and Konan. They saw it. That he was floating in the water. They positioned themselves parallel and Lefort got on board. And he...' her voice changed for the first time, although only slightly, becoming flatter, 'he saw him, he left him to his fate in the sea. He looked for the application where he knew it should be, he knew our boat.'

She paused for a long time.

'He took it and got back onto his boat. Then they left,' she faltered again. 'They thought they'd submit it, and if it was accepted, they could claim Jacques had given them the document – then it would have been three statements against mine.'

That was it. That was the story. The dark core of everything. And – what had happened to Lefort and Konan on Sunday night was this: they had suddenly found themselves in the exact same situation as Jacques Nuz ten years before. Hopelessly floating, without lifejackets, in a fierce storm in relentless Atlantic currents.

'And Le Menn?'

'He was almost directly behind them. Le Menn saw them, not everything, but the crucial part – that Jacques was in the sea and Yannig and Lucas were driving away. He didn't stop. He kept going. He didn't do anything. Not even afterwards. He was afraid of Lucas. He was a coward. He was always a coward.'

Things were falling into place in Dupin's mind, the pieces of a gruesome, brutal and terribly sad puzzle were slotting together. Just a few were still missing.

'How long have you known about it? How did you find out? Did you find the application that was deposited in the file?'

'It was a coincidence. I found it three months ago. I needed information from the very first applications, for the planned renovation of the annexe. I saw it then. And realised.'

'And you went to Lefort.'

Her voice changed a second time. It became completely hollow. Eerily hollow.

'He laughed. He said I could never prove it. And he was right about that.'

Dupin was silent. They had arrived at the rocks.

And how did you know about Le Menn?'

'Lefort told him. That I suspected it. Le Menn came to me. And he – he told me everything,' she replied much more quietly and calmly. 'You have to look for cracks in the rocks, deep, narrow cracks in the pools. You only see a small section of the mussel, a tiny little bit, if at all, and it's the exact colour of the rocks. Rusty. You...'

'Monsieur le Commissaire? Hello?'

It was Riwal. He was racing towards them and had called out from far away. It looked funny, the inspector charging at them and extremely agitated. A very bad moment to choose.

'Sorry! I need to speak to you, Monsieur le Commissaire!'

Dupin walked to meet him. In the darkest of moods.

'Riwal, now is...'

'Pascal Nuz has confessed. He has confessed to everything.'

Riwal said this sentence still half running, while wheezing and gasping for breath. He only came to a stop just in front of Dupin.

'Pascal Nuz did what?'

'Confessed to the murders. That it was him who put the sedative into the drinks. That he met Le Menn on the island yesterday, forced him onto his boat at gunpoint and finally, two or three nautical miles to the south of the archipelago, forced him to go overboard. He...' Riwal paused to inhale again deeply, he was still out of breath, 'he also said why. He wanted to avenge his son. The – *murder of his son*,' Riwal supported himself with his right hand on his hip, 'he is claiming Lefort and Konan killed his son.'

Dupin lowered his head. He was overcome by dizziness again.

He walked towards the waterline. Riwal didn't follow him. Dupin only stopped just before the gently lapping waves. The water was incredibly clear. Crystal clear. You could see every little stone and every mussel, pin-sharp on the gleaming white seabed.

Dupin didn't believe what he'd just heard. That wasn't how the story went. He stood there absolutely motionless for a moment. Then he walked back to Riwal. Riwal stood forlornly in the sand, looking at his shoes and smoking. He had in fact given up smoking for good six months ago. Solenn Nuz had simply kept walking and was now fishing in the cracks in the rocks.

'Was Le Coz able to verify Solenn Nuz's stated timings?'

'Yes. We've been trying to call you the whole time. Everything checks out. To the minute. As far as we could verify it in any case. And we have the phone records for Le Menn's phone calls now, which was not very easy. He spoke to the *Quatre Vents* twice yesterday, the bar has a business mobile, for reservations and things. He was called once, he called there once. Once at quarter past ten and once at eleven o'clock.'

So Solenn Nuz had in fact not been on Brilimec. Even though there was still some haziness surrounding the timing with all of the verified statements, it couldn't make a difference of three quarters of an hour or more. *She* hadn't been on Brilimec; *she* hadn't met Le Menn. And she couldn't have made or taken any calls from the *Quatre Vents* yesterday morning.

'The thing on the island, that really was Pascal Nuz,' Dupin said to himself.

'He still had a gun from before. From the Résistance. His own gun. That he fought with,' Riwal was visibly in turmoil. 'It was also him who called you about *Medimare* yesterday morning with a disguised voice, to put you on the wrong track.'

'And Pajot? What about Pajot?'

'He didn't want that. He didn't know that the three of them were out together. He has said many times that he didn't want that.'

Riwal sounded as though he wanted to defend him.

'And how did he do it with the sedatives? Is it plausible, what he's saying?'

'Ten tablets, dissolved in red wine. He showed us the tablet packet.'

All of it fit, it was true, but somehow it sounded too slick.

'And he simply came to you just now? Just like that?'

'Yes, a few minutes after you left,' Riwal spoke in a serious voice, 'you actually ought to have bumped into him on the path. He said you'd have known everything soon anyway.'

Dupin wanted to reply but couldn't. He couldn't speak any more. He had been gripped by a profound sadness. Everything, everything about this story was tragic.

He had never been in a situation like this before. He knew it hadn't happened like that. But he didn't know what to do. Or even what he was capable of doing anyway. And: above all he didn't know what he *wanted* to do. *Whether* he even wanted to do something.

Riwal had turned around and was walking slowly, still smoking and somewhat stooped, up the flat beach. Back towards the *Quatre Vents*.

Dupin had no idea how long he had just stood there. Finally, he looked towards the rocks. He saw Solenn Nuz. She was standing very straight, seeming to be balancing. He set off. She had already climbed along a significant portion of the steep rocky landscape and was getting close to the sand on the other side again. Dupin thought it over, walked up the beach to the end of the rocks and went around the stony area.

They stood about five metres apart. Solenn Nuz only saw him at the last minute, she had been entirely focussed on the ormeaux and her footing.

'Not great pickings today. Five pieces.'

'Your father-in-law has spoken to us. He has...' Dupin hesitated, 'he has told us everything.'

Solenn Nuz looked up, calmly. She looked Dupin hard and piercingly in the eye. He couldn't interpret her gaze. Then she lowered her head. She was still two or three steps away from the sand. She was silent. As was Dupin. She walked over to him and stood still, the baskets over her shoulders, the shovel in her right hand. All at once she seemed lost in her thoughts, as though she had forgotten that the Commissaire was standing next to her. With a calm movement, she turned her head toward the sea. She looked far into the distance. Dupin observed her the whole time. Looking at her from the side. He couldn't detect a thing.

Solenn Nuz stood like this for a while. Motionless. Then she turned around, without haste and began to walk up the beach. Dupin walked along beside her. They walked slowly, but steadily. With precise steps.

Once they had almost reached the end of the beach, the place where the marram grass began, Dupin knew that he had made a decision. He had already made up his mind just now. Once he hadunderstood the whole story. He just hadn't been aware of it yet.

'We know what happened. We know the whole story, Madame Nuz,' he broke off for a moment and made an effort to make his voice strong and definitive, 'for us, the case is solved.'

Dupin hadn't looked at her as he said this.

'The police know everything they need to know.'

Solenn Nuz didn't respond. They had reached the wooden stairs and were climbing the steps side by side. They had almost arrived at the *Quatre Vents*.

'You'll surely want to speak to your father-in-law.'

'Yes. I do.'

A little later, they reached the terrace. Riwal and Le Coz were standing in front of the entrance to the *Quatre Vents*. Even Le Coz was smoking now.

'Pascal Nuz is sitting in the bar. We've sent all the customers away. Louann Nuz went home. He is alone. He wanted to be alone.'

Riwal sounded uncertain, in a very odd way.

He hastened to add:

'We have recovered the gun. Le Coz took it from the house, along with Pascal. It was in his room, in a small box.'

'Madame Nuz wants to speak to her father-in-law. We will leave the two of them alone for a few moments.'

Solenn Nuz disappeared into the bar and closed the door behind her.

Le Coz had approached from the side. Now all three were standing very close together. For once it didn't bother Dupin. None of them knew what to say. It wasn't even an embarrassed silence. Not a void either. Each had fixed their gaze on something else.

They stood like this for a while.

'The case is solved.'

Dupin spoke clearly and carefully. It seemed like a signal to return to the reality which they had lost touch with for a short time.

'I'll let the pilot know, Monsieur le Commissaire.'

Le Coz got out his mobile.

'I'll inform Inspector Kadeg,' Riwal seemed happy to have something specific to do. 'And Kireg Goulch. The treasure hunt is over.'

Both police officers were walking in different directions and already had their phones to their ears. Dupin remained alone.

He sat down. Not at the 'operations table', but where he'd sat that first time on Monday, right at the wall. Where he had eaten the lobster. When he still thought he was dealing with a boating accident. With an accident that his inspectors and the resourceful Kireg Goulch would quickly solve.

He looked over the quay and out to sea. That spectacular spherical light lay over everything again. He would have to call Nolwenn. Above all, he would have to call the Prefect. Dupin hated all calls with him on principle, the ones during the normal 'working day', the ones during a case, but most of all he hated the calls *after* solving a case. But it was different now, after this case it was important that *he* was the one to talk to him at length first.

Riwal came back.

'Kadeg is up to speed. He was somewhat miffed that in the end he was, how should I put this, so far away from the action.'

Dupin could well imagine that.

'Call him again and tell him I'd like him to nail the mayor and the Director of the institute. That under no circumstances is he to let up, in either case. And that I will personally advise the Prefect of this.'

'Absolutely.'

There was understanding in Riwal's voice.

Le Coz was back too.

'I need to make a few long phone calls. You two wait here. Madame Nuz stays alone with her father-in-law until the helicopter is there.'

Dupin stood up.

Lost in thought, Dupin walked to the left this time. Between the old farmhouse, the sailing school and the oyster restaurant with the two pools beside it, past the big wall, with its surreal penguin. Further towards Bananec in the direction of the sandbank.

The events were swirling around in his head. The controversial story, the whole case.

He came to a stop. He had already been walking for a while and now found himself on the narrowest strip of the sandbank. The water had risen somewhat by now, flat turquoise lagoons glittered to his right and left, then it nothing but sea, endlessly, until the horizon. Saint-Nicolas behind him, Bananec in front of him. He got out his phone. Sixteen missed calls. Since his conversation with Solenn Nuz. Sixteen.

He dialled Nolwenn's number.

'Monsieur le Commissaire?'

Dupin thought about how to begin. He was finding it difficult.

'I'm up to speed. About the big picture. Inspector Riwal informed me.'

Dupin was glad. He hated these summaries. Especially in this case.

'It's all so – tragic.'

Dupin could hear that she suspected something.

'It is, Nolwenn. Tragic.'

'Poor Solenn Nuz. Unbelievable.'

Dupin briefly considered saying something more. But he didn't feel capable of it.

'You can tell me the details this afternoon or another time, Monsieur le Commissaire. You should just call the Prefect. He's trying every five minutes.'

Yes, he'd do that now. There was a small pause.

'All right, Nolwenn.'

'All right, Monsieur le Commissaire.'

There was something solemn in these words. A kind of pact. No, that wasn't it, it was without saying anything out loud that they had established a kind of pact. Which made Dupin strangely happy.

He hung up. And kept walking. Straight onwards, closer towards Bananec. With determined steps. He dialled the number. It took less than a second for the Prefect to pick up. Dupin held the phone a little bit away from his ear, he knew what was in store for him. The Prefect was bellowing so loudly in one of his well-known fits of temper that Dupin would have understood his words perfectly even several metres away from the phone. He held the handset at a safe distance and let the initial fury subside, during which he picked up something along the lines of 'another immediate transfer' amongst other things. Then he kept waiting until he detected a minuscule pause and broke in with impressive speed:

'The case is solved.'

The sentence didn't need to be any longer. It had a dramatic effect. For a brief moment nothing happened, then it was deadly silent.

'Ah. You mean the case is closed? You've got the murderer?'

The Prefect sounded confused.

'We have the perpetrator.'

Again it took the Prefect a little while to answer. He had to regather his nerve.

'Everything is cleared up?'

'Everything is cleared up.'

'I can stand in front of the press and announce the success of the investigation?'

'You can stand in front of the press and announce the success of the investigation.'

Everything always boiled down to this last point anyway. As soon as the Prefect could announce that his investigation had led to a swift success, he was satisfied. Dupin had experienced this often enough by now.

'I'll call a press conference for this afternoon,' he seemed uncertain, 'for early this afternoon. Can I do that, Dupin?'

'Yes, you can.'

'And who was it?'

It did mildly interest him after all.

'It's a very sad story, Monsieur le Préfet. Ten years ago, your friend Yannig Konan and Lucas Lefort let Jacques Nuz, the son of Pascal Nuz and husband of Solenn Nuz, drown in a storm. Wilfully. They...'

'I want to know who the murderer is.'

So his interest didn't extend all that far then.

'Pascal Nuz. His father. He avenged the murder of his son. He learnt three months ago that it was in fact murder. Ten years later. But the pain seems to have remained unchanged.'

'How old is this Monsieur Nuz?'

'Eighty-seven.'

'He planned and carried out multiple murders at the age of eighty-seven? By himself?'

Dupin didn't hesitate in his answer.

'We have his full confession. And it corresponds with all of the known facts.'

'He has filed a confession? Wonderful. So the press conference is settled. And that doctor who disappeared?'

'Pascal Nuz forced him to go overboard way out from the Glénan. He'll have drowned.'

'Why did he do that?'

'Le Menn stood idly by while Konan and Lefort let Jacques Nuz drown. To understand that...'

'You will explain that to me in detail. Of course I need all the details. But not now.'

Of course.

'And another thing, Dupin!'

'Yes?'

'It's not correct to speak of Monsieur Konan as my friend. Bear that in mind. Not everyone whom I know is my friend.'

It was disgusting. Dupin didn't reply.

'So it wasn't about hunting for treasure then.'

Dupin wasn't sure whether that was meant as a simple observation or a smug comment.

'No. We do know that two of the three dead were treasure-hunters in any case and that they had been going to a particular spot noticeably often in the last few months and that underwater archaeologists suspect there are still numerous sunken ships in the area around the Glénan – but it wasn't about that in this case, you're right there.'

'A particular spot, you say?'

The enquiry had come swiftly. Dupin couldn't help grinning.

'Unfortunately we couldn't identify it exactly. But everything is sorted now.'

The Prefect was silent, you could practically hear his mind at work. But he reconsidered.

'And what about Monsieur le Directeur Le Berre-Ryckeboerec? And the mayor of Fouesnant, Du

Marhallac'h? He's actually regarded as a reasonable man, he…'

'Corruption, the evidence is overwhelming. Kadeg has taken this on.'

Dupin wouldn't yield a millimetre. Ever.

'Is that so? The evidence is clear? Does Kadeg think so too?'

'Absolutely.'

'Do you believe the state prosecutor will not see it differently under any circumstances?'

'No way.'

The Prefect seemed to be reflecting for a moment.

'If that's the case, he's a black sheep and will hopefully receive severe punishment.'

'And the Director of the institute,' Dupin knew that this was a weak spot, but he saw no reason to reveal the vulnerability, 'manipulated the regulations on the sale of the institute's research results, licenses and patents in a demonstrably large number of cases, thus causing economic damage to the institute.'

Dupin also knew that they had no proof of any kind for it. He didn't care right now.

'We are investigating whether undue advantage existed and, if so, in what form. I'm sure that we will find something.'

'A very unpleasant chap. I had a number of dealings with him in the last two days. With him and his lawyers. They really would have…' the Prefect's voice had got a bit louder again at these sentences, sometimes a second outburst then occurred. But not this time.

'What I wanted to say was this: from now on you'll inform me of the state of play more regularly if you're on an investigation. Especially with these kinds of cases. Do you understand?'

Dupin didn't reply. He had almost reached the end of Bananec. A lengthy strip of land grown over with grasses, whose paradise beaches, just like on the western end of Saint-Nicolas, led to another, small island attached here during low tide. Dupin walked on. The Prefect seemed to have interpreted his silence as obedient acceptance of his dressing-down and to have thus achieved his goal.

'But that's not the subject at hand – correct, *mon* Commissaire? It's about the solved case now. And we've done it well!'

That was the red button to Dupin. Bright red. When the Prefect addressed him as '*mon* Commissaire' at the end of a case and switched into the plural.

'Tell me, when can you be here, Commissaire? Because of the press conference. I could hold it without you of course if it doesn't suit, but we should at least – have a thorough discussion, so that I know the details. I ought to...'

'Hello? Hello, Monsieur le Préfet?'

The connection had already become unstable at the end of Saint-Nicolas, there had been hissing now and again and a few times he hadn't been able to hear the Prefect for a few seconds.

'Dupin? -lo?'

'Yes, Monsieur le Préfet?'

'I – any more. I need to – information – absolutely the –.'

Dupin had taken another step. Successfully. The connection had dropped completely.

A few more metres and Dupin was standing on the flat accumulation of sand off Bananec, which had never even been designated an 'islet'. It was another four hundred metres to Guiriden's sandbank which he had gone past yesterday, about the same distance again from there to Penfret.

Dupin looked around. It was an incredible panorama. He was standing on the remains of sand that the rising tide was relentlessly conquering. Standing in absolutely nothing. In the ocean. If he did a full turn, he could see the whole archipelago, no island hidden by another here. Today they all seemed inconceivably close. Almost crowded, lined up in a meticulous circle. As if they had rearranged themselves. The air was was tremendously clear.

Dupin could make out a boat that was clearly coming from Saint-Nicolas and seemedto be heading towards him. At first he'd thought it was making for the passage between Bananec and Guiriden, but it was making course towards him too plainly for that. It was a pointed, narrow boat. He recognised it now. It was the *Bir*. He saw Goulch on his raised captain's booth. The two young police officers in the bow. Dupin reached for his phone before realising that there was actually no reception here. Goulch signalled to him with both hands. After a brief moment of confusion, Dupin understood. Goulch wanted to take him on board and get him to the mainland.

Dupin had in fact intended to go into the *Quatre Vents* again. To see Solenn Nuz one more time. But maybe that wasn't a good idea. Perhaps it wasn't the appropriate time. He would need to speak to her again very soon anyway. Purely because of the formalities, because of the report. And the official statements. Dupin had sworn to himself yesterday never to set foot on a boat again. To travel only by helicopter from now on. But the advantage of the boat would be that he would be back quickly. And the *Bir* could drop him off exactly where he wanted, he wouldn't waste any time. And his interest in getting there, which was almost verging on a longing, was great. It was quarter past one. It would just about work out.

The dinghy had already been launched, one of the two young police officers was on board in his oversized tailored uniform.

Four or five metres from his almost-island, the little boat came to a stop. The police officer looked at him expectantly and politely. Dupin understood. This time he sat down for a moment, took off his shoes and socks, rolled up his trousers – and strode without hesitation through the Atlantic. Two minutes later Commissaire Dupin was on board the *Bir*.

Goulch nodded to the Commissaire, Dupin didn't know exactly what it meant, but it seemed to mean a lot. A profound understanding. Dupin nodded back with the same subtle, meaningful head movement.

Dupin was finding everything tough. This case. The 'solution'. Even his own decision. The decision to leave it the way it had been presented to him. But which didn't correspond to the truth, Dupin was sure of it. Was that right? He thought about the old man. He thought about Solenn Nuz. About Nolwenn's words. That the Glénan were her kingdom. A magical kingdom. And about the fact that Solenn

Nuz had had a dream, together with her husband. To live in this place. In *their* place. This dream had been brutally taken from her. For ever. What did Solenn Nuz deserve? She would be alone her entire life. One way or another.

Dupin was sure that he would be making things too easy for himself if he were to dismiss the question of what was 'right' as the 'wrong question'. After all it was a fundamental question, but perhaps it wasn't the only one? Or, there were two true answers. Perhaps he, Georges Dupin, was caught up in an impossible dilemma. They did exist.

Dupin realised how terribly tired he was. How utterly exhausted. So much so that even going by boat on the open sea on rough waters at top speed didn't bother him. He ought to stop brooding. In his state, that led nowhere. This case, he knew, would still be with him for a very, very long time to come.

The islands had been sharply outlined behind them just now, almost touchable and now, just a short while later, they were nebulous silhouettes, getting more and more blurred with every metre that the *Bir* covered as it sped away. He strained his eyes, scouring the horizon. Already, he could not have said whether they weren't just clouds over the sea that he was seeing – dust, hazy reflections of light on the brightly glittering sea on this silvery day. The Glénan had dissolved into infinite nothingness again. They had disappeared.

It was quarter past two when Dupin walked into the *Amiral*. He had walked down the long stone quay, where the *Bir* had left him ashore to the end with the large parking places, the picturesque old town and, on the other side of the street, the restaurant.

Girard was standing behind the counter, busy with an impressive knife and a paper-thin *tarte aux pommes*, the last of the lunch customers having long since moved onto dessert. He had seen the Commissaire immediately and called over one of the *garçons*, handing him the knife.

To his not inconsiderable relief, Dupin saw that his regular table was free. The table to the left at the back, right in the corner of the brasserie, from where you could see everything. The people in the restaurant, the people outside on the squares, but above all: the three harbours. The new yacht harbour to the right, the local fishermen's harbour on the left and the large open-sea harbour behind it. And between the harbours, the old fortress that had defied everything for five hundred years, never conquered by anyone, a large sundial fixed to the wall facing the *Amiral*. Underneath the sundial gleamed the words: '*Le temps passe comme l'ombre*' – 'Time passes like shadow.' Sometimes it doesn't, Dupin thought, sometimes it stands still forever.

It was invincible, indestructible, this fortress. Everything about it conveyed that it would stand there forever. Dupin was glad to be close to it today. To have something so unshakeable to hold onto.

'Exhausted? Are you done?'

Girard was standing next to him.

'I'm done.'

'Was it bad?'

'The worst.'

Girard looked at him with a warm, undramatic gaze.

'I saw – real dolphins.'

Dupin couldn't help smiling. He had more or less whispered this absurd sentence, but knew that Girard, even if he had heard it, wouldn't say anything about it.

'*Entrecôte frites*? Red? The usual?'

'Absolutely.' Something else occurred to him: 'And before I forget: I have a visitor tomorrow evening. I could do with a table for two. Around eight or so.'

'Noted.'

Commissaire Dupin leaned back. 'The usual.' There they were. The words that made everything all right. On this day. At the end of this day. And of all these things. That's how it was. That's really how it was.

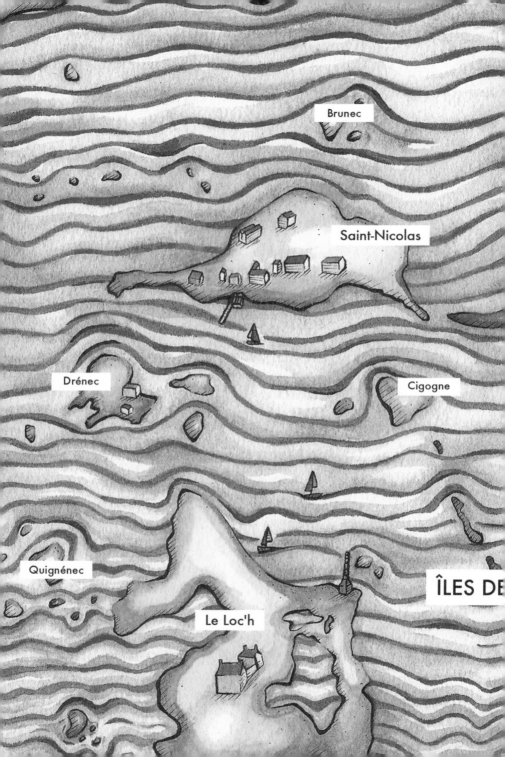